THE FACE STEALER

THE FACE STEALER

Sarah Rayne

**SEVERN
HOUSE**

First world edition published in Great Britain and the USA in 2025
by Severn House, an imprint of Canongate Books Ltd,
14 High Street, Edinburgh EH1 1TE.

severnhouse.com

Cover and jacket design by Jem Butcher Design

British Library Cataloguing-in-Publication Data
A CIP catalogue record for this title is available from the British Library.

ISBN-13: 978-1-4483-1402-7 (cased)
ISBN-13: 978-1-4483-1403-4 (e-book)

All Severn House titles are printed on acid-free paper.

MIX
Paper | Supporting
responsible forestry
FSC
www.fsc.org   FSC® C013056

Typeset by Palimpsest Book Production Ltd.,
Falkirk, Stirlingshire, Scotland.
Printed and bound in Great Britain by
TJ Books, Padstow, Cornwall.

The manufacturer's authorised representative in the EU for product
safety is Authorised Rep Compliance Ltd, 71 Lower Baggot Street, Dublin D02
P593 Ireland (arccompliance.com)

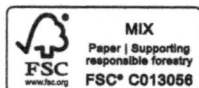

Praise for Sarah Rayne

"The story is dense, complex, and twist filled, and readers
will be riveted by this suspenseful, provocative read packed
with depth, drama, and charm"
Booklist on *The Murderer Inside the Mirror*

"A playful puzzle with an elegant veneer and
abundant twists"
Kirkus Reviews on *The Murderer Inside the Mirror*

"Superb . . . Lovers of British historical mysteries with
a dash of romance and gothic atmosphere will clamor
for more"
Publishers Weekly Starred Review of *Chalice of Darkness*

"In this taut, Gothic-style mystery, Rayne offers a gripping
plot with plenty of suspense and period ambience"
Booklist on *Chalice of Darkness*

"Frightful fun with haunted history and a blustery thespian"
Kirkus Reviews on *Chalice of Darkness*

About the author

Sarah Rayne is the author of many psychological and supernatural suspense novels, including the Nell West & Michael Flint Haunted House Mysteries, the Phineas Fox Mysteries and the Theatre of Thieves Mysteries. She lives in Staffordshire.

Author's acknowledgement

Grateful thanks are due to my good friend, the talented sculptor Gillie Nicholls, who so patiently explained and demonstrated to me how the 'Stone Heads' of this book could be created.

Author Acknowledgment

ONE

London, autumn 1909

Mikhail Volkov was trying not to be overawed by his surroundings, but he thought that to sit in the audience at the almost-legendary Amaranth Theatre in London – even to be in London itself! – and watch the Fitzglen theatre company performing a comedy by Mr Oscar Wilde was enough to overawe anyone. The Fitzglens were very famous, although Mikhail suspected he was one of the few people in the audience who knew they might also be considered infamous. He was, though, as sure as he could be that he had found the right family. There could not be more than one theatrical family who, in secret, were what the English called society burglars.

When Jack Fitzglen made his first appearance, brief applause greeted him, and the audience seemed to sit up more attentively, as if this was what they had been waiting for. Mikhail sat up as well, because from all he had been able to find out, this was the man who controlled the theatre, and the man who planned and directed most of the thefts. Jack was younger than he had been expecting – he was probably only a few years older than Mikhail himself – but from the moment he stepped on to the stage, he had the entire command of it.

The dialogue was slick and sharp – Mikhail was pleased that his own English was equal to following and appreciating it. English people liked this kind of light, dry humour – he knew that, and listening to it, he understood why. There were ripples of appreciative amusement from the audience, and then – Mikhail was not sure how it came about – there was a moment when Jack Fitzglen paused before responding to another character on the stage, and turned slowly to look at him. Several pleased voices behind Mikhail murmured, 'The Fitzglen Pause', and there was a sense of satisfaction as if this was something for which they had been waiting.

Jack Fitzglen judged the Fitzglen Pause to exactly the right second. When he delivered his next line, it brought a ripple of laughter, and a second outbreak of applause.

During the interval, Mikhail drank a glass of what he thought was very good wine, then approached one of the uniformed men by the exit and asked if a note could be taken to Mr Fitzglen's dressing room.

'An old friend whom I promised to contact when I was in London,' he said. 'I am here on a visit from Russia, you understand, and wish to meet him briefly again.'

It appeared to be an acceptable request, and the man took the note and said it would be delivered to Mr Fitzglen after curtain fall. If Mr—? Ah, if Mr Volkov would kindly wait in the bar after that, he would bring a reply.

'Thank you,' said Mikhail, and sat down again, his mind going back over what he had written, which, after considerable thought, said this:

My dear Mr Fitzglen,

I am writing to you because I believe your family may be able to help me, and I hope a letter from a total stranger will be acceptable.

Recently, a grave crime was committed in my village of Cympak – which is near the Russian–Siberian border. It is a crime which has its roots in the past, and I believe it may involve your own family, both in the past and in the present. This is why I have travelled to London to meet you. It is possible that the very special skills I believe your family to possess could help me to uncover the truth and prove my innocence, which I must do if I am not to face imprisonment.

If it is possible for you to grant me an interview, I could explain everything.

I am writing this in the interval of your performance this evening of Mr Oscar Wilde's *The Importance of Being Earnest*, which I am enjoying greatly. It is a pleasure to see the work of such a wonderfully talented writer brought so vividly to life.

    With kindest regards,
    Mikhail Volkov

He had not, of course, written the note in the interval. He needed to snare the Fitzglens' interest, and had made and discarded several drafts earlier in the small room in his Shepherd's Bush lodgings. He thought the final sentence was justified, because he knew he would enjoy the play.

The missive was duly borne away, after which Mikhail finished his wine and listened to the comments from various members of the audience. It appeared that the play was receiving considerable acclaim, and that the critics had written about 'Jack playing Jack', which was a reference to the character of Mr Jack Worthing. Somebody remarked that the *Evening Standard* had written how 'London audiences are wild over Jack Fitzglen's Wilde performance', but went on to say that it was very likely that the Fitzglens themselves had influenced the article, if they had not half written it.

'And wasn't Jack Fitzglen seen dining with the critic's wife quite recently?' demanded the man.

There was a vague murmur of assent, then another voice from the far end of the bar said, 'Forgive me, sir, but aren't you Mr Theophilus Gilfillan?'

'I am, sir, and proud of it.'

'Thought so,' said the speaker, then, to the rest of the group in general, 'Never trust a word a Gilfillan says about a Fitzglen – or vice versa if it comes to that. Arch-enemies and foes, those two families are, since – well, probably since Shakespeare romped around London stages. And,' he added, 'aren't the Gilfillans currently rehearsing an Oscar Wilde piece themselves?'

Theophilus Gilfillan said, loftily, that it so happened they were.

'Ha. Just as I thought. Drawing up new battle lines. Sworn rivals, you see,' said the speaker to his listeners.

Mikhail knew he should step away from this conversation, because it was little better than outright eavesdropping, but there was a press of people all around him, making it difficult.

A third person was observing that the two new Fitzglen girls were giving very creditable performances. It was nice to see the younger ones making a favourable mark, wasn't it?

'Oh, those two,' said Theophilus Gilfillan, in a slightly dismissive tone. 'They're twins, I think. I've heard that one is rather a saucy baggage—'

The man who had commented admiringly about the twins said, 'I don't think we want to hear any rehashed, regurgitated scandal stories you might have picked up. And isn't that the bell for the next act?'

After the final curtain fell – which it did to tumultuous applause and some cheers – Mikhail returned to the bar. There was no sign of the uniformed man, so Mikhail ordered another glass of wine and sat down to await a response to his note. He was just deciding that Jack Fitzglen would probably not even reply when the attendant appeared.

'Mr Volkov, if you have time and if you can come with me now – and if you don't mind the informality – Mr Jack Fitzglen could see you in his dressing room.'

Mikhail did not say that he would have been happy to see Jack Fitzglen in whatever venue suggested at any time of the day or night. He followed the man along several bewildering corridors, past closed doors and up a narrow flight of stairs. As they went, he looked with interest at this world that existed behind the plush splendour and rich velvet, and the gilt and mahogany and glittering crystal chandeliers. There was a cheerful untidiness and a sense of purpose, which he liked. Pieces of scenery and ladders and wicker skips stood against walls, there were scents of timber and paint and sawdust, and people scurried about, calling out largely incomprehensible things about flying a flat or moving stage braces, and how somebody had missed the half-hour call. A worried-looking man darted out of one of the rooms, demanding to know whether anyone was repairing Miss Daphnis's flowered hat, because somebody had sat on it by mistake after curtain fall, and Miss Daphnis refused to appear on the following night in a sat-upon bonnet.

The attendant stopped outside a door, knocked on it and, appearing to receive a satisfactory response, opened the door and gestured to Mikhail to go in.

The voice that, a couple of hours earlier, had caused a packed audience to sigh admiringly, said, 'Mr Volkov? I'm Jack Fitzglen, and I'm immensely intrigued by your note.'

The curious thing – the thing Mikhail knew he would never forget – was the instant conviction that Jack Fitzglen was someone he could trust. Even though you know – almost certainly – that he's an incorrigible thief and a dyed-in-the-wool robber and cat-burglar? said his mind. Even then, thought Mikhail.

The room was quite small. Various garments hung from rails, and there were several large mirrors, and narrow shelves containing what Mikhail supposed was stage make-up. In one corner, a smallish man with very bright eyes was pinning together sections of a lady's elaborate hat. He smiled at Mikhail and continued with the pinning. A dark-haired man, slightly younger than Jack, was half lying, rather languidly, on a battered sofa; Mikhail recognized him as the actor who had played Algernon Moncrieff earlier.

'My cousin, Byron Fitzglen,' said Jack, indicating the young man. 'And the gentleman repairing my Great Aunt Daphnis's bonnet is my dresser, Augustus Pocket. Sit down, Mr Volkov.'

'You could call me Mikhail, please,' said Mikhail, hopefully, taking the chair indicated.

'Oh, that's much friendlier. Gus, don't go – if there's a tale to unfold, you'd better hear it. Gus,' said Jack Fitzglen to Mikhail, 'knows every one of this family's secrets.'

'And often manages to extricate us from the worst of their consequences,' put in Byron.

'You don't mind if I finish removing the final traces of Mr Worthing?' said Jack, replacing the lid of a jar of some kind of thick cream and reaching for a comb. Under the stage lights, his hair had looked almost golden – in here, it was the colour of honey.

'Your note was very interesting,' he said. 'We'd certainly like to hear about this crime from the past—'

'And also how you think our family could help,' said Byron, but he said it with what Mikhail thought was genuine curiosity, rather than challengingly.

Choosing his words carefully, Mikhail said, 'I wrote that I feared imprisonment for a serious crime. I am innocent, though, and I have tried to look into the origins of the crime. That was when I discovered various facts about your family that seem to be woven in.'

He had no idea how this would be received, but Jack Fitzglen said, 'I shouldn't be at all surprised at anything you found out about this family. Byron is always unearthing all kinds of things. He's been writing what he calls the Fitzglen Chronicles for years – although it has to be said that a good many of his discoveries turn out to be gross exaggeration or even outright fiction, and most of them can't be allowed into print anyway.'

'What have you found, Mikhail?' asked Byron, not at all discomposed.

Mikhail reached into his pocket for his notebook, and as he opened it, he said, 'I have written here part of a chapter from an old book. A Russian book, but I have translated into English.'

'Thank heavens for that.'

'It was in a dim old shop, in a small town near to Cympak,' said Mikhail. 'A marvellous place to spend time in, and the shelves yielded an astonishing result.'

Jack and Byron exchanged brief grins. 'We have one or two dim old bookshops that are marvellous to spend time in, too, and their shelves can also yield astonishing results,' said Byron.

Again, there was the sense of an understanding and almost of kinship. Mikhail handed the notebook to Jack Fitzglen. 'My English is perhaps not as good as it could be,' he said.

'Your English seems excellent to me.'

'But not for reading aloud and to people such as yourselves.' He waited, and Jack, who was already turning over the pages, glanced up, then nodded an acceptance and began to read.

'The sun is setting over the river in a fiery blaze of magnificence, and I am lying in my bed watching it. For once, I am alone in the bed, but that enables me to write this entry – to set down my private recollections of a journey that someone has already said is so glitteringly splendid it is lighting up the river banks for miles around, and will be remembered for a very long time.

What I shall remember is how today ended, and even as I write this, I am looking hopefully towards the door, in case *he* returns. That sounds like the dreaming of a moonstruck, love-bitten damsel of fourteen, rather than the thoughts of a lady of (moderately) mature years, but I do not intend anyone to read these pages, so I can write that tonight was one of the most marvellous experiences I have had for a very long time.

It is an experience that, for once, I must treat with discretion, though, for there are jealous people who may plot against the gentleman who lay in this bed earlier tonight and cause him harm. The gentleman who lay in this bed . . . Even to write that brings a fresh wave of delight. I describe him as a gentleman, for he has the manner and the manners of one – but he has the eyes and the smile of a rogue. It was, of course, the rogue that attracted me . . .

One day, I will probably have to burn this private journal, but not yet. I have no intention of dying for a very long time, and if any of my servants sell my diaries after I have departed this world, may they be visited by the Ten Plagues of Egypt and suffer each of the curses of the Bible in turn.

I shall write my memoirs for history, of course, and history may make what it likes of my life – although I shall try for a degree of discretion and moderation.

But whatever I write, those memoirs must never include the secrets I am sharing in these pages. Above all, there must never, anywhere, be any account of the truth about the Stone Heads.'

To Jack Fitzglen, the remarkable thing about these brief paragraphs was the vivid images they conjured up. A glittering river cruise – a lady who had waited for a lover while the setting sun lit up the river beyond her window. But within the images was a darkness. The possibility of a jealous plot against the lover. And at the end, those words: 'There must never, anywhere, be any account of the truth about the Stone Heads.' Reading that, Jack almost felt as if something that had lain hidden for a very long time had lifted its head and breathed dank coldness into his face.

He looked at Mikhail. 'Who wrote this? And when?'

'It was written by the Princess Sophie Friederike Auguste von Anhalt-Zerbst-Dornburg.'

'I've never heard of her,' said Jack.

'Yes, you have,' said Byron, abandoning his languid post and sitting up with enthusiasm. 'Her English names were Catherine Alexeyevna Romanova, weren't they, Mikhail?'

'Yes. But,' said Mikhail, 'she was more generally known as Catherine II, the Empress of Russia. To most people since, she is simply Catherine the Great.'

There was a brief silence, during which Jack thought: Catherine the Great. And now I'll have to ask who the lover was. The lover who had had the manner of a gentleman and the eyes and the smile of a rogue . . . It can't be what I'm thinking, of course – but the dates would fit, and it might explain why this young Russian has come to the Amaranth.

Almost against his will, he said, 'Is it known who the gentleman was? The one she waited for?'

'She does not name him in the extract I found,' said Mikhail. 'But the book's author had added a footnote.' He reached into his pocket for the rest of his notes. 'I did not write out a translation of it, but I can tell you the English.'

'Yes, please.'

'It says: "It is a loss that only scraps of these private memoirs – credibly attributed to Catherine the Great – have survived. However, in the fragments I was able to find, it is indicated that the lover on that extravagant river cruise was an Englishman."' Mikhail looked up from his notes and met Jack's eyes. He said, 'The author goes on to say the lover's name was Harry Fitzglen.'

Jack thought he had been prepared to hear this, but it still came as a shock. After a moment, he said, softly, 'Highwayman Harry.'

'The man who founded this family and created this theatre,' said Byron. 'My God, was Harry Fitzglen one of Catherine the Great's lovers?'

Mikhail, clearly choosing his words carefully, said. 'The index – the credits? – at the back refer to the extract being from a "private publication".'

'It sounds as if a disgruntled servant found the journal after Catherine died and saw a chance of making a bit of money from it,' said Byron. 'She even refers to the possibility.'

Jack was still studying Mikhail's notes. He said, 'What are the Stone Heads? You've given them capital letters.'

'It is what they have always been called,' said Mikhail. 'They are believed to be the likenesses of children who vanished about a century and a half ago.' He leaned forward earnestly. 'It was never known what happened to those children, but the belief has always been that they were murdered. No one ever knew why, or who the murderer was, but the legend is that the Stone Heads were created – sculpted or carved – soon after the deaths, or perhaps shortly before. What is known is that the sculptures were locked away in a vault in St Nicholas's Monastery in Verkhoturye.'

'Where?'

'It is in the Ural Mountains,' said Mikhail. 'It is sometimes called the Gateway to Siberia, and I think it is often regarded as one of the centres of Russian Christianity. The monastery is very old – it stands at the top of a steep mountain track, from where it frowns down on the villages. It is perhaps a little under half an hour's walk from my village of Cympak.'

'Did you ever see these Stone Heads?'

'They have been kept locked away by the monks for a great many years. But everyone knows the legend.'

Jack thought: That isn't quite an answer, but then Mikhail said, 'It is believed they contain some secret – something so dangerous those long-ago monks dared not allow it to become known.' He paused, then said, 'About three weeks ago, it was discovered that the Heads had vanished.' He had been twisting his hands tightly together, but he seemed to suddenly realize it and forced himself to stop.

'And you were accused of taking them?' said Jack.

'Yes. It was said I knew the monastery better than anyone in my village – that I would know how to reach the crypt through the stone passageways under the main building. And so I do. After my parents died, I was taken in by the monks, and I spent several years with them. I learned English at their hands, and later I was able to teach others – I am responsible for history and literature at Cympak's little school, and I have enjoyed that work. But Mr Fitzglen – Jack – I would never have done anything to harm anyone in my village. And you have my word that I did not take the Stone Heads.'

Jack could hear that the emotion behind the words was genuine, but again he sensed evasion. There's something he's not telling us, he thought. Something that might incriminate him? Something he's too frightened to disclose?

But he only said, 'These Stone Heads would be valuable?'

'I think very valuable. The mystery that always surrounded them – the belief that there is some secret that has had to be kept from the world—'

'Would make them worth stealing,' said Jack, thoughtfully.

'Yes, of course it would.'

'There is something else I must tell. An English clergyman had been staying in Cympak. He was charming and persuasive, and he told everyone he was travelling through the remoter areas of Russia to preach Christianity—'

Jack glanced at Byron, then said, 'Might this clergyman have also collected donations for English charities?'

'He did. He took over local halls for his talks and sermons in the area,' said Mikhail. 'He came to Cympak's own little local church and also the school where I teach. He was interesting and spoke well, and people were drawn to him – especially when he described how he turned to religion after discovering that his family were criminals. He told how he found out that they were thieves and cheats and forgers, and how it affected him very deeply. But he also said he had never betrayed them – they were famous and successful, and if he had told the truth about them, no one would have believed him.'

Jack said, 'And the Heads vanished at the same time as the clergyman?'

'Yes. It is because of that clergyman – because of the story he told of his family and because of his name – that I have come to London to find you.'

'You want us to trace the clergyman and the Stone Heads and get them back.'

'Yes.'

Jack looked at Byron. 'A charming and persuasive gentleman posing as a man of the cloth, persuading people to hand over their money,' he said. 'And historic and valuable sculptures vanishing around the same time. Who does that suggest to you?'

'There's only one person it can be, isn't there?' said Byron. 'Saintly Simeon Fitzglen.'

TWO

Gus Pocket had set the long table in the Green Room with notebooks and pencils. It was already well after half past eleven, an hour when the theatre was usually settling into its after-show silence, but the Amaranth was never entirely quiet. Gus had sometimes imagined how, after audiences had left and the actors had shed their costumes and their characters, inquisitive ghosts tiptoed out of the shadows to see what the old place was up to, or perhaps even gathered in corners to hold critical discussions about the evening's performance.

He had collected a platter of cheese and fruit from the crush bar, along with a couple of bottles of wine, and he was glad he had done so, because Mr Rudraige Fitzglen, arriving slightly out of breath and inclined to be indignant at being summoned so abruptly to a family conclave, was very appreciative. It had been, he said, something of a scramble to divest himself of the costume and the character of Canon Chasuble in order to attend this sudden late-night meeting; consequently, he had not had time for his customary after-performance snack, and he dared say he was in a bit of a dishevelment.

'Don't worry, Uncle Rudraige; we're all in a dishevelment,' said Mr Byron, who had followed him in and who, so far from being dishevelled, had wrapped himself in what looked like a velvet opera cloak. Gus thought it had been part of somebody's costume from a melodrama staged the previous year.

Miss Cecily was certainly dishevelled when she came in – she was still wearing her Miss Prism costume, and her hair was escaping its pins, but this was not unusual. She had seated herself next to Mr Volkov and was asking him about his journey from Russia, which she was sure must have been exhausting – the language problem so difficult. But his English was extremely good, said Miss Cecily; she had particularly noticed that when Jack made the introduction.

Mr Ambrose was his usual composed self, and was already setting out his famous accountant's notebooks in case any calculations were needed. The family was inclined to tease him about his notebooks and the columns of figures in different-coloured inks, but they all acknowledged that he kept a very cunningly disguised record of all profits from filches. He had concocted several complicated schemes which got around nuisances such as income tax, and discouraged officials from asking awkward questions about large payments into bank accounts. Only last month, the proceeds from the acquisition of two mink cloaks by Miss Daphnis, while attending a very grand society dinner, had been classed as 'Proceeds of sale of valuable Chinese wallpaper removed from Miss Fitzglen's boudoir walls and sold to Sir Humphrey Pomfret to be rehung in his garden room'. Byron had been able to write a genuine-looking receipt for Ambrose's records, although, as he said, it was not likely they would be expected to pay tax on the sale of 200-year-old Chinese wallpaper, even if it had actually existed.

Jack, taking his customary place at the head of the table, glanced to where Gus was ensconced in the window seat, ready to take notes, and smiled. The family – Great Uncle Rudraige in particular – often had the way of forgetting, or misremembering, what was agreed at these meetings, so Jack always asked Gus to take notes.

Everyone listened to the story of how Simeon Fitzglen appeared to have stolen from a Russian community several valuable and historic stone sculptures – resulting in Mikhail coming to London. When Jack finished, Rudraige, who was usually the first to speak out, said he had thought they had got rid of the black-hearted villain, Saintly Simeon, for good and all.

'But now it seems he's come back into our lives, like the ghost reappearing at the feast,' he said, cutting himself a large wedge of cheese and adding biscuits and Gentleman's Relish. 'If we aren't careful, he'll bring shame and disgrace on the family all over again.'

'He always did,' remarked Daphnis. 'He knew the Fitzglen rule perfectly well, but he never kept to it.'

'I've explained to Mikhail,' said Jack, 'how we never filch from people who can't afford to lose money or belongings, or anything such as treasured family mementoes.'

'It was Jack's father who instilled that in most of us,' said Ambrose. 'Aiden Fitzglen, that was. A remarkable man.'

Jack said, 'Thank you,' and then, looking round the table, he said, 'You do see that if Simeon really has appeared on the scene, and if he's still using the Fitzglen name, we need to track him down and put a stop to whatever game he's playing.'

'My word, we certainly do,' said Rudraige, drawing down his brows in the frown that had sometimes caused the first few rows of the stalls to draw back and gasp.

'He was expelled from this family several years ago,' said Jack to Mikhail.

'And very firmly indeed,' said Daphnis. 'It was good riddance to bad rubbish.'

'He always donned a religious guise,' said Cecily to Mikhail. 'In fact, I believe there were two occasions when he even passed himself off as an archdeacon. He was a very attractive man,' she added, somewhat wistfully. 'And Jack, I'm sorry to say this, but he was remarkably like your father to look at.'

'He was an out-and-out villain,' said Rudraige. 'And never mind posing as an archdeacon; I happen to know that he once convinced a distinguished university debating society that he was a bishop.'

'And delivered a stirring lecture on *The Origin of Species* and Charles Darwin,' nodded Byron. 'He'll certainly be the one who took the Stone Heads.'

'I wonder how he knew about them,' said Jack, looking across at Mikhail. 'It sounds as if they were very strictly guarded – and for over a century, so you'd expect them to have faded from people's awareness.'

He thought there was another of the moments when Mikhail seemed to flinch, but then he said, 'In such places as Cympak, memories are long, and the legend of the Stone Heads is a persistent one. It would not be difficult for him to hear of it.'

I suppose that's a fair enough answer, thought Jack, but I still have the feeling he's hiding something.

'Simeon would be alert for just that kind of story, anyway,'

Ambrose was saying. 'Anything that might lead him to something valuable.'

'And once he heard about those Heads, he'd go after them at once,' nodded Rudraige.

Jack said dryly, 'If Highwayman Harry heard about the Stone Heads, he would probably have gone after them at once, too.'

'Would they have been around in his day?' asked Ambrose.

'Catherine refers to them in that fragment of her memoirs,' said Byron. 'And clearly, when she wrote them, she had met Harry.'

'"Met"?' said Rudraige, with a chuckle. 'That's throwing roses at it.'

'Don't be coarse, Rudraige. Still, it's a shame we've only got that fragment of Catherine's private memoirs,' said Daphnis.

'There was nothing else in the book that related to this or to Harry Fitzglen,' said Mikhail. 'I have brought the book with me, and I will translate any parts for you. But it is a collection – "anthology" is the word, I think? – of information about many famous people. There were quotations from autobiographies and textbooks, and accounts of events in history by learned people, but there was no more about the Tsarina, or any of her Court. She wrote her memoirs in much detail elsewhere, but they are . . . I think you would say "official versions".'

'Not so candid,' said Byron, grinning. 'Simeon will have sold the Stone Heads by now, of course, but if we could find him, it might lead us to their present whereabouts. Mikhail, how large – how heavy – would they be?'

'I think the size of a living person's head – but children's heads, you understand.' He indicated with his hands.

'And if they are stone, taking them won't be like scooping up a handful of emerald necklaces or a silver snuff box,' said Jack, thoughtfully.

'Or openly carrying out a Gainsborough as if you're a museum attendant about your lawful occasions,' added Byron, winking at Mikhail.

Ambrose said, slowly, 'Could we trace Simeon through

some kind of Church directory? What's that famous one – Crockford's, is it?'

'But Simeon isn't a genuine churchman,' said Daphnis.

'That wouldn't prevent him getting into Crockford's,' said Jack. 'Mikhail, you said he told people he was collecting donations for various charities. Can you remember the names of any?'

Mikhail frowned for a moment, then, sounding apologetic, said, 'I do not have a very clear memory, but I think he talked of a Society for Ecclesiastical Restoration. Does that sound right?'

'It certainly sounds authentic,' said Jack. 'If it's genuine, it would give us a good starting point.'

'But we'd need to be wary,' pointed out Rudraige. 'We can't risk Simeon finding out what we're doing.' With the air of mentally rubbing his hands in glee, he said, 'If we're going to infiltrate Church societies, we'd better use disguises.'

'We had,' said Jack, and saw Gus's dismayed expression. The family loved disguises and the creation of false personas, but Gus always prophesied doom and disaster would result from them. Jack supposed it might do so one day. But not yet, he thought. Not with this filch to embark on. With the forming of the thought came the familiar sensation of delighted anticipation. There was nothing like the start of a new filch – the planning, the discussing, the working out of who should do what and when and how.

'Whoever dons the mantle for this could seem to be a Church researcher of some kind,' said Byron. 'Compiling notes for a thesis, maybe.'

'We'll need to be wary about who makes an approach,' put in Daphnis. 'Simeon knows most of us well enough to see through almost any disguise. I don't think any of us could risk it. The Fitzglen eyes are very distinctive.'

Jack caught himself wondering if the long-ago Harry, who had had the manners of a gentlemen and the smile of a rogue, had possessed the narrow Fitzglen eyes.

'What about one of the twins?' said Ambrose, rather hesitantly. 'They aren't very well known yet, and we'll want to bring them a bit more into the offstage profession at some point. You didn't think it worth including them in this meeting, Jack?'

'I thought we shouldn't overload them with the complication of Saintly Simeon so soon,' said Jack. 'He won't be much more than a vague family legend to them, and they haven't been in London very long. This is their first real appearance on the Amaranth's stage.'

'They'd never manage a disguise and an infiltration of a Church society,' said Daphnis. 'They'd giggle at the wrong moment, or Phoebe would get up a flirtation with a curate and spoil the whole thing. Her mother was just the same when she was Phoebe's age. By the way, did anyone notice that Phoebe missed a cue tonight in Act Three?'

'Petronella said Phoebe had been trying to achieve the Fitzglen Pause,' said Cecily.

'Oscar Wilde's plays don't allow for the Fitzglen Pause,' said Daphnis. 'I told them so myself afterwards. I said if Phoebe did it again, you would probably drop her over the edge of the stage into the orchestra pit, Jack.'

'Oh, we're quoting Gilfillan maxims now, are we?' said Byron, with glee. 'Isn't that one of their standard threats to players who need too many prompts or overact? To be dropped into the orchestra pit?'

'There are worse punishments,' said Jack, and was glad to hear that he sounded completely uninterested, because the Gilfillans were nothing to do with this – in fact, they were nothing to do with any of the Fitzglens whatsoever.

Byron said, thoughtfully, 'What about Todworthy Inkling? Would he know someone we could use in the search for Simeon. He loves an intrigue.'

'Yes, and he has a good many acquaintances in various walks of life – not just people in the book world, but historians and scholars and academics,' said Jack, at once. 'We could be open with him about needing to find the sculptures – simply say they've been stolen and we've been asked to trace them.'

'He'd be interested in the legend, too,' said Byron. 'I'll go along to the bookshop tomorrow morning to talk to him. We need him to fence those pieces you lifted from that Maida Vale house last week, anyway, Jack.'

'The Poetry Society,' nodded Jack. 'You read your latest epic poem to a drawing room full of enthralled ladies, while I got in through the scullery window and went up to the lady of the house's bedroom. Three diamond necklaces and a pair of white jade figurines,' he added, and everyone nodded, pleased, because jade always fetched a very good price, and Jack had an unerring eye for the best.

THREE

Mr Todworthy Inkling's lively imagination had, it seemed, been stirred by the story of the Stone Heads.

'He listened very intently,' said Byron, lounging in Jack's dressing room after the evening's performance. 'And then that acquisitive gleam appeared – you know that look: it's for all the world as if a wrinkled walnut's chuckling over a good joke – and he rubbed his hands together, and said he believed he knew the very person. We're to go along to the shop tomorrow for a meeting.'

'He does understand we must have someone we can trust?' Jack was putting on a dress shirt which Gus had ironed earlier, since Mr Jack was attending a late supper party at the Thespis Club, and Gus was not having him appear at such a distinguished gathering wearing a crumpled shirt.

'He does,' said Byron. 'I'm guessing he's dredged up someone from his Cambridge University days. As for trusting people,' he said, suddenly, 'I suppose we can trust Mikhail himself, can we? There were a couple of times when I thought he seemed evasive.'

'Such as when we asked him how Simeon could have heard about the Stone Heads?' said Jack. 'I noticed that. But probably he was only searching for the English words to reply.'

'However,' said Byron, 'on a more positive note, I've discovered that Church organization he mentioned – the Society for Ecclesiastical Restoration – is genuine. Its exact title is the Ecclesiastical Society for the Restoration of Sacred Buildings, and it has offices in Chancery Lane, quite close to the Maughan Library. I think we must certainly investigate there.'

'You're thinking Simeon had created a link with them before he travelled to Russia?' said Jack. 'And tracked down the most valuable artefacts he could find that he thought would appeal to them?'

'It's a good possibility. He might have filched half of

Russia's historic treasures, for all we know, and had half a dozen innocent Church societies lined up to buy them. But this Society in particular sounds as if it would be interested in the Stone Heads. Sculptures for decaying churches, and so on.'

'And they'd buy them from him in good faith,' said Jack, 'because it was the helpful and entirely trustworthy Reverend Fitzglen, and they thought they knew all about him. Byron, you're right – this is a line of enquiry worth pursuing. Gus, where are you? Oh, you're there. Listen now, I think you'd better come with us to Tod's tomorrow. You know Tod as well as any of us, and if he's putting up someone a bit questionable for this, you'd see through it. You always spot the doubtful ones and the fakes.'

'That comes from having grown up on the streets as a boy, and watching my pa lift wallets from the toffs in Bond Street,' said Gus, sagely. 'You develop an instinct for what's real and what isn't. Shall you be home for breakfast tomorrow, Mr Jack?'

'No idea,' said Jack, and grinned at Byron. 'That was Gus's polite way of asking if I'll be staying out all night.'

'Or,' said Byron, 'whether you might be entertaining an unexpected guest in your own rooms for breakfast.'

In fact, Jack ate a respectable solitary breakfast in his rooms next morning, and as midday chimed from St Martin's, he and Byron, with Gus in attendance, made their way through the maze of streets and alleyways leading off St Martin's Lane.

Jack always enjoyed visiting Inkling's; as Byron often said, it felt like stepping back into the previous century. They went through the door bearing a plaque proclaiming it to be *Inkling's Emporium, Rare Books, Manuscripts and Folios, Items of Interest Bought and Sold, and Quests for the Unusual Undertaken*, and picked their way through the cluttered rooms and between hazardously lopsided shelves to Todworthy Inkling's private quarters.

He beamed a welcome, readjusted the purple plush surcoat which was his latest choice for day attire, adjusted the crimson velvet smoking cap without which he had never been seen, and cleared several stacks of what looked like seventeenth-century manuscripts from chairs for them to sit down. After this, he waved an introductory hand to the figure seated by the desk, its head tilted expectantly, the eyes behind rimless spectacles inspecting the three newcomers with interest.

'Miss Vera Gilchrist,' said Tod, and stood back, beaming. 'Aha! Not what you were expecting, Mr Jack.'

'No, it isn't.'

'She is a very learned young lady. Ideal for your mission,' said Tod, resuming his chair behind the desk, revolving his thumbs, his eyes in his seamed face twinkling.

'I'm glad to be meeting you both,' said Miss Gilchrist.

She could have passed for any age from twenty-one to forty-one. She was wearing a plain costume that was either dark grey or a very drab green, with a hat that did not quite match pulled down over her hair. The rimless glasses were perched on her nose, and she was clutching a slightly battered bag.

Jack looked at her and was aware of a wholly unexpected – but certainly not unfamiliar – emotion taking hold of him.

'Miss Gilchrist is Scottish,' said Tod.

'So her voice suggests,' said Jack, expressionlessly.

'I'm from Edinburgh,' explained Miss Gilchrist, earnestly. 'But I attended Girton College at Cambridge.' She fixed Jack with a very straight stare. 'It was thought strange of me, for ladies did not, in the general way, enter universities then,' she said. 'Indeed, I believe they do not do so very often now. We were not awarded degrees, you know, and we had to obtain permission to attend lectures; even then, we could not sit exams without special dispensation—' A pause. 'I am talking too much. Nerves, of course.'

'I wouldn't have thought you ever suffered from nervousness,' said Jack, and heard the suppressed anger in his tone.

'Wouldn't most ladies be nervous at meeting the famous Jack Fitzglen?' she said, levelly.

'What exactly was your field of study?' said Jack, ignoring this.

'Theology,' said Vera Gilchrist, promptly. 'I had a particular interest in Church history.'

Jack leaned back in his chair and folded his arms, his eyes still on her. 'Not an interest in the theatre?' he said. 'Not how to step on to a stage and fool an audience into thinking you're someone other than your real self?'

'Oh, damn you, Jack,' said Vera Gilchrist, all traces of the Scottish accent vanishing. 'Tod, I told you we wouldn't fool him.'

'Viola Gilfillan,' said Jack. 'Of course you didn't fool me. Tod, I can't believe you've tried to foist a Gilfillan on to us.'

'I knew you'd realize,' said Viola, pulling off her hat and loosening the tightly bound hair beneath, so that strands of copper-coloured hair like rippled silk escaped. 'Although I didn't think you'd do it so quickly, and it's very annoying, after I took such trouble. The Scottish accent was good, though, wasn't it?'

'It's the accent you used when you played Lady Macbeth last season,' said Jack.

'I wouldn't have seen through it so quickly,' said Byron, studying Viola. 'Gus, would you?'

Gus said it was difficult to know, and Miss Gilfillan was a very fine actress.

'Diplomat,' said Viola, grinning at him. 'Look here, Jack, Tod's told me a bit about what's needed, and I'm intrigued by these ancient Russian sculptures. As for infiltrating Church commissions and scholarly religious boards, I could do it with complete aplomb. Is "aplomb" the word I mean? Anyway, Tod and I have worked out a very good character for me – I'm assistant to a professor of theology living in Edinburgh. Professor Pilkington. A dear muddly academic, and he gets into frightful tangles with his research, which is why he has to have my help. He's a lifelong bachelor, so I think I could be a distant niece, which makes it all entirely respectable.'

'You can portray yourself as his fifth wife or his tenth illegitimate daughter for all I care; you're still not coming in on this, Viola,' said Jack.

'I could give a very convincing performance. As a professor's assistant, I mean.'

'Miss Gilfillan is extremely gifted,' said Tod.

'I don't care if she's Sarah Siddons and Anne Bracegirdle

rolled into one,' said Jack. 'In any case, the family would never agree to it.'

'Then don't tell them.'

'And aren't you about to appear in *Lady Windermere's Fan*?' demanded Jack. 'Which you're certainly staging as an attempt to outdo our run of *The Importance*. You won't, of course.'

'We'll have *House Full* notices up within the week,' said Viola at once. 'But I can consign Lady Windermere and her fan to my understudy for a night or two.'

Byron said, cautiously, 'Jack, for Viola to help with investigating Simeon's trickery might be a good idea.'

'Saintly Simeon?' said Viola, sharply.

'You know him?'

'I know *of* him,' she said. 'I've heard some of the stories, and they're particularly unpleasant. How he relieves vulnerable people – older ladies in particular – of their life savings to finance fictional schemes. If he's likely to be brought to justice at the end of all this, I'd certainly like to help.'

There was a short silence, broken only by the popping of the gas jets, which Tod clung to on the grounds that he did not trust electricity.

Then Byron said, 'Jack, we should remember Viola is one of the very few Gilfillans who know the truth about us. And she's never betrayed us.'

'I don't care,' said Jack. He strode angrily to the small, grimed window and stood glaring at the cluttered yard beyond.

Gus, sitting quietly in his corner, thought it was as if Mr Jack had suddenly retreated behind a thick curtain. What he had not expected was that Miss Viola would go to stand next to him and lay her hand on his arm. After a moment, he turned to look at her, and she said something, but so quietly Gus could not hear it. But there was a moment when something seemed to pass between them – almost a sizzle of light, a little like when the new installation of electric light had had to be fitted in the Amaranth two or three years earlier, and wires and cables had fizzed alarmingly and spat out flashes of blue light.

Byron said, softly, 'It was inevitable that Jack would realize who she was, Tod. I don't believe they could both be in the same room and not recognize each other. She could don Pompey's furred fox and lambskins, and he could put on Shylock's gaberdine – and they would still know one another.'

Tod Inkling said, 'I've never known if it's love or hate between those two.'

'I don't think they know themselves,' said Byron, his eyes on the figures framed in the window. But when, at last, Jack turned back to the room, he said, 'Jack, an idea occurs to me – something that might provide a way through this.'

'Well?'

'Don't growl at me. I think it would be perfectly acceptable for Viola to approach this Society asking about the Stone Heads. She could say her professor is writing a treatise or a monograph or something about religious sculptures, and he's heard on some academic grapevine that these unusual effigies were recently brought to this country from Russia.'

'And he thinks they could help with his research,' said Viola.

'Yes. But there's a caveat,' went on Byron. 'It's that if you do this, Viola, someone must accompany you.'

'In case I give you all away or ruin the entire plot?'

'You won't do that. But a companion is quite a good idea,' said Tod, thoughtfully. 'Mr Jack?'

'It's a terrible idea. The whole idea is impossible. In any case, who could Viola take with her?' said Jack. 'If Simeon is tangled up in this and likely to be around, he would instantly see through any disguise one of us adopted.'

'Jack's right,' said Viola. 'The Fitzglen eyes are unmistakable.' She looked at him, and again Gus felt something shiver on the air between them.

Byron said, 'But it doesn't necessarily have to be a Fitzglen who'd come with you.'

A sudden silence fell, and Gus realized they had all turned to look at him.

'Bless us and save us all,' said Todworthy, waving aside Gus's protests. 'Of course you can do it, Augustus Pocket, and if we can't fit you up with a credible disguise, we don't deserve to be part of the filching profession. That's excepting you from that description, of course, Miss Viola.'

'Oh, don't except me, Tod; I'm loving stepping into the criminal underworld,' said Viola, cheerfully. 'Gus, do say you'll come with me. We'll put it right with Jack; don't worry over that.'

Gus could not think how to say he would prefer to have nothing to do with the Stone Heads, or that, to his way of thinking, they would be better left wherever they might have come to rest. He waited and, at last, Mr Jack said, very grudgingly, 'If anything goes wrong with this mad scheme, don't expect me to rescue anyone.'

'Nothing will go wrong,' said Mr Byron. 'Gus, don't look so gloomy – this isn't a real filch. It's a legitimate quest to find and restore stolen sculptures.'

'It's an adventure,' said Viola. 'We're going on a quest for these mysterious sculptures. And we have no idea what we're likely to find at the end of our journey.'

Gus did not dare say that what they might find at the end of their journey was exactly what was worrying him.

Russia, early 1770s

Harry Fitzglen was not in the least worried about what he might find at the end of his journey – he had frequently found that it was possible to turn unexpected quirks of fate to advantage. And as he rode out of the dark forest road and around the curve of the carriageway, almost directly below him was something very unexpected indeed. A line of immense barges – easily six or eight of them – moored on the side of the river, their prows and bows festooned with lights and glowing lanterns that sent radiance into the night sky. Even from up here, in the concealment of the trees, he could make out immense gilt candelabra on the decks, all with dozens of lit candles. Music reached his ears faintly – violins and pipes and lutes, even harps. The entire spectacle was lighting up the night – it was lighting up Harry's mind, as well, because here, clearly, was wealth and luxury. And wealth and luxury meant opportunities.

He had expected to see the river, because it was where he

had been heading, so that he could follow it until he came to the next prosperous-looking town. He had not, however, thought it would present this brilliant and extravagant spectacle.

His lips curved in a smile, and he clicked his horse into a gentle canter. It would not do to go galloping eagerly down to that luxurious fleet of vessels as if he did not want to waste a minute in boarding one of them. Instead, he would approach at a leisurely, measured pace – a pace that befitted a gentleman who lived his life surrounded by, and well accustomed to, such splendour.

He had been travelling across Russia for several weeks, enjoying his journey, finding interest in the different people he met. He was pleased that he was able to converse with most of them; he had what he thought was a fairly good command of French and also some German, and lately he had been gratified to realize he was acquiring a smattering of the Russian language. A beautiful although complex tongue, it was, and it varied considerably from region to region, which could be difficult. But in the last week or two, Harry had been able to converse surprisingly well, and the people with whom he had talked had been friendly and welcoming. Perhaps the ladies had been especially welcoming – a reminiscent amusement flickered over his mind when he thought about some of them. He had something of a weakness for raven-haired, porcelain-complexioned ladies, preferably of impeccable lineage, but it was not a strict rule. And he invariably behaved as a gentleman, never disclosing names or betraying liaisons after the event.

Two nights ago, he had spent a pleasant and profitable evening just outside the city of Sevastopol – a beautiful place, proud of its new status which had been conferred by the Empress, and delighted to welcome all travellers. His destination had been a palatial residence on the outskirts, and the exhibition it was holding of rare and valuable icons. It had been absurdly easy to go through the imposing portico unchallenged – the trick was to walk in as if you had every right to be there, and Harry had done so with panache. His evening attire was as well cut as anyone's, and although he disdained the fashionable powdered wigs that many gentlemen wore, he conformed to the extent of combing his black hair into a semblance of tidiness, tying the ends neatly at the back with a black satin riband, although the front flopped over his forehead as usual.

He had mingled with the guests, and had wandered through the rooms in leisurely fashion, appreciatively sipping the wine that was being served, falling into conversation with various members of the company. Asked about his travels, employing a mixture of French and as much Russian as he could, he explained he hoped to make for a particular area north of Yekaterinburg.

Ah, a beautiful city, Yekaterinburg, smiled the listeners, and were pleased to talk about the history of that area to this extremely charming traveller. A French gentleman, was he? Yes, he was almost certainly so. The French had such style.

Harry listened to all the discourse, then said, 'I should like to get as far as Verkhoturye – the Gateway to Siberia, it is called, yes? I am told it has an interesting history.'

It was slightly disconcerting when an abrupt silence came down at the mention of Verkhoturye. Several people looked uneasily at one another from the corners of their eyes, and Harry wondered if he had said something that had unwittingly struck an offensive note. But he did not think he had, and so he smiled, sketched a half-bow and moved on to one of the other rooms.

Examining a small silk icon, embroidered with glowing colours and surrounded by a gold frame, he caught a snatch of conversation close by.

'A beautiful exhibition,' a man's voice was saying. 'Some very rare pieces.'

'Let us hope the English Thief has not heard about them,' rejoined the companion.

Harry edged closer, amused at the unmistakable capital letters the speaker had used. 'I heard he was travelling in this part of Russia,' said the man.

'But who is he? Somebody told me he's a nobleman's son who became bored with the rigid life of the English Court.'

'I heard he was a nobleman's bastard,' said the first speaker, rather scathingly. 'And that he lives by his wits – although if even a quarter of the stories are true, he lives very well indeed. But I doubt anyone knows the truth. I doubt, too, that he would dare to so much as approach this place.' There was a complacent glance around.

'If he does get in here, I'd wager he'd clear half of the cabinets and shelves inside twenty minutes and have made off into the night with the spoils before anyone noticed.'

Harry had not cleared half of the cabinets or shelves, of course; he would not have dreamed of being so extravagantly – and so riskily – acquisitive. What he had done was to appropriate six of the smallest icons, all of them beautiful, all of them valuable – among them the gold-framed embroidered silk piece. None were signed – it had never been customary to sign icons, which was an advantage, because it meant a whole provenance could be created for each piece. He enjoyed that part of his work.

But the speaker had been wrong about the time it took him to take the items. It had been just under fifteen minutes.

And now, standing on the outskirts of the forest, looking down at the glittering fleet of river craft, he thought this might be a very suitable hiding place for the icons and for himself. Just for a little while, just until the inevitable hue and cry had died down. It was very easy to visualize the well-heeled people who were doubtless aboard those vessels, among whom he was unlikely to be noticed.

Was there one of the animal barges somewhere, where he could safely take his horse for a night or two? That was important. Such a large fleet of vessels would surely have to have horses on hand for part of their transport. Stable barges, they were called in some countries. And there, at the end of the line, was just such a boat – he recognized it for what it was, and he could see people moving back and forth on it.

The smile curved his lips again, and he rode forward.

It was some little time before he walked along to the largest craft, but as he did so, the music and the lights and the warm rich scents seemed to reach out to enfold him.

He paused at the top of the walkway, seeing that ornate tables had been set up at the far end of the long deck, laden with exotic foods on silver and gold platters. It would be absurd to refer to the meal as supper, because clearly it was an outright banquet. But were there empty chairs at this banqueting table? If he had to ask one of the soft-footed attendants, it would instantly mark him out as a stranger, as one who had not been invited. It was all right, though; several chairs were empty, and Harry walked with studied nonchalance to one of them and sat down as if he had expected a place to be reserved for him, nodding to the people on each side. He was starting to feel as if he had stepped into a dream, and it was no exaggeration to think of this as an Arabian Nights' fantasy, or to imagine that he was aboard Cleopatra's fleet.

The music swirled around him, and people smiled and addressed comments to him. He was presented with platters of food by liveried attendants, and a gold-rimmed chalice at his place was filled with something that might have been spiced wine, but that could equally have been the Ambrosian draught of the gods, sent down from Olympus for the occasion.

Finally, he looked along the table to the figure who sat at the table's head. She was richly dressed, and several ropes of pearls were around her neck, but Harry gave them only the most cursory glance, because it was the lady herself who was taking his entire attention. She had dark eyes, and there was a look almost of calculation in them, as if she were assessing everything she saw – weighing it all in her mind and reaching a conclusion. She had strongly marked cheek-bones, and lips that might relax into humour if there should be something at which to smile. Her hair was elaborately dressed but, unexpectedly, it was unpowdered. It was dark, with red lights glinting in it, and Harry had the curious impression that red lights glinted in her eyes as well, in the way devils were sometimes depicted in paintings. But then a small breath of wind stirred the lantern lights, and the light shifted and the devil-impression vanished.

With a twist of amusement he realized that although this was not, of course, the famed, extravagant Egyptian ruler's legendary fleet he had boarded, it was the fleet of another equally famed and equally extravagant ruler.

Catherine Alexeyevna Romanova.

The Empress of all the Russias.

And she was looking straight at him with the unblinking stare of a creature who has seen and marked out a new and particularly desirable prey.

FOUR

Russia, early 1770s (cont'd)

Harry could not decide if he was surprised when the soft-voiced attendant came to him at the end of the banquet, and murmured in his ear that Her Imperial Highness would be interested to receive the unknown traveller in her private chamber.

It was not couched as a command, but it was certainly not a mere suggestion, and Harry murmured an acceptance and followed the man. He was outwardly calm and composed, but his mind was spinning. She is going to seduce me, he thought. That astonishing and powerful lady has beckoned me to her bed. And if I accept her beckoning, will it be because I find her alluring and desirable, or simply because of who she is? Seduction by an empress was not a possibility that had ever occurred to Harry, and he wondered what would happen if he were to politely decline. Would he be thrown into some dungeon and left to rot for insulting a crowned head? Marched to the scaffold for committing lèse-majesté? But you're not going to decline, are you? said his mind. She must be easily fifteen years your senior, but that doesn't matter.

The chamber to which he was shown was richly furnished, hung with silken drapes and strewn with velvet cushions. Thick skin rugs lay on the floor, and a massive tester bed, with more silk curtains, faced the door. There was a seductive drift of perfume – was she brewing the love potion of the gods in order to entice him? Standing there, Harry could almost believe it was Aphrodite's fabled cup of desire that was being distilled for his delectation, but when he looked across at the figure lying on the bed, he knew that no aphrodisiac was necessary.

Her dark eyes were watching him with speculation. Then,

in a soft voice, speaking in French, she said, 'Well, M'sieur? What are you thinking? Perhaps that I am shameless to summon a complete stranger to my bedchamber?'

Harry said, 'I am thinking that this is one of the most beautiful rooms I have ever seen, Your Majesty, either on land or on sea. And that you are one of the most remarkable ladies I have ever encountered.'

At once, she switched to English. 'You have seen many, I am sure. Rooms and ladies, both, yes?' As he hesitated, 'I have it right – you are English?'

Harry spread his hands in a gesture of acknowledgement. 'You have the gift of discernment, madam,' he said. 'And your own English is very good.' Yes, seen closer to, she was easily fifteen years older than he was; even by the kindly candlelight, he could see the fine lines at the corners of her eyes.

She laughed, and said, 'So I did read your thoughts. And I believe you are also thinking I was probably born a great many years before you. I was, of course. Does it matter?'

'Not the smallest bit.' He sat on the side of the bed, took her hand and waited, because, presumably, some sort of etiquette would be brought into play now. Did you make the first move into the bed of a queen – an empress – or did you wait for the equivalent of a royal command?

She studied him, then said, 'I am glad you accepted my—'

'Invitation? Command?'

She smiled, but said, 'The young men of the Court will tell you that I have certain requirements when choosing a lover.'

Harry said, gravely, 'I have heard stories of how you fling the unsatisfactory ones into the river the next morning, or dismember them and feed them to jackals and hyenas.'

There was a moment when he thought he had miscalculated, and that he might find himself subjected to that very fate or one unpleasantly similar, but then she laughed, and suddenly seemed much younger.

'Do they really say that of me?' she said, with delight. 'It has a splendidly biblical sound. But it is only the gossip of the envious, of course.'

'Of course.'

'The only real qualification I require in a lover is the ability to' – this time the smile was mischievous – 'the ability to make love throughout an entire night,' said Catherine Romanova, demurely. 'I use polite wording, you understand.' She reached for one of his hands, and her fingers curled around it. My God, thought Harry, his senses reeling, even the touch of her hand is enough . . .

'Well, sir? Will you disappoint me? Have you that ability?'

Harry smiled at her. 'Shall we find out?' he said, and without particular haste, but certainly without wasting any time, began to remove his clothes.

Catherine's private memoirs, early 1770s

In this private journal, I can write that the minute I set eyes on the dark-haired young Englishman, who so unaccountably appeared on my barge, I had a single, absolutely overpowering thought: That one is for me. And then: Is this the one I have always hoped might one day appear in my life?

As for his ability to maintain— Well, I shall only write that he certainly did not disappoint me. (I write those words with a reminiscent smile.)

The most beautiful sunrise was bathing the river when I awoke, and the river banks looked as if they had been painted with scarlet and gold.

Breakfast was brought to us – a discreet knock on the door heralded it, but the trays were left just inside, and the two attendants withdrew without looking over at the bed. They are well trained.

I do not trouble about making a grande toilette for breakfast, even in the presence of a lover, and my Englishman did not seem to care anyway. He was tousled and unshaven, and he looked like an aristocratic gypsy.

The morning sun streamed through the small windows, turning the honey transparent and making the warm, fresh bread glisten. My companion cupped his hands about one of the breakfast bowls of warm mead that had been served, and drank with appreciation. As he held the bowl to his lips, I watched, and recalled the uses those hands had been put to during the night.

He caught the thought at once – he has a remarkably perceptive mind – and smiled at me. 'You did not object to any one of the things my hands did,' he said.

'You can read thoughts as well as all else?'

'I think,' he said, consideringly, 'that we are a little in accord. Strange, isn't it? The English wanderer and the imperious, imperial Empress. Perhaps we are both "spirits of another sort".'

'That is a quotation?'

'William Shakespeare,' he said, and, annoyingly, I felt at a disadvantage for not recognizing the line by the famous English dramatist. It is rare for me to feel at a disadvantage, and to counteract the feeling, I said, 'You admire playwrights and plays?'

'I do. If my life had taken a different path, I might have taken to the stage. So might you. We both enact roles for those we meet, yes?'

And now he really was seeing far more than anyone else ever has. Into my heart? Into the sadnesses, and the ache for things I have lost, and into the darknesses? But haven't I always known that one day someone would do that?

I said, 'I do not yet know your name.'

'Do you need to know?'

'I think I do.'

The smile came again. 'Harry Fitzglen, ma'am.'

'Where do you go after this, Harry Fitzglen?'

'I am a traveller,' he said, lightly. 'A wanderer of worlds.' His hand came out to trace the lines of my lips. 'Did you know that a French philosopher once said that to travel is almost like talking with men and women of other centuries?'

After a moment, I said, 'That was René Descartes, I think?' and I was absurdly pleased I had recognized the words and to see his eyes light with appreciation.

But he only said, 'I see I was right to say we are both spirits of another sort. I like to think that when I travel, I am talking with people from other centuries, Catherine.' He considered me, then, in a solemn voice, but with amusement in his eyes, he said, 'And now have I committed another sin in addressing you by your name?'

'There are very few people who call me Catherine – very few who would dare to. My husband even—' I frowned and shut off that particular memory, and said, 'What I think you would call my family name was Sophie.'

I had not realized I had been going to say this, but I was glad I had done so, because there was again the feeling of sharing something private.

'Sophie,' he said, trying it out. 'It turns you into someone entirely different. It clothes you in a disguise. I do not think there are many people who know – or even are aware of – Sophie.'

He was watching me from the pillows with a quizzical look that was not really open to misinterpretation, and I glanced at the gilt clock near the bed. There were three-quarters of an hour before I must be in the part of the barge furnished as a state room to meet my advisors and discuss the next stage of our journey. Three-quarters of an hour . . .

I took from his hands the bowl of mead, set it down at the side of the bed and let him pull me against him.

Later

I swept into the meeting with as much formality and panache as possible. This is expected of me.

The papers were set out charting the next part of our journey. It had been worked out before we embarked, of course, and there are to be a number of stops. I shall be taking official possession of new provinces; I shall be welcoming nobles and diplomats aboard these barges and entertaining them lavishly.

I had known, in a general way, of the various towns we were to visit – some of which were to bear my name. The voyage was to end in Constantinople, and I had been looking forward to that.

I am not looking forward to anything now, though. For

placed before me were details of an addition to our schedule
– an extra place for us to visit.

'It has an interesting history,' said the fleet captain, jabbing
at the map with his finger. 'I have charted the journey, and it
will only mean one extra night. We have all agreed it will be
a good place for you to visit, Highness.'

'Messages will be sent ahead to prepare the people
there for your journey,' said someone else, and there were
murmurs that there would be a fine welcome – that this was
a place with much history, many interesting legends, an ancient
monastery . . .

I listened and nodded, and somehow hid the tumult in
my mind. I agreed that such a small detour made little
difference.

But it made an enormous and terrifying difference. Because
the place that has much history and interesting legends is
Verkhoturye, and the ancient monastery is the Monastery of
St Nicholas.

Verkhoturye. Even to write that causes a sense of menace
to close around me, because that is the place where a tangle
of bloodied skeins came to rest – skeins that almost ten years
ago were shut away in the dark for ever. Even now, there are
nights when I feel as if reproachful eyes stare at me, as if to
say, 'You are the one who condemned us to this dark lonely
silence.'

But I could think of no rational reason to give for not visiting
Verkhoturye, and so I smiled and agreed.

Harry had always considered that new places held opportunities,
and that most would be found to contain items of elegance
and value that could be discreetly removed – although he
would acknowledge that matters could occasionally go
disastrously wrong. There had been times when he had had
to flee a house or a city. He would always regret that, following
a certain night in Paris, he would probably never dare risk
visiting that beautiful city again.

But tonight, preparing to escort his lady to the evening
banquet, she suddenly said, 'It has been decided that we shall

make an extra stop on the voyage. A detour – I have that word right?'

'We have the word, certainly. Where is the detour?'

She paused, then said, 'To a place called Verkhoturye,' and it was as if the name dropped into the warm bedchamber like a spear of ice. Harry's mind at once went back to that curious silence that had fallen at the Sevastopol exhibition when he had so casually mentioned he might travel to Verkhoturye.

But he only said, 'You do not want to go there?'

'I cannot prevent it,' she said, evasively. 'The plans have already been made. And it is a place with an interesting history – it is often called the Gateway to Siberia. But—'

She stopped, and Harry hesitated, then said, 'But there are places in the world that hold darknesses, I think.'

There was no mistaking the gratitude with which she turned to him, but she only said, 'Shall you remain with me until after Verkhoturye.'

'Are you commanding me?' He traced the lines of her face with the tip of his finger. 'Command me, Sophie,' he said, softly.

She gave him a half-smile, but said, 'I would never command you. But I would wish you to be with me.'

'We have a saying in my country – that your wish is my command. I will accompany you to Verkhoturye.'

Taking his place at the long table on the banqueting deck, Harry sifted in his mind the possible reasons for his lady to be afraid of Verkhoturye. It could be anything from a discarded lover plotting vengeance to a full-scale insurrection, involving half a dozen disgruntled states and an army of exiled crowned heads intent on deposing the House of Romanov. He was aware that Emperor Peter III had died in very questionable circumstances, and also that time did not necessarily count when it came to such things. Harry thought he was not going to risk becoming mixed up in the echoes of a ten-year-old murder and ending up on the gallows. Not even, said his mind, slyly, for the sake of a Russian empress in whose bed you have spent the most astonishing nights you can ever remember?

He smiled at the memory, but even as he did so, he was again wondering what there could be at Verkhoturye that had brought that look of unmistakable fear.

Catherine's private memoirs, early 1770s

I do not think there is another man alive – at least, no man I have ever met – who would have sensed my fear regarding Verkhoturye.

But my English lover sensed it, even though he could not possibly have understood the reason for it. And he will be with me when we go there. There is a faint far-off comfort in that.

I wore the green brocade tonight. My maid – the sulky wench, Anya – was annoyed – she is waiting for me to throw out this gown so that she can have it for herself. She will have a long wait, since I have no intention of discarding it yet. But she dressed me with her usual attention to detail, and unlocked the jewel case so that I could wear my emeralds, as well.

My English lover found the gown and the emeralds very alluring. He found it even more alluring when I removed the gown so that I was wearing the emeralds and nothing else.

I do not entirely trust him, of course, and I would not be surprised if, when he finally departs, some of my jewels depart with him. But, strangely, I do not think I should mind. I would like to think of him making use of a few of my jewels for some profitable investment. The purchase of land, perhaps – in England, in London – on which he will build a property that will endure long after he and I have both gone.

These are thoughts and speculations that should drive back the fear, but I know the nearer we get to Verkhoturye and what lies in its lonely darknesses, the more intense will be the fear.

I still do not know if I acted in the right way all those years ago, but, even now, I cannot see what else I could have done. But I had not allowed for Quintus.

Quintus. Even briefly allowing his name into my mind brings the familiar cold dread. I have never written of that particular dread before, and it is probably madness to do so now, but perhaps writing it down will exorcise it.

So I will write that there have been times over these years when I have felt Quintus's mind brush mine. It is almost as if he and I think about one another at the exact same moment, and that in that moment, our minds lock together—

No. I cannot – I will not! – believe that there may be times when he reaches out to me. And that at those times his mind finds me.

FIVE

Quintus had been in the Verkhoturye Monastery of St Nicholas since the day shortly after his ninth birthday when his father had taken him up the steep path leading out of Cympak. Once at the monastery, his father had delivered him into the hands of the monks. There had been no farewell; his father merely said he hoped Quintus would follow the path of obedience and devotion, and that he would remain safely within the monastery walls.

It was almost sixteen years since that day, but Quintus could still remember watching his father walking away to enter a small, enclosed religious house many miles distant, where he intended to spend the rest of his life.

Quintus had no intention of spending the rest of his own life in the St Nicholas monastery. He hated it. It was an old building, its fabric eroding despite the monks' care, and it had mean, slit-like windows that seemed to stare balefully down on the huddle of villages below, as if daring enterprising sinners to climb the path to request admittance. Spiteful winds hissed and whispered along the draughty corridors, never quite forming themselves into words, but sounding as if they were sending out warnings of things crouching in the shadowy corners.

This was a place that would have many layers of memories, of course, but over the years, Quintus often wondered if some of the memories were not from the past, but from the future. Occasionally, he even had the feeling that they were trying to warn him – to say: don't take such and such a course of action; or: at all costs, avoid treading a particular path that lies in wait.

The years slid along, dreary and uneventful, and Quintus could see no means of leaving. In any case, he had nowhere to go, and no money with which to travel. And always, deep within his mind, was the knowledge that to venture into the world could be dangerous for him. There were things that could never be known . . . things that must remain hidden . . .

He applied himself to his studies, to the work allotted to him, but all the time, impatience and resentment were clawing at the edges of his mind, because there must be a way in which he could leave this place and safely enter the real world. He clung to the hope that one day he would find it.

And then, finally, without warning, the day came.

He was summoned to Father Abbot's study, where Father Abbot was frowning over a letter.

'Brother Quintus, I have asked you to come here because we have been called on to send a member of this community to an extremely exalted residence. To minister to the spiritual needs of the household's servants.' He looked up from the letter and studied Quintus. 'You will know we are sometimes asked to send one of our community out into the world in such a way?'

Years of practice had bred in Quintus the ability to conceal his feelings – to appear humble and accepting. He said, 'I do know that, Father.'

'You have been requested – by name – for just such an appointment.' He frowned, then said, 'I am surprised, and you are very young for such a task. But I believe you are equal to it, although you will find it very different from the serenity and peace here. I think it will be very worldly, filled with the clamour of ambition and greed – perhaps also of intrigue.'

Quintus waited to be told where the worldly, greedy, ambition-filled destination might be, and Father Abbot said, 'You are going to St Petersburg. To the Winter Palace of the Tsar.'

It was the last thing Quintus had expected, but it was as if something had ignited a brilliant light directly in front of him. It was the escape opening up at last, and it was an escape into a world that would contain people of power and influence.

The Winter Palace. The most glittering residence of all the residences belonging to the Emperor of all the Russias – Peter III – and his wife, Catherine Alexeyevna Romanova. It was barely six months since they had succeeded to the Imperial

Throne – the monks might be remote from the world, but they knew what went on in it, and Father Abbot had arranged for services to pray for the health and wisdom of their new rulers. He had especially prayed that His Imperial Highness, Peter, could be led to a better, more generous, understanding of Russian Orthodoxy. Quintus had even heard him say it was difficult to feel loyalty for a tsar who was already attempting to secularize all Church land and serfs.

But if this appointment meant Quintus would escape St Nicholas's Monastery, he did not care if Peter Romanov worshipped devils or cavorted with Satan's emissaries across half of Russia.

He said, deliberately humbly, 'I shall do my best to fulfil whatever is wanted.'

'You will care for the spiritual needs of the servants in Their Highnesses' private apartments,' said Father Abbot. 'You will be known as Father Quintus, rather than Brother. That is the tradition for monks who go out into the world.'

'I understand.'

Father Abbot glanced back at the letter. 'I do not know why you have been particularly asked for,' he said, with a slight frown. 'As you know, it is not in our creed to pry into the minds or the lives of a brother – but can you think of any links your family might have with the Imperial family? Is there any association of any kind with any members of the Court?'

'No,' said Quintus. 'I know of no links whatsoever.'

He had expected to be impressed by St Petersburg, but the opulence and the magnificence – the sheer size – of the Winter Palace stunned him. It was a realm – an entire world – in its own right; it was as if a massive glittering city had been raised from the earth's core.

For several days after his arrival, he felt almost blinded by the immense rooms and the vast dome-ceilinged apartments and halls – he felt as a man emerging from a dark room into strong sunlight might feel. But he set out his books and writing materials in the room he was given, and he made himself known to the people for whose spiritual care he would be responsible, presenting himself as a man of humility and piety, but also as a man not unaccustomed to grandeur.

Early on, he found what was known as the Grand Church, and he stood for a long while staring in. It was an immense, cathedral-like place, with soaring pillars and domed ceilings that glowed with paintings of saints and religious scenes.

How would it feel to stand before the elaborate altar at the far end of the nave, with the Imperial Court assembled before you? Could he do that if ever he were called upon? He waited for doubt to assail him, but it did not. This was something to strive towards. Something to aim for.

For the moment, however, he had his own small domain in the far more modest chapel, which, it seemed, had been recently created. Even though it was intended for the use of the servants, it still contained riches: mosaic panels and elaborate rood screens, and gold ciboria and jewelled plates and patens.

The servants grumbled cheerfully about the work required of them, telling one another that it would take a year to clean the Palace from one end to the other – a thousand rooms, there were, and the mosaic floors alone must stretch for miles.

As for the Tsarina, no one knew whether to be shocked or intrigued by the fact that although the Tsar had accompanied her to the Winter Palace, he had returned to Oranienbaum soon afterwards. They discussed this at length, dwelling on the Empress's custom of entertaining a gentleman when the mood took her. Her favourite was the handsome artilleryman, Grigory Orlov, who was frequently to be seen leaving her bedchamber at hours when God-fearing souls were virtuously asleep in their beds. And never mind folk saying he was a son of a noble house, said the gossips – being noble did not give him the right to dip his wick wherever the fancy took him – begging pardon, Father Quintus, if that was an ungodly thing to say.

The female servants said that, in the Empress's favour, the gentleman was dashing and attractive, although the same could not be said for his younger brother, who was currently staying in the palace, and who bore the marks on one side of his face of a duelling scar that had the effect of twisting his lips into a perpetual sneer. Still, wouldn't you rather have even a sneering duelling scar on your pillow of a night than a

grimacing gargoyle, which was all you could say for the Tsar
himself? They then hastily suppressed their giggles, because
to be heard describing His Imperial Highness as a gargoyle
might result in a spell in the dungeons, if not worse. His
Imperial Highness was known to have a vicious temper.

It was several weeks after Quintus's arrival at the Palace when
the event that was to wrench his entire life off its moorings
occurred.

There was to be a very elaborate banquet, and preparations
had been going on for several days, with servants rushing back
and forth, polishing and mopping and scrubbing, and minions
scurrying in quest of dried lavender and aromatic pastilles,
since guests must not be subjected to the aroma of gravy and
goose-fat the minute they arrived. It was thought there would
probably not be more than a hundred guests, although this
could not be relied upon, because the Empress had a way of
adding upwards of a dozen extra people at the last minute.
That made it impossible to know how many roasted swan and
stewed peacock to prepare, because if the numbers at table
were not what you had expected, you were left with a surfeit,
which was all very well, but could be a nuisance, especially
as the chefs refused to send leftovers of any kind to table.

The upper servants were given permission to watch, from an
upper gallery, the procession of the Empress and her guests
into the banqueting hall. Quintus had not intended to be part
of this, but he was somehow swept along and squashed into
a corner that looked down on to the wide antechamber.

Guests were already standing respectfully along the sides,
their jewels glinting, their eyes on the immense doors at the
far end which bore the crests of the Houses of Romanov and
of Holstein-Gottorp.

At last, there was a fanfare of trumpets, bewigged flunkeys
threw open the gilded doors, and she was there, framed in the
massive ornate doorway. Catherine Alexeyevna Romanova.

She was clad in silk and brocade and glittering with jewels,
and as the procession passed under the gallery, she glanced
up, as if to see if people were watching her – almost as though

their presence amused and pleased her. The servants all bowed their heads at once, the women curtseying. Quintus did not bow, though; he looked directly at the Empress and, incredibly, she looked back at him.

In that moment, he felt as if he had been seized and shaken. Then the moment passed, and the procession moved on, but he was left with the inescapable feeling that the woman walking with such ceremony across the polished floor was destined to be immensely important in his life. The astonishing thing was the equally strong conviction that he was destined to be immensely important in hers.

It was late the following evening when Quintus, half drowsing over a book in his room, was roused by a knock on his door.

'Father, your presence is requested. Please to come with me.'

Quintus, somewhat startled, saw that it was almost midnight, but he supposed someone was ill or even dying, and in need of spiritual comfort or final absolution. He therefore took from the desk drawer a small flagon of unction for the anointing of the dying, murmuring softly the lines of the Parting of the Soul as he did so. He had been present at deaths in the monastery, and he knew the litany well.

He had expected to be taken to a bedchamber, but at the end of a marble-floored corridor were double doors, on which the servant knocked, then threw open. Beyond was a high-ceilinged library, with shelves lined with gilt-lettered books. Two men sat at a leather-topped desk. They were not exactly in shadow, but the light from the flaring candelabra did not quite reach them, and Quintus could not make out their features.

After a moment, he said, 'Why have I been brought here?'

The men exchanged glances, and Quintus felt a tremor of apprehension. There was something wrong about this. He glanced behind him. The doors had been closed by the departing servant, but he could reach them in six or seven paces, and be on the other side of them. But then where would he go?

He waited, and one of the men said, 'You are here, Father – in this Palace and tonight in this room – because we want you to be part of a plan.'

The apprehension increased. 'What plan?' said Quintus.

A pause, then, 'A plan to remove the Emperor,' said the man.

Silence came down, almost stifling in its intensity, but at last Quintus said, 'I don't understand.'

'Of course you understand. You are not stupid, Father Quintus.'

He came out from behind the desk, and Quintus saw the scar that twisted one side of his face, and realized who these two were. The scar-faced one was Alexei Orlov; the other was his brother, Grigory, the man known to be the Empress's lover.

He said, 'But to remove the Emperor could only be achieved by—' He broke off, hardly believing what he had been about to say. But Alexei finished the sentence for him.

'—by his death,' he said. 'Yes. We intend that Peter III will be assassinated.'

Assassinated. The word fell like the blow of the executioner's axe, and Quintus's mind flinched. This is too dangerous, he thought. And yet he was aware of a sly voice whispering that wasn't this precisely the kind of opportunity he had waited for? Mightn't this be the chance to be part of something immense and vastly important – something that, if achieved, would shake the entire country – perhaps other countries, as well – to its roots? And something that would mean Quintus himself would acquire power and wealth and influence?

'For our plan to work,' Grigory Orlov was saying, 'we must have the presence of a man of religion. A priest – a monk.'

'You understand, of course, that what we are planning is necessary,' said his brother. 'The Tsar is already a danger. He is forcing on to the country new religious practices – his own pro-Prussian policies. He is ruthless, and he will become more ruthless. He believes that occupying the Imperial Throne allows him to sweep aside the feelings of others.'

Quintus said, 'And if this . . . this plan succeeds, who would rule in his stead?'

'The Empress Consort,' said Grigory, impatiently, as if it

should have been obvious. 'Catherine. She will be Empress Regnant – she will reign and rule in her own right.'

Quintus stared at them, then said, 'You are asking me to commit mortal sin. Murder.'

Murder. The word seemed to shape itself within the shadows, as if a blood-dabbled fingertip had scrawled it across the dimness.

'Yes. But we do so in the knowledge that it would not be the first murder you have committed.'

Grigory got up from behind his desk, his brother at his side, and as the candle flames flickered, Quintus saw their faces more clearly. He saw the light fall across the eyes of them both.

The eyes. It was many years since he had looked up and seen those two pairs of eyes watching him through blazing firelight. Sixteen years.

Then Grigory said, softly, 'I think you will help us, Father. For you know us now, don't you? It is many years since we met, but it was a day I do not think any of us have ever forgotten. We were all much of an age – perhaps nine, and ten or eleven years old.'

Quintus said, in a low, hoarse voice, 'You were in the carriage outside the house that day—'

'Yes, we had stopped, because our coachman had to repair a damaged wheel. And because of that, we saw what you did.'

'Later, we heard you had been taken to the old monastery and hidden there from the world, so that no one should ever know – so that you should never be punished,' said Alexei. 'There was no evidence to betray you, was there? But we knew what you had done, and we stored the knowledge away. Even then, we understood how the actions of others can be turned to advantage in the future – even the smallest of actions.'

'But that was no small action, Father Quintus.' A brief but expressive gesture of hands, then Grigory said, softly, 'We have been calling you Quintus. But we should more accurately call you Leonid.'

Leonid.

The candlelit room blurred, and for a dreadful moment, Quintus thought his legs would no longer support him, and he would fall to the ground. His mind was spinning him back to his childhood – to a day when a nine-year-old boy's rage had filled an underground workroom.

To the time when he had been Leonid.

SIX

Growing up in the remote village, impatient with the dullness of their lives – where the only thing to do was attend the local church and sit through tedious lessons in the schoolroom that always smelled of boiled cabbage – some of Cympak's children had found a way to make their lives exciting. It was a way that was forbidden and sinful – they all knew that – but it was being forbidden and sinful that made it exciting.

They had formed themselves into a small group of street thieves. For most of the time, there were ten of them, although there were three or four older ones who sometimes joined in. At the beginning, it had surprised them to find how easily their plan had unfurled and how many opportunities were open to them. This was mostly because Cympak lay at an intersection of several larger towns and thoroughfares, which meant affluent travellers frequently came through in their splendid carriages. They were richly clad and disdainful, uncaring if their carriages churned up mud that splashed the streets and quite often the people in them. Usually, they were bound for grand houses, mansions and even palaces, although sometimes there were ladies journeying to St Nicholas's Monastery to make a retreat which they thought would atone for all the sins they committed during the rest of the year. The children hated these people – the older ones said it was a hatred born of envy, but whatever it was, they all relished taking the jewels and the pouches of coins from the travellers. Quintus – who had been called Leonid then – hated them the most.

The children became very skilled – stopping carriages with various stories, usually that there was a rockfall farther along or a broken carriage blocking the way. That meant they could swarm inside the carriage to adroitly relieve the passengers of jewels and money, then vanish into the maze of streets and alleyways almost before the shocked occupants realized what had happened.

The stolen goods were sold to the goldsmiths and the jewellers in one of the towns, usually with a story about it being a grandmother's legacy, or a sick mother's attempt to raise money to pay for a physician. The children were careful to keep long intervals between these trips; between times, the items were stored in the cellar which was the studio for Leonid's father, and was where he made household goods – flat-bottomed bowls that people could use for storage, and platters – at times, roof tiles for repairs. Travellers occasionally came to the house, wanting a likeness in stone or clay of their wives or daughters.

There was a kiln for firing the various objects; it was immediately behind the house, and it was reached by a narrow, low tunnel leading out of the cellar. When it was firing, it would glow with the heat gradually building up inside it, but at other times it was a cold, sinister shape, like a hunchbacked man crouching in the shadows, the fire-holes near its top like empty eye-sockets.

There was often the sound of dripping water in the cellar, because of the river that ran under the house's foundations. When Leonid was very small, he thought the dripping sounds were footsteps. Once, he asked his mother about this, thinking she would say that of course there were no creeping footsteps.

But the look he always found frightening came into her eyes, and she said there might well be footsteps or even someone rowing secretly along the underground river. Satan's emissaries were always in the world, looking for sinners to carry off to hell, which was why Leonid must be sure never to fall into sin.

Leonid did not really think anyone would bother to row along that dark old river looking for sinners; anyway, there was an iron gate in the cellar sealing the river off. It did not do so completely, though, and occasionally, if the river was swollen from rain, greenish slimy water seeped under the iron gate and lay on the cellar floor for days. But the gate could only be raised by the immense wheel at the side, which no one had operated for years, and which probably did not work now anyway.

Even so, he tried never to enter the cellar by himself – except when there were spoils from the thieving expeditions to hide. There was a crevice in the kiln tunnel, near the roof, and between visits to the gold and silversmiths, the jewellery and coins could be stashed there when Leonid's parents were out.

Most of the children spent the results of their thefts almost immediately, but Leonid saved his. In a few years' time – perhaps when he was fifteen – he would have enough money to leave Cympak. He hated the village and the narrow minds of the inhabitants, and he hated his parents, as well.

He sometimes thought he did not know them very well. When his father was not working in the cellar, he often walked up the steep narrow path to the monastery, so that he could join in the monks' various services and observances and rites. His mother spent a great part of her days in the local church. When it was not a day for school lessons, Leonid had to accompany her so that he could pray with her to be saved from hellfire. The church was small and cold, and they sat in front of what most people said was a rood screen, but Leonid's father said was an iconostasis – a half-wall composed of icons and tiny paintings. Usually, such screens were made up of religious images, he said – saints and martyrs and various angels who defended mankind – but the Cympak screen was almost entirely made of faces with slanting, peering eyes and grinning mouths.

Sometimes, the faces caught the light from the altar – where what was called the Eternal Light, which was never allowed to go out, burned. It made the eyes in the screen glint redly. Leonid's mother said the faces were representations of devils who had found their way into the church centuries earlier, but had been caught and imprisoned in wood and stone. Often, after a visit to the church, Leonid would wonder if the heads his father sometimes created trapped a part of those people's real selves.

One afternoon, when his father was at the monastery and his mother in church, Leonid took the results of the latest theft to the cellar to hide them. There were some pieces waiting to be fired in the kiln; when his father returned, he would expect Leonid to help fire it. It was a long process – it could take over a day for the kiln to become sufficiently hot, but Leonid had done it a number of times, and it was easy enough.

The theft had been a particularly profitable one; the travellers had been bound for some kind of grand gathering in Sevastopol. This, of course, meant more carriages would come through Cympak in the next day or two – the group had been pleased about that.

There were soft sounds of water dripping in the cellar when he went in, and little rivulets of water had trickled under the gate, which meant the river was swollen from recent rain. Leonid propped open the tunnel door, and he was just stashing away the bags of jewels when, behind him, the cellar steps creaked, and a harsh, angry voice said, 'Leonid – bring me those things you have just hidden.'

His mother. Of course it was. If a sin was being committed, you could be sure she would ferret it out.

But he said, 'I was only putting some – um – old toys away.'

'You lie,' she said. 'You are hiding things. Money and jewellery – like the ones I found hidden in your room earlier today.'

She crossed the floor, not taking her eyes from him, and anger spiked across Leonid's mind, because she had been spying on him – perhaps she had even sneaked back from the church to catch him.

But there was nothing to do but obey her, and he reached up for the little bag and handed it over.

'You are a thief,' she said, snatching it and peering inside. 'A sinner, and there will be a terrible punishment ahead for you. But I shall take you to the priest, and perhaps you might be saved. The priest might send you to a labour village for you to pray for forgiveness.'

Leonid stared at her, sickening fear clutching him, because he knew about the labour villages – everyone knew about them, and they were terrible places. There were harsh punishments – whipping . . . scourging—

He made to dart across to the steps, not knowing where he would go, only wanting to get away from her, but she caught his arm, twisting it painfully behind his back. He managed to pull free, and backed to the open door of the tunnel. 'You would not send me to one of those places!' he shouted. 'Not your own son!'

'I do not recognize a thief and a liar as my son,' she said.

'My father would not let you send me there!'

'Oh, your father will not be interested,' she said, contemptuously. 'All he ever wanted was to spend his filth in me.'

Leonid's mind was reeling; he had never heard her speak like this – he had never heard anyone speak like this. The thought that she was not entirely sane was not a new one, but it seized him more violently than it had ever done before, and with it came a bolt of fury. He grabbed her arm and dragged her into the tunnel.

She struggled and screamed, clawing at his face, but he managed to snatch up a long-handled iron shovel lying near the kiln. It was thick and heavy, and he brought it smashing down on her head. She slumped at once, and Leonid pushed her against the tunnel's wall, then darted to the kiln itself and, using the shovel's handle, began frantically to prise off the bricks covering the fire-holes. They were a tight fit, but finally they tumbled to the ground, leaving a yawning blackess at waist height. A sour smell gusted out, and Leonid flinched, then dragged his mother's unconscious body to the kiln. He levered off more bricks until the opening was larger, then lifted her and crammed her through it, head first. There was a dull clang as she fell on to one of the iron trays inside.

But the fall seemed to have revived her, because, almost at once, there was the sound of scrabbling against the inner wall, and then screams of rage and fear, and shouts of how he would be punished – how he would have to face the devil's servants, who would seize him when he least expected it. Leonid scarcely paid any attention to the threats; all he could think was that he must silence her. Supposing his father came back early and discovered what had happened? He snatched up the bricks he had removed, and frantically thrust them in place to seal the kiln.

But he had only wedged in a few when he became aware of other sounds in the cellar behind him – footsteps and soft creaks. There was a dreadful moment when he thought it really was the devil's servants creeping up on him, and he spun round, having no idea what he might see.

Beyond the tunnel door were two boys, standing at the foot of the old wooden stairs. One was about his own age, the other perhaps a little older. Both were richly clad. Leonid stared at them, then said, as sharply as he could manage, 'Who are you? What are you doing in this house?'

They were staring into the tunnel – they were certainly staring at the kiln – but the elder boy only said, 'We are sorry to intrude into your house, but our carriage met with an accident—'

'A broken wheel,' said the other one. 'We were waiting for it to be mended—'

'—and we heard screaming,' said the first. 'We came down here and saw . . .' He paused, his eyes still on the shadowy outline of the kiln and on the scattering of bricks still lying against its walls.

Leonid thought: What did they see? How long have they been here? But almost at once, he saw an explanation that might satisfy them. 'I was the one you heard screaming,' he said. 'I hurt my hand carrying the wood over to fire the kiln for my father's work.'

They hesitated, but they were still looking at the kiln. If the screaming started again, they would certainly go into the tunnel to investigate. But then they glanced at one another, nodded and went back up the stairs, and Leonid heard the outer door close. He waited for the sound of carriage wheels going back down the street. It seemed a long while before they did.

His mother had stopped screaming, but she might start again at any moment, and his father could return soon. Leonid's mind was tumbling with the memories of how she had threatened him with the fires of hell – not just this afternoon, but throughout most of his life. They had ruled her life, those fires. With this last thought, a smile curved his lips, and he went across to the corner where the dry wood for firing the kiln was stacked. There was not very much of it – his father had intended to collect more in the morning, and bring it in – but there should be enough for what he wanted now.

He began to feed the dry wood through the partly open fire-hole. There was no sound from within; most likely, she had been smothered by the dark sourness, but he could not take any chances.

When he had pushed in as much of the wood as there was, he began systematically to put the remaining bricks back over the vents. It was necessary to seal the kiln before he began firing it.

When Leonid's father returned, he was pleased to hear Leonid had started the firing process. Leonid was a good, thoughtful boy to have done that, he said.

It was not until they were seated at the little table overlooking the street that he commented on how late Leonid's mother was tonight.

'Perhaps she stayed at the church to help with something.'

'That's likely. Have you finished your supper? Then we'll go down to see how the kiln firing is progressing.'

Leonid was at once aware of apprehension, but he had to follow his father, and hope everything would be all right. But as soon as they entered the cellar, he knew it was not. There was something dreadfully wrong – something that was going to reveal what he had done, only he could not work out what it was . . .

His father was saying, in a puzzled voice, 'It should be almost at full temperature by now, but it's only about three-quarters of the way. You can't have put in enough wood – didn't you bring in the extra pieces?'

'I didn't think they were needed.'

'Of course they were needed.' He frowned, then said, 'And you haven't put in those bowls and the two pots, either. I left them out for you to do that. There's all that smoke, too – I don't understand why . . .'

He took a step nearer, and Leonid, managing to keep back, saw a look of extreme horror come into his father's face. He pointed, with a hand that was shaking, and said, 'There's something lying just under the fire-hole. It— Oh, dear God, that's your mother's steel cross.'

It was then that Leonid realized it was not only the cross

that was about to betray him. There was something else, something much, much worse.

The tunnel and the cellar were filled with the smell of roasting meat.

His surroundings seemed to spin around him but, through the confusion, he was aware of his father running forward, reaching up to the bricks sealing the fire-holes, and scrabbling frantically at them, tearing them away, only managing to dislodge two. But that was enough to allow the glow from within to send a dull radiance into the cellar. It was enough to allow the stronger stench of something that was not the usual one of clay pots and bowls being baked to gust out more strongly.

As the stench met him, Leonid's stomach lifted, and he retched, then was sick, messily and humiliatingly, over his own feet.

When, finally, he straightened up, wiping his mouth on the back of his hand, he saw his father huddled near the tunnel opening, sobbing, rocking back and forth, and cradling his hands. Even in the uncertain light, Leonid saw they were scorched and raw, blisters bubbling up on the skin from where he had torn away some of the bricks.

His father said, in a gasping, choking voice, 'I can't get in there to reach what's left of her . . . Too hot . . . But you put her there, didn't you? You threw her in, then you started the firing. No one else could have done it.' He shuddered, and then, as Leonid took a shaky step towards the tunnel, his father waved him back. 'Leave it be,' he said. 'Don't look on the results of your evil, sinful work.'

Then, wincing with pain, and with extreme difficulty, he picked up the steel crucifix and half threw, half pushed it through the small aperture he had managed to unseal. Leonid heard it fall with a dull clink inside the kiln.

It had been Leonid whose rage had filled up his father's cluttered, fire-drenched workshop that day. But it had been Quintus – renamed, even perhaps reborn – who was taken to the monks at the Monastery of St Nicholas.

'It is the only solution I can think of,' his father said, as they approached the monastery. 'No matter what you are, I cannot let you face punishment for what you have done. The monks need only know I am entering a monastery of my own – that I am handing you into their care. But I shall never see you again.'

He fumbled for the massive iron door knocker with hands that were tightly bandaged, but which, despite the bandages, were visibly damaged.

As he did so, he said, 'This is the fifth day of the fifth month. From now on, you can be known as Quintus to remind you of this day. Leonid must disappear. No one except the two of us knows what you have done. No one else will ever know you for the murderer you are.'

Leonid – Quintus – had stared at him, and thought: But someone does know. Two boys came into the cellar and saw what I did – I know they saw.

But surely it was all right. Surely inside this remote monastery he would be safe.

SEVEN

But Quintus was not safe. Because now, some fifteen years after that day, he was looking into the eyes of two men who did know him for a murderer – the two who had seen what he did that day. Staring at them, the memories came scudding back – the screams of his mother, the stench of slowly roasting flesh . . .

'Well, Father?' said Grigory Orlov. 'Now we have recognized one another, I think you will see you have no choice but to do what we want.' He moved closer. 'You must play the part we have created for you in our plan.'

'The plan to assassinate the Tsar,' said Alexei, a lick of unmistakable pleasure in his voice.

It was easy to understand what was behind the plan. Everyone inside the Palace – and probably a great many people outside it – knew Grigory shared the Empress's bed on most nights. With the Tsar dead, with Catherine occupying the throne in her own right, he would gradually gain control of her. Quintus had no experience of such relationships and no wish for them, but it was clear that Grigory was aiming to have control of Russia himself. But Quintus remembered Catherine's unwavering stare and the firm set of her jaw, and he thought: Is that a lady who will allow a man – any man – to gain control of her to that degree? But alongside these thoughts was another: If I were part of such a plan, I could also be at the Empress's side.

As if hearing this thought, Grigory said, 'If you were to do this, Father, your rewards would be very rich ones.'

'You promise that?'

'We promise it. Also, we promise that you would be completely safe.'

Quintus thought: Rich rewards. A promise that I shall be safe. But he still hesitated, and then Alexei said, softly, 'You have committed one murder already. What difference will it make if you commit a second one?'

As if from a great distance, Quintus heard his voice say, 'You are right. It makes no difference at all.' He met their eyes. 'I will do it,' he said.

Private journal of Catherine, 1762

This evening, Grigory and his brother, Alexei, sought audience with me. This is unusual – Grigory has a way of simply entering my apartments when he chooses. One day, I shall tell him it is arrogant and it assumes I will always be prepared to receive him, which I may not be. Also, it causes sly mirth among the servants.

But tonight he had donned his formal manner, and he and Alexei were accompanied by a young monk who is newly come to the Palace, and has been appointed to look after the spiritual needs of some of my servants.

Grigory said, 'Highness, may I present Father Quintus. He has a very concerning story to relate.'

I recognized Father Quintus. A day or two earlier, he had been on the gallery with the servants, looking down on the banquet procession. It is absurd to even write down this next thought, but I shall do so. I shall admit that as he looked down at me that evening, I felt as if something had smeared a cold darkness across my mind. I had thrust the feeling away, but facing him in my apartments tonight, it returned.

But he bowed respectfully enough, and when he spoke, his voice was pleasant, his manner deferential.

'Your Imperial Highness,' he said, 'I am deeply saddened to bring you the information that your . . . that His Imperial Highness . . . is at the heart of a wicked plot.'

I said, 'What is the plot, Father? And how do you come to know of it?'

I thought his eyes darted briefly to Alexei, almost as if for reassurance or even permission to continue, but then, with the air of one reaching a decision, he said, 'A confession was made to me yesterday.'

In the iciest of all my icy voices (I can sound extremely

icy if the occasion requires), I said, 'You are not about to disclose the secrets of the confessional, I hope?'

He paused and looked again at Grigory and Alexei. Then, with a curious note of decision – almost as of someone burning his boats – he said, 'Yes. That is what I am about to do, Your Highness. The rules that bind us are strict – nothing told in the confessional can ever be revealed, but—'

'Yes?'

'There is one exception,' said Father Quintus, and now there was what I can only describe as a woodenness about his words. I was strongly reminded of players who stand on a stage and declaim words written in a script for them. But, at first, I did not understand what he was trying to tell me. One exception to the secrecy of the confessional, he had said. Then, quite suddenly, I did understand, and a coldness swept over me.

'You refer to the confessing of treason,' I said. Treason. The act that even the most powerful rulers fear. The word seemed to shape itself threateningly on the air.

'I do, Highness,' said Father Quintus. 'If a penitent has committed – or is planning to commit – an act of outright treason, then not only must absolution be denied, but the treason itself must be made known. That is a ruling made more than fifty years ago, I believe.'

'You are correct,' I said, speaking tersely to hide my growing horror. 'It was a ruling made by a fearful and nervous tsar.'

'And it is known as the Spiritual Reglament,' murmured Grigori. 'It was created by an ancestor of your imperial husband's, Highness, after his son confessed to a priest he intended to assassinate his father and claim the throne.'

His casual display of familiarity with the Romanov lineage annoyed me. Does he think he stands equal with my family because he shares my bed? No lover is that good! But what he said was correct. It had been Peter I, who, half a century ago, terrified of the threat posed by his son, had woven the Spiritual Reglament into Russian ecclesiastical law.

I said, 'And you have received such a confession, Father Quintus?'

'It was made to me last night, Your Highness.' There was

again that impression that he was repeating by rote, a carefully learned lesson.

I made an angry, dismissive gesture. 'I do not believe you. No one would dare raise a treasonous hand against an emperor of Russia again,' I said, and looked at Grigory, hoping, I think, for reassurance.

But there was no reassurance, and Quintus said, 'Your Highness, the confession was not of treason against the Tsar. The planned treason—'

'Continue.'

'—is against you, Your Highness.'

It was as if the cold darkness closed suffocatingly down on the two of us, but at last, with a fair assumption of calm, I said, 'Who is it who has made this confession?'

I saw at once that I had disconcerted him, and it lent me resolve. I said, 'Tell me who it was, damn you!'

Quintus looked briefly at Grigory, then said, 'I do not know who it was.'

'But you were in the confessional with the man! Close to him! You must have known! I command you to tell me! Or must I have you flung into a prison cell and left to the rats to chew on!'

'I cannot tell you,' said Quintus. 'You might threaten me with the worst prison cell – the most fearsome tortures you have, Your Highness – but I do not know who the man was. I have only been in your service for a very short time, and this was a . . . a stranger.' There was another of the glances at the Orlov brothers. 'I did not see the man, of course – the confessional is dim, and there is the screen— And it was not a voice I had ever heard.'

'Clearly, though, it will have been someone who had been in the Tsar's service,' said Grigory, almost eagerly, and Quintus sent him a look that could have been gratitude.

'And someone who has come very recently to this Palace, Highness,' put in Alexei, quickly. 'It must be so, for how else would he have had access to Father Quintus? How else could he have made this confession – even known of the Father's presence?'

'Someone who secretly left the Tsar's service and came

here to warn you,' said Grigory. 'But whoever he is, be sure, Highness, that we shall find him, and question him.'

'And learn who is at the heart of the plot?' I said, and I was pleased to hear my voice had regained a degree of control.

'Your Highness, it is already known who is at the heart of the plot,' said Father Quintus. 'The penitent told me.'

'Then tell me also, damn you.'

His eyes seemed to look straight down into my soul. Then he said, 'It is His Imperial Highness himself.'

In a whisper, I said, 'The Tsar. You are telling me that the Tsar intends to murder me.'

'Yes.'

Midnight

If this is true, it may explain why Peter left the Winter Palace so soon after our arrival, and returned to Oranienbaum. If you are plotting to kill someone – and that someone your own wife – you would want to put a considerable distance between you. If I were going to kill someone, it is what I would want. Not that I am going to kill anyone – I hope I will never need to.

Father Quintus told his story woodenly, and certainly with some reluctance, but I think that was because Grigory and Alexei had exerted pressure on him to reveal the secrets of the confessional to me. Perhaps, also, because he was a little overawed at being brought into my presence? I have just reread that last sentence, and I am inclined to scratch it out, for I do not believe Quintus is a creature who would be overawed by anything. No matter.

What is of matter is the substance of the story, and, to my shame, I believe it. I believe my husband intends to kill me, and that some wretched servant has reneged on the plan and sought absolution. And it is this confession that Quintus has carried to me.

However I look at this, I believe it to be true. Worse, I believe Peter may be enjoying planning it, and savouring carrying it out. Even in our early years, there was a sadistic streak in him. His idea of humour was brutal, invariably involving whippings or beatings or the public ridicule of underlings. He would leap from his bed at midnight, and order the servants to assemble, then force them to march and drill like soldiers until the early hours of the morning – heedless that most of them were dropping with fatigue. On those nights, I always sensed a strange aura about him. Saints are frequently depicted with their heads surrounded by an aureole of light, and it is fanciful to write this, but I used to think an aureole of darkness might surround my husband. There were even times when I flinched and involuntarily put out my hands to prevent that darkness streaming out to me.

Our nights together were embarrassing. I can still remember how he would sweatily and gruntingly try to bring himself to a condition that would allow him to consummate our union. I was barely sixteen then, and I did not entirely understand. I certainly had not the knowledge to help him to achieve physical arousal.

The fact that I quite speedily acquired the knowledge – and very pleasurably indeed under the tutelage of one or two skilled and sympathetic gentlemen – is not, I feel, really relevant.

Later

Dawn is breaking outside the Palace, and Grigory and Alexei have left. Earlier, I had dismissed Quintus to whatever part of the Palace he inhabits, and the three of us talked for most of the night. And now a plan has been made. In three days, I shall travel to Izmailovsky, to deliver a speech to the Russian Imperial Guard there, openly telling them that my husband is plotting to murder me, and asking – no, commanding! – them to protect me from him. I have no idea if they will swear allegiance to me over their Emperor, but Grigory and Alexei have convinced me this is the only course of action.

I should set down that I am aware Peter has achieved some notable things – he proclaims religious freedom, which I certainly agree with, and he has encouraged education. I will acknowledge all of those things.

But I will not acknowledge his right – divine or otherwise – to murder me.

I do not think I shall sleep soundly until we are at Izmailovsky and I have secured the Guard's protection. I have considered sleeping with a sword under my pillow in case a murderously inclined agent from my husband manages to get in. I have even wondered if I could command a detachment of the household guard to remain on constant duty outside my door – although I can all too easily imagine the talk that would create. That is not to say that a number of the guards are not extremely good-looking, and it might help to pass the three days until we set out for Izmailovsky . . .

I have selected the gowns for Izmailovsky. For the speech to the soldiers, I shall wear amber velvet, with my hair threaded with topazes. This may be a mission of diplomacy and an appeal for help, but I see no reason not to look my best. I am ignoring Anya's predictions that it will rain, bedraggling the elaborate hair arrangement and ruining the amber velvet gown. She says it to unnerve me – she frequently tries to do that – but I will not be unnerved, and certainly not by such a sour-faced gloom-monger. I can deal with her, perfectly well. I can even deal with that manipulative Alexei Orlov, if I have to.

But I do not know if I can deal with Father Quintus.

EIGHT

London, 1909

The Fitzglens were delighted to hear of the plan to infiltrate the Ecclesiastical Society, and agreed that it could well lead to finding the Stone Heads. As for Gus taking part in the proceedings, this was thought a very good idea indeed.

'Because,' said Ambrose, 'none of us can approach that Society in case Simeon might be lurking around and recognizes us.'

'That's why Gus will present himself as an assistant to a researcher,' said Byron. 'He'll be from – which university did we decide on, Jack?'

'Christ Church, Oxford. We're keeping everything as religious-sounding as possible.'

Gus, who was aware that Mr Jack was disliking deceiving the family just as much as Gus was himself, said he would do his best. He added, rather doubtfully, that he did not know if he would succeed, to which Mr Rudraige said stuff and nonsense – Gus would play the part to the manner born – and bore him off to The Punchbowl to tell him about Simeon.

'I didn't say anything in front of Cecily or Daphnis,' he explained, 'because Simeon's expulsion distressed them – well, it distressed Cecily at any rate. We found out he'd been cheating members of our audiences, you see – offering subscription memberships, whatever they might be – for all kinds of privileges within the theatre world in general, and the Amaranth in particular. I think some sort of affiliation membership of the Thespis was even one of them. I'd never heard such a meaningless term in my life, and nor had anyone else in the family; as you probably know, the Thespis is *very* strict about who it allows in – it's nearly as bad as Boodle's or the Carlton, and you practically have to prove you're descended from

Burbage or Garrick. But a great many people were taken in by Simeon's scheming.' He drained his glass and gestured to the barmaid to refill it.

'And it was the final straw,' he said, as the new glasses were set down. 'We might be thieves and villains, Gus, but as you know, we have certain codes.'

'Mr Aiden's codes,' said Gus, nodding, and wishing, as he often did, that he had known Mr Jack's father.

'Indeed so,' said Mr Rudraige. 'Handed down from that rascal, Highwayman Harry, so it's always said. Thankfully, we managed to pay almost all of the money back to the people Simeon had duped. We managed to keep it from the newspapers, too. That was due to Byron's grandfather – he knew all the reporters, and one or two newspaper editors, too, I think. We told Simeon he could no longer regard himself as a member of the family, and we never wanted to see or hear from him again.'

Gus listened, spellbound.

'I wish I could say nothing in his life in this family became him like the leaving of it,' said Mr Rudraige.

Gus, who had tried to study as many plays as possible, in order to understand and be part of the Fitzglen world, was pleased he could say, 'That's *Macbeth*, isn't it?'

'It is, and credit to you for recognizing it. And Simeon's leaving was certainly not becoming to him or anyone else,' said Mr Rudraige. 'We escorted him through the stage door; Daphnis and Aiden came with me – oh, and Freddie Fitzglen, the twins' father. Byron's grandfather was there, too, making notes of everything, exactly as Byron does now. Jack and Ambrose were only very young then; they were told to remain inside, but they watched from an upper window. And Bill the Chip carried down a couple of stage weights so we could wedge the street door shut in case Simeon tried to batter his way back in.'

'Did he try to batter his way back in?' asked Gus, trying to picture the scene.

'He did not, but,' said Rudraige, 'he had the infernal impudence to stand in the middle of Sloat Alley and hurl curses at the stage door at the top of his voice – he had always been able to send his voice to the very back of the theatre – and the entire street heard him. People came out of their shops to listen, and the barmaids here even ran out with trays of drinks – I believe The Punchbowl did rather well out of the whole thing.

'Simeon didn't mince his words. He launched into a speech, scorning the whole family as scurvy companions; he called poor old Freddie Fitzglen a lily-livered poltroon and a three-inch fool. Lydia leaned out of the window of the crush bar, shouting down insults, and Cecily had to pull her away before she started throwing ale tankards at him.

'Then Simeon said we were all nothing but stuffed cloak-bags of roasted guts. Mind, we'd just been doing *Henry IV*, which is full of the most energetic cursing,' said Mr Rudraige. 'And whatever else I might say about Simeon, I will admit he was a magnificent Shakespearean player – people used to say he was nearly as good as Irving or Charles Kean – not that I ever saw Kean act, because he was well before my time, you understand.'

'Of course,' said Gus, and Mr Rudraige beamed, said they would have another glass of port and one of The Punchbowl's mutton and ale pies to go with it, and waved to the barmaid again.

Byron had put together a disguise for Gus, which Gus supposed could have been worse. There was a grey suit, which Byron said had originally been of very fair quality; he suggested its wearer had known better days, but had fallen on threadbare times.

'It's all exactly right,' said Jack, who had accompanied them to Todworthy Inkling's shop. 'I know you're hating it, Gus, but you'll make a splendid job of it. All you have to do is play the part of Miss Gilfillan's assistant.'

'Miss Gilchrist, let's remember,' said Viola Gilfillan, coming out of Tod's office to greet them. She was wearing a porridge-coloured costume, which she said she had found in an old skip at the Gilfillan theatre. She had added a hat shaped like an upended saucer which was tied in place with a piece of grey chiffon, and which hid her hair almost completely. Gus did not think anyone could possibly recognize her as the dazzling Viola Gilfillan.

She said, 'Gus, I think you should keep your own name, don't you? We want everything to be as simple as possible. Jack, I don't suppose the rest of your family know I've been lured into helping with this imbroglio, do they?'

'They do not. And if you so much as breathe a word to them or to any of your own family, Viola, I'll wreak such revenge on you that it will out-Herod Herod, and you can howl away twelve winters and make the beasts tremble, and—'

'Prompt him, Byron; he's forgotten the rest of the speech,' said Viola, as Jack paused. 'But I shan't breathe so much as a syllable to anyone. I don't want it known that I'm fraternizing with the enemy any more than you do.' She looked at Gus. 'Well, fellow criminal,' she said, 'it seems the game's afoot. Really, this is all turning out to be great fun. I can see why you all cavort around London in disguises when you're pilfering and plundering. Ready, Gus? Then en avant.'

If Gus had never expected to find himself joining forces with a Gilfillan, even less had he expected to embark on a journey in a motor car. But when they walked out of Inkling's Emporium, Viola gestured with pride towards a monstrous contraption, which, as far as Gus could see, consisted solely of metal and chrome and violently scarlet paintwork, with a kind of iron grille at the front that bore an unpleasant resemblance to a grinning mouth.

A smell of smoke and grease hung on the air, which, in itself, was disconcerting, because the alleys and little streets around St Martin's Lane usually smelled of horse dung and soot, and quite often spillage of ale from a brewer's dray that had come to grief on the uneven cobblestones. There was somehow a comforting familiarity about those odours. There was nothing comforting about the fumes of motor oil.

But Mr Jack and Mr Byron were inspecting the vehicle with interest. Mr Jack was even saying he was considering acquiring one of his own, and asking incomprehensible questions, most of which Miss Viola – who Gus was trying to think of as Miss Gilchrist – waved airily aside, and said she left that kind of thing to other people.

She flipped several coins to the cluster of street urchins who seized delightedly on the bounty, shrilly assuring her they had guarded the machine as asked. As she prepared to climb into the vehicle, Mr Jack suddenly said, in a more serious voice than Gus had ever heard him use to her, 'Viola, you'll be wary if you encounter Simeon, won't you? He has the reputation of being a very charming rascal when he likes—'

She paused, then said, 'I will be careful, Jack. But I'm becoming rather accustomed to gentleman who are very charming rascals.'

They stared at one another, and Gus thought there was another of those moments when either or both of them were about to say more. But the moment passed, and Miss Gilchrist climbed into the seat behind the driving wheel. Gus reluctantly got into the seat next to her, and there was a grinding of wheels and cogs. As the motor began to move ponderously forward, he had the thought that it was smoother and faster than an omnibus, but that he hoped they did not collide with anything.

However, they reached Chancery Lane without incident, and stopped in front of a tall, stone-faced building, with a brass plate proclaiming it to be *The Society for Ecclesiastical Restoration of Sacred Buildings*. There was also the information that Prebendary Dr J.D. Oldyce was in residence for enquirers between eleven of the morning and three of the afternoon on Mondays to Fridays.

'It's two o'clock,' said Miss Viola, and Gus heard that she was already speaking in Miss Vera Gilchrist's Scottish burr. 'A very civilized time for us to call. Let's go in and hope we aren't struck by celestial lightning for all the lies we're about to tell.'

It appeared that Dr Oldyce would be very happy to see two unexpected visitors.

'The Society does not receive many enquiries from outside the Church,' he explained, ushering them into a room with bookshelves and metal cabinets. 'So it's always a pleasure

when the wider world comes calling.' He indicated to them
to be seated, took a place behind a large desk and asked how
he could be of help.

Viola opened a notebook and launched into a description
of Professor Pilkington, and how he was currently engaged in
writing a treatise.

'Religious sculptures,' she explained. 'Their symbolism for
worshippers.' She regarded the prebendary earnestly, and Gus,
who had taken an unobtrusive place near the window, thought
you had to allow that she had the character and the voice of
Vera Gilchrist to perfection.

'I am the professor's emissary this afternoon,' went on the
earnest Miss Gilchrist. 'He is presently immersed in notes and
diaries and papers – do you know, I have to extricate him from
it to come to his meals, or he would not eat enough to keep
a flea alive.'

Gus had a brief but vivid image of a mild old gentleman,
happily working at a desk in a cluttered library, oblivious to
the world – and then reminded himself that Professor
Pilkington was a figment of Miss Viola's imagination, his
character embellished by Mr Jack and Mr Byron.

'Clearly a scholar,' said the prebendary, nodding in sympathy.

'Indeed so. But he has heard of a set of sculptures recently
brought from Russia which he thinks might assist his research,'
said Miss Gilchrist. 'Stone heads, so it seems, with a very
strong monastic link – a Russian Orthodox monastery, of
course, but I think it would be right to say there are many
similarities between their practices and those of the Church
of England – and, indeed, Catholicism. The professor is keen
to trace what he calls the echoes – one to the other, you know.'

Dr Oldyce, clearly interested, said, 'Indeed yes.'

'He thought that an organization such as yours might have
been approached regarding the pieces. Hence our visit.'

'Your description matches a very recent commission we
accepted,' said Dr Oldyce, and beamed.

Viola leaned forward. 'A commission? To sell the
sculptures?'

Dr Oldyce winced slightly at the word 'sell', but said, 'An
agreement to try to place them for the owner. We have a

list of authorities and landowners who are engaged in renovation of dilapidated churches. They are always looking out for suitable pieces – sculptures, statues, rood screens, stained-glass panels . . . And although the provenance that accompanied these particular pieces was sparse, and the documents were written in Russian, once we had them translated, it was agreed that they were genuine.'

'It's good to hear there was a reliable provenance.'

'Yes, sadly, there are extremely clever and cunning forgers in today's world.'

'Sad, indeed,' said Viola, straight-faced.

'For that reason, if for no other, we are most careful about all documentation. We keep very detailed records, in case there should be a query later on.' As he said this, Gus saw the doctor's eyes flicker to the two cabinets in the corner of the room. He knew Miss Viola had noticed it as well, but she only said, 'Could I ask if you have been able to find a . . . a home for the sculptures?'

'I see no reason not to tell you that we found a very good home for them, Miss Gilchrist. A speedy and satisfactory arrangement was reached. I believe the pieces will be part of restoration to a thirteenth-century church.'

'That sounds very suitable. Can you tell me where the church is? The professor would probably want to communicate with the new owners.'

Dr Oldyce looked worried. 'I do not think I can,' he said. 'I am extremely sorry, but we are strictly bound by confidentiality, you understand.'

'Of course. And we're very grateful for all you have been able to tell us.'

'I am extremely sorry I can't help you further,' said Dr Oldyce. 'The professor's work sounds very interesting. But you will at least take a cup of tea before you leave?'

Gus knew Miss Viola would seize any chance to prolong the interview, and he was not surprised when she said, 'If it would be no trouble?'

'None whatever. I will go along to see about it at once.'

The door had hardly closed before Miss Viola was out of her chair and crossing to the two cabinets in the corner. 'Gus, we've probably got five minutes,' she said. 'Stand guard at the door while I search these cabinets.'

'What?'

'Did you see how the doctor glanced across at them when he referred to keeping records of provenance documents?'

'Yes, but—'

'The documents for the Stone Heads are in that cabinet; I'd put money on it.'

'But dare we risk—'

'Of course we dare. Think how delighted Jack will be if we can find out where the Stone Heads are.' Her eyes shone when she said this. She wants to please him, thought Gus, and he went to the door and pulled it slightly open, so he could see into the corridor.

Viola had snatched a notebook from her bag, and was already opening the deep drawer of the main cabinet. Folders were stacked upright inside, and as she began to sort through them, Gus could almost hear his heart pounding with tension.

'Miss Viola, do hurry – I can hear voices nearby—'

She muttered something that sounded to Gus like a curse, then suddenly said, 'I've found it!' There was the sound of papers being rustled. 'Russian stone pieces, circa mid-seventeen hundreds. It must be the one – oh, and there's a dispatch note with an address. The Manor, Mallory Abbot, Suffolk. No name, though.'

Gus risked looking back over his shoulder. Miss Viola was scribbling notes furiously, and turning over two or three sheets of paper, frowning and writing more notes. Then she returned to her seat, and said, 'Even without the name of the buyer, I think Jack's going to be delighted with this.'

Footsteps sounded in the hallway, together with the chink of crockery, and Dr Oldyce's voice said, 'The promised cup of tea.'

'It is very welcome,' said Miss Viola.

NINE

'It seems we've found the Heads,' said Jack, setting down Viola's notes the following afternoon on Tod Inkling's desk. 'They're at The Manor, Mallory Abbot, Suffolk.' He looked at Viola and Gus, his eyes bright. 'I have to say, you've both succeeded brilliantly.'

'We enjoyed it, didn't we, Gus? It was very exciting.'

'It was nerve-wracking,' said Gus.

'The documents we found,' said Viola, 'clearly weren't the original ones – you do understand that? I think they were transcripts – they were all in the same handwriting and on the same notepaper. I copied them as exactly as I could.'

Byron said, 'I'd imagine any papers that accompanied the Heads would be sent with them to The Manor.'

'And it's likely they'd have been written in Russian anyway,' said Jack. 'But clearly the Ecclesiastical Society kept copies of the translations for their own files.'

'Let's hear what they say,' said Byron.

'The first one,' said Jack, looking at Viola's notes again, 'is addressed to Father Abbot – presumably at St Nicholas's Monastery. There wasn't a date, Viola?'

'There might have been on the original, but there wasn't on the transcript.'

'Read it again, Jack.'

'"My dear Father Abbot,"' read Jack. '"Please accept my most sincere and heartfelt thanks for taking possession of the Stone Heads of four . . ."'

'Did you know there were four of them?' asked Viola, as he paused.

'I think four might have been mentioned. ". . . and for confirming the pledge and the promise to 'guard them for the sake of the lady whose name I do not dare commit to paper'."'

'There's no signature,' said Jack. 'It just ends with grateful thanks and blessings.' He stared at the notes, his mind going

back to the extract from Catherine the Great's memoirs that
Mikhail had brought to the Amaranth that first night. Might
the lady whose name could not be committed to paper be
Catherine? He reminded himself that Viola did not know about
the memoirs, or that, at best, she knew only the very sparsest
details, so he turned to the next page, which was headed
'Extract – probably from monastery's daybook'.

'I wasn't entirely sure what a daybook was,' said Viola.

'A detailed record of day-to-day activities, I think,' said
Byron. 'Tod?'

'Exactly that.'

'Whatever it is, it sounds like a kind of general directive,'
said Jack. 'It says: "The community must never forget that
the Heads are to be locked in the crypt, and the door secured,
with the keys held by Father Abbot at all times. Darkness must
be maintained in the crypt at every hour of the day and night
and every season of the year."'

Darkness at every hour of the day and night and every
season . . . Jack had a sudden disturbing impression of something that had been huddled in deep, lonely shadows lifting
its head, as if it had heard a sound or glimpsed a faint ray of
light. Then Byron's voice reached him, asking what else there
was, and he was pulled back to his surroundings.

'The next one is just a receipt,' said Jack. 'For two padlocks
delivered to the monastery.'

'To lock the Heads away,' said Byron.

'Yes.' Jack put the notes down. 'The important thing now,'
he said, 'is to find this Mallory Abbot.'

'That shouldn't be difficult. Tod, can I scour your bookshelves,
to see if there're any reference books about Suffolk?'

'Scour to your heart's content,' said Tod, indicating the
library ladder in the corner, and Gus got up to help wheel it
along and prop it against the shelves, most of which stretched
to the ceiling.

'Viola,' said Jack, 'this is all precisely what we wanted, and
we're very grateful. But—'

'But you can't let me stay on the stage for the next act,'
she said. 'That's only what I expected, of course, although it's
a pity because I've been enjoying it.'

'We'll tell you the outcome, of course.'

'So I should hope. And if it means Saintly Simeon ends up behind bars, so much the better. I suppose,' said Viola, thoughtfully, 'you won't feel able to tell the rest of your family about my part in it all, either, will you?'

Jack glanced at Byron, who was working his way along the bookshelves, then said, 'I don't think we can. I'm sorry.'

'I'm being written out of the script,' she said, sweeping the back of her hand across her forehead in the classic dramatic gesture of despair. 'Banished to a distant attic like the first Mrs Rochester.'

'Portrait turned to the wall,' murmured Byron. 'Name forbidden to be uttered by all succeeding generations.'

'But,' went on Viola, 'it's almost worth it to hear the word "sorry" on your lips, Jack. And it's given me a splendid hold over you. I can threaten to tell all at any point.'

'You'd do it as well, if it served your purpose, wouldn't you?'

'Without a second's hesitation. But you can keep my Professor Pilkington if it would help. In fact, you could tell the family that Gus posed as his assistant, and approached the Society to ask if the Stone Heads had passed through their hands.'

'Annoyingly, that's a good idea,' said Jack. 'I'll hate deceiving them, though. I'll particularly hate the fact that they'll accept the story unquestioningly.'

'You could hold a grand confession scene afterwards,' suggested Byron. 'Peppered with contrition and mea culpas.'

'Yes, we'll do that,' said Jack, at once. 'Gus, how do you feel about staging this deception to the family? It's asking a lot of you, but—'

Gus said, '"If a lie may do thee grace, I'll gild it with the happiest terms I have."'

At this, Tod Inkling, who had been filling his guests' glasses from the decanter of Malmsey, paused in mid-pour and turned to regard Gus with surprise.

Jack laughed, and said, '*Henry IV*, by God! Gus, you're a constant delight. We'll make a player of you yet!'

'Thanking you kindly, Mr Jack, but I would rather not. It's

true that I do pick up the occasional line here and there, though,' said Gus, modestly.

'Well, gild away to your heart's content when the occasion arises.'

'He's learned the art from the master, of course,' said Viola. 'Byron, have you found Mallory Abbot yet? You've been at the top of that ladder long enough.'

'I believe I have,' said Byron, descending the steps, clutching a battered reference book which he placed on Tod's desk. 'It's described quite clearly in this. *Venerable Church Edifices.*'

'A dull work, but informative,' said Tod, inspecting the page through his pince-nez.

'The church is St Osmund's – it was built in the thirteenth century, and,' said Byron, 'it seems that even at the time this book was printed, the building was in what the author describes as "a sad state of disrepair". Which presumably means it's been crumbling away since the Wars of the Roses. But I can't see at the moment how we crumble ourselves into it without arousing suspicion.'

'Well, clearly we'll have to do it under cover of night, and the best way would be— What on earth's the matter, Byron?'

Byron had leapt up off the desk's edge and was swirling his cloak around his shoulders. He said, 'It's almost six o'clock, and we're both on stage at half past seven. Gus, run out and flag down the next hansom that comes along, will you? Never mind if it's occupied – just throw the occupants out, even if it's got the royal crest on the panel and half His Majesty's government inside—'

'There's no need for any throwing out of anyone,' said Viola, standing up. 'My motor is outside – I can drive you to the Amaranth. I'll even stop at the top of Sloat Alley so you needn't be seen in my company.'

The journey was made to the accompaniment of several hiccupping spurts of steam from under the bonnet, and Gus's hat blew off halfway across Covent Garden, so that he had to leap out to retrieve it, but they reached Sloat Alley without major mishap.

Gus and Byron made for the Amaranth's stage door at once,

but Jack hesitated. 'Viola, how long would it take this contraption to reach Mallory Abbot?'

'I don't know. But there's a map in here, so we might be able to work it out.' She reached into a small compartment near the steering wheel and produced a large folded-up paper. Jack glanced about them, but although one or two people had slowed their steps to look with interest at the vehicle, none of them actually stopped. Byron and Gus had disappeared into the theatre, so he leaned over to study the map with Viola.

Unfolded, it took up a considerable part of the motor's interior, and had to be turned up and down and around several times before they located Suffolk. At length, Viola said, 'Mallory Abbot isn't marked – but then it did sound like a very small place.'

'Yes. The distance from London into Suffolk,' said Jack, who was not very familiar with road maps, but was not going to let Viola know, 'looks to be about ninety miles.'

'That's what I thought.'

'How fast can this contraption actually go?'

'I have driven it at nearly thirty miles an hour,' she said, proudly.

'Dear God. Does that mean to motor for ninety miles would take about three hours?'

'It must, mustn't it?' she said, frowning. 'Although I think you'd have to allow for breaking down. Punctured tyres or the engine over-heating. Say a bit over four hours to be safe.'

'But it could manage London to Mallory Abbot, there and back, in the same day?'

'I think so. It might like a rest between going and coming back, though.'

She replaced the map in its cubbyhole, and Jack said, carefully, 'Would you happen to be free this Sunday? It's the one day when neither of us need to be at our respective theatres.'

'I could be free. And on a Sunday, we could be perfectly open about going into a church to attend a service. And spy out the terrain,' she said, hopefully.

'We'd have to leave London very early, of course.'

'Seven o'clock?'

'Even earlier. Could you be outside my rooms at half past six? You know where they are, do you?'

'I do, as it happens,' she said. 'I could be there at half past six. Oh, and I've got one of those vacuum flasks. I'll fill it with coffee and bring some sandwiches so we can have breakfast on the road. Are Byron and Gus coming? Because, if so, I'd better make extra sandwiches—'

'I think it had better be just the two of us,' said Jack. 'It might be a fruitless journey, anyway. I can postpone reporting to the family for a couple of days – I don't think we need to let anyone know what we're doing.'

Viola considered him, then the three-cornered smile, loved by the critics and her audiences, showed. 'Anyone would think we were conducting a clandestine affair, wouldn't they?' she said, and reached for the gear lever preparatory to bouncing the car back into the flow of cabs and carriages.

It was annoying that Viola's words and the mischievous look in her eyes stayed with Jack throughout the evening's performance. It was even more annoying that, several times, he had a brief tantalizing image of the two of them half lying on a rug in a meadow, drinking coffee from Viola's vacuum flask and sharing a picnic breakfast.

'It's a pity about the meadow,' said Viola, as the motor finally rattled past a sign that proclaimed they were entering the village of Mallory Abbot. 'But I don't suppose there are many meadows where you don't find inquisitive cows.'

'Pity about the puncture just outside Colchester, as well.'

'Yes, but weren't those men nice – helping to change the wheel? And three-quarters of an hour is very fast for changing a wheel,' said Viola. 'We were able to top up the radiator a bit further on, too. And we saw something of Colchester while we waited for the engine to cool down. Still, I'm sorry it's taken a bit longer than four hours. We've probably missed all the morning services, haven't we?'

'We might manage evensong,' said Jack, dryly.

'You're such a pessimist. We've made very good time. The village looks rather nice, doesn't it? I wonder if that's

The Manor over there – glowering down on the landscape? I can't see any sign of the church, though, can you?'

'No, but since it's almost twelve o'clock, however much it's crumbled, it'll probably chime midday at any minute—' Jack broke off and grinned at her. 'Exactly on cue,' he said, as chimes rang out. 'Follow the tolling bell, Viola.'

The noon chimes had scarcely died away when they drew up at the lychgate guarding St Osmund's Church. Viola wrestled the motor car on to the grass verge, wrenched at what Jack recognized as a handbrake, then turned in her seat to look towards the church.

'It's certainly crumbling, isn't it?' she said.

'The bell tower looks as if it might collapse all the way down to the ground at any moment,' said Jack, leaning forward to get a better view. 'But the morning service must only just have ended, because there are plenty of people around. If we're quick, we can mingle with them. We might even go inside the church and look round.'

Viola untied the motoring veil from her hat, smoothed her hair into place in a tiny hand mirror and climbed out of the driving seat. A narrow path with overgrown grass on each side led to the church, and old trees dipped their branches inquisitively.

'The vicar's mingling with the congregation,' said Jack. 'We'll try to mingle, too. We're visitors interested in church architecture, remember.'

'I'll wax lyrical about the flying buttresses,' said Viola.

'Don't overdo it.'

The vicar was charmed to meet two visitors to the village, and delighted to hear his church had caught their interest.

'Thirteenth century, I think?' said Viola, gazing raptly at the grey stonework and the skewed bell tower.

'Indeed so.'

'You must have a constant struggle to maintain such a very old structure,' said Jack.

'We do, and I'm afraid funds are thinly spread, Mr – er—'

'Fitzglen,' said Jack, who had considered, and rejected, the idea of a false name for the expedition. 'Jack Fitzglen.' He shook the vicar's hand.

'I am the Reverend Hornbeam, incumbent of St Osmund's.'

'This is my cousin, Miss Vera Gilchrist,' said Jack, who had decided that using the Gilfillan name would be one risk too many.

He thought Viola glared at him, but she only said, 'I've been helping an uncle with research for a book. Professor Pilkington of Edinburgh, currently studying the way church interiors change over the years – how they adapt or how they're embellished in different ways by different generations. St Osmund's would certainly interest him.'

Jack thought that whatever he might at times say or think about Viola, he had to admit this struck a very useful note.

The Reverend Hornbeam explained that embellishments to St Osmund's had, to some extent, been forced on his predecessors.

'Considerable damage was inflicted by Oliver Cromwell's soldiers in 1644, and in a most irreligious fashion,' he said, and Viola murmured sympathetically about Cromwell's men.

'Didn't they even sometimes stable their horses in churches?'

'That is one of the legends, Miss Gilchrist, although I don't think it happened here. Happily, we have an excellent local fundraising committee who are doing sterling work. It is run by a very energetic lady: Mrs Marjorie Brundage. She is indefatigable in her efforts to restore the church,' said Mr Hornbeam. 'She recently acquired several sculptures – stone figures, which I believe came from Russia.'

'How interesting.' Jack managed not to exchange glances with Viola. 'Religious figures, presumably?'

'I believe not,' said the Reverend Hornbeam. 'But Mrs Brundage purchased them specifically to install inside St Osmund's, and we had arranged for a stonemason to assess what work was needed. The pieces were to be sited above the high altar or immediately over the pulpit.'

'But . . . not any longer?'

'Mrs Brundage is a very strong-minded, very energetic lady, and we are lucky to have her,' said Mr Hornbeam, gloomily. 'But she decided the figures were unsuitable for church use, after all. Accordingly, she asked me to store them in the Brundage mausoleum for safekeeping until she decided what to do about them – she did not care to enter the mausoleum herself, you understand, so I was her emissary. And once I had inspected the heads more closely, I agreed with her decision. I placed them on a very high shelf at the back of the mausoleum where they were unlikely to be seen accidentally. Not that anyone enters the mausoleum from one year's end to the next, of course, and it is kept locked.'

'A high shelf at the back of the mausoleum?' said Jack, thoughtfully.

'Yes. The verger had to help me with a stepladder, but between us we managed it.'

'It isn't often you come across a mausoleum nowadays,' said Viola.

'Indeed it is not, and, of course, it has not been used for many years. And—' A bell chimed in a somewhat peremptory fashion, and Reverend Hornbeam started, then consulted his watch. 'I had not realized the time,' he said. 'And I am expected at the Rectory – an early lunch and then a Sunday School class at two. Perhaps I might see you at evensong, though? I have enjoyed talking to you, and you might like to see the church in more detail. There would perhaps be features that would interest your professor, Miss Gilchrist.'

'I'm sure there would, and—'

'Although we would like to stay, we have to be back in London before nightfall,' said Jack, firmly. 'I think I can say we will be travelling here again before too long, though.'

'You would be most welcome any time. The Rectory is just beyond that wall,' he said, pointing.

As he set off, Viola looked expectantly at Jack. 'Well?' she said. 'Are we going to try to get the Stone Heads back right away?'

'It depends on how accessible the mausoleum is,' said Jack. 'I'm certainly going to see if I can find it. It's bound to be in the church grounds. Will you wait in the motor while I investigate?'

'No, I'll come with you. I don't much want to grub around in a mausoleum, but I don't want to miss anything.'

They walked around the side of the church, treading warily between the gravestones, most of which were leaning at slightly drunken angles, and many of which had their lettering almost completely obscured by moss and lichen.

'There it is,' said Jack, indicating a low building ahead of them.

'So it is. And I feel,' said Viola, pausing and staring at it, 'as if we're about to step into a Gothic novel. It's very dark, isn't it?'

Indeed, the mausoleum was so dark that once night fell it would probably blur into its surroundings. Even in the early afternoon light, it gave the impression that it might have clawed its way up out of the ground one night when no one was looking, and established its right to this corner of the churchyard.

'It probably looks dark because there aren't any windows,' said Jack. 'But then who'd want to look in? And anyone already in there wouldn't be able to look out.'

Viola gave a small shiver – Jack could not decide if it was genuine or simply for dramatic effect. 'You certainly know how to increase a lady's pulse rate,' she said.

Jack looked at her. 'Do I?' he said, softly.

'I shan't answer that,' said Viola, but she held his look, then a small wind stirred the trees, and the moment passed.

'I don't suppose,' said Jack, slowly, 'that any mausoleum looks hospitable, but—'

'But this one looks as if it's glowering and preparing to repel all who approach,' said Viola. 'There'll be stone shelves inside, won't there, with rows of coffins covered in dust and cobwebs. Dead Brundages – probably going back to the thirteenth century.'

'Yes, but Hornbeam said the forceful Mrs Brundage had the Heads brought here for safekeeping, so we'll have to investigate.' Jack hesitated, then said, 'You do know I wouldn't have actually stolen them from St Osmund's, don't you?'

'I've always known that you have a kind of code of honour.

But if stealing the Heads from St Osmund's was the only way to clear Mikhail's name, would you have done it?'

'Yes, I think I would. But I'd have made some kind of recompense.'

'Anonymously, presumably?'

'Of course anonymously,' said Jack, impatiently. 'Did you think I'd send a bank draft in my own name, with a note saying, "Sorry I filched your sculptures the other day, but here's a donation to buy some new ones"?'

As they went towards the mausoleum, Viola reached out a hand to take hold of Jack's arm. 'Only in case I fall over an uneven bit of ground,' she said. 'There are dozens of rabbit holes.'

'If we fall down one into a fantasy world, at least we'll fall together,' said Jack, closing his free hand over hers.

At what looked like the front of the mausoleum was a thick, heavy door. It was a good two feet below the level of the surrounding ground, and steps led down to it.

'I expect it will be locked,' Jack said. 'But I'll see if I can get in.'

'I suppose you've broken into at least a dozen properties.'

'I haven't kept count. But I've never broken into a mausoleum,' said Jack.

He went down the stone steps to the door, which was black with age. They're in there, he thought. The Stone Heads – the sinister-sounding sculptures that commemorate those long-ago children who might have been murdered. He pushed away the thought that the blind, dead faces might have turned to the door at the approach of an intruder.

There were bands of iron around the doorframe, and a massive ring handle with a substantial padlock. Jack grasped the iron ring and twisted it, but was not surprised when it scarcely moved. He knelt down to inspect the padlock, then reached up to examine the stonework beneath the eaves.

'It's all very secure,' he said at last, returning to Viola. 'There'll be a way to get in, but I can't see what it is at the moment. I'm not going to risk making a closer examination, because there are sure to be people around.' He frowned, then said, 'I think we'll have to return to London, and I'll report to the family. As far as today goes, I'll tell them I came down here to reconnoitre.'

'Why don't you stay in the village somewhere – there's sure to be a local pub or something – and break in tonight? Oh, but if a break-in were to be discovered within hours of talking to the Reverend Hornbeam, you'd be the obvious suspect, wouldn't you?'

'You're learning too many of the tricks of the trade,' said Jack.

'It comes from consorting with thieves and robbers.' She frowned, then said, 'Jack, there's something about all this that I haven't told you.'

They walked back to the lychgate, and Viola sat on the ledge just inside. Jack leaned against the lintel, his arms crossed, and waited. She was staring across the churchyard, and although the mausoleum was almost completely hidden behind the skewed clock tower and the trees, Jack knew they were both aware of its closeness.

Speaking slowly, Viola said, 'When Gus and I were at the Ecclesiastical Society's office, he stood guard at the door while I searched – we told you about that. You know about the transcripts I copied – the letter to the monastery and so on. But there was another document I copied. Gus didn't realize.' She paused, then said, 'But after I read it, I wished I hadn't found it. I wished I hadn't read it. I think I didn't tell you about it, because I wanted to shut it out.'

She was more serious than Jack ever remembered. After a moment, he said, 'Tell me. Bring the horror out into the daylight.'

'Because it might dissolve it?'

'It might.'

'I hate it when you're perceptive and understanding,' she said. 'It almost makes me think—' She shook her head impatiently and reached into the small bag she carried, drawing out a sheet of paper.

The lychgate was in a patch of afternoon sunlight that warmed the old wood and turned it to golden brown, and it should have been a tranquil and lovely setting.

But as Viola began to read, Jack had the feeling that, all

around them, the light and the warmth were being leached from the day – and that the huddled darkness he had sensed when he read the monks' directive to keep the Stone Heads locked in the crypt was lifting its head once more.

TEN

Mikhail had been very pleased that his English was allowing him to follow all that was happening.

Tonight, there was to be a meeting after the evening's performance to discuss the next step in regaining the Heads, and he had been asked to attend.

'We've made several discoveries,' Jack had said. 'All very promising. But are you happy for me to disclose them to the family, because this is very much your story, Mikhail. If you would prefer to keep some secrecy—'

'Please to tell everything,' said Mikhail, at once.

'Good,' said Jack, and smiled, and Mikhail thought that although he would not forget that the Fitzglens were thieves and lawbreakers, by this time he did not think he would care very much if they had stolen the crown jewels of every imperial family in the Western world.

Not three days earlier, he had been asked if he would like to help out with some backstage work, which he had greatly enjoyed. He had not entirely followed all of Bill the Chip's conversation, but he thought he had learned several new English expressions. Then, the following day, the twins, Petronella and Phoebe Fitzglen, had sought him out after the evening performance, and carried him off to a lively, noisy tavern in Sloat Alley called The Punchbowl. Petronella said they were not really supposed to go there, but Phoebe said everyone else did, and they would only drink lemonade, and no one would see them anyway.

'You're here because of some deep, dark plot involving Wicked Simeon, aren't you?' Phoebe demanded of Mikhail, when they were seated at a reasonably discreet corner table. 'Well, we know you are, because we've heard the Elders talking about it in whispers.'

'Except that most of the whispers were Great Uncle

Rudraige's, and his whispers are loud enough to bounce off the back row of the stalls,' said Petronella.

'We know about Simeon,' said Phoebe. 'We know our papa helped Uncle Rudraige and some of the others to throw him out into the street,' she added, and gestured through the rather grimy, diamond windowpanes. 'That very street out there, it was, and there was a dramatic scene with everyone shouting and hurling threats. I wish I could have seen it. It must have been splendidly dramatic, mustn't it?'

Mikhail murmured something non-committal, not liking to say he found the thought of somebody shouting insults in the middle of a busy London street somewhat alarming.

'Simeon's supposed to have been very good-looking,' said Phoebe. 'Very like Jack's father to look at, they all say. We didn't know him, of course,' she added, rather wistfully.

'Actually, we didn't know our papa very well, either, because we were only eight when he died,' said Petronella.

'That's sad. I'm sorry.' Mikhail wondered whether to tell them his own parents had died when he was around that age, but he remembered he was still being careful not to give away too much. He said, 'I know only that Mr Simeon is thought to have committed some crime, and—' He paused, searching for the right words, then said, 'and your cousins hope to put it right.' He would like to have suggested taking them out to supper some evening, but he was not sure of the etiquette surrounding such things in this country. Also, his small store of money would not last indefinitely, although Jack had insisted on paying him for the work with Bill, and would not take a refusal.

Mikhail made his way to the Green Room for the meeting, enjoying the cheerful activity everywhere, carefully negotiating the bits of scenery and pots of paint and odd pieces of furniture that were lying around. As he took a seat at the long table, he was already thinking everything was going to be all right. They would find the Stone Heads, and he would be able to return them to Cympak and prove he had nothing to do with stealing them, and life would go on as before. It was a bit startling to suddenly realize that the thought of Cympak and of life going on as it used to was not as alluring as it should have been. He was liking London very much, and he was starting to feel almost at home in it – even though the sheer size and the constant noise and bustle of everything were still overwhelming. But he was beginning to wonder whether, if he could find a way of earning money, he might move to nicer lodgings, and it had also crossed his mind to wonder if Jack Fitzglen might consider giving him more permanent work at the Amaranth. There must be a number of areas in which he could be useful. He would choose a suitable opportunity to ask, saying how much he was enjoying being part of the theatre, and how much he would miss it.

He would certainly miss the opportunity of meeting Petronella Fitzglen in places such as The Punchbowl. And Phoebe, too, of course.

The Fitzglens and Gus, seated at the long Green Room table, midnight chiming distantly from St Martin-in-the-Fields, listened attentively to Jack reading the notes made from the transcripts found in the Ecclesiastical Society office.

When he finished, there was silence for a few moments, then Great Uncle Rudraige said, 'So the Stone Heads were locked away in the dark by the monks. Do you know, I find that curiously disturbing. Don't shudder like that, Cecily.'

'It's that part about "darkness must be maintained".'

'Why would they find it necessary to hide the things so completely?' asked Ambrose.

'We don't know yet, but,' said Rudraige, 'I must say, Gus, you've done a splendid job with all this, although I always knew we'd make a successful villain of you in the end. You're a Fitzglen in all but name, dear old lad. For my part, I think there should be some form of financial recognition for this. Ambrose, don't you agree?'

He glared at Ambrose, drawing down his brows, and Ambrose wrote down a figure in his account book, frowned at it, crossed it out, wrote down another figure, showed it to the others, then nodded.

'Very well deserved,' said Daphnis, firmly.

'But I don't want financial recognition. Mr Jack, I really don't—'

'It's no more than what's due to you,' said Jack, aware Gus was feeling guilty about the deception involving Viola. 'And it will please us all if you accept.'

'You can take that bright-eyed young lady from The Punchbowl out for an extravagant supper,' said Rudraige, as Ambrose counted out some coins from a tin cash box and passed them to Gus. 'I noticed how eagerly she refilled your glass the other night.'

Cecily had taken the notes from Jack and was reading them quietly to herself, dabbing her eyes with her handkerchief.

'It's dreadful,' she said, 'to think of those dead children you told us about, Mikhail – how they vanished, probably murdered, all those years ago. And now this permanent darkness closed down over their likenesses – all that was left of them. It's too upsetting, and – oh, thank you Gus – what exactly—?'

'A tot of brandy, Miss Cecily,' said Gus, handing her the glass. 'Very restoring.'

'We'll all have a tot,' said Rudraige. 'Now then, Jack, what are we going to do about this mausoleum in – where is it? Mallory Abbot? Because we need to move quickly.'

'Yes, because there's no knowing how long they'll be kept there,' put in Daphnis.

'It doesn't sound as if the mausoleum would be easy to get into,' said Ambrose.

'It won't be,' said Jack. 'There's an iron ring handle and a strong padlock on the door.'

'Padlocks aren't difficult,' said Rudraige. 'A tiny tension wrench inserted into the casing pushing up the key pins – your father had padlock-breaking down to a fine art, Jack. He even designed a tension wrench of his own – he and that villain Simeon worked on it together. Do you know, I can see the two of them now, working out that design. They were very much in accord in those days, and they were so alike as young men that you'd almost have thought they were twins . . . And when you think what happened – Simeon went to the bad, and Aiden died on that disastrous night that nearly destroyed the Amaranth—'[1] He fished in a pocket for his handkerchief, and blew his nose.

Jack said, 'I've still got the original of the miniature wrench my father made.'

'Have you really? He'd like that,' said Rudraige, cheering up. 'Do you know, he and I used it one night when we were breaking into a house in St John's Wood—'

'What's the mausoleum built of, Jack?' asked Byron, before Rudraige could wander too deeply into the realms of reminiscences.

'Solid stone, as far as I could tell.'

'Sometimes you can chip away a bit of stone or a few bricks just under the roof, though. Then you can reach down inside to the inner door hinges.'

'It looked a bit too solid for that,' said Jack, but even as he spoke, he was wondering whether to tell them that the beginning of a fragile plan was already unfolding in his mind – that he was starting to see a way to get inside the Brundage crypt which would not involve outright breaking in. But he would let the plan develop a little more.

'Do we believe the documents are genuine?' demanded Daphnis, suddenly. 'They sound authentic, but if Saintly Simeon is involved in this – and I think we should assume he is – they're exactly the kind of thing he would have cooked up.'

'Much as it pains me to say it, if he did cook them up, they'd have been convincing,' said Byron.

'The Ecclesiastical Society seems to have accepted them as genuine, though,' said Jack. 'And they deal with this kind of thing all the time, so you'd expect them to have an eye for a fake.'

'They might well be genuine,' said Rudraige. 'Simeon could have lifted them at the same time as the sculptures. Remarkable documents, though, every one of them.'

Jack thought if ever there was a moment when the ideal cue was given, this was it. He said, 'There's actually one more I haven't yet read out. It's very brief, and someone –

[1] Chalice of Darkness

presumably, the translator – has added a note at the top of the page, which says, "The original of this looked like a child's writing . . . Suggest it might be part of a folksong or a nursery rhyme, or possibly a chant for a children's game."'

As Jack said this, he was aware of a reaction from Mikhail, and when he looked across at him, he saw what almost seemed to be fear in the boy's eyes. He knows what's coming, thought Jack, and he's afraid of it. At once, his mind went back to Viola seated in the lychgate of St Osmund's, saying she wished she had not found this final paper, and also that she wished she had not read it.

But Mikhail did not speak, so Jack said, 'Whatever its origin, I think it sounds a bit sinister.'

'Folksongs sometimes can be sinister,' said Daphnis. 'Nursery rhymes, too.'

'Oh, they can, Daphnis. I remember being terrified as a child by "Oranges and Lemons" and the part about "Here comes a chopper to chop off your head". Mamma had to take the nursery rhyme book away from me, because—'

'What do the lines say?' asked Daphnis, in a voice that was not quite exasperated, but sharp enough to halt Cecily's flow.

Forcing his voice to be as expressionless as possible, Jack read from Viola's notes.

'*Beware, beware, the Face Stealer's hands,*

'*Run for your life if he comes.*

'*He'll carve out your face, then he'll throw you away.*'

He paused, then said, 'Below that is another line:

'*Never be caught, never be caught, never, never, NEVER be caught.*'

The words lay on the air as if waiting to press down, and for some moments no one spoke. Then Ambrose said, slowly, 'It's a warning among children, isn't it?'

'And very disturbing,' said Daphnis. 'Jack, you were right to call it sinister.'

'This is certainly a tale to harrow up the soul,' said Rudraige. 'Read it again, Jack.'

'*Never be caught by the Face Stealer's hands*

'*Run for your life if he comes . . .*

'*He'll carve out your face, then he'll throw you away . . .*'

'Then there's the warning about "never be caught".'

Cecily said, tremulously, 'It's "Here comes a chopper to chop off your head" but in a different guise, isn't it? Ambrose, do you happen to have any sal volatile? Oh, thank you.'

The pungent scent of ammonia filled the Green Room, and Daphnis raised her eyes to the ceiling as if in entreaty, then said, 'Mikhail, have you ever heard that rhyme? Is it a local children's song, perhaps? Something from your own village?'

For a moment, Jack thought Mikhail was not going to answer, then he said, slowly, 'The lines are a little familiar. But I have no idea where they come from.'

His tone was vague, but Jack thought the look on Mikhail's face was the look of someone confronted with a nightmare.

As the words of the old rhyme fell like stones on the room, Mikhail felt as if something had reached up out of his past, and as if clawed hands were trying to drag him down into a deep dark well.

'*Never be caught by the Face Stealer's hands*

'*Run for your life if he comes . . .*

'*He'll carve out your face, then he'll throw you away . . .*'

The shabby, comfortable Green Room blurred, and he no longer heard what was being said; all he was hearing were the words of the old rhyme, chanted in the small yard outside Cympak's little school. All he was feeling was the same horror that had swept over him on that morning.

ELEVEN

I t had seemed to be an ordinary school day in Cympak. Earlier, Mr Blokhin's arithmetic lesson had been disrupted, because two of the livelier spirits in the class had hidden in the stationery cupboard behind the teacher's high desk, and pretended to be ghosts while Mr Blokhin, a timid soul, was explaining the complexities of long division. They had groaned sinisterly, tapping eerily on the door, and poor Mr Blokhin had fled the room in terror, which the children had thought a great joke. Mikhail had had to seek him out and calm him down, and explain it had been a bad joke by thoughtless pupils. After this, he had summoned the two girls in question to deliver a reprimand.

'What on earth gave you the idea of pretending to be ghosts?' he said.

The culprits glanced at one another, then the younger one said, 'It was something the English church gentleman said.'

'The English—? Ah, Reverend Fitzglen.'

'Yes.' They giggled a bit shamefacedly, and the elder girl said he had talked to them – a lovely voice he had, they all thought – and told them stories about England, which they had enjoyed. He had asked about their own local stories, so they had recounted one or two.

'He was very interested in the history of Cympak and the other villages,' said the younger one, hopefully.

'I see,' said Mikhail, and smiled, but set them both a punishment which involved writing an abject apology to Mr Blokhin, and half an hour's homework studying long division.

Returning to the empty classroom, he thought he would seek out the Reverend Fitzglen to ask what kind of tales had been discussed – he was staying at the little local tavern, so he would be easy to find. Probably, the tales would be perfectly harmless; the Reverend had been courteous and friendly, and everyone had liked him. He had come to the school to talk to

the children about his home – about England and its history
– and twice he had taken the pulpit at the local church, to
address the congregation, and to tell them about his travels
and the organizations for which he was raising money.

The local priest had been delighted to welcome such a
distinguished English churchman, and everyone agreed that
the Reverend Fitzglen had an extremely good command
of their language, although occasionally an unusual way of
pronouncing some of the words. The ladies, however, said this
was attractive and added to the Reverend's charm, and they
had been eager to contribute to the charities described.

As Mikhail sat down to mark the weekend essays about the
poetry of Alexander Pushkin, which he was trying to enthuse
his pupils into studying, he could hear shouts and laughter
from outside. He smiled, because they were imaginative, his
pupils – even the mischievous creation of ghosts in the
stationery cupboard had been inventive. They were playing
some game now, and chanting a rhyme along with it – he
visualized them in a circle, hands linked, perhaps counting
one another out around the ring.

And then the words of the children's chant reached him,
and a deep unease brushed his mind.

'Beware, beware, the Face Stealer's hands,
'Run for your life if he comes.
'He'll carve out your face, then he'll throw you away.
'Never be caught, never be caught, never, never, NEVER be
caught.'

The Face Stealer, thought Mikhail. I've never heard that
rhyme before, but I know what it's referring to – anyone in
Cympak or the surrounding villages would know. It was
the old legend – the handed-down warning of a murderous
malevolence that had once stalked the night streets. Mikhail
had never completely believed the story, but he had never quite
disbelieved it, either.

And now from somewhere had come this rhyme. Was it
from the time of the old legend itself? Did that mean it was
waking – or had been woken? No, of course it did not. But
even if the story was true, it had all happened more than a
hundred years ago.

He went over to the window and looked out. The children had formed a circle, but facing outwards, their hands linked. One of the taller boys was prowling around within the circle, raising his hands in an exaggerated gesture, as if about to snatch the children – then dodging back if they caught him trying to grab them. There was much giggling, but Mikhail thought some of the younger ones seemed uncertain. He could not grasp the entire meaning of the game, but it seemed to be based on the traditional premise of a villain prowling along to catch prey, trying to remain hidden as he did so. Macabre. But weren't children often drawn to the macabre – enjoying it because of not really understanding it?

The singing was continuing, and he opened the window as unobtrusively as he could, and leaned out to hear it more clearly.

'*Beware, beware, the Face Stealer's hands*

'*Never be caught, never be caught, never, never, NEVER be caught.*'

Then came a second verse, chanted faster, the tall boy matching his prowling to the pace of the rhythm.

'*He'll snatch you all up in his murderer's hands,*

'*He'll carry you off to his lair down below*

'*Where the iron teeth clang and the river-light glows, and the water lies waiting for prey.*

'*And the iron will clang down and you'll never get free;*

'*You'll scream and you'll fight, but you'll die in the flow.*

'*He'll carve out your face, then he'll throw you away –*

'*Into the green waiting stream.*'

Mikhail was never able to remember much about the rest of that day, but somehow he got back to his house – the house that had belonged to his parents and in which he had been born.

He knew the house's memories, just as it knew his. After his parents died when he was eleven, in the cholera epidemic that everyone had said was brought to the area by travellers from China or Japan, he had had to leave it for a time. The local priest and people in the village said an eleven-year-old could not live on his own, so Mikhail had been taken to the monastery and handed into the care of the monks for a few years. The monks had been kind; they were used to taking in children, they said. It was something they had done several times over the years.

Mikhail had always been grateful to them, and he was grateful, too, that their tutoring had enabled him to later teach at Cympak's own little school, and to return to live in his family's house.

His family's house . . . This house in which he was sitting now, his mind in chaos.

The little clock on the mantel was showing half an hour before midnight when, finally, he went through the stone-floored scullery and the little washhouse beyond it, and stood before the scarred old door that led down to the cellar. Throughout his childhood, this door had been kept firmly shut and bolted, and it was a strict rule that he must never go down there by himself. His parents had not made any secret of the reason, and Mikhail had known it was because of the deep cellar with the river gate with its iron teeth . . . It was because the river itself, despite the heavy iron gate and the teeth-like grille, sometimes oozed and trickled through crevices and lay in slimy puddles on the stone floor. It was shivery to think of all that immediately below the house – Mikhail had usually managed not to think about it very much.

But he was thinking about it now.

'*He'll carry you off to his lair,*' the rhyme had said. '*Where the iron teeth clang and the river-light glows and the water lies waiting for prey . . .*'

The bolt was still on the door; it was rusty, but it scraped back easily enough. The door swung slowly inwards, creaking like old bones disturbed from a forgotten tomb, and there, at the bottom of the wooden steps, was the cellar, bathed in green water-light from what lay beyond the iron gate.

At the far end was the door that opened on to the short tunnel leading to the old kiln. The kiln had belonged to a sculptor who had lived in the house a very long time ago. Mikhail's father had sometimes said he would try to find out how to fire the kiln – assuming it could be fired now – and if so, they might even be able to start their own business.

Earthenware dishes and bowls and pots, he said, his eyes
shining with enthusiasm. He had been a dreamer, Mikhail's
father, but his dreams had been good ones.

But the tunnel door was firmly closed, and Mikhail's entire
attention was on the river gate. It was perhaps six feet in height
and seven or eight feet wide, and its surface was dull and
pitted, but even from here, he could see that at the lower edge
were the spikes – like huge black teeth driven into the floor,
locking the gate down. The opening mechanism was on the
left. Would it still work? Could you winch it up, causing
the gate to rise slowly and inexorably – and, if the river was
high, see the water come slopping in. Once raised, it would
be easy to push through it something you did not want to be
found. To push it into the river and let it be swept away for
ever. And then the gate could be lowered, and no one would
ever know what had been done.

'And the iron will clang down and you'll never get free;
'You'll scream and you'll fight, but you'll die in the flow.'

The legend of the Face Stealer had faded over the years, but
it had never quite gone away, just as it had never lost its horror.
And now it had come back, and with it had come a new horror
– the fact that the Face Stealer had almost certainly lived and
worked in Mikhail's house. Or was his imagination getting
out of hand? No, the rhyme had been dreadfully explicit: *'The
Face Stealer's lair / Where the iron teeth clang and the river-
light glows.'* Mikhail forced himself to acknowledge that the
Face Stealer had committed his appalling crimes in the cellar
of this house – firing the kiln so that he could immortalize his
victims' features in stone or clay before raising the iron gate
and consigning their bodies to the river. That being so, he did
not think he would be able to live in the house, unless he
could make some attempt to lay its dark past to rest. But how?

The monks believed in evil, and they taught that to banish
it, you had to have the courage to confront it – to look it in
the eyes. And there was the ancient belief that in order to
exorcise a demon, you must first know its name and then
address it by that name, they said, solemnly. This was not
likely to be of much help in banishing the evil memories from

Mikhail's house, and he had no idea of the Face Stealer's name anyway, even if he had thought it would do any good to pronounce it and order its memory to dissolve.

He certainly could not look into the eyes of the Face Stealer himself – but might there be a way in which he could look into the eyes of the victims? His mind flinched from the idea, which was very likely a ridiculous one anyway. Or was it? He realized that he would not rest until he had tried. Before he could give way to weakness, he closed the cellar door, reached for a warm coat and scarf, and went out, locking the house's outer door behind him.

The streets were lit only by the occasional flaring lamps outside a few of the houses, and here and there by a faint overspill of light from a window. It was a cold night, with no one abroad, and Mikhail did not think anyone saw him as he made his way through the village. Had the Face Stealer really once prowled these shadow-filled streets? Had he looked at those lighted windows and paused at doors, listening and waiting for a chance to snatch up a new victim? Or had he hidden in the shadows – perhaps in that narrow alley between the cobbler's workshop and the little bakehouse, or in the passageway that led to the wool-spinner's house – waiting for his victims to come unsuspectingly along so he could pounce on them? But why had he done any of that? Why had he created likenesses of his victims? And why had those likenesses been hidden away?

As he left the village streets, a watery moon slid briefly from behind the clouds, shedding just enough light to show him the way. The night was not entirely silent, of course, and there were faint rustlings and scuttlings in the thick under-growth on each side of the steep path winding up to the monastery. It was important to remember they were only night creatures.

The monastery came into view, rearing up as if it had been watching for him, starkly limned against the scudding clouds. The monks would be in their cells at this hour, but a single light burned above the main door. Mikhail knew it was a tradition across most of the world that travellers were welcomed into religious houses and given shelter for the night; the light flaring through the darkness now would be part of that tradition – a signal that the monks of Verkhoturye welcomed all comers.

He went warily around the dark, high walls of the main building, to the garden door which he had so often used when he was living and studying here. It was often propped open in order to carry in the produce from the garden – the monks were proud of their vegetables, and the mushrooms that grew freely, and the fruit bushes. But they frequently forgot to lock the door, and it was through this door that Mikhail hoped to get in.

There was a bad moment when he thought it was locked, after all, but then it swung inwards. He paused, half expecting to hear someone come along to find out who was there, but nothing stirred. Or did it? Had the deep shadows in the corners shifted slightly, as if something crouched within them? He stood very still, but nothing moved, so he stepped inside and began to walk, as softly as possible, through the dim corridors.

The stairs going down to the crypt were at the end of several long passages with stone archways overhead, and narrow windows set at intervals in the walls. A faint light came through them, and despite his care, Mikhail's steps echoed in the emptiness. His heart was racing furiously, because if he were to be heard – if he were to be caught . . . But the monks knew him and surely they would not punish him very severely.

Twice, he spun sharply round, thinking footsteps were padding after him, and the second time he thought he caught a glimpse of something – the hem of a cloak? – whisking into hiding behind a pillar. He retraced his footsteps, looking about him, but there was no one to be seen. Imagination running riot, that was all.

The stone passages branched off several times, but Mikhail was fairly sure he was going in the right direction. Yes – here was the low stone arch, with the names of the monastery's founders carved into the sides, along with a hope that they were now enjoying everlasting life. Beyond it, narrow steps led down. Mikhail, keeping one hand on the wall to retain his balance on the sharp curves, went cautiously down. Again, he thought the shadows slithered, but again nothing seemed to be moving, and he went all the way down the twisting steps, because, having got this far, he would not succumb to nerves.

He had known the crypt would be in darkness, and he had brought a tinder box and matches. He lit two of the matches and held them up, and the small flames showed up the pitted surface of the old walls and the plain stone coffins that held the remains of the monastery's founders. Mikhail walked slowly between them, trying to suppress the feeling that he was intruding on something that should be left in its own dark silence.

The matches had burned down, and he had to light more before he saw, directly ahead, the low door set deep into the thick old walls. His heart leapt, because this was surely what he had come to find – this was the prison, the hiding place of the Face Stealer's grim work.

The door was smaller than he had expected – no more than five feet in height and perhaps three feet wide. At the top was an oblong-shaped window – not glazed, of course, but with thick black bars. On one side was a massive lock, which was certainly much newer than the door itself, secured by a large padlock. Mikhail hesitated, then managed to wedge several matches in crevices in the walls. They shed an uncertain light, but they should burn long enough for him to see what he was here to see. He lit two more, then, holding them up, went up to the barred window and leaned as close to it as he could.

At first, he thought there was nothing beyond the door – only deep, thick shadows and veils of cobwebs that stirred from the slight disturbance of the air caused by his approach. He was aware of a stab of disappointment – after all the handed-down tales, was there nothing at the heart of the old legend? He struck another match and held it closer to the door. It did not look as if it was ever opened, but wouldn't someone come down here from time to time, just to make sure the Heads were still here? And if this really was just an empty old room, then why were there bars and a padlock?

Then, very gradually, he began to make out dark shapes in the dimness. Outlines of things that seemed to be turned towards the door, as if watching it. The match burned down, scorching his fingers slightly, and he gasped, then, although his hands were shaking, forced himself to light two more, which he set in the old brickwork. Then he looked back through the bars into the shadowy room. There would not be anything there after all, of course; it had simply been the clustered shadows . . .

But there was something. Mikhail could see shapes in the gloom – shapes that seemed to look towards him with blind, dead eyes. His heart began to pound with fear, but also with excitement, because it was as if he was looking at a legend – at something no one living today might ever have looked on.

These were the stone memories of vanished children. The graven faces of the little lost ones who had vanished over a century earlier, almost certainly slaughtered by the Face Stealer, their bodies flung into the river below Mikhail's own house.

Mikhail leaned as close as he could to the bars. 'I can hardly see you,' he whispered, 'but I think a tiny memory of each one of you was captured inside those stones, and perhaps that fragment of memory is still here, and it's hearing me. If so, then this is a promise that I will try to find out what happened all those years ago.'

With the whispered words, there was a sense of movement within the room. Mikhail's heart skipped several beats again, but then he thought it could only be the tiny flames casting shadows. To be sure, he struck another match and held it as close to the bars as he could.

Panic swept in, almost smothering him, and he gave a choking cry, recoiling so violently he fell back against a jutting ledge of stone.

From just beyond the barred aperture had come unmistakable movement, as if something was coming towards him. Mikhail managed to get to his feet and forced himself to stand by the doors again, and to look through the bars. Of course, what he had seen had only been the shadows and, of course, nothing was inside that room that could have moved – that could seem to be pressing its face up against the bars . . .

Its face . . . *Its face* . . .

But it was not just one face; it was three – no, four – of them, looming out of the thick darkness. Even in the erratic light, the features of each held no emotion – no clue as to the feelings that must have scalded through them at the last. No, he was wrong – one did hold emotion. It was different, somehow twisted – unchildlike. Resentment and hatred glared from the dead features.

But they're not dead, thought Mikhail, wildly. They're moving. They can't possibly be alive, though – it's the flickering of the matches. But even as the thought formed, the movements came again – movements of creatures huddled together, as if for warmth, pressing against the bars as though trying blindly to know who was looking in at them.

Mikhail had no idea how long he stood there, motionless with horror, until the last of the tiny match flames suddenly sputtered out, plunging the crypt into complete darkness. Panic overwhelmed him afresh, and he ran frantically back towards the steps, groping wildly through the darkness, banging into jutting stone walls and the tombs of the long-ago monks, eventually reaching the stairway and clawing his way up it to the main part of the monastery.

He ran for all he was worth along the echoing corridors, uncaring if anyone heard, fell through the garden door and half ran, half slithered down the narrow path to the village. An icy rain was driving into his face, and several times he skidded on the wet path and almost fell, but he went determinedly on, pushing away the nightmare images of the sightless faces that had looked out at him.

TWELVE

Returning to his house – the house so unmistakably described in the song – was more than he could face yet. The lines the children had sung, just a few hours earlier, ran through his mind over and over.

'*He'll carry you off to his lair down below*

'*Where the iron teeth clang and the river-light glows, and the water lies waiting for prey . . .*

'*And the iron will clang down and you'll never get free . . .*'

He paused on the outskirts of the village. The familiar outline of the church was ahead of him; that would surely be somewhere he would feel safe. But supposing the priest came in and found him? He turned in the other direction, going towards the schoolhouse. Could he get in? Yes, there was a flimsily shut window. Mikhail forced it open and climbed through. The familiar scents of chalk and dust and ink closed reassuringly around him. I'm safe, he thought, as he went into the teachers' private room and shut the door.

He lay on the battered sofa, wrapped in his coat and a rug, but sleep was impossible. Every time he closed his eyes, the dreadful images of the Heads swam into his vision. They had moved – they had come to the door and looked through the bars at him. No, it was impossible. There would be a logical explanation for what he had seen – he must believe he would find it.

It seemed a very long time before light finally began to streak the skies, but eventually it did so, and Mikhail forced himself to walk through the streets to his house. Unlocking the door, he wondered suddenly if his parents had known of its past. Had they acquired it from the descendants of the Face Stealer himself? Might they even have inherited it from those descendants? His father had insisted the cellar was always locked – was that because he knew what had been done down there? Or simply because the old river gate made it dangerous?

The house was exactly as he had left it, but as Mikhail set a kettle to boil for a cup of coffee and found bread in the larder, he knew he could not remain here. He was not even sure if he could remain in Cympak.

The coffee warmed him, and he managed to eat a slice of bread and honey with it. But sitting at the table – the table his mother used to polish every week, so that the room smelled of lavender beeswax – he wondered if the Face Stealer had sat by this window and eaten his meals here. Had he actually lived here – slept here, perhaps even in Mikhail's own bedroom? – or had it simply been his lair, the hiding place to which he brought his victims? The place where, once the doors and windows were locked, he could descend to the cellar and create those eerie, pitiful likenesses of the children he had stolen away?

But the question as to why he had taken the children seared Mikhail's mind again. Had it been straightforward madness – always supposing madness could ever be called straight-forward – or had there been some darker, more twisted motive?

Mikhail finished his coffee, pulled on fresh clothes and tried to tidy his hair, which always seemed to look like a dishevelled floor-mop, no matter what he did to it, then returned to the schoolhouse. He thought he managed the day's classes well, but as the afternoon wore on and darkness began to steal forward, he was increasingly aware he could not face going home. He spent a second night on the schoolroom sofa, hoping the nightmare images would have receded, but they were still there. He was grateful when dawn came.

Halfway through the following day, the headmaster stopped him in the corridor and asked if he was quite well, and later that same afternoon, Mr Blokhin wanted to know if Mikhail might be coming down with an illness. There was a lot of illness about, he said, seriously, and you could not be too careful.

To both of them, Mikhail said he was quite all right, thank you, only a little tired. But the feeling of being pulled deeper into a nightmare persisted, and he spent the next two nights on the schoolroom sofa, returning briefly to his own house shortly after dawn for a change of clothes and to force down a few mouthfuls of breakfast.

It was at the end of what he thought was the fourth day – although he was starting to lose all sense of time – that the headmaster sent a message to ask if Mr Volkov would please step into his study after his class was over. Mikhail was not surprised; he supposed his erratic behaviour had been noticed, and that the headmaster intended to speak sharply about it. But when he entered the study, the headmaster had two other people with him. One was the local priest. The other was Father Abbot from St Nicholas's.

'Mr Volkov – Mikhail – a very grave matter has come to my attention,' said the headmaster, indicating to him to sit down.

Mikhail sat, but his heart was clenching with panic. Then I *was* seen going in there! he thought. And probably half the inhabitants heard me running out later, like a mad thing pursued by the demons of hell. He wished his mind had not presented him with this particular vision, but he waited to see what was to come.

'Four nights ago,' said the headmaster, 'you were seen inside the monastery around midnight. You spent time in the monastery as a child, and you probably knew of an outer door likely to be unlocked.'

'The garden door,' said Mikhail, seeing no point in evasion or denial. 'It was often missed when everywhere was locked for the night.'

'Ah. You went down to the crypt,' said Father Abbot. 'Several of the brothers were keeping an all-night vigil in the chapel – I was with them. But I heard footsteps and I went out to investigate. I recognized you, of course. And I was forced to conclude that you were wanting to get at the monastery's deepest, most closely guarded secret.'

'The Stone Heads,' said Mikhail, almost to himself.

'Yes.'

Mikhail looked at him for a moment, then said, 'Why did you not come down there to challenge me?'

'I know something of the Heads' history and the legend,' said Father Abbot. 'And it is a very dark legend. I suspected that some ungodly force might be driving you, and I was not prepared to confront you – or such a force – without due preparation.'

His eyes held Mikhail's, and after a moment, Mikhail said, very levelly, 'But you could have called some of the Brothers to join you. If you thought I intended to make use of the Heads for some . . . some sacrilegious purpose, surely a group of men who had spent their lives in God's service could have fought that? And there must be at least twenty or thirty Brothers in the Order. That would have created a formidable army against the powers of darkness.'

'I hope you are not intending to be frivolous,' said Father Abbot, coldly.

'I am not,' said Mikhail. He frowned, then said, 'I certainly entered the monastery, and I went down to the crypt. It was because I was afraid the ancient legend might be waking. The children had been singing an old rhyme about the Face Stealer—'

'I heard them, as well,' said the headmaster. Mikhail thought he said this reluctantly, but at least it gave some credence to his explanation.

He said, 'I wanted to find out as much as I could about the Heads and the old story. But other than entering the monastery clandestinely, what have I done that is so very wrong?'

Father Abbot said, 'What is so very wrong, Mr Volkov, is that, since your visit, the Stone Heads have vanished.'

There was an abrupt silence. Mikhail felt his mind spin in disbelief. He thought: Then the Heads got out! – but this was so wild and so impossible a thought that he pushed it away.

The headmaster said, 'You must see, Mikhail, that the logical conclusion is that you broke into the crypt and stole the Heads.'

'Of course I did not!' said Mikhail, angrily. 'Search my house for them, if you wish.' But his mind flinched from this prospect, because the cellar would be found, and it would be linked to the Face Stealer and the Stone Heads. And Mikhail himself would be linked to them. He tried to think this would not matter, but he knew it would matter very much.

He stood up. 'I did not steal the Heads,' he said. 'You have my word I did not – and I give that word in the presence of two men of God. If that is not enough for you, there is nothing more I can do or say.' Before they could reply, he walked out of the room.

Somehow, he got back to his house. They would come to search it, of course, although probably they would have to get permission from some authorities somewhere first. But Mikhail did not think it would be long before he was formally accused of stealing the Stone Heads, and taken to a gaol somewhere and made to stand trial.

He locked the street door against the world and sat down, trying to think logically. To believe the Heads had escaped because of his intrusion on their brooding darkness was patently ridiculous. That impression of them moving to stand at the barred window could only have been a trick of the light. Mikhail repeated this to himself several times and was faintly reassured.

If the Heads had vanished, it was because someone had stolen them. Could that have been done? It was common knowledge that every Father Abbot held the keys to that room, each one passing them to his successor, but keys could be stolen if you knew where to look, and even without a key, padlocks could be broken open.

But it did not seem very likely that anyone from Cympak would have done that. Apart from all else, the local people were unlikely to know how to dispose of such things. Also, the story was so much a part of Cympak's history, and the history of the villages adjoining, that nobody paid it much attention anymore. It was just an old legend—

Except that it was not an old legend any longer, because someone had revived it, and that someone had caused the schoolchildren to start singing the Face Stealer rhyme. With the intention of stealing the Heads? But who might that someone have been?

Even as the question formed, a name dropped into Mikhail's mind.

The Reverend Simeon Fitzglen. *Fitzglen.*

Mikhail ran up to his bedroom, and reached for the old book recently discovered on one of his rare trips to the nearby town. When he could manage these trips, one of his greatest pleasures was to spend time in the bookshops – often an entire afternoon. Sometimes he bought a book or two; sometimes he only talked to the various booksellers who came in, and to other customers. There was always a great sense of companionship between people who read and bought books; Mikhail enjoyed these small, brief exchanges.

On his last trip, he had found a book mentioning Cympak, and he had bought it for that reason. It had also contained extracts from various memoirs and autobiographies with links to the village, which he thought might be interesting. He had wondered whether he might read some of it to his pupils and perhaps set them an essay.

He turned the pages, unsure whether he was remembering correctly or whether his memory had been tricking him. But it had not; here it was. Almost an entire chapter describing how Catherine the Great had made some kind of ceremonial progress through the area including Cympak and Verkhoturye in the early 1770s – and how an English traveller named Harry Fitzglen had become her lover during that journey. There was some proof of this, explained the author, because it was recorded in the Empress's private journal. A few copies of this journal had been printed shortly after her death – the authenticity could not be entirely relied on, of course, and the author himself had only been able to find partial copies. However, it was not unlikely that such a document had been put into circulation shortly after the Tsarina's death by venal or resentful servants who had found the journal among Catherine's private possessions. As to the existence of the Englishman, Harry Fitzglen, that, too, was very likely; it was generally accepted that Her Imperial Highness had taken a great many lovers.

Mikhail thought someone like Catherine the Great would certainly have been surrounded by people who would have seized greedily on a chance to make money by selling such a thing for publication after her death. However, that was something that could be investigated later if it seemed important.

What was relevant was that an English gentleman called Harry Fitzglen had entered the Empress's life in the early

1770s. And a century and a half later, another Englishman, also called Fitzglen, had come to Cympak. Had Harry known about the Stone Heads? Had it been a story he might have passed down in his own family, until it reached the Reverend Simeon Fitzglen? If so, when Simeon left Cympak, had the Stone Heads gone with him? And if they had, how could he be tracked down?

With this thought, the glimmer of a plan began to form in Mikhail's mind. Simeon Fitzglen had talked about his family one night, sitting with Mikhail and the priest in the church hall, after delivering a stirring lecture to locals.

'I cut myself off from them,' he had said, with sad solemnity. 'They are quite famous and even distinguished – a theatrical family in London. But when I discovered the truth about them, I could no longer regard myself as one of them. I did not judge them, though,' he said. 'We are all sinners in our own ways.'

'Indeed so,' said the priest.

'But it was a grave shock to discover that my cousins, my uncles and aunts were irreclaimable thieves,' said Reverend Fitzglen, sorrowfully. 'What in England are called society burglars.'

Mikhail, hoping for a tale of bold adventure and gallantry, had said, 'Robbing from the rich to give to the poor?'

'Ah, the old fairy story,' said the Reverend, indulgently. 'But I am afraid they were not – are not – a band of benevolents. They rob solely for their own ends.' He spread his hands ruefully. 'I could not betray them, but I could no longer be one of them. I turned to God.'

Mikhail had had the oddest sense that he was hearing something frequently repeated – a tale told many times, honed and polished along the way. To elicit sympathy? And, with the sympathy, donations?

Remembering that conversation now as he sat in his own house, the plan that had nudged his mind moments earlier solidified. His first response was to push it away – I can't do it! he thought. It's too great an undertaking – it would mean a journey – a very long journey . . . But then he thought about what might be ahead if he remained here, and he took out the little box where he kept his wages from the school, and counted the money. He lived quite simply – the school provided a substantial midday meal, so he only had to buy items such as milk and bread. He seldom bought clothes, and books were his only real indulgence. It meant his wages had mounted up surprisingly substantially.

But he had no idea how much it cost to travel on trains for such a distance, or what lodging houses charged, and after a moment, he went into the bedroom that had been his parents'; in the corner was a small cabinet containing the few pieces of jewellery his mother had inherited from her grandmother, and also a fob watch that had been a gift to his father sometime or other. I won't sell any of these things unless I absolutely have to, he said silently to the memories of his parents. But if I do, you'll understand it's because I need to prove my innocence.

If he could reach London, he would seek out Simeon Fitzglen's family, and ask for their help in tracing him. A theatrical family, the Reverend had said. Famous and distinguished. It ought to be easy enough to find them.

He would do it. Once in London, he would find a single room in some respectable house where he could live for a while. His money would not last for ever, and he would have to find work, but there must be schools or institutions who would be willing to employ a young man who could teach the Russian language to English students.

He began to be aware of excitement. It would be an adventure. A quest. And hadn't he always thought he would like to leave this tiny place and see the wider world?

He looked out a big haversack that had been his father's, and rummaged in cupboards for clothes to fold inside. He added two or three of his favourite books to the haversack, making sure to include the one with the reminiscences about Catherine the Great and Harry Fitzglen.

Then, before he could succumb to doubts or fears, he pulled on his jacket and went out of the house. No one was around as he locked the door and set off on the road that took him away from Cympak.

Towards England and London and the Fitzglens.

THIRTEEN

Great Uncle Rudraige had invited what were often called the Fitzglen Elders to a convivial Sunday lunch at his house.

'And since Jack's going to disclose a plan for getting into that mausoleum and retrieving the Stone Heads,' he said, brandishing a carving knife and attacking a roast beef joint with gusto, 'I haven't included young Volkov. I thought we should keep the details to ourselves, at least until it's all sorted out.'

'In any case, Mikhail was going to have lunch at The Punchbowl with the twins,' said Cecily. 'Phoebe had bought a new hat to wear.'

'The boy's having lunch with that precious pair?' said Rudraige. 'He'll be lucky if he comes back in the same condition as he went out, because that saucy Phoebe is a minx if ever I saw one—'

'She's a very practical-minded minx, though,' said Daphnis. 'I shouldn't think she'd get seriously entangled with a penniless Russian.'

'He mightn't be penniless if he gets the Stone Heads back,' remarked Ambrose.

'Rot! He'll return them to their rightful place in that Russian village. What was its name – Cympak? He struck me as entirely honourable. Now then, Jack, let's hear this plan.'

'I love hearing a plan for a new filch,' said Cecily, cosily, 'because— Oh, Byron, did you know the edge of your velvet cravat is trailing in the gravy? You'd better take it off and let me sponge it before it dries in.'

Byron said, 'But then I'd be seated at the table in an open shirt, and I wouldn't for worlds wish to cause a maiden blush to bepaint your cheek, Cousin Cecily.'

He regarded her with guileless eyes, and Cecily, with unusual tartness, said, 'I daresay I've seen a gentleman's bare neck before now,' and held out her hand for the cravat.

'My idea,' said Jack, 'is not to break into the Brundage mausoleum furtively under cover of night, but to enter it openly. To go to Mallory Abbot as our real selves,' he said, taking from his pocket a folded sheet of notepaper and propping it up against the mustard pot. 'This is only a draft letter, but it explains what I've got in mind. I've addressed it to "Mr and Mrs Brundage", although from what I learned when I was there last weekend, it's "Mrs" who's the driving force behind all the fundraising.'

'I do think it was unnecessarily furtive of you to go off to that place without telling anyone,' complained Rudraige.

'No, he was perfectly right,' said Daphnis. 'He needed to spy out the land, and he didn't want hordes of us milling around.'

'I don't see why not. I can be very unobtrusive if the occasion calls for it,' said Rudraige, indignantly.

'Let's hear the letter,' said Byron.

'My dear Mr and Mrs Brundage,

I hope you will forgive this approach without a formal introduction, but I was recently introduced to the Reverend Hornbeam, and I understand from him that you are an integral part of the plans to restore the Church of St Osmund.

The Fitzglen Theatre Company is currently engaged in arranging the performances of appropriate plays in the grounds of churches where restoration and renovations are being undertaken. Such performances will be given at this Company's expense and without any cost to individual parishes or church authorities. However, audiences would be required to pay for their seats, thus raising much-needed funds. In addition, individual churches would be brought into prominence and in the process could attract the attention of potential benefactors, such as local businesses or financial institutions.

I am sure you will be aware that "open-air" theatre has a venerable history, stretching as far back as ancient Greek drama, commedia dell'arte and the medieval mystery plays.

These performances will, of course, only be possible where conditions and church facilities permit, but I believe that St Osmund's would be most suitable for our scheme. Therefore, we would very much like to include it in our itinerary.

With that in mind, I would be happy to come to Mallory Abbot to meet you and hold a preliminary discussion to explore the possibilities.

With kind regards,

I am yours very sincerely,

Jack Fitzglen

Director and Actor-Manager, Amaranth Theatre, London.'

He laid down the letter and looked round the table.

Then Daphnis said, slowly, 'It's an unexpected idea, Jack. It's not a ploy we've ever tried before.'

'Open-air theatre isn't something we've ever tried before, either,' said Rudraige.

'I think it's a marvellous idea,' said Byron. 'And you've phrased the letter very cannily, Jack. You've praised these Brundages for wanting to restore their church—'

'And assumed they'll know about theatre history,' nodded Cecily. 'Didn't the Church used to dramatize stories from the Bible for their congregations?'

'Yes, because most of the populace couldn't read,' said Ambrose, 'and it was a way of getting the Bible message across to them. I don't much care for that suggestion that we'd perform without any kind of fee, though.'

'I didn't think you would. But wouldn't it be worth it if it meant we could get at the Stone Heads?' said Jack.

'Yes, but it won't be cheap to stage something of this kind.'

'We can juggle the finances a bit, surely.'

Cecily said, eagerly, 'Lydia has had an invitation to a very grand reception next week, and she's asked me to go with her.'

Lydia, the twins' mamma, did not actually appear on the Amaranth's stage – Daphnis said she did not need to, because she spent most of her time acting anyway – but she attended

very high-class assemblies: dinners and receptions for diplomats and politicians, and, even occasionally, minor royalty.
She almost always managed to leave, quite openly, wearing
furs and sometimes jewellery belonging to other guests.

'The reception is in Cadogan Square,' said Cecily, proudly.
'And Lydia thinks some very valuable items will be left around
that we can discreetly pick up. Furs in the ladies' room and
rings left in the wash handbasins. She's going to look very
grand – dowager-like, feathered hat and slightly out-of-the-
fashion gown. I'm going to be a meek younger sister. A bit
twittery and anxious, you know.'

Jack managed not to catch Byron's eye.

'And so,' went on Cecily, 'we can use whatever proceeds
we make there for Jack's idea.'

Everyone nodded approvingly, and Ambrose made a note
in the appropriate column of his account book.

'You do see,' said Jack, 'that once we're in the church
grounds, we'll have fairly open access. We'll be rehearsing
and preparing – everyone will be coming and going. Bill the
Chip and his team will be putting up a small temporary stage.
And if we can't remove a few pieces of stone sculpture in that
situation and get them back to London without being caught,
then we aren't worthy of the Fitzglen name.'

'I'll bet Highwayman Harry would have gone romping in
and lifted the Heads with great panache,' nodded Byron. 'I
say we go ahead – Brundages permitting.'

'I agree,' said Rudraige, who was now passing round large
helpings of apple tart and custard. 'It will be a completely
new experience for us, and I'm all for new experiences. By
God, we'll get those Heads back and be avenged on that rascal
Simeon. Jack, send that letter at once.'

'It will probably be ages before there's a reply,' said Daphnis.

But it was not ages at all. A reply arrived three days later.

My dear Mr Fitzglen,
     I was most interested to receive your letter with the
details of your proposal for the staging of a dramatic
performance in the grounds of our church.
     Sadly, Mr Brundage's health is frail, and he leaves

most estate matters and decisions to me – hence this letter coming from me alone. I have, however, explained to him what is mooted.

I believe St Osmund's Church would lend itself admirably to your plan – although, of course, whatever you stage would need to have due regard to the surroundings. However, such an event would certainly assist in the raising of monies for the Church Restoration Fund – a cause in which I am actively involved, so your scheme will certainly have my support.

You may care to know that this village was named for Abbot Thomas de Mallet, who founded the church in 1280, before he entered the monastery.

I look forward to hearing more of your plans.

With kind regards from myself and my husband,

Marjorie Brundage (Mrs).

'It only arrived today,' said Jack, placing the letter on Byron's desk. 'And you were the nearest one likely to be free, so I came straight to your rooms.'

'She doesn't mention the Stone Heads,' said Byron, reading the letter. 'Although there's no reason why she should. I still wish we knew why those sculptures had to be hidden a century and a half ago. It was Highwayman Harry's time, as well, you know.'

'Yes, but I don't expect we'll ever know what Harry got up to when he was in Russia, so—' Jack broke off, seeing Byron's expression. 'You've found something.'

Byron grinned like a delighted imp. 'I have.'

'What?'

'I'd like to say I've got hold of the Title Deeds to the Amaranth, but it isn't quite that. It's fairly close to it, though – what's apparently called the Epitome of Title. As far as I understand, it's a kind of schedule of the actual documents and Deeds – a sort of index.'

Jack said slowly, 'I suppose I knew Title Deeds existed for the Amaranth – yes, of course I did – but I've never given them a thought.'

'Neither had I until a couple of days ago.' Byron had opened a drawer in the desk, and he took out several pages of faded parchment, most of the pages curling at the edges, all bearing deep creases. 'This is what I cajoled out of Arthur Challis,' he said, handing the pages to Jack. 'You've met old Challis, haven't you?'

'The solicitor? Yes. We use him when we can't avoid needing conventional legal help. He's a crony of Tod Inkling's, isn't he?'

'He is, and he's also a cousin of that publisher in Holborn who's going to put out a collection of my poems— Well,' said Byron, 'he's going to read them at any rate. But it means Arthur is inclined to look favourably on this family at the moment, and he was interested when I told him I was compiling a history of the Fitzglen family. I gave him the expurgated version of it, of course, but the upshot was that when I asked how far back his association with the family went, he said, "Oh, well, dear boy, it goes back to my grandfather and to *his* grandfather and so on back." When I asked if I might see any documents he had relating to the theatre, he tutted and muttered, and said it wasn't really in accordance with correct practice. But then he said he supposed that since an historical book was being written, he dared say I could be loaned the Epitome of Title. After which he burrowed into a few old deed boxes, opened one or two creaking safes, and finally produced this. But he's only letting me have it until the end of the week; even then, I practically had to pawn my soul, Faustian fashion, and sign a contract in blood like Theophilus of Adana.'

'Cheap at the price, I should think.'

'I'll work on Challis to see if he'll let me see the actual Deeds,' said Byron, as Jack began reading the faded papers. 'They might tell us a bit more. But what is clear from this short document is that Harry bought the land from the Bedford Estate.'

'I've certainly heard of the Bedford Estate,' said Jack. 'In fact, I think we have to pay some kind of annual rent to it – ground rent, I think it's called. It's increased every five years, and it gives Ambrose nightmares each time. He goes around grumbling about some law or other passed in the thirteenth century, although I've never been able to make out if he believes it's a law that works to our advantage or against it.'

'I've managed to turn up one or two references to the Bedford Estate,' said Byron. 'It looks as if, in Harry's day, they owned most of Bloomsbury and a fair chunk of Covent Garden, as well – in fact, I think they still do.'

Jack was scanning the list with the appended notes, most of which appeared to be couched in heavily legal terms. He said, 'For Harry to be able to buy land in central London means he must have been an immensely successful highwayman. Or did he have a few other professions we don't know about?'

'Look at that last item,' said Byron. 'It's one of the complete documents that is attached to the Epitome – probably because it's quite short and, legally speaking, I shouldn't think it's terribly binding. But it goes a fair way to explaining how Harry could afford the land. I think it might be regarded as a kind of promissory note, although, whatever it's called, it's written in what seem to me quite strong terms.'

Jack turned the fragile pages with care and began to read aloud.

'I pledge and guarantee that the items deposited with Messieurs Challis and Partners, detailed and described in the inventory herein, are an earnest of my good faith and intent, and that they shall be sold per auctionem by Messieurs Challis and Partners, in conjunction with Messrs Rundell and Bridge of Ludgate Hill – who, if they do not possess the knowledge to accurately value and profitably sell the pieces, ought not to be representing themselves as appointed goldsmiths and jewellers to the English Court.

'Such sale is to take place no more than fourteen days from the date of this document, and seven days thereafter the purchase price as agreed will be paid by me to Messrs Challis and Partners by means of bank draft drawn on Coutts Bank in The Strand – which bank will attest to my ability to honour such obligation, and if it does not, I shall withdraw my custom and take it to Hoare's, since if Hoare's was good enough for Samuel Pepys, it is good enough for me.

'If any man questions my intention to complete this transaction, I cordially invite him to call me out, when I will fight him until he retracts such accusation.'

At the foot of the page, in exuberant characters, was the signature Jack had been hoping for. Harry Fitzglen. The ink must originally have been black – it had faded with the years to a dull brown, but the vigorous scrawl still managed to convey triumph and delight at the prospect of acquiring what, even in those days, must have been an extremely valuable piece of land. He was elated to be buying it, thought Jack. After a moment, he said, 'He was a fiery and determined gentleman, our ancestor, wasn't he? I wish I could have known him. Is the inventory attached, as well—? Oh, yes, it's the next page.'

The inventory bore a heading, announcing that these were 'Items lodged with Messieurs Challis & Partners by Harry Fitzglen Esquire'. Jack supposed that as he was about to become a man of property, it would have been considered that Harry could be accorded the title of esquire.

The inventory was businesslike, but unexpectedly descriptive.

Item: one multi-stranded necklace, comprising in all six strands of emeralds and diamonds, with gold claw clasp.
Item: triple-rope-strand of emeralds, on 24 carat gold link chain.
Item: two cuff bracelets, each 3″ in depth, 24 carat gold, each with 12 emerald studs.
Item: two bangle bracelets in 24 carat gold, with harlequin pattern in emerald stones.
Item: two emerald and diamond rings.
Item: hair ornament of emerald studs, set in 24 carat gold.
Item: large brooch, 4″ by 2″ emerald and white gold.

Authenticity and value of all pieces certified and attested to by Rundell and Bridge, Jewellers & Goldsmiths of Ludgate Hill, London.

Jack set the pages down, frowned, then said, 'If these pieces were the spoils of one of Harry's filches, then it's one of the most colossally profitable filches I've ever heard of. Those wouldn't be pieces you or I could scoop up from a lady's dressing table while she was asleep, then swim down the drainpipe with them in a pocket. They'd be locked in a safe or even a bank deposit box.'

'What about the possibility that they weren't the proceeds of a filch? That the jewellery was a gift.'

'From Catherine?' said Jack.

'Isn't it a possibility? The extract from her private memoirs that Mikhail found certainly indicated a romantic connection. I'm phrasing that politely, you understand.'

'Yes,' said Jack, slowly. 'But—'

'But it isn't getting us any nearer to the truth about the Stone Heads,' nodded Byron. 'I bet Harry did know about them, though. Could Catherine have told him when they were in bed? Not that I'd know much about what ladies tell gentlemen in bed,' he said, with a sideways grin. 'That's more your area of expertise.'

'For all we know,' said Jack, disregarding the last part of this, 'Harry and Catherine might simply have been ships that pass in the night.'

'With the departing ship having on board a small fortune in jewels?' demanded Byron. 'Never. Harry was more than a passing ship to Catherine. Remember she wrote that she was concerned he might be in danger from jealous-minded people?'

'If you aren't careful,' said Jack, 'you'll start believing Harry was the love of her life.'

FOURTEEN

Private journal of Catherine, 1762

At times, I wish there was someone – I will be honest, and say a lover – with whom I could discuss my life. Someone I could trust – someone who would understand and sympathize. But if there were such a one, would he think I had too easily accepted Father Quintus's account that Peter was plotting to assassinate me? Would he even wonder whether I had been influenced by Grigory?

He is my creation, though, this lover, and I shall allot to him perception and sympathetic comprehension. The ability to enjoy the ridiculous and the amusing. As well as that, he must, of course, be a sensitive and inventive lover. I doubt such a person exists, but it is a curious comfort to think that he might, and that one day he could walk into my Court.

The full details of the plotting and subterfuge that surrounded what happened to Peter can never be told in any official account. But I can set them down here.

As I prepare to travel to Izmailovsky, I am dreadfully aware that I am about to incite violence – a battle – against my own husband. But isn't he inciting his own battle, his own violence, against me? I disliked and even feared Peter from the outset – I discovered, early on, that he possesses a cruel and sadistic streak. But I never imagined he would plot to kill me. Grigory is right, though, to say I must fight back, and that I must defend myself. Clearly, he believes Father Quintus's story of the confession made to him. I believe it, too – or do I? Could it possibly be some wild, complex plot? But I cannot believe that. I do not think a professed monk would lightly invoke the Spiritual Reglament. Listening to Quintus that night, I could not think why a monk would make up such a tale. As I write this, I still cannot.

I truly believe Peter intends to kill me.

The details of the journey to Izmailovsky and my meeting with the Imperial Guard can be saved for my official memoirs. Here, I shall merely record that Grigory and Alexei accompanied me, and that the sight of the assembled soldiers was splendid and imposing.

I spoke to them as directly as I could, asking for their protection. When I finished, the musicians sounded a stirring fanfare, then their captain – he may have held a higher rank, but I never knew what it was – dropped to one knee, placed his right hand on his heart and said, 'We pledge that you will be kept safe, Your Highness. I and my men will follow you into hell and beyond.'

The promise to follow me into hell was immensely gratifying, although the part about 'beyond hell' gave me pause, because I do not think even Dante visualized a place beyond hell.

Later, there were documents to be signed – hastily drawn up, but seemingly legal – announcing themselves in elaborate script and flowery language as Instruments of Abdication. It was an extraordinary sensation to see those words set down on paper. The sense of betrayal against Peter clawed at my mind again, but I signed everything.

'All that is required now is His Highness's signature,' said Grigory, and the documents were borne away to Oranienbaum and Peter. With them went the captain, a detachment of soldiers and an assortment of senior churchmen. Grigory and Alexei accompanied them – neither would miss being part of such an historic event, of course!

It was a curious feeling to know I was deposing an emperor. Especially since the emperor was my husband.

I am back at my beloved Winter Palace again, and writing this in my bedchamber by candlelight. It is a night when I am trying to conjure up that imaginary lover. He would understand my tangled emotions – he would smooth away the guilt and dispel the disturbing images that are troubling me. Because earlier, a letter from Grigory, brought by one of his servants and sent from Oranienbaum, was delivered to me. If I copy it here, perhaps it will bring my make-believe lover a step nearer to me – it will feel as if I am talking to him.

'Early this evening,' Grigory writes, 'His Highness, the former Tsar of the Russias, fled the royal residence at Oranienbaum and made for the military base of Kronstadt on Kotlin Island. It was at once clear to all of us that he believed the fleet there would take up arms in his name. We pursued him, and far from fighting for the dethroned Emperor, the men at Kronstadt opened fire on his boat. They forced him back to the main shore, and their commander shouted that he was no longer recognized as Emperor and that Russia was now ruled by the Empress Catherine.

'I wish I could describe properly the remarkable experience of that battle – the blazing energy and determination that drove everyone. The constant cannon fire drew the ordinary people of the island to its shores – many of them armed with makeshift weapons to prevent your husband reaching St Petersburg. They are your people, Majesty, and they fought for you with all their strength.

'The deposed Tsar was taken captive easily enough. He has been taken to Ropsha, where he is closely guarded.

'I must remain here for a little longer, but I shall be with you again as soon as it is possible. Alexei is with me, and also Father Quintus.'

Alexei would have remained with Grigory, of course, but I was surprised that Father Quintus had also stayed with them. Surely his part in all this was simply the revealing of the assassination plot? I cannot think how he might be further involved.

But I am thankful that at least he will not be here in the Winter Palace for a while.

'You told our story to the Tsarina well,' Grigory Orlov had said to Quintus. 'The confession of an unknown man – a renegade servant of the Tsar—'

'It sounded believable,' said Alexei. 'It sounded as if there really had been such a man – such a confession.'

Quintus did not remind them how they had coached him in the story they had created, making him go over and over the fabrication of a confession of planned treason until they were satisfied. He had kept faithfully to the story, and he had seen that the Tsarina had believed it. And beneath his apprehension at what was now ahead, he was becoming aware of a curious satisfaction at knowing he had been able to fool a powerful empress.

Grigory said, 'And now, Father Quintus, you know what you must do when you reach Ropsha. And if you carry it out successfully, you know what will be your reward afterwards.'

Power and wealth and influence at the Empress's Court. That was the lure they had held out, and it was a lure that had wound itself tightly around Quintus's brain. But in response to Grigory's words, he merely nodded and said he would do what had been agreed.

'You know the outcome if you renege.'

'I shall not renege.'

If he reneged, they would disclose how, on that long-ago afternoon, he had murdered his mother. They would be believed because of who, and what, they were, and Quintus might have to stand trial. Would they hang him for a crime committed when he was nine years old? He had no idea.

He had never felt any regret for what he had done that day in Cympak. The thefts he and the other children had committed had been his means of escaping Cympak. But his mother had found out, and she had been going to send him to one of the appalling labour camps, there to atone for what he had done. Quintus could not have borne it, and he was still glad he had prevented it.

And now, all these years later, there would be no regret for what he would do at Ropsha. What did it matter if he committed two murders rather than one? A man can only be damned once.

He travelled to Ropsha in a small, unmarked coach – Alexei Orlov had arranged that, and the coachman was apparently one of his own servants.

It was a strange journey. From time to time, the coachman sang odd little songs to himself. When they stopped to rest the horse, Quintus asked about the songs, and the man grinned, gap-toothed.

'I makes them up,' he said. 'Rhymes is company on a long journey – I often have to make journeys for the Count – his brother, too.' He sent Quintus a sly look. 'I've driven those two on their travels ever since they were boys,' he said, taking a swig from a bottle filled with some black viscous-looking liquid, and offering it to Quintus, who shook his head.

'All kinds of places we been to,' said the coachman, wiping his mouth with the back of his hand, and replacing the bottle's cork. 'All kinds of things we seen.'

The sly eyes darted to Quintus again, and Quintus knew the creature was telling him he had been in Cympak on that long-ago afternoon. He had been those two young Orlov boys' coachman, and he had seen what had happened, just as they had. Quintus's heart lurched with fear, but he waited, saying nothing, and after a moment, the coachman said, 'I writes songs in my head to pass the time on a journey. Gleb the Rhymer they call me.' He clambered back on to the box, winding his muffler over his face, and hunched over the reins like a malevolent imp bent on reaching hell before the gates were closed against him.

The journey took longer than Quintus had expected, and although they had started early, it was growing dark when they finally reached Ropsha. The carriage bowled along a tree-lined highway with glimpses of houses and cottages and fields beyond them, but at last Gleb pulled the horse to a halt and jabbed a finger in the direction of a rearing outline directly ahead of them.

'Ropsha Palace,' he said, and sat for a moment, staring through the dimness. 'A bad old place, with a bad old reputation. A rascally prince used to keep his prisoners in there – seize anyone who di'n't agree with his laws and throw them into the dungeons and chain 'em up till they died.'

Half to himself, Quintus said, 'Prince Fyodor Romodanovsky.'

'That's him,' said Gleb. 'Terrible cruelties he dealt out on them as spoke against him. He's long since dead, but there's

folk hereabouts as'll tell how, on certain nights, you can sometimes hear the echoes of his prisoners, sobbing and pleading
for mercy. That's the prison over yonder, where that bell tower
is.' He pointed again. 'Wait long enough an' you'll hear the
bell clanging out for the soldiers to change duty. What they
guard in there, I ain't got no more idea than fly to the moon,
but when that bell sounds, it comes at you like the crack of
doom. I made up a rhyme about it – might sing it on the way
back. Folk'll hear me singing it through the darkness, and it'll
give them a shiver.' He leaned closer and said, in a treacly
voice, 'I likes to give folk a shiver,' and Quintus flinched from
the rancid stench of the man.

He said, 'Aren't you taking me up to the prison?'

'No, I ain't. I ain't going any nearer to that place. Come
back at midnight for you, I will.'

'All right.' Quintus got down from the carriage, lifting his
small carpetbag with him. 'I'll wait for you by this oak tree,'
he said, and hoped that, come midnight, he would not be
locked in the prison tower, hearing the bell that tolled like the
crack of doom for himself.

The carriage rattled away into the smeary dusk, but for a
few moments snatches of Gleb's rhyme drifted back. Quintus
caught something about the tolling bell marking a dying man's
heartbeat, and then a warning against listening to its voice.
*'It'll snare you into its iron embrace, it'll snap its brazen lips
on your face . . .'*

He set off towards the tower. He would not think of long-
ago prisoners, whose ghostly screams might still linger on the
night, or macabre chants about death bells; he would only
think of getting to the man who was held captive here. The
man who, until a few days ago, had been the Tsar of all the
Russias.

The carpetbag could be safely hidden beneath one of the
nearby hedges, but first he removed from it three small items
and placed them in a small cloth bag, which he slung over
one shoulder. As he set off, a spiteful wind was snatching at
the boughs of the trees and whipping through the grass. Quintus
wrapped his robe more firmly around him, and went on,
keeping to the cover of the trees.

The light was fading fast, but the time would favour him. It was not so late that a lone figure might be challenged as a prowler with sinister intent, but nor was it so early as to provide sufficient daylight for anyone to make out the lone figure's features.

He had not brought the plan of the palace with him – 'Incriminating if you are caught,' Grigory Orlov had said – but he had studied it so intently before setting out that he could see it clearly in his mind.

Ahead of him now was what must be the prison wing – a low, crouching outline huddled against the trees, with dusk lying over it like a shroud. Even in the dimness, it was possible to see that at one end was a door with a small, narrow window next to it. The window was too narrow to climb through, and the door had an immense lock. But Gleb had talked about the prison bell ringing for the changeover of guard, and Quintus smiled, because those words had shown him how he might get inside the place. He stepped into a patch of dense darkness and sat down with his back against a tree. It would not matter how long he had to wait for the bell to sound; his years in the monastery had taught him patience.

But the bell tolled sooner than he had dared hope, and by the time the third chime died away, he was halfway across the ground to the door. Once there, he stood against the wall on one side of it, pressing back into the shadows.

And now came the sound of marching feet and barked orders, and the guards appeared. There were six – no, eight – of them, all with rifles, the leader bearing aloft a lantern, which gave out a wavering light. They halted, and there was the rattle of keys, then the scrape of the door opening. From inside came the steps of the sentries coming off duty. Under cover of the sounds, Quintus moved forward and fell quietly into line behind the newly arrived detachment. Even if they should look back, the wind was making the lantern's flame flicker so wildly it was casting grotesque shadows everywhere. It was unlikely they would notice an extra figure among those distorted shadows.

Immediately beyond the door was a narrow, low-ceilinged stone passage, with wall sconces flaring at intervals. Several low doors opened off it, with tiny, barred apertures near the top. The sentries marched to the far end of it, then turned right. Quintus stood very still, willing them not to look back – but they did not. There was the sound of more doors opening and shutting, and of voices, and then nothing. The bell's chimes stopped, and Quintus, his heart beating furiously, began to walk along the passage, peering into the cells as he went. His heart was pounding – at any moment, someone could appear and demand to know who he was, but he was wearing his monk's garb, and in the small shoulder bag were the tools of his trade. It should be easy enough to say, in a voice of quiet authority, that he had entered with the departing sentries – legitimately and openly – and had been sent to administer spiritual comfort to the prisoner. By the time someone had gone to the palace to verify the story, Quintus would either have done what he had come to do or, if necessary, made good his escape.

Half-rusted chains lay on the ground or hung from the stone walls of several of the cells. In the uncertain light, they might have been iron bones from which the flesh had long since shrivelled. There were manacles and fetters, and everywhere was the stench of human exudences and human despair.

Quintus reached the intersection where the guards had turned right. He hesitated, then turned left. At once, he saw a dim light flaring outside one of the doors. His heart leapt, and he glanced to where the sentries had vanished earlier. But all was quiet, and he went towards the lit cell. Thick bars bisected the small aperture, and Quintus looked behind him along the passage again, then went up to the cell and peered through the opening.

The man he had come to find lay on a narrow bed, his head turned to the door. Quintus was relieved to see he was not chained or tied up in any way, which might have made his task difficult.

The prisoner came to stand at the door, pressing his face against the bars. He said, 'No, monk, they have not chained me,' and Quintus recoiled slightly, because it was as if the man had reached into his mind and scooped up his thought.

But he only said, 'No unnecessary sound, if you please.

There is not much time, but I am here to render a service, sent by Her Imperial Highness.' He had decided that to suggest the Tsarina was behind his visit would indicate compassion, although he had no idea whether Catherine had any compassion in her nature. Very likely, the man who had been married to her for fifteen years would not know either, because from all accounts they had lived virtually separate lives for most of those years.

'Is that service to set me free?' said the prisoner. He pressed closer against the bars, and the flickering wall light fell across his face, showing the smallpox scars, and the unmistakable cruelty and cold calculation in the small eyes. A sour smell came from him, and Quintus had to repress an instinct to step back.

He said, 'Not to set you free yet, sir. It may be possible to arrange that later; for now, I am here to bring you spiritual comfort and strength.'

'Be damned to spiritual comfort; just get me out of this rat-hole. If there's a gun hidden in that bag, I can shoot the guards one by one as they come along, and we can get the keys and be off into the night. Those we don't shoot, I'll strangle with my own hands.' He pressed closer to the bars. 'I'm perfectly capable of doing so,' he said, in a slurred whisper. 'And if you do rescue me, I shall reward you.' He grinned – a sly, greedy grin, showing discoloured teeth. 'Riches such as you've never imagined I'd give you,' he said. 'Think about that. Think what you could do if you were wealthy – think of the soft, sweet life you could lead. The women you could take to your bed.'

There was a moment when Quintus was eerily aware of the man's mind coiling persuasively around his own, and then a moment when he felt his resolve wavering. Could he accept what was being offered? But even as the thought formed, he knew that he dared not. The guards would easily overpower their prisoner, even if he had a gun. And he knew the stories about Peter Romanov's many cruelties, and also how he seldom kept a promise or was loyal to anyone. Even if an escape could be managed, he would almost certainly be recaptured within hours. And then? He would not hesitate to name

Quintus as his rescuer, and Quintus would find himself on the scaffold.

He pulled his eyes from the intent stare, and took from the cloth bag the items he had brought. Two discs of unleavened bread, a tiny flask of wine and a small, silver, six-pointed cross – the distinctive emblem and symbol of the Orthodox Church.

He held them up so the prisoner could see them, and said, 'I am here to administer to you the Holy Sacrament.'

'Oh, keep your ridiculous bread and wine,' said Peter Romanov, in a scornful, sneering voice. 'You may stick them down your own gullet, or shove them up your arse for all I care. Wait, though, I'll have the wine – it's a while since I tasted wine. Give it to me.' It was the imperious demand of one accustomed to instant obedience.

Quintus hesitated. 'It is for the administration of the Sacrament,' he said.

'Then administer it, damn you, but be quick about it. We needn't bother with confession – unless—' He pressed closer to the bars. 'Unless it would excite you to hear a catalogue of my sins,' he said. 'Would it? They'd make lively telling, my sins.' Again, there was the sense of something dark and threatening twisting around Quintus's mind.

But he said, quietly, 'Confession before the Sacrament can be set aside in certain circumstances. As can the need for the full ritual. Those who sent me here believe that for you to receive the Sacrament will give comfort and strength for what lies ahead of you. I shall ask that you are cleansed of your sins by Jesus Christ, who gave his body and his blood for all our sins.' Before the prisoner could speak, he began to intone the words.

'Take, eat, this is My Body . . . Take and drink, for this is My Blood of the new covenant, poured for many for the forgiveness of sins . . .' Do it, thought Quintus, managing to avoid directly staring at the man. *Take and drink . . . DRINK, curse you . . .*

Peter Romanov pushed away the proffered bread, but grabbed the flask through the bars. Holding it to his lips, he drank the entire contents in four gulps. Then he thrust it back through the bars and wiped his mouth with the back of his hand.

'Damned rubbish you use for your Sacrament,' he said, then broke off, a look of puzzlement clouding his eyes.

Quintus, replacing the flask in his bag, looked quickly along the passageway. But it was all right – no one was there. And yet there was something different. It was as if the shadows suddenly leaned closer – or as if the flaring wall lights became still. He frowned and turned back to the Tsar. How long would it take? How would it happen?

But it was happening already. The puzzled look vanished, and the prisoner's face twisted in a spasm of pain.

His hands went up to his throat, and he gave a kind of wet choking gasp, then half fell against the door.

'Help me . . .'

The words rasped into the cell. Then, as Quintus did not move, the prisoner groped on the ground, and his hands closed on what Quintus saw was a tin drinking cup. He banged it against the door's surface, over and over, the sounds echoing loudly in the enclosed space. Quintus knew the guards must hear, and he went swiftly along the passage to the main door, and pressed into the shadows alongside it.

The guards were running towards the prisoner's cell, calling out as they went.

'Probably a trick of some kind,' one of them was shouting. 'But—'

'It'll be a trick, all right,' said another. 'Pounce on us the minute we get the door open. Watch out for him.'

As he said this, screams cut through the prison, and Quintus shrank deeper into the shadows. But the guards were all running towards the cell, and it was unlikely they would look along the passage towards the door.

'He must be ill,' shouted one of them. 'Who's got the cell keys?'

'He'll be faking,' said another voice.

'Don't sound like faking to me. For God's sake, get the door open—'

From where he stood, not daring to move, hardly daring to breathe, Quintus could not see what was happening, but he could hear frantic orders being shouted, and he could feel panic filling up the passage. There was a command to fetch a physician – 'Quickly, we daren't let this one die in the cell—'

'We're supposed to save him for a different fate,' said the man, who had called the cries fake.

'Hold him down,' said one of the others. 'Do it, damn you – grab his arms and ankles. He'll kill himself thrashing like this—'

The screaming was going on and on, dreadful, sickening. It appeared that a physician had been summoned – though Quintus had no idea by what means – because, in a very short time, there was the sound of an arrival at the main door, and two guards ran up to unlock it. Quintus stayed where he was, but everyone was running back and forth in panic, and no one looked towards his corner. A man wearing a dusty-looking black cloak, carrying a large bag, was admitted and taken quickly along the passage. Quintus, his mind working fast, fell into step behind them. He must know what the outcome was – he must be sure that the prisoner had died and that he had not been able to tell what had just happened.

No one questioned his presence, and he was able to stand quietly in the cell doorway. The physician was bending over the figure who was writhing in pain, the hands flailing wildly, and he was trying to hold a phial to the prisoner's lips.

'Hold him still,' he said, sharply, to the guards. 'Tilt his head back— No, he can't take it.' He glanced around the cell. 'There has been no sickness? Vomiting?'

'No.'

'Then we shall have to try another method.' He took from his bag a length of tubing with a wide cup at one end. 'Unfasten his breeches,' he said, 'and pull them off— And now turn him on his front and spread his legs – no, much wider than that. Good. Get a bucket, one of you,' he said, then leaned over the struggling figure. 'Sir, try to keep still—'

'Pain . . . Such agony . . . Do something . . .'

The words came out in bubbling fragments, but the physician said, 'I am trying to help you. I need to rid your body of whatever is poisoning you.' To the guards, he said, sharply, 'Keep him still. Hold his arms and legs—'

The guard who Quintus thought had issued the order to

send for the physician suddenly looked across to the cell door and saw Quintus. In a sharp, challenging voice, he said, 'Who are you? What are you doing here?'

'I was ordered to attend,' said Quintus. 'I am Leonid.' It felt strange that the name of his former self should come so readily to him, but the name of Quintus must not be uttered. He said, 'I was told a man was dying—'

The guard shrugged, as if this was something to be expected, and turned back to where the physician was unrolling more of the tubing. 'I am afraid this will be unpleasant,' he said, looking at the watching guards.

It was more than unpleasant. It was appalling and sickening. As the tube was forced up inside the prisoner's body, his screams increased, filling up the small room. Quintus began to have the feeling that, with every one of them, the strange darkness of Peter Romanov's mind was being poured into his own mind.

As the fluid was pushed through the tubing, the prisoner struggled even more, but presently, there was a wet bubbling, and a dreadful stench began to fill up the room, causing several of the guards to back away, their hands covering their mouths.

But although the physician worked diligently, applying the grisly treatment twice more, it was to no avail. The man who had been Tsar of all the Russias died after several hours of squalid agony, and did so to the sound of his murderer softly intoning the prayer designated for one whose soul is departing and who cannot speak.

FIFTEEN

Quintus had expected to be greeted by the Orlov brothers with praise and admiration for what he had done. He certainly looked forward to the warmth and the lights of the Winter Palace, after the grim darkness of Ropsha, and the cold, uncomfortable journey in Gleb's carriage.

But although there was warmth and also lights at the Palace, there was no praise or admiration from Grigory and Alexei Orlov.

He sent a message to Grigory reporting his return, and within a very short time, he was summoned to a small room he had never seen before – a bleak sliver of a place, with only a couple of wooden chairs, and a neglected air that suggested it was hardly ever used. Quintus felt a stab of unease, but then he thought the Orlov brothers would be wanting to keep everything unobtrusive until the news of Peter Romanov's death had officially reached the Palace. Until then – and also for some time afterwards – there must be nothing to attract suspicion. Quintus understood this. Even so, it was not the reception he had expected.

Grigory Orlov was seated on one of the wooden chairs, with his brother lounging on a window ledge. Neither of them asked Quintus to sit down, so he stood just inside the door and, since it appeared that the niceties were not being observed, launched, without preamble, into what had happened at Ropsha. He made sure they understood how adroitly he had dealt with his task, but as he talked, his unease grew. Something was wrong.

When he reached the end of his account, Grigory studied him for a moment, then said, 'It is gratifying to hear that our plan worked, Father.' He glanced at his brother, then said, 'But you realize that you can no longer be allowed to remain here.'

The words slammed into Quintus's mind like a blow. Then anger surged up.

He said, 'There was to be a reward—'

'I do not recall any reward being mentioned,' said Grigory, examining his fingernails.

'Yes. You promised me money,' said Quintus. 'A place at Court, even. You gave me your word!'

They exchanged glances, and pitying contempt showed in both their eyes.

'You have been dreaming, Quintus,' said Grigory. 'You performed for us a service – the word we gave you was that we would not disclose what we saw all those years ago. Your mother's death in the cellar of your family house. You will not have forgotten it.'

'We certainly have not,' put in Alexei. 'We have kept the memory of it ever since.'

Quintus stared at them. They were going to cheat him. They had made use of him, and now he was to be thrown aside. For a moment, bitter fury almost overwhelmed him.

'As for a place at Court,' said Grigori, 'you cannot possibly remain in any of Her Imperial Highness's palaces. You will return to your monastery. We only had you brought here to carry out our plan. Surely you realized that?'

'My coachman has been ordered to take you back to Verkhoturye in one hour's time,' said Alexei, and smiled, the scar on the side of his face twisting the smile into a sneer. He said, 'No doubt the monastery will be happy to have you back, Leonid.'

Leonid. There it was – the reminder of what that long-ago boy had done, and how these two men had seen it.

There was nothing to do but allow himself to be hustled out of the Palace, his few belongings hastily thrust into his carpetbag. Gleb the Rhymer was waiting in the small courtyard outside the servants' quarters, a huddled bundle of mufflers and wrappings.

As they set off, resentment was scalding through Quintus like acid. The Orlov brothers had blackmailed him into committing murder – and the murder of a crowned emperor at that! – while they remained in safety in the Winter Palace. And now, with the plan accomplished, they were sending him back to a place where they believed he would not pose any threat.

Because they could hold their own threat over him – the threat of making it known how he had killed his mother. And their word would be believed over the mewling denial of a monk from a remote monastery.

As the carriage jolted along, Quintus's mind was churning with everything that had happened. It was a wild, cold night, but he could hear Gleb singing to himself as he had done on the journey to Ropsha. The wind was gusting all around them, and he could not make out what the man was chanting, but it did not matter. It was nothing to Quintus if a coachman made up songs and sang them to himself as he drove through the night.

The journey seemed endless, although he was so wrapped in misery and anger that he was scarcely aware of the hours sliding past. Presently, he made out Cympak's little church and the schoolroom that adjoined it. Here was the cobbled square; at the far end, he could see the narrow street leading down to his own family's home by the river. He had no idea if anyone lived in the house now, but among his possessions he still had a key to the place.

The carriage turned on to the mountain track and jolted slowly upwards. Finally, it went through the wide stone arch into the big courtyard, and Quintus got down. He stood for a moment, staring up at the grey walls, remembering the years of restrictions – remembering how he had maintained the pretence of obedience and piety through those years, believing one day he would escape.

Gleb did not immediately drive away. He sat on the coach's box seat, not looking at the monastery, but staring down at the little cluster of villages.

Then he said, 'I been thinking, and I reckon my master owes me something for what I done these last two days.' The small, mean eyes slewed round to look at Quintus, and a half-leer curved his lips. 'I'd say Alexei Orlov'd be glad if I kept my mouth shut about that journey to Ropsha,' he said. 'I went into the local tavern while I waited for you that night – did you know that, Father Quintus? Friendly kind of place it was. Some o' the guards go in there when they're off duty. Hear all kinds of interesting things from them, I did.'

He was still looking over the dark landscape, then he said, thoughtfully, 'I got a mind to give up coaching – I done it many a long year, and I been looking for a place like this for a while now. Cympak – that's the place down there, you said?'

'Yes.' Quintus was aware of faint unease brushing across his mind.

'Looked like the kind of place I'd take to,' said Gleb. 'Folk there'd be glad to have someone to take them to and fro – move things, deliver provisions and the like. Alexei Orlov'd let me keep the old nag, I reckon, and maybe even the carriage, too. Providing,' he said, 'that I ask him in the right way.' Again, there was the greedy, knowing grin.

Quintus had no idea how to answer this, but before he could speak, Gleb clicked to the horse and began to turn it around. As he did so, he began singing to himself, much as he had done on the journey to Ropsha.

'I writes songs in my head to pass the time on a journey,' he had said. 'An' I sings them to myself. Bit o'company, it is.'

But this time the singing was not about Ropsha's prison and the tolling bell marking a dying man's heartbeat. This time it was entirely different. And even through the gusting wind that whipped around the hillside, Quintus could hear the chanting with dreadful clarity.

'Beware, beware, the murderer's sin . . .
'Beware him stealing his evil way in . . .
'Hide from him for there is nothing of good . . .
'Drink not the sacrament masked as God's blood . . .'

As the carriage jolted farther away, the chanting faded, and then it was beyond sight, and Quintus was alone.

His mind was tumbling with panic and fear. Gleb knew. He knew what had happened in that prison cell – he had talked of being in the local tavern and hearing what the guards said. And no matter whether the guards had realized the truth – and no matter how much Gleb had gleaned from them, and also from Alexei Orlov's orders about the journey – he had strung together facts and gossip and guesses, and from them had made up one of his repulsive rhymes.

Stealing his evil way in . . . The sacrament masked as God's blood . . .

He knew Quintus had poisoned the deposed Tsar, using consecrated wine.

As Quintus reached up to the monastery's massive bell-rope, the irony of the situation gripped him. Fifteen or so years ago, he had committed a murder that must never be discovered – his father had brought him to this place to be safe from discovery.

And now Alexei and Grigory Orlov had sent him to this same place, and again it was to keep from the world the truth about a murder. They knew Quintus himself would not talk about it, and they themselves would certainly not speak of it either.

But there was someone who might talk. Because it seemed as if within a couple of miles of the monastery there would be living someone who knew – or had guessed – most of what had happened. A man who, if he saw any advantage in it, would not hesitate to tell people that Quintus was a murderer.

Private journal of Catherine, 1762

It is terrible to know you have removed your husband from his rightful throne and taken that throne for yourself. But deposing a ruler sometimes happens; it has happened in my own family, and I expect it will do so in the future.

I had been prepared for guilt and remorse over deposing Peter; what I had not been prepared for was to learn that he had been murdered. I am horrified and devastated – I am also furious to realize that I trusted Grigory and Alexei, who had persuaded me that the situation was completely the reverse – that Peter was intending to murder me. I had not thought I was so gullible. I will certainly never be as gullible again.

I had assumed the Orlov brothers would arrange for Peter to go into exile, and that it would be an exile of comfort – even luxury. It was what I believed happened to dethroned royalty. There are any number of palaces – here and across Europe, and very likely in England, too, for all I know – where exiled or deposed monarchs are housed in such a way. I had thought that would be Peter's destiny. I had not thought his destiny would be to die inside the torture mansion of Ropsha.

Grigory has been assiduous in arranging how the official announcement should be couched – and what reason should be given for Peter's death. Most of his suggestions include terms unfamiliar to me, which shows how much I have been protected from what my mama used to call the sordid aspects of the human body. I daresay most of the terms would be unfamiliar to the general populace, as well; there was something about colic and something else about apoplexy. But I finally agreed to a form of announcement which seems to be thought acceptable.

'And which,' Grigory said, unemotionally, 'will not arouse any suspicion in anyone's mind that the Tsar was poisoned.'

He held my eyes levelly, and the terrible word hung on the air between us like a branding iron.

Poisoned.

Grigory or Alexei will not have administered the poison to Peter themselves. I know that with absolute certainty – they would not take such a risk. And although it has not actually been said outright, I know, with the same certainty, that the murder was committed on their orders.

It is difficult to write this but, incredibly, I am starting to believe that Grigory is calculating how soon he can marry me. I suppose I should not be surprised – such a marriage would give him what he would see as total control over me. But if he believes I would agree to either the marriage or the control, he does not know me well at all. I am many things, and a good deal of them are reprehensible, but I could never, for an instant, contemplate marrying a man who, even if he did not hand Peter the poisoned chalice himself, ordered some wretched catspaw to do so.

As for the catspaw . . . I do not need to wonder who that was. Father Quintus. Is this why I have always felt a menace from him? Could I have sensed what was ahead – what Quintus was destined to do?

Whatever my feelings, I certainly cannot allow any part of this to become known. If it were to be revealed that Peter was murdered by people so close to me, I should instantly be suspected – branded as a murderess. I daresay I am a coward, but that is something I cannot face.

I think I am safe, though. The Orlov brothers will not incriminate themselves, and it is already in my mind to try to set them both at a distance from the Court, although I do not think I can do that until after my Coronation later this year. Shall I face my Coronation, my anointing as Russia's Empress, with serenity, knowing by what means I have achieved it? But I must do so.

I do not think there is any threat from Quintus. He has already been banished – he is once again inside the Verkhoturye monastery – and he will never dare speak of what happened.

And yet, even though I know he is many miles away, in the seclusion of the monastery, I am still afraid of him.

Quintus had been received unquestioningly by the monks, and given his old room. Father Abbot had welcomed him and been interested in hearing about St Petersburg.

After a while, the announcement of the Tsar's death reached the monastery, of course. Father Abbot received a letter, which he read to the community – there was no hint of anything suspicious, but it was possible some of the monks might see a connection between Peter's death and Quintus leaving the Winter Palace, so he would have to tread carefully. He avoided the company of them as much as possible – taking up his former tasks, labouring in the garden and in the woodturning and stone masonry workshop. He was submissive and obedient, and he was just beginning to feel safe when the monastery's kitchener sent him to help with unloading supplies from a dray that had driven up from the village.

'One of the local men has brought them up – some of the village children are with him to help,' he said. 'Inquisitive little creatures, but it won't do any harm for them to see the monastery and understand something of our way of life.'

Not thinking much about it, Quintus went along to the side gate, where the dray had drawn up. Two of the younger monks were already there, lifting down various boxes and sacks. The children were helping. There were three of them – two boys, one perhaps nine or ten, the other a little younger, and a girl who was strikingly like the elder boy. Brother and sister, perhaps. They were all staring up at the soaring arches and pillars, slightly overawed by their surroundings, but also clearly curious. It was rare for children to come up here, and Quintus guessed they would be taking everything in so they could tell their schoolfriends about it later.

And then he looked at the figure on the dray. He had not got down to help with the unloading; he had remained where he was, huddled into his scarves and mufflers. But even with the scarves partly concealing his face, Quintus knew him.

It was Gleb the Rhymer.

Panic swept in at once, but it had to be beaten down, because no one must realize Quintus knew Gleb. After a moment, he managed to step forward and reach for the remaining crates. The children were livelier now, clearly enjoying this small adventure, calling to each other to look at that bit of stonework shaped like a face, and that carving with words in a strange language.

One of the young monks was pointing out the stone carvings to them, translating the words. The children listened; then, told to get back on the dray for the return journey, they did so, swinging their legs over the sides, chattering about what they had seen, and what the man in the robe had said.

Quintus watched Gleb turn the cart around. As he did so, he looked over his shoulder, and the small, artful eyes met Quintus's. The dreadful knowing smile showed briefly, then, as Gleb prepared to take the cart through the wide stone arch and back down to the village, he started to sing.

The children joined in with him, their shrill, piping voices mingling with his gravelly tones. At first, Quintus tried to think it would only be some harmless rhyme, but he knew it was not. He knew it was the rhyme Gleb had sung on the journey from the Winter Palace.

'Beware, beware, the murderer's sin,
'Beware him stealing his evil way in.
'Hide from him for there is nothing of good,
'Drink not the sacrament masked as God's blood . . .'

He glanced at the two young monks to see if they had heard, but they were carrying the crates into the monastery. The cart had passed through the stone arches now, but Quintus could still hear the singing. He walked across the courtyard and stood for a moment, watching the cart jolt its way down the track. The chanting came again, and then four new lines.

'Beware the black robe and the murderer's lure;
'Take not the cup for it holds tainted wine.
'Drink not from the cup and run for your lives
'For the black robe and hood hides the murderer's wiles.'

SIXTEEN

When Quintus could think clearly again, he wondered if it would be possible to tell Gleb to stop singing frightening rhymes to the local children. But he did not think Gleb would pay any attention. Might the children in some way be warned to keep away from Gleb, though? Quintus began to consider how this might be done.

The monks could not, of course, come and go as they pleased, but there were occasions when a visit to one of the villages had to be made, and especially to Cympak, which was the largest of the villages and had its own church and a schoolroom – the same schoolroom where Quintus, as Leonid, had attended lessons. And the same church where his mother had spent countless hours on her knees.

It was over fifteen years since he had lived in Cympak, and it was not very likely he would be recognized. The years had changed him, and his name had changed, as well. Surely no one would connect that long-ago boy called Leonid with today's Brother Quintus? The schoolmaster of that time had long since left the area, but even if anyone did recognize him, Quintus could say, quite openly, that he had spent his early years in Cympak, then had entered the monastery. It sounded perfectly normal. And no one would know what had happened that day, or how his mother had died. After Quintus's father left him at St Nicholas's, he had travelled to some remote and strict monastic order, to live out his life in silence and prayer and fasting. Quintus had never heard from him again.

He approached Father Abbot with a diffident suggestion that the local children might be interested in a brief talk about the Winter Palace. It would teach them a little about the history of their people and the Romanov dynasty, he said.

Father Abbot approved the idea. He suggested that as well as telling the children about the Romanovs and the Palace, Quintus should lead them in prayers for the departed Tsar and his grieving family. Quintus agreed, even while he was thinking it was grotesque to lead prayers for the soul of a man he himself had murdered.

The schoolmaster, suitably approached, approved the suggestion as well, and if the reverend gentleman who presided over the church was not best pleased at having his domain appropriated by a monk, he did not say so.

Quintus had never actually given a talk, but it was impossible to be part of a religious community and not become accustomed to speaking before a roomful of people. He took his turn at being Reader at supper – reading aloud from various religious works and treatises for the other monks. He sometimes acted as Responder at services as well, taking his place in the rota with the other monks.

It turned out to be relatively easy to compose what he felt was a suitable talk. He included details about the Romanovs and about Russian history, and wove in descriptions of the Palace from his brief time there. He thought this should snare the children's interest – he needed to do this, and he very particularly needed to snare the interest of the three who had been with Gleb that day. He had only seen them that once, and for a fairly short time, but he would know them.

It felt strange to enter the church and the schoolhouse again. The church still had the rood screen with the icons – the faces Quintus's mother had said were really devils who had been captured in wood and stone and left there as a warning to sinners. As Quintus walked past them, he had to push away the impression that their eyes followed him – that they whispered slyly to one another that here was a sinner – here was a man who twice had committed murder.

The schoolhouse had the same desks, and rows of books that looked as if they had not been taken down since Quintus's time here. Even the remembered smell of boiled cabbage still clung to the walls.

The children assembled in the little hall. They were well behaved and they listened attentively to the talk – Quintus thought they were probably pleased to have an interruption to the normal school day. There were perhaps thirty of them, all ranged on wooden benches, the smallest at the front, sitting cross-legged on the floor. And four rows back were the two boys and the girl he had come here to find.

After the talk, the schoolmaster's wife beamingly brought large jugs of lemonade, which the children greeted with delight. While it was being distributed, Quintus was able to fall into conversation with the two boys and the girl.

He was friendly, but he was firm. He said he had seen them on their visit to the monastery, and that Father Abbot had been most upset and a good deal worried about the song that had been chanted on that day. He understood, said Quintus, that they had learned the song from the man known as Gleb the Rhymer—

They broke in eagerly, explaining how Gleb told good stories and how they liked learning his songs. There was a game being made up as well, to match one of the rhymes.

Quintus said, 'But some of those songs are wrong and harmful – not only to you, but also to God. God would be hurt and angry to hear what you were chanting that day.'

They looked at him, as if uncertain how to respond, and Quintus said, 'You must promise you will not sing it again, or have any more to with Gleb. I am sure your parents would not like to know about any of this.' He waited, and when they did not speak, he said, 'But I am sure there is no need for me to talk to your parents. I have your promise, do I?'

They nodded vigorously and, when Quintus stepped back, clearly took it as dismissal and went off to join their friends.

Taking his leave of the schoolmaster and his wife, he thought he could feel pleased at the way he had managed everything. You did not need to be a high-ranking diplomat or a nobleman of the Imperial Court to handle a difficult – indeed, potentially dangerous – situation.

It had been a sunlit afternoon, but as Quintus walked through the village, the sky was becoming overcast. He went towards the path leading out of Cympak, thinking he must hurry if he was to outrun the impending storm. But when he reached the edge of the square, almost of their own volition, his steps slowed. At the far end was the narrow street that wound down to the river and to his family's old house. Quintus stood very still, the memories crowding in.

He had never known whether his father had returned to the house after taking Quintus to the monastery that day. Might he have done so, waiting for the kiln to cool, then tearing away the bricks, so he could reach what was in there? Or had he simply walked away from Cympak for ever? Had anyone gone to live in the house since? And if so, had the kiln been opened? With sudden resolve, he crossed the square and made his way down the familiar street, pulling the hood of his cloak over his head, partly against the flurries of rain blowing in, but also to avoid recognition. But no one was around – probably, people would be in their homes, sheltering from the impending storm.

And now, in front of him, set apart from its neighbours and from the village, was the house. No lights showed in the windows, but that did not mean no one lived there. Surely it would not have stood empty all these years? Eventually, he reached into the pocket of his robe for the key. He had kept it with him through the years in the monastery and through the time at the Winter Palace, and now he took a deep breath and slid the key into the lock. It resisted slightly, as if long unused, then turned, and the door swung open. Quintus stood for a moment in the doorway, listening. It was curious how you could sense if a place was occupied or not, and he knew at once that this was an empty house. He must return to the monastery before long, but the compulsion to explore the house was overwhelming.

His footsteps echoed in the emptiness, and there was a musty dankness everywhere. Rain slid down the windows, leaving grimy streaks. Clearly, the house had not been lived in for a very long time – there was no furniture, and only a few pots and crocks in the scullery, and a box of candles and a tinder, which he put in his pocket.

There remained the cellar. And the tunnel leading out to the kiln.

As he went down the steps, the stairs creaked and swayed slightly. Like old bones that had been lying in the dark for more than fifteen years and were struggling into life . . . No, he would not think like that.

The cellar was exactly as it had been all those years ago.

There were the shelves and the boxes and stone jars used for storing wax and clay, the sacks that had contained plaster for mixing. Probably, everything had dried out by now. In the far corner was a large stack of the wood that had always been kept down here for firing the kiln.

Quintus looked across at the old river gate. 'Never try to operate the wheel, and never even go near it,' his father always said, and Quintus never had.

The wheel was crusted with verdigris, and the spokes had partly corroded. The gate itself had patches of mould; clearly, it was years since the mechanism had been operated. But equally clearly, the river still sometimes slopped into the cellar, because trickles and puddles lay slimily across the ground.

Quintus went across to the door leading to the kiln tunnel. As it swung in, a dank stench came at him, and he flinched, then lit one of the candles, annoyed to realize his hands were shaking. When he held up the wavering light, it fell over the pitted stone walls and the arched roof. The stones were black; rotting vegetation trailed from the roof and drifted against his face like questing fingers. He shuddered and pushed it away.

For a child, it had been exactly six steps along the tunnel to where it came out into the open. For a full-grown man, it was less, and after only three steps, he was standing in front of the kiln itself.

It was like a crouching deity, squat and dome-shaped, its chimney rising up against the rainswept sky. Thick mats of weeds had grown over it, and clearly it had been cold and dead all these years, the vents and the fire-holes bricked up. Had his father returned to the house that day, waited for it to cool and removed what was inside, replacing the bricks afterwards? Or had he simply walked away, leaving what was in there to its lonely darkness?

Quintus wedged more candles at intervals in the crevices of the tunnel's walls, then unearthed a long-handled implement – part hammer, part chisel – from an old toolbox. Re-entering the tunnel caused the candles to flicker wildly, distorting his shadow, almost making it seem that dark shapes were leaning forward to see what he was doing.

Chiselling away the bricks over the vents was easier than

he had expected – they had dried and cracked, and several came away in a sudden tumble, crashing on to the ground. As they did so, a dreadful stench gusted out of the kiln, like the breath of an ancient tomb suddenly opened up. Quintus flinched, but forced himself to hold one of the candles close to the small opening he had made. There would not be any trace of what he had done all those years ago, of course; what had been sealed up would have eventually burned, and long since disintegrated.

But it had not. He had always believed the bones would have been completely consumed, but he was remembering now that he had not fully fired the kiln that day. Lying inside the kiln, huddled over but unmistakable, was what had been a living human being. Bones – charred but recognizable . . . hands and fingers and spine . . . a skull, half turned to the vent, as if seeking light . . . There was a heart-stopping moment when the bones seemed to move, as if struggling to reach out with hands that once had been living and warm and covered in flesh, but then he saw it was only that the scattered dust had stirred from the ingress of air when he knocked away the bricks.

On the top of the grisly fragments lay a thin chain and a crucifix, and Quintus saw again his father scrabbling at the ground with his scorched hands, then throwing the crucifix into the kiln. The crucifix was one of several that had been given to the women of Cympak by some visiting church dignitary. It had survived the heat, though; Quintus thought iron would have survived even the fiercest heat.

He reached for the hammer again and began to chisel at the remaining bricks, knowing he could not let that terrible thing remain in there. Because she's alone and in the dark? asked a faintly mocking voice within his mind, but Quintus knew it was not that; it was because that, even bricked up like this, there was still the possibility that she might one day be found. And that it would be realized who she was – and that her death might be traced back to him.

The final bricks fell away easily, making an opening large enough for him to reach in and grasp the edges of the iron tray with its grisly burden. It was necessary to move with extreme care, but he managed it, and carried it back to the cellar.

What now? Bury the fragments in the garden beyond the kiln? But his mind shied away from that – the house was set apart from the rest of the village, but it was still possible that someone would see him. Also, he did not think he could stay away from the monastery for long enough to complete the task.

It was then that his eyes fell on the old river gate and the massive wheel that would raise it.

The ancient mechanism probably no longer worked, but Quintus seized the wheel and began to drag it around. It was more than half rusted into its moorings, and at first he thought it would not budge, but then, with a half-creak, half-screech, it yielded slightly. A tremor seemed to shake the ground, and with it came the sound of a deep groan, as if something in the bowels of the ground was struggling to move. The wheel moved again, and a thin line of black appeared at the base. It's lifting, thought Quintus, with a sudden surge of hope, and he dragged at the wheel again. The gap widened and, with painful slowness, the gate began to rise. The iron teeth that had been sunk into the ground appeared – slime and river weed dripped from them, and thick brackish water oozed down on to the ground immediately below. The stench of wet decay came into the cellar, and Quintus flinched, then forced himself to look through the gap.

Even with the gate less than half lifted, it was possible to see the river. It was lower than he had expected, and there was a narrow stone shelf running alongside it. A faint greenish luminescence clung to the water's surface, and it was moving sluggishly, slopping against the stone ledge, but not quite spilling over it.

Quintus turned to what lay on the ground, but as he bent to lift it, a sound from above reached him. He straightened up, listening intently. Surely it had only been the rain pattering against the windows, or the creaking of the old, warped timbers in the house, or even the echoes of his own hammering.

But the sounds came again, and they were not creaking

timbers or rainfall. Someone was inside the house. He realized too late that he had not locked the street door – years inside a monastery did not teach you about things like securing property, largely because you did not own property.

Light, quick footsteps came towards the cellar, and soft giggling. Children. Would they come down here? Had he time to run up the steps and shut the cellar door? But they would hear if he did, and meanwhile the charred bones lay on the ground for them to see. Quintus looked frantically around for something he could fling over the charred bones, but there was nothing.

There was a new sound from overhead now. Chanting. Cold fear washed over him, because the children were chanting the rhyme he had heard on that afternoon outside the monastery and that he had heard again in the schoolroom today.

The words reached him clearly.

'*Beware, beware, the murderer's sin . . .*
'*Beware him stealing his evil way in . . .*'

There followed a muffled giggle, then a girl's voice said, 'Is this where he steals his evil way in?'

'Yes, I told you. It's the Black Robe's lair,' said a boy's voice.

'He isn't real, though, is he?' said the girl, nervously. 'The Black Robe? It's just a story, isn't it? And a game?'

''Course he isn't real,' said the boy. 'But he might once have been. And it's a good game and a good song.'

'That man told us not to sing it.'

'Yes, but he won't know if we do.'

'And it's why we followed him here.' That was the younger boy. 'I dared you, remember?' he said.

Three small figures appeared at the top of the stairs, and they were the three he had spoken to earlier, of course – the three who had been with Gleb at the monastery that day. Quintus had already known they would be. They came down to the cellar, their eyes bright with curiosity and excitement at this forbidden adventure, and Quintus moved to stand in front of the iron tray. But the children had already seen it, and their eyes widened with horror. The girl gasped and recoiled, pressing a hand to her mouth as if to choke back a scream.

The older boy took her free hand, and they began to back away towards the steps. But the younger boy stood his ground, staring accusingly at Quintus.

'The rhyme's true, isn't it?' he said. 'We thought it was just a song – we came here because it would be an adventure—'

'Something to tell our friends,' said the girl.

'But it's all real,' said the boy. 'You're a murderer. You killed someone like the rhyme said. And you burned the body, and now you're going to throw the bones into the river.'

'We should tell somebody,' said the girl, starting to back away to the steps. 'Our parents . . . the priest—' She looked at the boy who was still holding her hand, as if asking for confirmation, and he nodded and pulled her towards the steps.

Quintus moved at once, darting forward so that he barred their way. He had no idea yet what he would do, but he knew they must not be allowed to tell what they had seen. They already knew some tale of a black-robed killer and tainted wine from Gleb's rhyme; now, they had seen what was left of the body that had partly burned in the kiln, and they had realized Quintus was about to throw it into the river. His mind was churning frantically, but before he could think what to do, the boy was saying, angrily, 'Let us go. Get out of the way. We're going to tell what we've seen.'

He tried to thrust Quintus aside to reach the steps, but Quintus pushed him away. The boy half fell back with the force of the push, his foot skidding on one of the wet patches from the river overspill.

He fell against the wall on the side of the gate, and cried out, reaching up to grab something to save himself. But his hand met only the iron spikes, and even from where he stood, Quintus saw the spike bite into the boy's fingers. He shouted in pain, recoiled and, in doing so, lost his balance altogether and fell through the yawning opening. There was a dreadful crunch as he hit the stone edge, and then a splash as he fell down into the river.

The other two cried out and rushed forward, kneeling on the ledge and reaching frantically out to him. He grabbed their hands.

'Help him!' screamed the girl, half turning to Quintus. 'Please . . . You must get him out!'

But before Quintus could do anything – or even think what he should do – the river swirled and slopped closer, as if suddenly aware of possible victims. As the boy struggled, his head starting to sink beneath the surface; he was still clutching the hands of the other two children. They both cried out, but they were already toppling forward. As they fell into the river, it subsided slightly, almost as if relishing what it had managed to snatch into its depths.

Quintus remained where he was, staring into the dimness. Gone, he thought. I can't possibly rescue them – I can't even see them. Or can I rescue them? If I bring lights over – more candles . . . my father's old oil lamp – mightn't I see them? Mightn't they be clinging to something further along the tunnel? If so, I might be able to pull them out. But almost immediately came another thought: Trapped in there, drowned in the underground river, those children will never be able to tell anyone what they have seen.

It was a terrible thought but, once formed, it bit down into his mind, and he seized the wheel and began to turn it back to lower the gate. It protested again, but at last, with agonizing slowness, the gate began to descend. The trailing river weed stirred, but eventually, with a clang that echoed through the cellar, the gate came all the way down; the spikes drove home, and the river tunnel was sealed.

Quintus drew in a deep, shaky breath and half fell to the ground, against the wall. He was aware of an extraordinary mixture of emotions, but uppermost was the knowledge that the river flowed for many miles in its underground journey, and that when the children's bodies were finally washed up on a distant bank, there would be nothing to connect them with this village, and certainly not with Quintus himself. No one would ever know what had happened.

But you know, said a sly voice in his mind. You know what happened, and you know what you did.

But I didn't kill them! said Quintus silently to the inner voice.

You didn't try to save them, though, did you? it said. And you might have saved them if you had tried.

But no one will ever know what's happened! cried Quintus silently. I can seal up the kiln, and leave this house and never come back here. I will be perfectly safe.

On the crest of this thought, he got to his feet and went into the tunnel again. It took longer than he had thought to seal up the kiln – some of the bricks had shattered when he knocked them out earlier, but he managed to force several of the broken pieces into the vents, and even to smear dust and dirt over them. It looked as if no one had touched it for a very long time. Quintus was aware of a huge relief. Once the tunnel door was closed, the kiln would sink back into its dark, cold silence. He would lock up the house, and its secrets would be locked up inside it. As for the river gate, there was no reason for that ever to be lifted again.

He closed the tunnel door and turned back to the cellar, holding up the single candle he had used to make his way back down the tunnel. It was then that his eyes fell on what still lay on the iron tray.

It took more resolve than he would have thought to raise the gate again, but it had to be done. As he struggled with the mechanism, he was aware of the tangle of his emotions. He had no remorse over his mother's death – the cold, cruel bitch had deserved it, and she deserved to have what was left of her tipped into the dark river. He had no remorse over the poisoning of the Tsar, either.

But the three children . . .

He wound the gate to about a third of the way up, then lifted the iron tray and, very slowly and cautiously, tipped what lay on it over the stone edge. He stood for a moment, watching it sink slowly into the green waters, and he was about to step back and operate the mechanism to lower the gate when he saw, on the narrow stone shelf, a huddle of three small shapes.

They were all dead, of course. He saw that at once. Either they had managed to half climb out of the river, then collapsed from having been submerged and died there from their ordeal, or they had drowned, and the river had swelled and surged and washed up their bodies on to the stone lip.

They could not be left there, though. Not because of the risk of someone finding them – although Quintus accorded a brief acknowledgement to this possibility – but simply because he could not leave them like that.

He dragged the small bodies through the gate and laid them on the cellar floor. Then he lowered the gate, and sat down on the ground, staring at them.

You could have saved them . . . It was infuriating that those words kept echoing through his head. What was important – what he must hold on to – was that, with the children dead, he was safe. They could not talk about seeing the charred bones Quintus had taken out of the kiln, and they could no longer sing the chant about the black robe and the tainted wine.

After a long time, his thoughts began to arrange themselves into a curious calm, and he knew what he was going to do.

Stacked in corners of the cellar were most of the tools of his father's trade. His father, when commissioned to create the likeness in clay of some rich man's son or daughter, or the pampered pet of a lady, liked to say he was giving those people and those animals a kind of immortality. 'Once they are fired in the kiln's heat, they will live for always,' he would say.

Immortality.

The making of clay or stone heads was a lengthy task, and it required great attention to detail. Quintus would have to dispose of the bodies long before he could hope to complete such a task, but the river was at hand for that. He would, though, have to think of a way to manage the lengthy firing of the kiln.

But his mind was going back to the skills learned by watching his father – and, to some extent, by his time in the monastery's workshops. He knew how he could take a likeness of each of the children, from which he could then fashion and sculpt their heads, taking as long as necessary to do so.

He arranged the three small bodies so that they were all lying on their backs, and closed their eyes. Then he lit more candles and set them around the cellar. He would need better light later on – he would try to find his father's oil lamps – but for the moment there was enough light for what he was about to do.

Most likely, the chemicals and pastes his father had used were dried out, but some might still be usable. The tub of wax, when he found it on a shelf, had certainly long since hardened, but after several abortive attempts, Quintus managed to soften a reasonable amount over the candle flames. He scooped out the warm soft wax, then, carefully and with infinite attention to detail, he spread it thickly over each child's face, patting it into place, smoothing it over as much as possible. It would cool and set quite quickly, after which he would be able to lift each one away.

It would give him three death masks, from which he could create three life-sized heads of the dead children.

SEVENTEEN

I n the days that followed, Quintus was careful to keep the mantle of the quiet, submissive and devout Brother Quintus.

But two nights after the children's deaths, when midnight Matins had finished and the monastery bell was tolling one o'clock, he stole out of his room and went stealthily through the silent darkened halls. In the sculleries, he took two oil lamps, together with a box of candles, then unlocked the garden door and slipped out. He had just under five hours; Verkhoturye did not celebrate three o'clock Lauds as some other religious houses did, but he must certainly be in his place for Prime at six. He left the garden door unlocked – during those night hours, it would not be noticed.

No one was abroad as he walked down the narrow mountain path and then through the darkened streets. He would have preferred to wait longer before returning to the house, but what he had to do must be done without delay.

The wax he had spread over the children's faces had cooled and set exactly as he had wanted. He removed each one carefully and studied them all under the light of the oil lamps. The masks were what his father had called a back-to-front image – a reverse impression – but after Quintus had scraped out the clinging fragments of wax, he had a clear, clean image, and he was able to press three mounds of soft clay down into each mask. There was a heart-stopping moment when he removed them two nights later, but his care was rewarded; he had a precise likeness of each child which he could now fashion and refine, then fire in the kiln. First, though, he must dispose of the bodies.

The river gate lifted more easily than before, and the bodies were small and light; it was not difficult to tip each one into the river. Quintus did so quickly and dispassionately, but as the small shapes were swept into the dark echoing tunnels, he knelt to say prayers for them. It was a pity he did not know their names, but all prayers were supposed to be heard. Even the prayers of a murderer.

He worked absorbedly on the clay heads, stealing out of the monastery each night at the same hour. He remembered clearly how his father used to buff and smooth the features of his subjects, adding handfuls of clay to plump out cheeks, or scraping it away to sharpen the line of a jaw or the arch of an eyebrow. Quintus had set the death masks on a ledge, and by the third night, he found himself almost believing that these reverse images of the children watched him. At times, he thought he could feel their warm, living faces beneath his hands, and on several occasions, he caught himself looking sharply over his shoulder to the stairs, thinking he had heard sounds overhead. Twice, he was compelled to run up the cellar stairs and make a search of the house. Each time, there was nothing to be found, although once he thought a face peered through a downstairs window – a shadowy outline that whisked away when Quintus approached it. Of course, it was only his imagination playing tricks. Or he might have heard footsteps going along the deserted street above – although it was a lonely part of the village, and no one was likely to be abroad at this hour.

But sometimes, as he walked quietly through the shadowy village streets, going furtively between the monastery and the house, the feeling of being watched – and of someone creeping along behind him – persisted.

Finally, the heads were ready for firing, and Quintus sat down to consider how this could be managed. It could take at least a day – generally, nearer two – for the kiln to reach the necessary heat, but he could not be absent from the monastery for two days, or even for one day.

The oil lamps had burned low, shadows were creeping in from the corners of the cellar, and the children's faces were looking at him. They were open and innocent and guileless, and Quintus suddenly wondered what it might be like to convey quite different emotions in a sculpture – sadness, say, or passion, not that he knew much about what people meant by passion. But what about fear or menace? Menace should be easy – there would need to be a snarling look to the lips, or a sly narrowing of the eyes. Fear would be difficult, though. The eyes would have to be wide and staring, the mouth stretched in a soundless scream . . .

With this last thought, one of the lamps sputtered out, and there was a loud creak from the stairs, and then a movement within the shadows. Quintus spun round, scanning the dimness, and the movement came again. Then came a hoarse whisper.

'I know what you did, monk . . .'

Horror and panic engulfed Quintus, but with it was the realization that someone had indeed been following him and watching him, and whoever it was had got into the house and crept down here. He looked about him for something – anything – to use as a weapon, and his eyes had lit on the long-handled hammer when the voice came again. It was chanting, but now it was not the lines the children had sung – these were different, and they were far more damning.

'*Beware, beware, the Face Stealer's hands,*
'*Run for your life if he comes.*
'*For he'll snatch you all up in his strangler's hands*
'*And carry you off to his lair down below,*
'*Where the iron teeth clang and the river-light glows*
'*And the water lies waiting for prey.*'

Gleb the Rhymer. There was no one else it could be. He was here – he had come out of the shadows, and he was walking towards Quintus, a grinning, goblin figure, still chanting his macabre lines.

'*Never be caught, never be caught, never, NEVER, ever be caught.*
'*He'll carve out your face, then he'll throw you away –*
'*Into the green waiting stream.*'
'*He'll carve out your face, then he'll throw you away;*
'*Never be caught, never be caught, never, never, NEVER be caught.*'

The words burned into Quintus's mind like acid, but he managed to say, 'How dare you come in here! Get out, before I throw you out into the street.'

'You won't do that, Brother Quintus,' said Gleb, coming towards him. The dying lamplight cast shadows across him, making him look even more grotesque. 'I knows all about you, and I'd tell folk – the priest at the church, and your Father Abbot.' He came closer.

'Scared you just now, di'n't I?' he said. 'I likes scaring folk – I told you that. And I been watching you. See, I know what you did at Ropsha that night – I followed you and I saw. I know what you did here four nights ago, too. You got rid of those little'uns, 'cause they were singing my rhyme – the rhyme I wrote so's folk'd be warned about you. You let them drown in the old river.'

'No—'

'You murdered the Tsar,' said Gleb. 'How much did they pay you to do that? How much is an emperor's life worth – and how much are you worth because of it, monk?' He looked about him. 'Nice little house this,' he said. 'Don't fit so well with them vows you'll have taken. Poverty – ain't that the first of them? You ain't poor,' he said, sneeringly. 'Only got to look at this house to know that. If I had this house, I might keep my mouth shut about what you did to the Tsar – and what you did to them kids an' all.' His eyes went to the row of heads, waiting by the kiln for firing. 'You killed them and you stole their faces,' he said. 'That's what I put in the rhyme – in the new verse. The Face Stealer, I called you. Folk won't like that. They won't like to know what you did. They're searching for those children now, so you got to think how you'll stop me telling what you done.'

Quintus said, 'You saw nothing at Ropsha, because there was nothing to see. I was on an errand of mercy that night – the Sacrament to be administered—'

'Errand of mercy, my arse,' said Gleb. 'You poured poison into the Tsar, and he died in writhing agony. No use shaking your head an' clenching your fists, for I know it. I told you I went into the tavern that night and heard all the talk. The guards all knew what had happened. But,' he said softly, and again there was the calculating look around the cellar, 'we could strike a bargain, you and me.'

Quintus said, coldly, 'I don't bargain with the likes of you. Get out.'

'If you want me to get out – and to keep quiet – you got to pay me,' said Gleb. 'In money or with this house. Don't mind which. But you give me one or the other, Brother Quintus, or, sure as there's a hell, I'll tell everyone what you done.'

For a terrible moment, Quintus was hearing the Orlov brothers that night in the Winter Palace.

'We saw what you did,' Grigory Orlov had said, and the knowledge had flared between them of how a long-ago boy called Leonid had pushed his own mother into the kiln's heat in this very cellar. 'You have no choice but to do what we want,' Orlov had said.

And now this revolting creature was making almost exactly the same threat. Do what I want or I'll tell how you killed the Tsar and let the children drown, he was saying. And he had started to tell people already – he had written it into his macabre rhyme. Had he been singing it in Cympak? Fear closed its cold fingers around Quintus, but with it came the beginnings of an idea.

Speaking slowly, he said, 'There might be an arrangement. If you perform a small task for me, afterwards you can have this house – and money with it.'

Greed showed in Gleb's eyes, but he said, 'Tell me first. Then I'll see.'

Quintus indicated the half-open tunnel door leading out to the kiln. 'The kiln has to be fired,' he said. 'To finish the work to the sculpted heads. That means at least a day of continuously stoking it with wood – bringing the heat gradually up to what's necessary. You understand?'

'Yes?' The creature was not quite won over, but he was listening.

Quintus said, 'It's not something I can do myself – I'd be missed from the monastery for that length of time. But you could stay here for the next two days – there's wood stacked in that corner, and if there isn't enough, there'll be more kindling and fallen branches outside. I'd show you what to do – it's easy enough. Afterwards, once the heads are completed—

Well, I have no further use for this house. You can live here
or sell it – whichever you wish.'

The small eyes narrowed, calculating, considering. Then
Gleb said, 'How do I know I can trust you?'

'If I go back on my promise, you know enough about me
to tell your tale in the village anyway.'

There was a moment when he could feel Gleb's sharp little
mind considering, then he said, slowly, 'All right. But only
two days, mind. After two days, you come here and give me
the keys and any papers 'bout the house.'

'The Deeds, yes,' said Quintus. He had never seen Deeds
or documents relating to the house or its ownership, and he
had no idea if any even existed. But in two days' time, it
would not matter.

The plan, so suddenly conceived, was easy to put into action.

Quintus arranged the three heads inside the kiln, positioning
them on the shelves, setting them where he wanted with the
long-handled shovel. After that, he showed Gleb how to stack
the wood in the stoke holes, leaving him to finish the task
while he returned to the monastery.

He still had no idea if he could trust Gleb to do what was
needed, but on the following night, when he returned, the
remembered scents of hot wood and brick and stone were
already emanating from the kiln, and smoke was issuing from
its chimney. Quintus felt a jab of concern at seeing it – would
people be curious as to who might be in the house, when it
had been empty for so long? But it was some distance from
the main village, and the tunnel sloped steeply down, with the
kiln at the bottom of the slope. It was unlikely anyone would
notice.

'This time tomorrow,' he said to Gleb, 'your work will be
done.'

'And this house'll be mine.'

'Oh, yes.' Quintus looked about the cellar, as if making
sure everything had been done, and reached, in an almost
absent-minded way, for the heavy iron tray.

It could only have been coincidence that the oil lamps flared
at that moment, but it was almost as if a giant invisible breath

had blown on them, causing them to send shadows dancing across the cellar. Two figures stood starkly out against the walls – the hunched-over one that was Gleb, and a taller one behind him. The taller shadow raised its hand, and the heavy tray was briefly outlined against the wall. Then it came smashing down on the crouching figure. In the last second, Gleb realized what was happening, and turned, flinging up a hand in defence, but it was already too late. There was the sickening sound of metal crunching on bone – once, twice, three times – then Gleb gave a gasping grunt and fell forward.

After a moment, Quintus forced himself to bend over the motionless figure and feel for a heartbeat. There was no heart-beat, of course – the blows had been heavy and telling, and the creature was dead. It was no more than he deserved.

He looked towards the kiln. It was glowing, and it would be at least a day, probably two, before it would be sufficiently cool to retrieve the heads. That was all as planned, but in the meantime, there was Gleb's body. He remembered his idea of creating a contrast to the children. Could he do that? Could he create a dark variant to the guileless faces of the children? Even as the thought formed, he was reaching for the tub of wax, then turning up the wick of the larger oil lamp to soften it. There was deep satisfaction in spreading the warm wax over the creature's dead face, masking and blinding him. In a few hours, the wax would set and he could create a death mask. From that, he could make a fourth head – one that would portray not innocence and youth, but fear and malice and ugliness.

And once he had the mask, Gleb's body could be tipped into the underground river.

As he worked on this fourth sculpture, Quintus thought he had never realized that revenge could feel so good. You could keep all your religious ecstasies and spiritual transcendings; you could keep your sexual ecstasies, too – not that he had ever experienced such things, nor wanted to.

He had checked the kiln several times – it was starting to cool, and tomorrow, with dawn streaking the skies, he should be able to take the children's images out. As for Gleb, he could not fire the kiln all over again, but for a single item, he might use the ancient method, taught him by his father, of pit-firing. There were patches of clay in the soil behind the house, and it was a simple enough matter of creating a mound at the side of the kiln – a little like a small, low beehive – and then piling dry grass and branches around it. Once the grass and twigs were lit, the fire would be sufficiently small and insignificant to escape notice. When Gleb's likeness was packed inside, Quintus would cover the whole thing with the big iron tray that had been the cause of his death. He liked to think of Gleb slowly roasting in the ground.

He liked, as well, to think how thoroughly he was being revenged on the creature. Revenge. With the word, there came into his mind the realization that there were other people to whom he owed revenge. Grigory and Alexei Orlov, who had cheated him out of the rewards they had promised him, of course. And Catherine herself. Wasn't she at the heart of all this – the éminence grise?

It had been easy enough to deal with Gleb, but revenge against the Orlov brothers and the Tsarina would need to be entirely different. It would have to be on a much larger scale than a simple blow to the head and a body disposed of in an underground river. It would have to be on a scale so vast it could threaten thrones and topple dynasties . . . He began to think what form such a revenge might take.

EIGHTEEN

London, 1909

The Manor
Mallory Abbot
Suffolk

My dear Mr Fitzglen,
    The date you propose for your performance here at St Osmund's Church seems quite suitable. The vicar, the Reverend Hornbeam, tells me you have also approached him, and I understand he is in favour of the proposal, and very interested in all the details.
    As I explained in my previous letter, my husband's health is unreliable, which I am afraid precludes my inviting any of you to stay here. However, I am sure that, as theatricals, you will have encountered all manner of unconventional living and sleeping arrangements, and I think you and your company will find our local tavern, The Swan, perfectly comfortable. It is a respectable place, although I have once or twice had to bring to the attention of our local magistrate the fact that the landlord is sometimes lax in the observance of the licensing laws.
    I am a regular contributor to several local magazines, so I shall take pleasure in penning a little article for them, letting people in the area know about your visit here. With that in mind, perhaps you will be kind enough to let me know what your play is to be.
    Cordially,
      Marjorie Brundage.

Jack put the letter down and looked around the table.
    'It seems we're accepted at Mallory Abbot,' he said. 'So

we'd better consider the next part of our plan for getting into the mausoleum.'

'We'd better discuss what we're going to be putting on, as well,' said Daphnis, picking up the letter and reading it. 'It's all very well for the lady of the manor to ask that we let her know what the play is to be, but we don't know that ourselves.'

'Why don't we do one or two Shakespearean extracts?' suggested Cecily. '*The Dream*, or scenes from *The Tempest*?'

'Or how about the garden scene from *The Importance*?' suggested Ambrose. 'We've just finished the run, so it wouldn't need any rehearsal. It's an outdoors setting, so it would be easy to stage.'

'*The Dream* is too sprite-ish and fairy-fied,' said Rudraige, waving a dismissive hand. 'And we don't want Wilde's muffins and gentility, either. We want something in keeping with a crumbling old church. How about that old Brooke Warren melodrama, *The Face at the Window*? I know it's over ten years since it was written, but it's still a rattling good yarn. D'you remember, Daphnis, we talked about reviving it a few years ago?'

'I remember you wanted to play the killer who peered through windows at his victims,' said Daphnis.

'Le Loup,' nodded Rudraige, pleased. 'He howled like a wolf before each killing. I even rehearsed howling in the Amaranth. Very menacing and dramatic, it was. I got Bill the Chip to bring the thunder sheet up from the cellars, as well.'

'You did, and half of Sloat Alley thought a rabid wolf was rampaging through London,' said Jack, 'and the street preachers started proclaiming a biblical-strength storm and the end of the world being nigh.'

'We can't stage howling-wolf murders in an English church-yard,' said Byron. 'But listen, have any of you read any short stories by a writer called Montague Rhodes James? M.R. James, he calls himself for his fiction. No? He's a Cambridge don – a medievalist and quite distinguished – in fact, I think he's Provost of King's College. But he also writes splendidly eerie ghost stories, and some of them have been published in an anthology – *Ghost Stories of an Antiquary* is the title. As a person who aspires to publication myself – in a modest way, of course, but—' He caught Daphnis's eye, and said, 'Anyhow, I've read the stories, and there's one in particular that might work very well for an out-of-doors church setting. The title is *The Treasure of Abbot Thomas*.'

Jack said, 'Abbot Thomas— Didn't Marjorie Brundage's first letter mention an abbot called Thomas? Gus, have you got it? Thanks. Yes, here it is. "You may care to know that this village was named for Abbot Thomas de Mallet, who founded the church in 1280, before he entered the monastery." The story might appeal to them on that score alone.'

'It centres on an antiquary who uncovers information he believes will take him to the hidden treasure of a disgraced abbot from the 1500s – the Abbot Thomas of the title,' said Byron. 'The antiquary uncovers clues from a stained-glass church window, and concludes that "ten thousand pieces of gold are laid up in the well in the courtyard of the old abbot's house".'

'We can't create a well,' said Ambrose, frowning. 'Unless there's already a well in that churchyard – is there, Jack?'

'I didn't see one, but we could use the mausoleum itself,' said Jack, enthusiastically. 'It would give us a genuine reason to ask for it to be opened. Byron, this sounds like a very good idea.'

'It does,' said Rudraige. 'Who'd play the antiquary, though? It doesn't sound like your role, Jack.'

'I think it's Byron's part,' said Jack.

'I'd like to play it,' said Byron, at once. 'There's a rector in the story who helps unravel clues to the treasure's whereabouts – Ambrose could play that. Ambrose, you're good with clerical parts. We'd have to tweak the original a bit, though. The story tells how Abbot Thomas apparently trafficked with devils and demons, and when he stashed the treasure away, he set a Guardian over it. In the tradition of all good ghost stories, the Guardian wakes and attempts to wreak vengeance on the hero for disturbing the hoard. It's atmospheric rather than gruesome, though,' he said, catching Cecily's worried look. 'We won't be sending ladies into swoons.'

'What about lighting?' demanded Rudraige. 'We can't run cables and wires across a churchyard and risk tripping folk up. And if you're thinking of using gaslights, I'll tell you now, I'll have nothing to do with it. You won't remember the explosion halfway through the opening night of *A Blot on the 'Scutcheon* in Drury Lane – well, of course you won't, no more than I do myself, for it was over fifty years ago – but it blew out half the stage – ten folk in the stalls had to be taken to St Thomas' Hospital, and Robert Browning – the author of the piece – was in the stage box. Not that Drury Lane was ever a stranger to fires and disasters, of course,' said Rudraige.

'We could have flares in iron stands – sconces and torchères and the like,' said Jack. 'But we'd need to get the author's permission for this, wouldn't we?'

'Yes, and the story's probably subject to copyright,' said Ambrose, 'which could mean we'd be liable for royalties. And we aren't getting paid for this performance, remember.'

'What about Cecily's Cadogan Square fur filch?' asked Byron. 'Didn't we say it would fund this?'

'Unfortunately,' said Daphnis, dryly, 'that wasn't as successful as we expected.'

'Daphnis, I have apologized for that. Anyone can mistake coney for chinchilla. And Lydia did pick up a couple of quite nice rings in the ladies' washroom.'

Byron said, 'I wouldn't have thought royalties would be much for a single one-act performance. And I don't think obtaining permission to use the story would be difficult. Tod Inkling was at the same Cambridge college as James – there's a good twenty years between them, but you know Tod – he never likes to sever any academic ties, and he still attends a good many university gatherings. The Marlowe Society and the Cambridge Apostles' Conversazione, and yearly dinners and whatnot. As a matter of fact, I happened to call in at Tod's shop earlier,' said Byron, with deliberate nonchalance.

'Did you indeed? And you happened to mention this James man, I suppose?'

'I did, and it turns out that Tod does know him,' said Byron, triumphantly. 'So I suggest we ask him to approach the professor and arrange a meeting. It should all be perfectly easy.'

*   *   *

It turned out to be very easy indeed.

Professor James, invited to lunch at Rules with Tod Inkling, Jack and Byron – the probable cost of which had sent Ambrose into deep dejection – was delighted to be meeting two leading members of the distinguished Fitzglen theatre company, and charmed to think his story might be of use to them for a stage production.

'But I must explain, Mr Fitzglen—'

'Jack, please.'

'Jack, I must explain that I wrote those tales for relaxation and to entertain a few friends and students around Christmas. I read them aloud, you know—'

Byron said, hopefully, 'Curtains drawn against the winter night and firelight flickering on the walls—'

'Well, yes, usually. The publication of them was almost an afterthought.'

'They're beautifully eerie,' said Jack, who had read the anthology with enjoyment. 'And splendidly chilling. And if you give us permission to adapt *The Treasure of Abbot Thomas* for this single performance, we'll do our best to treat your work with respect,' he said.

'I'm sure you will, and it would be very exciting to see it on a stage. I would like to be present on the night, if it could be arranged.'

'Of course you'd be present. You'd be our honoured guest,' said Jack, at once.

'I don't care overmuch for fuss and publicity, you know, but it would be an interesting experience, so— Oh, roast beef, is that? My word, yes, I will have some. Dinners in Hall are perfectly acceptable,' he explained in an aside to Jack and Byron, as the deferential waiter plied carving knife and fork and proffered horseradish sauce. 'But you'll remember them from your time there, Todworthy—?'

Tod Inkling, addressing himself to the distribution of Bordeaux, the cost of which was going to send Ambrose into even deeper depression, said he remembered all too well.

Byron said, 'We'd show you a draft of what we intended, of course.'

'And any suggestions would be more than welcome,' put in Jack.

'I should hesitate to make suggestions to such eminent gentlemen of the theatre.' But it was said with a mischievous smile.

Jack said, at once, 'On the contrary, we'd be grateful for your ideas.'

'That's very amiable of you,' said the Provost of King's College, helping himself to cauliflower. 'Forgive me for asking this, but the name Fitzglen . . . Are you by any chance related to Simeon Fitzglen?'

'I believe there is a very distant connection,' said Jack, not looking at Byron or Tod. 'He isn't really known within our branch of the family, though. Have you met him?'

'He delivered a lecture to one of my student groups,' said Professor James. 'A very good speaker, but we made the decision not to invite him a second time.'

Jack said, carefully, 'Perhaps he might have been a little too persuasive when it came to donations to various causes?'

'Quite so. Especially,' said M.R. James, with unexpected acerbity, 'since they were causes that neither I nor my fellow dons had ever heard of.' He glanced at them both somewhat apologetically.

'I'm afraid every family has its rotten apple,' said Jack.

'Indeed so.' There was a gesture as if to dismiss unsatisfactory and probably untrustworthy clerics who lectured to Cambridge students.

Jack said, 'The main characters for the play are all worked out, and they'll be very much as you wrote them. Byron is playing your antiquary, and our cousin, Ambrose, will be the rector. And we thought of having a kind of prologue, with Abbot Thomas himself stashing away the treasure and setting the Guardian to watch over it.'

'Played by your Great Uncle Rudraige, of course,' said Tod Inkling, smiling.

'Who else?'

'That would be very effective,' said the professor, thoughtfully. 'Shall you be allowing the Guardian itself to make an appearance?'

Jack grinned. 'We shall,' he said. 'I'm going to make a brief dramatic entrance in the last scene, wearing a *very* sinister black cloak.'

'And exuding menace before he's vanquished,' put in Byron.

'Well, I'm liking the sound of all this very much,' said the professor.

'One other thing we would like to do,' went on Jack, 'is to weave in a slight romantic thread. Would you be happy about that? It would only be very light. There are a couple of youngsters who've just joined the company – twins. They could be the daughters of an innkeeper, and help the antiquary.'

'Adding a touch of romance to balance the darkness,' said their guest, thoughtfully. 'That's a very good idea.'

'Audiences like the hint of a happy ending to come,' explained Jack.

'Of course. And being under the aegis of the church, for the evening, you'll want to show that the darkness – the abbot's Guardian – is soundly defeated, and that love triumphs.'

Jack said, 'Exactly. But we won't lose your marvellous darkness, I promise you.'

'The only thought I would tentatively put forward,' said Professor James, 'is that you remember that what cannot be seen is almost always more frightening than what can. But you don't really need me to say that.'

'The midnight shadow rather than the midnight figure itself,' said Byron, thoughtfully.

'How percipient of you. Yes. A glimpse of the ghost's shirt-tail rather than the ghost itself, and— Have we mustard anywhere? Oh, thank you. You'll both recall Gloucester's words in *Richard III* – well, of course you will. "Thus I clothe my naked villainy with odd old ends, stol'n forth of holy writ . . ."'

Jack said, '"And seem a saint when most I play the devil."'

'Just so. Dear me, how enjoyable all this is. Tell me, Todworthy, shall we have time for me to browse in your bookshop before I return to Cambridge?'

As Jack and Byron walked back through Covent Garden, Jack said, 'Interesting to hear Professor James had encountered Saintly Simeon.'

'Simeon's reach knows no boundaries,' said Byron. 'Still, I hadn't realized he had managed to infiltrate the hallowed halls of King's College. But at least James and his learned cronies saw through him.'

'James is no fool, despite that gentle amiability. But on a different topic entirely,' said Jack, 'I had another letter from the lady of the manor this morning.'

'What does she say this time?'

Jack reached into a pocket and passed the letter to him. 'There's an enclosure,' he said. 'Don't drop it in a puddle, if you can help it. But look at the second paragraph.'

'"You will be interested to hear I submitted an article to the *Church Messenger*, with a preliminary announcement of your company's performance here,"' read Byron. '"I daresay you will be glad to know of this publicity, so I am enclosing a cutting."' He unfolded the cutting, and read it.

'"Mallory Abbot is delighted to announce it is to host what is sure to be a memorable performance by a famous London theatre company. The entertainment will be staged in the grounds of the historic Church of St Osmund, with all proceeds donated to the church's Restoration Fund. More details will be given in our next issue." That's all fair enough, isn't it?' said Byron.

'Read on.'

'"Readers will be interested to know that St Osmund's has recently been the grateful recipient of a set of four most unusual sculptured heads, believed to be Russian and dating to the mid-eighteenth century. The sculptures have been most generously bestowed on the church by Mrs Marjorie Brundage." She isn't slow in advertising her charitable works, is she?' said Byron, replacing the cutting in the envelope. 'It's not exactly what we'd have wished, though. We don't want the whereabouts of the Heads trumpeted abroad too much.'

'No. Still,' said Jack, 'I don't suppose the *Church Messenger* has a massive circulation. It's not very likely that it will be seen by anyone who might upset the filch.'

'I doubt if anyone in this country will even have heard of the Heads, anyway,' said Byron.

NINETEEN

My dear Reverend Fitzglen,

I am pleased you took the trouble to seek me out after Evensong at St Osmund's on Sunday. I had not realized my little piece for the *Church Messenger* would reach such a wide audience, although I am a regular contributor to several such publications, of course.

I was very interested to hear you had encountered mention of the Russian sculptures in your travels. I acquired them through the Ecclesiastical Society for the Restoration of Sacred Buildings; the provenance is rather sparse, although genuine, I am sure, but I should like to learn more of the sculptures' history. You spoke of staying in this area for a while to pursue your charitable work, so perhaps you would care to dine at The Manor one evening?

As you suggest, I am sending this letter poste restante to the post office in Melford Abbot. I quite understand you do not want the bishop troubled with your correspondence while you are staying with him, and also, if you are travelling around the county, then of course as a 'man of affairs' (if I may borrow the term), you will want to receive your letters as soon as possible.

With kind regards,
Marjorie Brundage.

Dear Reverend Fitzglen,

I look forward to your company at dinner on Tuesday.

By a curious coincidence, the theatre company who are to stage the performance at St Osmund's share your surname. If they should happen to be connections of yours, we might arrange for you to meet.

Our small community is greatly excited by this forthcoming theatrical evening. There is to be a buffet supper afterwards in the church hall. I had offered to organize it, and as an experienced hostess (we entertained the Lord Lieutenant last month), it would have been well within my capabilities. However, it seems that some of the other ladies had already volunteered, and Reverend Hornbeam feels it will be diplomatic to let them take on the responsibility. Doubtless they will be glad of my help, though.

I recently sent to the *Church Messenger* details of the evening, and they have today printed this at my request:

GHOST STORY EVENING AT ST OSMUND'S CHURCH
THE TREASURE OF ABBOT THOMAS
Adapted from the story by the famous and distinguished author and academic, Mr Montague Rhodes James, of King's College, Cambridge.

A chilling tale that unfolds a long-ago secret. Presented in the church grounds by the Fitzglen Theatre Company of London, under the direction of Mr Jack Fitzglen.

To commence at 7.00 p.m. on the date above. Seats can be reserved from the church hall in advance, or can be purchased on arrival.

A buffet supper will be available afterwards, from approximately 8.45 p.m.

Come along and enjoy the spine-tingling tale.

I think it reads very well. I thought it best to stress that it is a ghost story, so that people will not bring along young children, and will be prepared for a certain atmosphere within the piece. I did ask Reverend Hornbeam if he thought it was suitable, but it seems he was at university with the author, so I am reassured that it will be acceptable. I am sending a copy of the magazine to Mr Jack Fitzglen, who will, of course, be pleased at this publicity.

Naturally, I shall attend the performance, and I could reserve a seat for you – we might sit together for the evening. My husband will not be accompanying me; as I told you, he is some years older than me and in poor health, meaning he seldom goes out.

Cordially,

Marjorie Brundage.

Dear Reverend

I am so pleased you enjoyed our dinner. It was a pity my husband was unable to join us, but I feel we had a very companionable evening.

It is interesting that you are indeed connected to the Fitzglen theatre people, although I am sorry to hear of the long-standing estrangement. Mr Jack Fitzglen and a cousin – Mr Byron Fitzglen – are to dine at The Manor on their arrival, but I quite understand that you would prefer them not to know you are currently working in the area. I shall take care that your presence here is not mentioned.

Thank you for telling me a little more of the history of the Russian sculptures – the Stone Heads, as you call them. At present, they are in the Brundage mausoleum – Reverend Hornbeam most kindly took them along and locked them in there on my behalf. I did not feel I could enter such a place myself. However, it is a very secure building – there is a padlock on the door, and the key is kept in my desk. My original idea was to have the sculptures incorporated into the fabric of St Osmund's, but after I had studied the documents from the Ecclesiastical Society for the Restoration of Sacred Buildings, I felt it would not be suitable. In light of our discussion, I am now sure of it. The four additional pieces, which you appear to think are death masks – actually taken from the dead bodies of the murdered children themselves – would certainly be inappropriate in a church. I found that a very affecting story, although no doubt you thought me a weak, foolish woman for succumbing to emotion at the tale. (I shall have your handkerchief laundered and will return it when next we meet.)

In view of all this, your offer to make enquiries regarding the disposal of all the sculptures – the heads and the masks, alike – is most welcome. Perhaps a museum might be interested? I should hope to regain most – if not all – of the price, of course, and we could come to some arrangement regarding your involvement.

I certainly concur with your request that they should be kept from what you describe as 'prying, prurient or intrusive eyes'. As you say, ill-intentioned people too often seize on old legends and make greedy use of them.

I hope the bishop is pleased with the work you are doing for him. Your description of it was most interesting, and the charities for whom you are raising money sound very worthy. As promised, I enclose a bank draft for a contribution. It is made out to you, which you had intimated was the most straightforward way for you to distribute it to the various causes.

With grateful good wishes,
      Marjorie.

My dear Simeon,

In view of what I feel to be our deepening friendship, I believe I can now address you with this informality.

It is kind of you to enquire about my husband's health. I am sad to say it seems to be declining markedly – only two nights ago, he took one of his turns, and I had to send for our doctor. It is a great responsibility to ensure Rodger follows Dr Wallingford's instructions and takes his medication. He is a difficult patient – he frequently throws bottles of pills across the room, swears at me and orders me from his sight. I fear he now needs a firmer hand than I can supply, but there are no other family members who might share the burden, so I must do the best I can.

I believe, though, that I must start to face the fact that he may not be long for this world. It will be a sad loss, and although I shall have The Manor, which has always meant so much to Rodger (having been in his family for so many generations), money and a house and a position in the county cannot replace the loss of a loved one.

Yours,
　　Marjorie.

Dear Simeon

Your letter with its offer of your help with my husband reached me this morning, and touched me very deeply.

It is immensely kind of you to suggest you move into The Manor for a while, to help take care of Rodger – and you worded the suggestion so delicately and tactfully.

I believe Rodger would accept the administering of the pills and potions from another man more readily than he does from me. I also think he would accord a clergyman more respect, and would desist from throwing medicine bottles, and also (you will forgive this allusion) from sometimes deliberately emptying the contents of the utensil usually referred to as bedroom china on to the floor by way of protest. (The housemaid had to hang the bedroom carpet out in the kitchen garden for three days after one such episode.)

I am sure it would be thought perfectly proper for you to come to The Manor for a little while for the sake of Rodger's health and that no one would look askance at such an arrangement. You could have the apartments that adjoin his rooms – there is a bedchamber and what was once a dressing room, which could be adapted as a study for you. As you say in your letter, you could easily continue your work from The Manor – indeed, its very address may add a certain cachet to your fundraising activities.

Perhaps we could meet discreetly and discuss the details of this a little further in privacy?

Rather annoyingly, the theatre people will be here the day after tomorrow, so it will not be possible for you to take away the Heads until they have left. But a few days' delay can hardly make any difference, and Mr Jack Fitzglen and his colleagues are unlikely to be using the mausoleum for their play. In any case, I shall make it clear that it cannot be opened up.

With warm regards,
Marjorie.

'I had not realized you would want to use our mausoleum for your play, Mr Fitzglen.'

Jack and Byron had dined in draughty grandeur at The Manor, where their hostess had had the air of one being gracious to the serfs, but watchful in case they made off with the silver when no one was looking. The food consisted of stringy chicken, indifferent vegetables and some puckered fruit salad. Jack was extremely glad that he and the rest of the company were quartered at the friendly, comfortable Swan in the village, and he tried not to remember that its evening menu had included steak and ale pie, with treacle pudding by way of dessert.

At this mention of the mausoleum, Rodger Brundage, who resembled an elderly gnome in a dinner jacket, said cheerfully, 'Oh, you'll find the mausoleum crumbling away and covered in mould, Mr Fitzglen. I shouldn't think anybody's gone in there for years.'

He had had to be helped to his chair at the table, but he was bright of eye, interested in the discourse and certainly amiably disposed towards the two guests. Jack, making a vague, suitable rejoinder regarding the mausoleum, thought it sounded as if Marjorie had not told her spouse anything about the Stone Heads.

Byron, who was heroically eating his way through the

withered raspberries in his dish, explained that they would only want the mausoleum for a very short scene at the end of the play. 'It would be very atmospheric,' he said, 'and it would draw attention to the wonderful old church and your own family's history.'

'Church is falling to bits, and the family's not much better these days,' observed Rodger, cheerfully, and waved to a hovering maidservant to bring the port. 'My wife'll tell you I'm not allowed this stuff,' he said, conspiratorially, as the decanter was placed on the table. 'Hides the brandy from me, as well. Lot of nonsense. And port's a gentleman's drink, ain't it?'

Jack said he believed the King himself was particularly fond of port, to which Rodger Brundage chuckled and said the King was believed to be fond of a good many things folk were not supposed to know about.

'I must make sure to introduce you to my Great Uncle Rudraige after our performance, sir,' said Jack, who was liking their host. 'The two of you would find a good deal in common.'

'Oh, my husband won't be attending your performance,' said Marjorie, at once. 'His health will not be up to it.' She produced what Jack thought of as a sad, brave smile.

'Stuff and nonsense,' said Rodger Brundage, indignantly. 'Not much wrong with me. I'm looking forward to it, Mr Fitzglen. There's a bath-chair arrangement around somewhere – we'll use that, and I'll make a grand entrance. Ha! That'll upstage you all.'

'I was glad,' said Marjorie, as if he had not spoken, 'that I was able to place that notice about your play in our magazine. I daresay it will ensure a good audience for you.'

'I'm sure it will,' said Jack, politely. 'But as for the mausoleum, as Byron said, we would only want it opened for a very brief time.' The thought flickered in his mind that they would probably only need ten minutes to remove the Heads, anyway. He said, 'And we would be very careful of the structure.'

'I'm so sorry, Mr Fitzglen, but—' The smile was one of the falsest Jack had ever encountered. 'I'm afraid the mausoleum is unsafe. We have even considered demolishing it, and – ah – reinterring the remains in the churchyard.'

'First I've heard about it,' said Rodger.

'And I could not have it on my conscience to allow anyone to enter it in its present state,' said Marjorie, as if he had not spoken. 'Will you have a little more port?'

'It looks,' said Jack, as he and Byron walked back to The Swan later, 'as if we'll have to break into the mausoleum, after all. Infuriating, isn't it? Getting in there is the whole point of coming to Mallory Abbot.'

Byron glanced at him. 'But you're already working out how to break in, aren't you?' he said. 'And you're looking forward to it, as well. You've got that glint in your eyes.'

'There's nothing quite like the anticipation of a break-in,' said Jack, and grinned. 'But it had better be a midnight break-in, and I think it'll have to be after the performance tomorrow evening. If we go in before that, once it's discovered the things are missing, we'd be suspected. We need to grab the Heads and be back in London before anyone realizes they're gone.'

'It might be some time before anyone realizes it anyway,' said Byron.

As they approached The Swan, Jack said, 'We'll have to work out how to do that closing scene with the mausoleum still locked. We wanted the Guardian to emerge from its depths in the last scene, but it might work if he's hidden in the shadows, and steps out just as the antiquary's about to break in to get at the treasure's hiding place. If the lighting's right, it would look as if he really had emerged from inside to confront the intruder.'

'Well, you're playing the Guardian,' said Byron. 'And if you can't conceal yourself in a shadowy corner and leap out menacingly on cue, then nobody can.'

'It's only just on ten o'clock,' said Jack. 'Let's find Bill, and see what we can come up with.'

My dear Simeon,

I entirely understand you think it will be better to remove the Stone Heads without anyone realizing it.

I am therefore thinking your earliest opportunity will be after the Fitzglen play. It is to end around nine o'clock or shortly after, and then will be the buffet supper, which I expect will last for about an hour. I do not know how long it will take Mr Fitzglen's company to clear away their paraphernalia, but I understand they intend to do so immediately, as they are returning to London by an early train the next morning.

St Osmund's should therefore be deserted by midnight – or one o'clock at the latest. You will understand that I cannot undertake to meet you there – it is many years since I have had cause to actually go into the place – and so I am enclosing the spare key with this letter, which I shall send by registered post. I am sure you will be discreet and watchful, but I must warn you that there may be one or two people around, even at such an hour. Reverend Hornbeam sometimes celebrates Lauds at six o'clock, and the service is often attended by early morning workers on their way to their work, or by vagrants, who doubtless are grateful for an hour's sojourn in a warm, dry place. Mr Hornbeam is known for his benevolence and inclined to hand out a few coins from the parish poor box, or parcels of food which his housekeeper prepares for the needy. Rodger has always supported this practice, but for myself I consider it absurd and unnecessary pampering of layabouts who could work if they had a mind to.

I hear that the author of the story on which the play is based is travelling here specifically to see it. I understand he is a distinguished academic gentleman. No doubt I shall be introduced to him – he will perhaps be interested to hear of my own literary efforts.

Marjorie.

My dear Doctor Wallingford

I am sorry it was necessary to call you out to The Manor late last night. Rodger had seemed so unwell,

although by the time you reached us, as you saw, the
worst was over.

I find these attacks worrying, and for that reason I
am arranging for a friend to stay at The Manor for a
while. He is a clergyman, and very willing to take over
much of the responsibility for my husband's health –
especially administering his medication – and he will
also keep a firm hand on Rodger's drinking habits,
which have become extremely liberal of late. I try to
maintain your ban on alcohol, but I suspect he bribes
the servants to bring him brandy and port.

My friend has a little medical knowledge, having
pursued mission work in several countries. He
understands about my husband's medication, so I feel
quite happy to trust him. He will take up residence
here next week.

Sincerely yours,
    Marjorie Brundage.

TWENTY

Reverend Hornbeam had apologized to Jack for what he termed the basic dressing-room facilities provided.

'I am sure it is not what you are used to, Mr Fitzglen,' he said. 'It is actually our parish committee room. But you have tables, mirrors, chairs, and the Ladies' Needlework Committee have provided screens to allow a little privacy for – hum – donning costumes.'

'Most of us have toured at various times, and we've had to put up with far worse than this,' said Jack, surveying the room. 'This is perfectly acceptable. Everything we need.'

Later, hearing the buzz of talk as the audience started to arrive, he thought it did not matter where you staged a play or where you prepared for it – the anticipation was the same. Even among such a small cast – Rudraige, Ambrose, Byron and the twins, and Jack himself – there was already the familiar feeling of nerves strung tightly up, but also of delight at what was ahead.

Gus was here, of course, helping wherever he was needed. Rudraige had been struggling with the abbot's robe, and Ambrose had discovered that several buttons of the cassock he was to wear were missing. Gus helped Rudraige to drape the robe around his shoulders, then went off in search of needle and thread for the cassock buttons. Returning, he said it looked as if there was a good house.

'All the seats are taken,' he said, sitting down to sew on the errant buttons.

'Jack, Bill the Chip does know to fade that music after my entrance?' demanded Rudraige, who was gluing on false eyebrows to give a suitably villainous appearance to the abbot. 'Because at rehearsal this morning, it practically blasted me off the stage with the wretched belly-aching row.'

'I took a great deal of trouble finding that music,' said Byron, injured. 'It's from a suite called *Gaspard de la Nuit,*

and it's a new piece by a French composer called Maurice
Ravel. It's supposed to suggest a malevolent goblin dancing
in cold moonlight. I think it's only been performed once in
public – I had to get special permission for us to make the
recording.'

'How did you manage that?' demanded Rudraige.

'I happen to know one of the musicians,' said Byron,
off-handedly.

'Never mind what the thing is called or whether it's been
performed a dozen times or not at all, I don't want it drowning
my opening lines,' said Rudraige.

'Byron's borrowed one of those concert phonographs for
us to use,' said Jack. 'It means Bill can control the volume.
He'll turn it down very slowly on your entrance.'

'I remember the time,' said Rudraige, 'when you had to put
a sock in the actual horn to muffle the volume. Literally
put a sock in it. Well, anyhow, I shan't speak until Bill has
got the sound sufficiently low. You won't mind that, will you,
Jack? An extended version of the Fitzglen Pause, it would be.'

'I don't care if you extend the Fitzglen Pause until the Last
Trump sounds, as long as we finish in time to break into the
mausoleum at midnight,' said Jack.

Mikhail was glad he had managed to find evening wear for
the performance. Gus had helped him search the Amaranth's
wardrobe room, and they had discovered a dinner jacket that
fitted almost as if it was tailor-made, along with a dress shirt
and bow tie. Gus had insisted on taking the shirt away to be
laundered, and had sponged away a few splatters of make-up
on the collar of the jacket. Mikhail felt very smart in the
clothes. He was looking forward to Petronella seeing him in
them.

He was also looking forward to seeing the performance,
especially as at the start of all the preparations, Jack had asked
if he would help Byron to adapt the original story.

'There would, of course, be a fee involved.'

'If you think my English is good enough, I am very pleased
to help,' Mikhail said. 'A fee is not necessary.'

'It's certainly necessary, and Ambrose is arranging it,' said

Jack. 'You've already made two excellent suggestions, and you've taught schoolchildren about literature and history, so you'll understand about structuring a story, no matter what language it's in. And,' he said, smiling, 'you'll probably be able to restrain Byron when it comes to ghostly figures.'

Daphnis and Cecily had told Mikhail that they would make their entrance after the audience was seated and would take their places in the front row with him at their side.

'I think I should go in quietly on my own earlier,' said Mikhail, in slight panic.

'Certainly not. You're as much part of all this as anyone,' said Daphnis. 'You helped Byron to write the piece.'

'And we'd like you to walk in with us,' put in Cecily.

As they made their way to their seats, heads turned, and there was a ripple of interest as people pointed them out and told one another who they were. Mikhail found himself sitting between Daphnis and Cecily, with the twins' formidable-looking mamma two chairs along. Daphnis said quietly, 'Mikhail, do you see the elderly gentleman in the centre of the second row to our left?'

'The one wearing a hat like a squashed red drum and a purple velvet coat?'

'Yes. That's Todworthy Inkling.'

Mikhail had already noticed Mr Inkling, but had thought he might be a fellow actor who had come from a nearby pantomime, either not bothering or possibly forgetting to change out of costume. He was glad he had not said this.

'The distinguished-looking gentleman with him,' said Cecily, 'is Professor Montague Rhodes James from Cambridge University.'

'The real author,' said Mikhail, trying not to stare too openly.

'Yes. I was introduced to him earlier. We got on rather well. I was glad I had put on my feather boa – he seemed quite fascinated by it.'

'Cecily, if you flip that wretched feather boa in my face again, I swear I'll throw it on the fire when we get home,' said Daphnis. 'And now be quiet, the music's starting.'

The goblin-dancing music discovered by Byron floated

across the stage, and Rudraige Fitzglen, as the sixteenth-
century Abbot Thomas, made his entrance into the flickering
torchlight. He did so unhurriedly, taking no notice of the spatter
of appreciative applause, and made his way to the desk that
was strewn with papers and scholarly-looking documents. As
he shuffled through the papers, Daphnis said in an undertone,
'Please God, don't let him get the scenes out of order.'

'He has the lines written on the documents?' said Mikhail,
startled.

'Of course he has, the wily old rascal.'

The Abbot studied the documents, not speaking, then the
music faded, and Rudraige Fitzglen embarked on his opening
speech.

*'In the years to come, there will be talk and speculation in
Church circles about me. I may come to be known as the
wicked Abbot Thomas von Eschenhausen. Wicked. I find I relish
the prospect of being remembered as wicked, even though that
is probably committing a very strange sin. But there are worse
sins a man can commit.*

'For tonight, I shall make a plan to hide my treasure.'

He stood up, looked about him, as if searching for hiding
places, then stared across at the crouching darkness of the
mausoleum, whose outline was just discernible. Bill the Chip
had gone to considerable trouble to position the temporary
stage so that it was near to the mausoleum, and now, in this
eerie light, Mikhail saw that Bill had got it exactly right.

The Abbot considered the mausoleum, then nodded, picking
up a small drawstring bag in one hand, and grasping a large
leather-bound volume in the other.

*'I see the place, and I shall do it. In here is the ancient
incantation – the means to protect the treasure. The words
that – if pronounced aloud – will call into being a Guardian.
A creature that will watch with endlessly seeing eyes and see
all comers.'*

He walked across to the mausoleum, the torch flares
distorting his shadow. He paused, staring at the dark outline,
then delivered the closing lines of what Byron had called the
Prologue.

'I have set the trap. I have invoked the Guardian to stand

sentinel. I wonder how many people will read or hear of the legend in the future, and covet the Abbot's treasure?

'It will take a clever or a fortunate man to find it, though. And any who dare to attempt to cheat the Guardian will find its wrath terrible.'

Then, in ringing tones: *'Depositum custodi! That is the charge I lay on the Custodian I have called into being. Depositum custodi. Keep that which is committed to thee.'*

When the interval came, moving among the audience, Mikhail had to remind himself that all this was actually happening, and when he was introduced to Professor James, he had to take a deep breath and make a conscious attempt not to seem overawed. But the professor was interesting and interested; he wanted to know about the adapting of his story, and talking to him, Mikhail forgot about being nervous. He was even able to exchange a smile with Mr Todworthy Inkling when Daphnis Fitzglen successfully and majestically headed off Mrs Marjorie Brundage's attempts to buttonhole the professor, who, by this time, had moved on to the Reverend Hornbeam, and appeared to be discussing Church architecture with him.

They resumed their seats, and when Lydia Fitzglen leaned forward to tell Mikhail she thought he had made a splendid job of adapting the play, he was able to say, quite composedly, that it had mostly been Byron's work, and even to add how much he was looking forward to seeing Petronella and Phoebe in the scenes ahead.

And now Byron and Ambrose, in the characters of the eager antiquary and the inquisitive rector, were poring over the Abbot's journal. It was age-spotted now and trailed thick cobwebs to indicate it had spent a few centuries hidden away. Mikhail smiled, remembering how Rudraige had insisted the most effective cobwebs were long pieces of stage hair, teased out slightly, but how Cecily had held that silk strands, slightly frayed, were better. In the end, they had used both, on the grounds that if one did not pick up the light, the other would, although Ambrose said most likely the whole lot would have dropped off or shrivelled up by the time they got to the scene where the grisly book was discovered.

At the entrance of the twins as the sympathetic tavern-keeper's daughters, there was an unmistakable stir of appreciation from the audience. Mikhail was extremely pleased; later on, he might see if he could escort Petronella back to The Swan, just the two of them.

Here was the scene in which Petronella pleaded with the antiquary not to break into the tomb-house to reach the sinister abbot's treasure. '*Don't do it, I beg you. Not if a hundred fortunes are in there.*'

Behind her was the scenery depicting the stained-glass window that held the clues to the treasure's hiding place. Bill the Chip and his assistant had constructed a narrow wooden frame, and Byron had designed and painted glowing colours on to thin pasteboard, with cryptic lettering from which the antiquary would work out the treasure's hiding place. Mikhail had been extremely impressed with the results of this – he had had no idea such things could be created for the stage. Byron had been pleased; he told Mikhail how, a couple of years ago, he had created a triptych, which the Fitzglens had sold, very profitably, to a museum in somewhere called South Kensington, which was apparently quite an expensive area of London.

Whatever the South Kensington panels had looked like, the stained-glass images on the stage tonight, their colours glowing from the flaring lights, drew gasps of admiration from the audience. There was murmured speculation as to whether it could be real glass, and several people could be heard asking neighbours if the lettering might actually mean something, and, if so, hoping it did not translate into anything irreligious.

Byron, as the antiquary, was still staring up at the painted scenery, brushing aside Petronella's entreaties to leave the treasure where it lay.

'*Let it be enough that you have solved the ancient puzzle,*' she said. '*The treasure of the long-ago abbot is ancient and evil. It should not be disturbed.*'

But the inquisitive antiquary was not to be dissuaded. He stole across to the mausoleum, glancing back over his shoulder several times. For a terrible moment, Mikhail was back in Verkhoturye, creeping down to the monastery's vaults, seeing, by the tiny match-light, the blind, cold faces within. He would never forget how the Stone Heads had seemed to move, to press imploringly against the barred door, as if hoping the intruder had come to release them.

Byron was at the door of the mausoleum now, plying hammer and chisel on it with vigour. Mikhail wondered if Marjorie Brundage would realize he was not actually pounding on the door, and that it was Bill the Chip who was creating the sounds from beneath the stage. At last, Byron stood back and gave a nod – indicating to the audience he had broken open the lock, thought Mikhail, pleased. Then he began to read aloud from the leather-bound book. He had told Mikhail the words they had imported into this part of the story were a very old form of Latin; Mikhail thought, whatever language they were, they had a ringing command to them.

When Byron stopped speaking, there was a brief silence, then the chilling music started again, very softly – cold, malevolent music that was enough to send shivers down the most robust of spines – and a figure in a dark cloak, sinister and menacing, stepped out of the shadows. The Guardian called from its darkness, ready to defend the ancient treasure, thought Mikhail. He was abruptly aware of the audience's sudden awareness – it was as if they immediately sat up straighter and looked more intently at the little stage. The Guardian's appearance has startled them, he thought. But then he thought it was not that at all; it was exactly the same reaction as when Jack stepped on to the Amaranth's stage. It did not matter that he was wrapped in the dark cloak or that this was a relatively small audience in a country churchyard: his presence had the same effect as it did on the London stage.

The Guardian moved forward, raising its hands as if to strike, and Byron fell back, the book falling from his hands. He landed half on his back, staring helplessly up as the Guardian came at him. The audience gasped, leaning forward as if willing Byron to escape, but Petronella was already running across the stage. She snatched the book up and, turning, flung it – not at the dark figure, but at the painted stained-glass flat. It split at once, and there was the sound of splintering glass – it did not matter that Mikhail and the other Fitzglens knew Bill the Chip was kneeling immediately behind it, rattling broken beer bottles in a bucket; it was tremendously effective.

The Guardian flinched, throwing up its hands in instinctive defence, then whisked the dark cloak about it and retreated – almost melted, thought Mikhail – into the shadows surrounding the mausoleum. Music – this time, gentle hymn-like sounds – came in, and the flares that had illuminated the stage were discreetly snuffed by Bill and his assistant tiptoeing around the edges. The lanterns positioned along the sides of the audience's seats were turned up and the play had ended.

As the audience got up from their seats, they could be heard telling one another that it had been a wonderful experience, so marvellously staged, so extremely well acted – and, of course, entirely appropriate for a church setting. Light triumphing over darkness – wasn't that the message it had intended to convey, and wasn't that the core of the Christian faith, anyway? They made their way to the church hall, still eagerly discussing the performance, and Mikhail, with Daphnis and Cecily, Lydia following, managed to get around to the dressing room.

The cast were divesting themselves of their costumes and removing their make-up – Rudraige had lost the spirit-gum remover and was glumly contemplating having to wear the false eyebrows for the next week. Somebody had apparently sat on the spectacles Ambrose had worn for the character of the rector, and Gus Pocket was sweeping up the fragments.

Byron, however, was stretched out on a chair, with his leg propped on a second chair, his face twisted in pain. 'I fell awkwardly,' he said, ruefully, as Mikhail and the others came in. 'When the Guardian came at me, I tumbled backwards. You'd think I'd have learned how to stage a graceful, painless fall, but there it is.'

'It looked very effective,' said Mikhail, tentatively.

'It felt agonizing,' said Byron. 'I've sprained my ankle quite badly. I can't put my foot to the ground. Jack, I bet you've never felled anyone with just a look before.'

'No, and I've never had to carry anyone off a stage before, either,' said Jack. 'It was a good thing Bill had doused the stage lights by that time, because the audience didn't realize what was going on.'

'It was so dark we nearly dropped him, and I almost went headlong off the edge of the stage anyway,' said Ambrose, as Cecily fluttered anxiously over Byron. 'But he really couldn't walk – he couldn't put any weight on his foot at all.'

'I think there was a doctor with Marjorie Brundage,' said Daphnis. 'Mikhail, could you try to find him?'

'Even if it means facing the Brundage herself,' put in Byron, as Mikhail went out.

Dr Wallingford, successfully detached from Marjorie's clutches, was reassuring. Nothing was actually broken, he said, having subjected Byron's foot to a series of proddings and twistings, which caused Byron to groan – 'Although I groaned very artistically, I think,' he said later.

'It's a severe sprain, and on no account must you walk on it for two days at least,' said Dr Wallingford sternly.

'But—'

'Don't worry, we'll carry you to the train tomorrow on one of Bill's trolleys,' promised Jack.

'I'll bind it up for you now, Mr Fitzglen, if someone can provide a large handkerchief or even a scarf – ah, yes, that will do very nicely, Miss Fitzglen.'

'Greater love hath no man – or woman – than to lay down a silk scarf for a cousin. Thank you, Cecily,' said Byron. 'And it's a rather fetching cerise-pink, which blends very nicely with the velvet cravat I thought of wearing for the buffet supper.'

Dr Wallingford, it appeared, had enjoyed the evening. 'And I especially enjoyed your performances, my dear young ladies,' he said, beaming at Petronella and Phoebe.

Mikhail was, of course, pleased that the doctor had admired the twins' acting, although he did not think there was any need for him to pat Petronella's shoulder quite so lingeringly. But the twins listened gravely, and thanked Dr Wallingford. As he turned away, Petronella sent Mikhail such a mischievous grin that he instantly felt better – of course she was not likely to be impressed by the doctor's florid compliments. In any case, he was years older than she was.

It was only later, when the audience had dispersed and arrangements were being made to transport Byron back to The Swan, that Mikhail realized with dismay that Byron would not now be able to assist Jack in breaking into the mausoleum later.

'I'll come in his place,' he said at once.

'No,' said Jack, and for the first time since Mikhail had known him, there was a sharp note of authority in his tone. 'I'm sorry, Mikhail, but it's a job for – well, for a professional.'

'I could keep watch, perhaps?' suggested Mikhail. 'Hide in the trees or by the lychgate.'

'The best thing for you to do is to return to The Swan and leave me to it,' said Jack. 'I can manage this perfectly well on my own.'

TWENTY-ONE

Jack supposed if you were going to break into an ancient mausoleum and steal sculptures to which a macabre legend was attached, you might as well do so at midnight and embrace the entire Gothic atmosphere.

It was easy to slip out of The Swan unnoticed – although Byron and Gus and the others all knew what he was going to do anyway, so it would not matter if any of them heard. The thought just flickered on Jack's mind as to whether they would all be in their appointed rooms. Gus had certainly been eyed very warmly by the flaxen-haired barmaid during their stay, and Jack also thought a very promising closeness was developing between Mikhail and Petronella. He liked Mikhail, and he thought he might make a very useful permanent addition to the Amaranth. Lydia would probably consider him a penniless adventurer, but Jack suspected that, despite his quiet politeness, Mikhail was quite capable of dealing with Lydia.

As he went towards St Osmund's, his mind was still partly on the evening's performance. It had been a means to an end, of course, but he was pleased it had gone so well and that the audience had so clearly enjoyed it. He was somewhat uncomfortable at having deceived Reverend Hornbeam, although it seemed as if the proceeds from the night had far exceeded expectations, so St Osmund's would be benefiting substantially.

As for Professor M.R. James, Jack thought he and Byron might arrange to meet him after all this was resolved, and relate the entire story to him. He had the feeling the professor would enjoy the tale, and would not put it past him to use it as a base for a future ghost story.

Around him, the trees stirred in the wind, and dipped their branches, almost as if curious to know who might be prowling around at such an hour. Twice, Jack turned to scan the darkness, because the sounds had been almost like stealthy footsteps, but nothing moved, and the sounds did not come again. Nerves, nothing more. He thought he could be forgiven that, though, because this was hardly a normal filch.

The mausoleum was directly in front of him now, and the familiar thud of excitement was starting to thrum through him. None of the family ever talked about this feeling, but Jack knew every one of them experienced it at the start of a filch. Even, he thought, with a smile, dear fluttery Cecily, nervously lifting fur coats from ladies' powder rooms.

A few hours earlier, the mausoleum had been the focal point of the play, but now it crouched silently and balefully in the shadows, the padlock across the door glinting like barred teeth. The rustling sound came from within the trees again, and Jack whipped round once more. *Was* there someone out there? No, it was all right. But the sooner he could get the Stone Heads and return to The Swan, the better. He reached into his pocket for the leather wallet containing the thin skewers and needles and hooks that would open almost any door. The wallet had belonged to his father, who had been a wily, intelligent member of the Fitzglen clan, and who was still remembered with great affection. Jack knelt down in front of the oak door, and saw the padlock was a conventional one. The tiny tension wrench that Aiden had designed and had made should deal with it easily, and when he slotted it in, he felt it connect with the key pins inside almost immediately. As the soft click indicated the padlock had released, Jack smiled an acknowledgement to his father's memory, looked about him again, then cautiously pushed the door inward.

He had expected a shriek of rusting, seldom-used hinges, but the door swung open with scarcely a sound, and Jack felt in his pocket for matches and the small candles he had brought, and stepped inside.

Darkness came at him, but he lit one of the candles, and by its light examined the door to make sure it could be opened from this side. He could prop the door slightly open, but it was just possible that some chance poacher might come along, and he was not going to risk anyone seeing the mausoleum was open. But it was all right; there was a handle on the inner

side, which, when he tried it, worked smoothly. He adjusted
the padlock so that it would look from outside as if the place
was still locked up, then went back in, closing the door.

Even with the candlelight to chase the shadows back, the
mausoleum was a terrible place. Four worn stone steps led
down, and as Jack descended warily, he was very aware of
the brooding silence all around him. He lit a second candle,
and now the small flames showed up a low roof, with cobwebs
dripping from it like boneless fingers. They stirred in the
current of air, and Jack shivered slightly and directed
the candles around the walls.

Along each side, at waist height, were deep shelves. I won't
look at what's on them, thought Jack, determinedly, but he
did look, and saw, set out in sad, neat rows, the coffins, all
thickly veiled with cobwebs. Here and there, a corner had
rotted slightly, or split with age or damp. Jack held on to the
thought that he was here solely to find the Stone Heads, that
once he had done so, he would scoop them up and make good
his exit, and that the whole thing should not take more than
ten minutes.

Reverend Hornbeam had mentioned placing the Heads on a
high shelf, and he had referred to using a ladder to reach it,
but Jack had swarmed up enough drainpipes and crawled along
enough narrow ledges to make him feel confident of reaching
almost any high shelf. He had considered, but rejected, bringing
one of Bill the Chip's ladders, because not even the stealthiest
thief in the world could steal unobtrusively and noiselessly
through dark church grounds lugging a ladder along.

At first, though, he could see nothing except the grisly
outlines of the coffins and the drifting cobwebs. He moved
around, holding the candles aloft, and then, without warning,
they were there. Cold stone faces, staring down, peering into
the darkness as if their blind eyes could see, and as if their
cold carved lips might suddenly smile. If they smiled, it would
be a mischievous smile, because they were children. Jack had
known this, of course, but he had not realized how young and
vulnerable they would look, and he was aware of a stab of
anger against the long-ago man who had been called the Face
Stealer, and who, if the legend and the old rhyme could be

believed, had slaughtered these children. He stood very still, holding up the candle as close to the Heads as he could. The uncertain light fell across them, showing up the details – and showing, as well, that one of the heads seemed to have been fashioned from darker, rougher stone. It was somehow disturbing – it gave the staring face a wizened look, as if it was intended to portray a much older person. Jack looked at it for some minutes. Presumably, it had simply been fashioned from different stone or clay, perhaps at a later date to the other three, but it held a malevolence, which was very much at odds with the gentle features of the others. It was almost as if some fragment of the living person had been trapped within the sculpture – and that whatever that fragment might be, it was nothing good.

The shelf was higher than he had expected, and the wall beneath and around it was smooth and flat. This was annoying, and Jack looked around for something to stand on. But there were only the coffins. Could he possibly drag one off its shelf and push it against the wall to stand on? But he would need two coffins, at least, one on top of the other. And, thought Jack, somewhat grimly, I'm damned if I'm going to start shunting coffins around in almost total darkness, and stack them up to reach up there. Most of them look as if they're half-rotting anyway, and I'd probably put my foot straight through the rotten wood. He was just accepting he would have to go back to The Swan for a ladder, after all, when a sound from beyond the door caused him freeze. It had been a scrabbling noise – an animal? But it had sounded more as if someone was out there.

Jack instinctively snuffed the candles and stepped back into the deepest of the shadows, remembering how, earlier, he had thought he had heard stealthy footsteps. It was just possible Gus or even Ambrose or perhaps Mikhail had followed him in case he encountered difficulties. Jack thought he would be extremely glad to see any of them at the moment, because they might help him to climb up to the shelf and get the Heads. But he would wait to see who it was before he made a move.

The door opened slowly, and Jack pressed back against the

wall, watching the slowly widening outline around the door's edges.

It was not Gus or Ambrose, or any of the Fitzglens, and it was not a man, either.

'Jack?' said a soft voice, and at once Jack came out of his shadowy corner.

'Viola!' he said, with relief and exasperation.

'Who else?' said Viola, coming down the steps. 'I wanted to be part of the last act, so I handed *Lady Windermere* to my understudy and motored down here.' But she looked around her and shivered, drawing her cape more closely about her shoulders. 'Although now I'm here, I wonder if I shouldn't have stayed with Windermere.'

'Yes, you should,' said Jack, relighting the candles and closing the door again. 'This was intended to be a very discreet manoeuvre.'

'I am being discreet. I motored down very unobtrusively – in the character of Vera Gilchrist,' she said. 'I bought a ticket for the performance, and after it was over, Tod Inkling recognized me, and waved me over to meet Professor James. We discussed the research I was collecting for my own professor. You remember my professor?'

'Vividly. But you can't stay here, Viola. Where's your motor? I'll take you back to it, and you can return London and Windermere and her fan.'

'The motor is parked on a grass verge near the lychgate,' said Viola. 'It's quite safe and more or less completely hidden in the trees. And I have no intention of returning to London until tomorrow at the earliest. I've taken a room at a very respectable hostelry in the next village – Great Mallory, it's called. I was looked at slightly askance – a single lady travelling alone, you understand – but I gave a very convincing portrayal of an earnest, rather eccentric academic lady, and they gave me a room. I stole out and drove here after everywhere was quiet.'

'And waited for me to appear,' said Jack, crossly.

'I guessed you'd come out here when everywhere was deserted, and I was right. I only had to wait a very short time before you prowled through the churchyard like a furtive ghost.

I prowled after you. I was very quiet,' she said, with an air of pleased hopefulness.

'No, you were not,' said Jack, at once. 'I heard something crashing around in the trees, but I thought it was foxes. Dammit, Viola, any churchyard is a lonely place at such an hour. You could have been pounced on by anyone.' He scowled, then said, 'But since you are here, before we go, I suppose you'd better see the Heads.'

'I thought you would never ask.' Even in the dim light, her lips curved into the mischievous three-cornered smile.

Jack led her to the corner and held up the candle so that its light fell across the high shelf, lending the Heads an eerie semblance of life.

Viola stared up at them, then said, softly, 'How sad. Those poor waifs. There's such trust in their expressions. But it's almost as if they're hiding up there – crouching in the darkness just under the roof, but peering down to see what's going on below. But that one at the very end – the one that's set a little apart from the others. That isn't a child, is it?'

She shivered slightly, and Jack said, 'No, it isn't. I wondered if it was someone who caught the Face Stealer in the act of killing – perhaps even confronted him – and was killed himself as a result.'

'And then was turned into stone along with the other victims,' said Viola. 'Sorry, I didn't mean to sound quite so biblical. Whoever he was, I don't think he was a particularly nice person,' she said. 'There's a look of sly malevolence, whereas the children—' She looked at them for another moment. 'What are those outlines just along from them, though? They're pushed quite far back, but I can just make them out. They're like the Heads, but there's something different.'

'They look like mirror images,' said Jack, holding up the candle as high as he could manage. 'Reverse likenesses.'

'Whatever they are, they don't somehow look solid, do they? Not like the main Heads. They're almost like masks. It looks as if each one is wedged or hung on to a stand.'

'They could be death masks,' said Jack, studying them. 'It's a grisly thought, but whoever sculpted the Heads might have taken some kind of wax impression straight after each one died.'

'And then created the Heads using the masks?'

'I think so, although I'm not very knowledgeable about sculpture. We'll speculate on all that later – when we actually manage to get the things into our hands. For now, Viola, we'd better get out of this place, because—'

He broke off and turned sharply to look towards the door.

'Someone's out there,' he said in a whisper, closing his hand warningly around her wrist.

'This is becoming more like Piccadilly Circus than a deserted mausoleum,' she said, softly, as he blew out the candle and pulled her towards a patch of denser shadows in the farthest corner. It was a kind of semi-alcove, and very narrow, but there was just room for them both. Jack put an arm around her, pressing the two of them against the wall.

The door opened slowly, and a figure was silhouetted against the night. There was the rasp of a match, and then a small lantern light flared up, showing the intruder to be a fairly tall man, dressed in dark clothes. It was still possible that this was an innocent visit, though, and Jack was just wondering if he dared reveal his own presence – although he had no idea what reason he could give for being in here – when the man lifted the lantern, shining it around the walls. Only then did Jack see that in his other hand he held a revolver.

Viola saw it as well – Jack felt her reaction, and he tightened his hold on her, feeling her heart beating fast against him.

As the man moved cautiously around the mausoleum, examining the walls, Jack thought that if it had not been for the revolver, he would almost certainly have challenged him. But an innocent, inquisitive local would hardly come in here with a gun, and in any kind of struggle, the gun might go off. And if that happened, Viola could be injured.

And then the lantern light fell across the man's face, and Jack felt as if something had closed tight painful fingers around his heart. The wild thought that if ever the dead walked, this was the kind of place where they would do so . . . But the dead did not walk. Or did they? Because the man's face, even

by the uncertain lantern light, was unmistakable. It was the
face of Jack's father.

The shadows swirled, and the stone walls seemed to close
in. It could not be Aiden; of course it could not – Aiden had
been dead for almost twenty years . . . Then fragments of
the family's talk dropped into Jack's mind, and he knew who
this was.

'. . . *a very attractive man, remarkably like your father to
look at . . .*' That had been Cecily.

And Uncle Rudraige had said: '. . . *they were so alike
as young men that you'd almost have thought they were
twins . . .*'

Of course this was not Jack's dead father. This was the
disgraced Fitzglen – the outcast who had cheated and deceived
people out of their money, and abused their trust, and who
had finally been banished from the family in that dramatic,
typically Fitzglen scene when Jack was still a child.

This was Simeon Fitzglen.

With the realization came anger, because how dared this
evil, heartless villain come sneaking and prowling in here to
steal a set of sculptures he had stolen once already? And over
and above that, how dared he look so much like Jack's long-
ago father that Jack had believed, in those crowded seconds,
that Aiden had somehow returned to him?

He felt Viola lean against him more closely, and wondered
if she had sensed something of his thoughts, because she
sometimes had the infuriating way of doing so. But even if
she had not, she would understand that they dared not reveal
their presence.

Simeon had seen the Heads now, and clearly he had not
known they would be so inaccessible. He looked around the
mausoleum, as Jack had done earlier, to see if there was
anything he could stand on. Jack tensed his muscles –
was this the moment he dared risk bounding forward? But
there was the revolver. And there was the knowledge that even
though this was not his father, if Jack launched an attack,
Simeon would look at him with Aiden's eyes, and if he did
that, Jack did not think he would be able to deal a single blow.
But once outside – once Simeon was going back through the

churchyard, it might be different. I'll follow him when he goes out, thought Jack. I'll persuade Viola to stay here, and I'll see where Simeon goes, and once I know that, I'll be able to outwit him. Make sure he doesn't get his hands on the Stone Heads.

Simeon had reached the door, and he was pulling it back. He stepped through it, pushing it shut behind him. Complete darkness closed down. In the softest whisper he could manage, Jack said to Viola, 'Stay here,' and started across the floor, not daring to light the candle again, and moving as quickly as the dense darkness allowed, praying not to trip.

He reached the steps and mounted them without mishap, then stood for moment, listening, because he needed to be sure Simeon had walked away through the forest before following him.

And then came a sound from the door's other side, and Jack felt a cold hand close around his heart, because he knew what the sound was.

Simeon was replacing the padlock and snapping it shut.

Jack and Viola were trapped inside the mausoleum.

TWENTY-TWO

Private journal of Catherine, 1762

It is almost autumn – a lovely season – and throughout the summer months I have hardly thought about Quintus. My Coronation, which took place at the Assumption Cathedral in Moscow last month, has occupied most of my time. It was a splendid, glittering ceremony, solemn and awesome, with soul-scaldingly beautiful music and inspirational prayers and vows. I felt proud and grateful and humble.

The Swiss-French court jeweller had designed a crown which he said he hoped would become known as the Imperial Coronation Crown of all Romanov emperors and empresses. It is a thing of such beauty – fashioned in two half spheres, one gold and one silver to represent the eastern and western Roman empires, the whole embellished with pearls and exquisite Indian diamonds. It shone with such radiance throughout the ceremony, and I felt it was genuinely a symbol of the immense responsibility that was being placed on me.

Celebrations took place throughout the land, and Moscow and many other cities were alight and alive with feasts and banquets and revels.

With all of that, if I thought about Quintus at all, it was only to remember that he was miles away, safely inside his monastery in Verkhoturye, and that he posed no threat to me. But today I know I was wrong – today I know the threat is reaching out to me. Because earlier a messenger delivered a letter from the Father Abbot of the Verkhoturye monastery. It is politely, albeit warily, phrased.

> To her most Serene Imperial Highness, Catherine Alexeyevna Romanova,
>
> Imperial Highness, I send this under the seal of my House's secrecy. The messenger who will deliver it

into your hands is Brother Kirill, whom I trust implicitly. He will carry back any reply you wish and that you feel able to make.

Two days ago, the priest of the local church in Cympak – one of the tiny villages that lies below this monastery – sought audience with me. He was deeply troubled. A gift had been made to his church by an anonymous donor. It had apparently been left at the door of the church during the night hours.

Anonymous gifts are occasionally made, of course, although I do not recall one ever being received in Cympak, which is a small place and has scant significance in the greater world. However, it lies on what is sometimes called the travellers' route, which means the carriages of the wealthy not infrequently pass through.

The gift is a set of sculpted heads – stone or possibly clay – which are almost exact replicas of three local children who vanished some weeks ago. The families have been hoping the children will be found safe and well – there were two boys, who were cousins, and a girl who was sister to the elder boy. Prayers and services have been held, asking that the children be found safe and well.

However, with the stone heads were what are clearly death masks – impressions that can only have been taken from the children's dead bodies, and the sculptures then created from them. With great distress, it is therefore being accepted by the two families that their children are dead. In sinister confirmation of this, a brief accompanying letter with the sculptures explained that they, and the masks, were intended as memorials to the children.

The little community is deeply disturbed. The two families would like to accept these strange pieces as memorials, but they, and almost everyone else, believe they can only have been sent to Cympak by the abductor – and therefore the murderer – of the children. If they are indeed dead – as seems almost certain – the parents have not the means to commission anything in the way of a carved panel or inscribed scroll within the church, and unless the bodies are found, there cannot, of course, be graves – something that might have brought at least a modicum of comfort. As a result, they are in deep distress, not knowing if they can or should accept these strange sculptures as something to mark their loss and perhaps in some small way assuage it, or whether there is a sinister purpose behind the gift.

It was only when the sculptures were examined more closely that the local priest sought my guidance. There is, I am afraid, a shocking and possibly dangerous aspect to the heads. It pains me to write that the danger is directed towards your Imperial Highness.

We have no means of knowing from where the gift came, nor the identity of the sculptor – who may well be a murderer – and we are chary of making enquiries for fear of drawing attention to the situation – and to your Highness.

I dare not send any more details to you in a letter, for although Brother Kirill is infinitely to be trusted, there is no knowing into what other hands this missive may inadvertently fall.

I have not travelled beyond these walls for many years, mainly due to the infirmity of age. I feel strongly, however, that it is imperative for you to know of the potential danger within these sculptures, and I therefore request, most humbly, that you come to Verkhoturye. It is not a request I make lightly.

We are a modest Order, but would offer the best of our hospitality to you and to any trusted members of your household who might accompany you.

I send you my blessings and assure you of my unfailing loyalty and duty to you and to the Imperial House of Romanov.

Father Ignatius

Father Abbot of the Order of St Nicholas, Verkhoturye.

When I read this, the words seemed almost to leap off the page and close icy fingers around my heart.

But now, alone in my bedchamber, it is not the unnamed danger that is twisting my heart; it is the three lost children. Two boys and a girl. That has revived memories I thought I had suppressed.

I have never set those memories down in these pages before, but I am compelled to do so now. My own memorial to the three lost children of my own.

My two boys – one taken from me so he could be brought up by others, because one day he will ascend the Imperial Throne. I have had almost no part in his life. The other who must be kept secret from the world, because he is illegitimate and might be seized by unscrupulous men who plot to place pretenders on thrones, or lead revolutions . . . Tsarinas are not supposed to give birth to bastards, to sons fathered not by their husbands but by enterprising and forceful lovers who have an eye to the Imperial Throne . . . I accepted what had to be, but it does not stop it from driving a knife into me.

As for the third loss – that little helpless one who only lived for a few months – that is the worst pain of all. I still see her small, trustful face in dreams, and I think I always will.

And so I have some understanding of how those parents would have seized gratefully on the unexpected appearance of the images of their lost ones, seeing them as memorials. I would seize just as gratefully on any likenesses of my children, all of whom are lost to me almost as completely as the three children who vanished in Cympak.

But my losses must be borne alone, and I must turn my mind to the warning Father Ignatius has sent. If it were not for the letter having come from the monastery at Verkhoturye, I might be tempted to dismiss it. But I cannot, for within that monastery is Quintus, and although Grigory and Alexei planned and were responsible for Peter's death, it was Quintus who murdered him – who administered poison to him in that stone cell at Ropsha. I think I have always known Quintus would one day re-enter my life.

Copying Father Ignatius's letter into this journal has made me wish that at my side could be that imaginary lover I have sometimes longed for – the man who certainly does not exist, but who, if he did, would understand the tangled emotions Father Ignatius's words have churned up.

I must face the fact that I shall have to travel to Verkhoturye. It will be difficult, but not as difficult as it would have been if the Court were still at the Winter Palace, for I am presently at my beloved Yekaterinburg, where I travelled for a brief stay after the Coronation. I derive great pleasure from being here; it is still what people consider a 'new' city, but I believe it could have great events ahead of it. More to the point, I think that from here Verkhoturye is only a single day's journey.

Any journey I make is invariably lavish and extravagant, involving servants and attendants and courtiers. Outriders flank my carriage along the highways, and often a detachment of the Imperial Guard gallops alongside as well. As we near our destination, fanfares of trumpets sound, and people come out to line the streets and cheer. It is all very splendid, and the demonstrations of loyalty are gratifying, but none of it allows for inconspicuous travelling. I have sometimes thought that for every hundred cheering people, there are as many more who are resentful at the sight of such a richly clad procession – especially in the poorer parts of the land. I know people are angry at the years of war, as well – the conflicts have lasted far longer than anyone ever imagined, and are causing much financial distress. And it is a war that has created strange bedfellows: Prussia with Great Britain, France with Spain and Saxony.

Earlier, I showed Father Ignatius's letter to Grigory. It could not be avoided. But I must write that a strangeness has crept into our relationship of late. Is that what murder does? Drives a wedge between people who once had been extremely close?

He tried to dismiss the letter's contents, and said it would all prove to be some unimportant tale by a religious house hoping for rewards or honours, but when he saw I did not accept his view, he changed direction, saying Father Ignatius would simply be exaggerating some small transgression – spinning gold from straw.

'And it will turn out to be tarnished gold, Highness,' he

said. 'He will be trying to garner favour with you. Monks can be very venal.'

I do not believe him. St Nicholas's Monastery is neither insignificant nor small; it is an old and venerable house and I cannot think its Abbot would have written such a missive lightly, and certainly not falsely. And haven't I known, since the night Peter died, that Verkhoturye harboured a menace? And that Quintus was that menace?

But when I said this, Grigory replied loftily that if there were to be any trouble from Quintus, he would know how to deal with it. He squared his shoulders and cracked his knuckles by way of a display of force, and looked at me, clearly waiting for swooning approval.

I do not, however, swoon when gentlemen crack their knuckles to indicate their strength, and nor do I think physical threats would deter Quintus. He would use subtlety and cunning by way of retaliation, and he would probably emerge the victor.

But Grigory clearly considered he had indicated his superior power and reasoning; he smiled at me with what was very nearly condescension, then reached for the lacings of my gown as if it was his right to do so. It is not his right, but I could not allow my annoyance to show, since I need his help to get to Verkhoturye.

Also, I will acknowledge that he is a good lover – very adroit, and possessed of remarkable stamina. The stamina on this occasion meant it was almost dawn before he left my bedchamber. After he had gone, I consoled myself by remembering I can have his head struck from his shoulders if I wish – there are sure to be any number of justifiable reasons for such an action.

Anya is shocked to her toes to hear that I am embarking on what I have told her is to be a very discreet journey, for which she will not be required. She asked, huffily, how I thought I should manage to dress or arrange my hair without her assistance. When I said I was quite capable of putting on a gown or two, and brushing my hair for myself, she sniffed and said she was never one to push in where she was not wanted, and asked if she should pack the amber silk and the peacock-blue brocade for the journey.

I do not dare take any servants on this journey, and I certainly dare not take Anya, who I suspect pries and spies into everything in case she can turn it into money. There has, though, been a little talk among the servants about the journey, but I think it is of a somewhat prurient – although also indulgent – kind. It seems most of the servants believe Her Highness is setting off to meet a lover – and nothing unusual about that, they say with sly relish. I have the impression they think for me to make a journey in this unusual way – one carriage only and not a single servant! – can only mean the lover is either disreputable or unsuitable, or possibly both. They have most likely decided I am about to leap into bed with one of Russia's enemies – some glittering-eyed sultan who serves the Turk, Mustafa III.

I should not dream of doing such a thing. Of course I should not.

Three days have passed since the arrival of the letter, but my planning and care has worked. Finally and at last, I am inside St Nicholas's Monastery of Verkhoturye.

The journey was made more swiftly than I had dared hope. It felt strange not to have at least three or four carriages following us, their roofs piled with luggage, and a retinue of servants crammed inside. But there are only Grigory, Alexei and me, as well as two coachmen who are part of the Yekaterinburg stables, and have their living quarters there. According to Alexei, they live their own life, entirely apart from the indoor servants, so they are unlikely to gossip or spread tales.

Twilight was falling when the carriage began the ascent of the mountain road leading to the monastery. The skies were dark and storm clouds were massing – there was the feeling that they were pressing down on us. Faint growls of thunder reached us, causing the horses to toss their heads uneasily. The nearer we got to the monastery, the nearer the storm seemed to get to us. It would have been absurd to think it was no storm, but rather the darkness inside the monastery sensing our approach and summoning its strength, and I did not really think it, or not for more than a moment or two here and there, anyway.

Halfway up the track, someone – presumably the monks – had placed flaring torches at the sides, which I told Grigory and Alexei was very welcoming.

'They are lighting our way to them,' I said, and frowned when Alexei said it was more likely the monks did not want stranded carriages or dead horses or injured Tsarinas littering their path. He had not wanted to come with us, of course; he was in favour of either ignoring the letter or sending a terse reply to Father Ignatius, saying anonymous gifts of sculptures in insignificant villages no one had ever heard of were nothing to do with the Court of Her Imperial Highness. But I had made it an order that he accompany me, and he had not dared disobey.

Whatever powers rule the elements appeared to have decreed that our first sight of the old monastery should coincide with the breaking of the storm in good earnest. As we rounded the final curve in the narrow road, thunder crashed deafeningly overhead, and lightning split the skies. And there, at the heart of the livid lightning, was the ancient Monastery of St Nicholas.

We were greeted by two monks who must have been watching for our arrival. One introduced himself as Brother Kirill; he has a face like seamed oak and extremely intelligent eyes, and is the monk who had delivered the letter.

The horses and the carriage and coachmen were taken to what I suppose are the monastery's stables. It had not occurred to me that monks would have horses, but this is a remote place and they would have to have means of bringing provisions out here.

I am writing this in a surprisingly comfortable room, where I am to spend the night. The walls are of thick stone, but they are softened and warmed with wall hangings. The hangings are dim with age, but they are still beautiful, depicting various religious scenes and saints. There is a marble-topped washstand, with a tall ewer filled with warm water, wrapped in a thick, soft towel. There are rugs on the floor, and the bed, although narrow, feels perfectly comfortable.

The windows are barred – I am unsure of the reason for that, unless it's thought the monks might try to stage an escape on some moonless night. Or perhaps, in the distant past, this place was a kind of stronghold or fortress used to house prisoners. Having spent large portions of my life in ancient strongholds with grim histories, bars and stone walls do not trouble me. And through them, even though night has fallen, I can make out soaring mountains against the night sky. The storm has grumbled its way out, and the monastery has the feeling of being shrouded in a quiet peace. And yet . . .

And yet somewhere inside this place dwells that cold darkness that is Quintus.

I shall close these pages for the moment, because footsteps are approaching my door.

The footsteps were followed by a polite knock on my door, and the reappearance of Brother Kirill, who explained that Father Abbot courteously requested my presence in his study at the tolling of seven. Therefore, I am making this entry hastily.

It is a new experience to be summoned by the head of a religious house. I shall remain in the rather plain garments in which I travelled – a gown of dark blue silk, which I feel is sufficiently subdued for the occasion. I have, however, added an azure surcoat and wound what are really very modest sapphires around my neck and wrists. I have even managed to put my hair into reasonable order – it is necessarily a much simpler style than I am used to, but I think it is reasonably becoming.

Note: I am aware appearance does not matter, especially in a monastery, and I am also aware that it matters even less when facing what is apparently danger. But I refuse to confront dangers of any kind with visible crumples in my gown, and with my hair in disarray.

TWENTY-THREE

Private journal of Catherine, 1762 (cont'd)
Verkhoturye, midnight

It is very late, and the monastery is shrouded in silence. But I cannot sleep – my mind is too full of emotions, and they are emotions for which I am struggling to find words. I am hoping that to write everything down will calm my mind, even though I am not sure my mind will ever feel calm again.

As I was shown into Father Ignatius's study, Grigory and Alexei entered, and we were bidden to seats.

The good father was much as I had expected: elderly and with a papery fragility to his skin – a mixture of age, ill health and the strict regime he will have observed for most of his life. His study had an air of dogged austerity, as if it was determined not to be taken frivolously – but the severity was softened by the rows of books that lined the walls, and by the leather-topped desk. On that desk were placed two large boxes. Father Ignatius indicated them, and said, 'Imperial Highness, you know from my letter what these boxes contain. But we – Father Kirill and I – decided that there were things about them that we dare not set down in a letter – that you must see them for yourself.' He nodded to Brother Kirill, who folded back the lids of each box, removed layers of cotton waste and lifted out what was inside.

I had thought I was prepared, but I had not been prepared for the heads to be so lifelike. They were not the work of a great artist, of course – that is a statement I think I can make with reasonable confidence, for I have seen – and often been presented with – sculptures created by some of the great craftsmen of this century and of previous centuries, too.

These sculptures certainly did not fall into that class, and yet their creator had captured something that made them compelling. They appeared to be stone – or, as Father Ignatius's letter had said, possibly clay. Three were children, but the fourth was an older man. He had a sly, furtive look about him, and his likeness seemed to have been forged from a different substance, for it was darker, the surface more coarse-grained than the children.

The children. It is difficult to describe, even now, in this quiet room, how deeply the sight of those children's cold, dead faces affected me. Children should not look cold and dead – nor should they look remote. The tragedy of the disappearance – and presumably the death – of them, and the anguish it must have caused their parents, fell upon me like a smothering darkness. A child – the most precious gift of all . . . Memories came scalding in, but I managed to push them away. They served no purpose, and I would not allow anyone to see how I felt – not even Grigory, who might have been thought to share the loss of our boy, conceived in delight, but exiled from my Court and my life. He does not share it, though; I have known that for a long while.

'The children have been identified by their parents as the three who vanished,' Father Ignatius was saying. 'The boys were cousins, and the girl is the sister of the elder boy.'

It was the girl whose image was the most deeply upsetting. I could too easily believe my own tiny daughter would have looked like this now if she had lived – tip-tilted eyes, a mouth intended for mischief . . .

I pushed the thoughts away, for Grigory was asking about the fourth head, and there was something in his tone that jarred unpleasantly. 'Who is he, that older man?' he was saying.

'We have no idea. He is not someone either I or Brother Kirill recognize.'

Grigory stared at this darker piece for a moment, his brows drawn down in a black frown. Then he made an angry gesture as if to brush away something unimportant, and said, angrily, 'I do not see, Father Abbot, why you considered it necessary for Her Imperial Highness to travel out here.'

'To do no more than look at some pieces of stone,' put in Alexei.

'But,' said Father Ignatius, 'have you not seen what is carved into the base of each?'

At the words, Brother Kirill moved one of the double-branched candlesticks so that its light fell more clearly across the heads, and I felt that cold darkness engulf me more strongly than it had ever done.

A number had been carved into each head. Odin – one. Dva – two. Tri – three. Chetyre – four. Brother Kirill had arranged the pieces so that the numbers read from left to right, in sequence. One to four. And next to each number were words.

Odin was inscribed with my name. *Catherine Romanova.*

Dva, the second one, with the words '*murdered her husband*'.

Tri, the third in the row, had the words '*Tsar Peter, III*'.

Chetyre, number four, said, '*Ropsha, 1762.*'

The words seemed to dance wildly before my eyes, then they settled into a sentence – terrible, accusing, damning.

Catherine Romanova murdered her husband, Tsar Peter III, Ropsha 1762.

For what felt like a very long time, neither I nor the Orlov brothers spoke. But at last, I became aware of Father Ignatius saying that neither he nor Brother Kirill knew the identity of the anonymous donor.

'And no more does the priest in Cympak,' he said. 'We do not know, either, if the donor is also the sculptor, or whether he – we believe it will be a man – commissioned the work from some unknown craftsman.'

I knew, of course, that whoever the sculptor might be, Quintus was at the heart of this. This was his revenge for being turned out of the Winter Palace after he had served Grigory and Alexei's purpose. Because of course those two would have held out the promise of rich reward for what they were asking of him. And then cheated him of it.

Grigory said, angrily, 'Whoever is responsible, the sculptures must, of course, be destroyed without delay. They must be smashed to fragments.'

I heard my voice say with authority, 'No!' and Father Ignatius looked at me with slight surprise. 'They are not to be destroyed,' I said. 'Whatever else they might be – whatever dark purpose might be behind their appearance – they are a memorial to those lost children.'

And that being so, I cannot bear to let them be lost, because I know what it is to lose children, and although I know it to be absurd, it is as if these three represent my own lost ones . . . I looked across at Grigory, willing him to sense my thoughts, but he did not meet my eyes, so I turned back to Father Ignatius, who was saying, 'A memorial to the lost children is certainly what the parents would wish. It would be a comfort to them. The heads need not be on display – it could be said that they are being kept quietly and privately, but in safety.'

'We could make it sound as if it were only a temporary arrangement,' said Brother Kirill, tentatively.

'That would be to tamper with the truth,' said Father Ignatius, with a touch of reproof. Then, in a completely different tone, he said, 'But I believe your Imperial Highness will understand me when I say that here at St Nicholas's Monastery we have always been your most loyal subjects – in all matters. Throughout this strange and troubling time, we shall hold firm to that loyalty.'

He looked at me very straightly, and I understood he was telling me that the carved accusation did not trouble him – that, in so far as he could, he would ally himself with me. I had no idea whether he gave credence to the words, but what I did know was that Peter had consistently annoyed and offended the Church. He had imperiously ordered the liberation of serfs on Church land, and he had certainly never troubled to conceal his contempt for Russian Orthodoxy. Meeting the bright, intelligent eyes of Father Abbot, I had the feeling that a friend had put out a hand to take mine, and it was astonishingly comforting.

I said, 'I understand, Father Abbot,' and he smiled as if satisfied.

But Grigory, on whom any display of subtlety or sensitivity is almost always lost, said, belligerently, 'The sculptures cannot be left intact. It is too dangerous. The accusation—'

'The accusation is the spite of some poor twisted – perhaps jealous – mind,' said Father Ignatius. 'Entirely false and without foundation. That is understood.'

'But it is an accusation that cannot be allowed to be

known beyond these walls,' said Grigory. 'I must insist that the heads are destroyed. It's the only way we can be sure that Her Highness is safe from dangerous rumour and speculation.'

Alexei said, 'Could the inscriptions be removed in some way? Scraped off with some suitable implement? I have not the knowledge of such things, of course—' A slightly dismissive shrug as if consigning such matters to the lowest class of tradesman.

Brother Kirill said, 'We had considered that, but it would involve several of the younger monks working on them – mostly the novices who are learning woodturning and stonemasonry. The words are very deeply carved, you understand. It would be a lengthy process.'

'You are saying your monks might talk?' demanded Grigory.

'They might do so quite innocently. But such talk could spread. There are also sometimes people from outside who come here with deliveries and suchlike,' said Brother Kirill. 'They might see the carved words.'

'The people of Cympak did not notice them,' said Father Ignatius. 'It was the children's likenesses that took their attention. Many of them are unable to read anyway. But if they came to hear of the accusation against Her Imperial Highness— Well, it is too great a risk to take. Instead, we have it in mind to keep the sculptures – and the death masks – locked away here. There is a small room deep within the crypt – a grim little place it is, but it is rare for anyone to go there. Once inside, with a stout padlock on the door, no one would know the heads were there. No one would see them or know of the carved words. Only Brother Kirill and I would know they were there.'

'That is the solution of weakness,' said Grigory, angrily. 'The things should be smashed to splinters.' His fists curled as if already around the handle of a hammer or a mallet. I winced, for I saw in my mind's eye that hammer, that mallet, being brought viciously and uncaringly down on the trustful faces looking at me now – grinding those faces to fragments. Eyes, cheekbones, lips, all reduced to unrecognizable shards.

Father Ignatius said, composedly, 'There is another aspect

you are not considering, Count,' and turned back to me. 'Highness, clearly you have a most vindictive enemy – someone with a mind so warped, but also so cunning . . .' He paused, then said, 'But whoever he is, I believe he will want to reclaim these heads, and that being so, they could be used to trap him. If it were to be made generally known – perhaps via the Cympak priest – that they are being kept inside the monastery, it is possible that your enemy will try to get at them.'

'In order to try again to make the accusation known to the world,' I said.

'Yes.' He smiled at me approvingly, and I was absurdly pleased. 'If that happens – if we keep careful watch – we should be able to imprison this creature. A suitable – and discreet – justice could then be administered. You would know how best that could be done, and how it could be managed without anything becoming known to the wider world.'

I looked at him for a long moment. His reasoning was sound, of course, but the path he proposed we tread would be a risky one. If Quintus were to be unmasked, however careful or discreet the justice meted out to him, he would turn on his accusers like a cornered rat and reveal what Grigory and Alexei had done. I glanced at them both, and knew we shared that realization. Surely it would be better – safer – to destroy the heads? But then I looked back at the desk, and the children's eyes seemed to meet mine, and I heard myself say, 'I agree to your plan, Father. And the heads must not be destroyed.'

Returning to Yekaterinburg in the carriage the following day, Grigory said, 'We know, of course, who is the enemy Father Abbot referred to.'

Alexei glanced warningly to the window, to remind him of the coachman seated on his box, but the windows were tightly shut, and Grigory had spoken softly.

'I should like,' he went on, his fists clenching, 'to drag Brother Quintus to face his punishment with my own hands.'

I said, 'I do not think Father Abbot's idea of using the heads as bait will succeed. He has no idea that the culprit is in their midst, and Quintus is no fool – he will recognize the trap for what it is.' I frowned, then said, 'Do you think Quintus was the actual sculptor of those heads?'

'I think it's likely,' said Alexei. 'His father undertook that kind of work in Cympak.' He glanced at Grigory, and I had the impression that something – some shared knowledge – passed between them.

But Grigory only said, 'Even if the monks did unmask him, I am not sure they would believe in his guilt.'

'Even then, they might protect him,' said Alexei. 'The Church – any church – is very good at looking after its own. They might deal with him themselves, privately, within the community.'

'If he were to be brought to open justice, he would incriminate us all,' said Grigory. 'He would be facing certain execution – he would have nothing to lose; he would fight for all he was worth, and there would be people who would believe the accusation. I am sorry to say this, Highness, but there is a good deal of resentment in the country. The war has gone on for so long.'

'I am aware of it,' I said, and added, sharply, 'You do not forget, I hope, that I had no knowledge of what was done to my husband.'

Grigory recognized the imperious note in my voice at once. It is rare I employ it with him, but there are times . . .

He said, 'I do not forget, Highness, but I still believe it would be far better and safer if those cursed sculptures could be destroyed.'

'Is there a way we could force Father Abbot to do that?' asked Alexei.

'No,' I said, quickly.

'Will Quintus acknowledge his ploy failed?' he asked. 'Mightn't it be the last we'll hear of him?'

'Oh, no,' I said at once. 'He will never accept failure.' I paused, frowning, then said, 'He intends to destroy us. I do not yet know what he will do next, but I am convinced he will think of another way to have his revenge.'

That single word, *revenge*, seemed to scribble itself on the air and hover there for a moment, cold and dripping and deadly.

Private journal of Catherine, 1762 (cont'd)

An entire month has passed since the brief, strange visit to Verkhoturye.

I had hoped that once we reached Yekaterinburg – and when later we were back in the Winter Palace – I would be able to forget Quintus. I had thought he would be driven from my mind by all the ceremonies and formalities I have to attend, and by all the state business and imperial duties I must deal with – there are a great many of those, and some are interesting and some are exciting, but a great many are tedious in the extreme.

I do not think I will ever be able to forget Quintus, though. I will certainly never forget the sight of those children. At night, in dreams, I see their imploring faces, upturned as if seeking the light, as if the blind eyes are pleading to be brought out of the darkness and able to look on the world once more. That is absurd and fanciful, of course; they are inanimate lumps of granite and clay.

Just as I will never forget those children, nor will I forget those words carved into the bases: *Catherine Romanova murdered her husband, Tsar Peter III, Ropsha 1762.*

I did not murder Peter, but I know Grigory is right to say there are sections of the people who would believe the accusation if they found out about it – and who would seize on it to cause violence and disturbance. But I trust Father Ignatius. He understands and he will keep the Stone Heads shut away.

I think I would do anything to ensure they are never seen again.

TWENTY-FOUR

Verkhoturye, 1771

H arry Fitzglen acknowledged – albeit reluctantly – that this Russian Romanov idyll would not – could not – last indefinitely. When it came to the parting, it would be a wrench – he thought it would probably be the most painful parting he had yet experienced, but he knew parting was inevitable. Catherine would know it as well, of course; they would talk about it when the time seemed right. But not yet, thought Harry. Not quite yet.

There was also the inescapable fact that he would soon have to start thinking about replenishing his coffers. There was a certain irony in the fact that while he was sharing the Tsarina's bed, he was within filching distance of more exotic and valuable jewels than he was likely to encounter ever again. Once or twice he amused himself by considering ways and means to steal the Imperial Romanov crown, but even as he did so, he knew it was a wild, impractical dream. I'm good, thought Harry, but I'm not that good. And where on earth would I dispose of the thing afterwards?

The icons taken from the Sevastopol exhibition would bring a very good sum of money when sold, but he did not think he could risk selling them in this part of Russia – perhaps not even anywhere in Russia. Hard on the heels of this thought came a memory of London and a sudden longing to be there once more; to be surrounded by a swirling London fog, to hear his own language spoken, to walk into a coffee house in Fleet Street or Maiden Lane and be welcomed by acquaintances. But for the moment, there was this place and there was Catherine – his lips curved in a smile as the name slid silkily across his mind.

As well as that, though, there was the mysterious place, Verkhoturye, ahead of them. Harry had not forgotten the abrupt

silence that had greeted him when he mentioned it in
Sevastopol, and he had certainly not forgotten Catherine's
unmistakable fear of the place. The nearer they got to it, the
more he was becoming aware of something drawing him in
– like one of the dark siren calls of the creatures of myth.
This was an absurd way to think, though, because what he
was really interested in was whether it might provide good
hunting ground for the polite removal of valuable objects.

There's only one way to find out, thought Harry, and that's
to reconnoitre the terrain. Accordingly, two nights later, when
the barges were moored for the night, and lights showed
intermittently in the cluster of buildings a mile or so inland,
he donned the dark cloak he had been wearing on his arrival,
added the deep-brimmed hat that shadowed his face, and
walked casually down to the shore. He did not think
anyone saw him leave, but it would not matter if anyone had,
because he would say – with a touch of arrogant surprise –
that he was taking a late-night stroll along the bank.

Earlier in the evening, someone had said that one of the
little places they would visit on their way to Verkhoturye's
heart was called Cympak, and had vaguely indicated it along
the shoreline. The name was a loose translation of twilight or
dusk, apparently, said the speaker, and somebody else chimed
in saying it was supposed to have come about because of being
in the shadow of the ancient Monastery of St Nicholas.

From the barge and from the riverbank, it had been
impossible to tell if Cympak and its environs was a shadow
place in truth, and it was certainly impossible to tell if it was
at all prosperous. Surely, though, there would be at least one
big house that would be worth investigating. But the closer
he got to the dark huddle of dwellings, the less likely this
seemed. A small church tower rose up against the night sky,
but the roofs of most of the surrounding houses were low and
shallow, and the streets were narrow and cobbled. It was a little
after ten o'clock, and here and there, a dim light burned from
a window, but as he stepped out into a small square with jutting
bow-fronted windows displaying various wares, he heard
laughter and cheerful voices and the chink of glasses. A tavern?
If so, it might be worth investigating; people in taverns talked,

and it was possible he would hear details of wealthy local residents, whose houses might be worth investigating.

As he went towards the sounds, he glanced with slight unease into the narrow alleys that led off the square. They were mostly in darkness, the buildings huddled together, some linked by overhead stone arches that spanned the street and blotted out any light that was trying to filter in. Several times, Harry thought something moved within the shadows, and once he heard what he thought were soft footsteps padding after him, but when he turned to look, there was no one to be seen.

The tavern was in one of the streets leading off the square. It was small, but there were flaring lanterns over the door, and, once inside, it felt warm and friendly. There was a long, low-ceilinged room with a fire crackling at one end, and men seated at small tables, quaffing what Harry thought would be local ale. As he stood in the doorway, a few of the drinkers turned to look at him. Several raised their tankards in his direction, in vague welcome, and a murmur of 'traveller' went round.

Harry nodded to them, made his way to the little bar in the corner and requested a tankard of ale.

'French?' said the aproned barman, and Harry nodded because it was easier to agree. He drank some of the ale, found it very palatable and smiled in appreciation.

He stood by the bar, pleased that his knowledge of Russian was enabling him to understand a fair amount of the various lively discussions, enjoying the warm, friendly atmosphere. But then, between one heartbeat and the next, the atmosphere changed – the talk and laughter faded, and, almost as one, the men turned to look towards the door.

'Out there again tonight,' said one of them, in a low voice. 'Hear him, can you?'

There was a low murmur of assent, and somebody said it was the hour anyway.

'He don't come so very often, but when he does, it's always around this hour.'

'One of these nights, we'll go out there and catch him,' said a third man.

'You won't catch him,' said the first. 'Haven't folk tried a number of times? He's too fly by half – he whisks into the shadows, and the darkness swallows him up as greedily as if he was part of it.'

The words lay on the air, and the moment lengthened. Then something moved beyond the window – a shadow, was it? Or was it only that the moon had gone behind a cloud or the candles in here had flickered in a draught of air?

Harry looked around the room, seeing a remarkable assortment of emotions in the faces – not fear, precisely, but certainly unease.

The shadow seemed to come closer to the window, as if it was pressing against the small panes of glass, trying to peer in, and Harry saw the men nearest draw back slightly. Whatever this is, he thought, they don't want to see it, or even admit it's there. In a moment, they'll start talking and laughing again – that game of cards in the corner will resume and everything will be ordinary again. Because there isn't anything there – or is there? But he knew there was something outside the tavern window, and the talking and laughing did not start again; the cards lay where they were, and he had the sense the men were waiting for something.

Into the strange uneasy silence came a voice, chanting softly, but not so softly the words could not be heard.

'Beware, beware, the Face Stealer's hands,
'Run for your life if he comes.
'For he'll snatch you all up in his murderer's hands
'And carry you off to his lair down below . . .'

At first, Harry thought he had misunderstood – that his knowledge of the language was not so good, after all – and then he looked about him and saw the expressions on the drinkers' faces, and knew he had not misunderstood at all. But was the rhyme a warning or a threat? Whoever this Face Stealer creature was, he had murderer's hands to snatch up his victims . . . Harry drew his cape more tightly around him and was glad he was in a room with other people.

Then the shadow seemed to dissolve, and there was only the dark street outside, and perhaps, after all, he had misunderstood. The men were already turning back to their

discourse and their card games, and although Harry caught
something from a couple of them about double-locking doors
and bolting windows, the moment had passed. He finished his
ale, nodded a farewell to the barman and made his way out
to the street.

It was approaching eleven o'clock, and apart from the lights
within the tavern and a scattering of candles in a few windows,
the streets seemed deserted.

Harry was about to make his way back to the barge, but a
church clock chimed the hour, and he decided he might as
well make his way towards the church and glance inside.
However modest it might be, if it were open – which probably
it would be – there might be something to learn about this
village, and also about Verkhoturye. And about the Face
Stealer? said his mind. But that had surely only been some
strange, quarter-witted local, wandering around.

He liked the church, which was small, but looked as if it
was well cared for, and when he tried the door in the deep
porch, it swung open smoothly. A pleasing scent of beeswax
mingled with incense greeted him, and moonlight slid through
latticed windows and lay across the polished wood of the pews.
Tall stained-glass windows were set into some of the walls,
casting harlequin patterns over the small altar. Harry
approached it quietly and slowly, not wanting to disturb the
serene silence. Laid out on the altar was what he thought was
an ornate Book of the Gospels, open at a page with beautiful
illuminated script; alongside it was a bronze altar lamp,
intricately carved. Beautiful, thought Harry, and he was aware
of a pang of regret that it was one of his unbreakable rules
never to filch from any kind of religious building.

After a moment, he stepped back from the altar, not quite
genuflecting, but making a brief half-bow of obeisance, when
a sound from outside sent his pulse racing. Was someone out
there? Yes, he could hear footsteps.

There was no real reason why he could not openly admit
he was travelling through the area and had come to look
at the local church when it would be empty – it was late, but
not as late as all that. But the recent memory of the sinister
figure who had stood at the tavern window was still with him,

and instinct caused him to step back behind a carved pillar, into deep shadow. He drew his cloak closely around him and stood very still. Probably, it would be the local priest, who had heard him and come along to investigate. If so, he would only glance around to make sure all was well, and then leave. Alternatively, it might be someone here to hold a night vigil, in which case Harry could be trapped until dawn. What was the earliest service held in the Russian Church? Prime, was it? Or Lauds?

The footsteps were soft and light, and after a moment, he realized they were walking all the way around the church. The dark cold he had sensed in the tavern brushed into his face again, and he was just calculating whether he could dart out of hiding, and be through the door and away into the night before the prowler realized it, when the chanting began.

And this time, he was not hearing it through the closed door and shuttered window of the local tavern. This time, it was coming from the open door of the church, and the words were very clear indeed.

He leaned cautiously forward, until he could see the outline of the door, which was still open. Silhouetted in it was a cloaked figure, the hood of the cloak pulled over its head, hiding the face. The hands were folded, monastic fashion, but there was nothing religious about the way the figure turned its head, as if searching every corner of the shadowy church.

The words of the chant reached him easily.

'Beware, beware, the Face Stealer's hands,
'Run for your life if he comes.
'For he'll snatch you all up in his murderer's hands
'And carry you off to his lair down below,
'Where the iron teeth clang and the river-light glows
'And the water lies waiting for prey.'

The whispering, slightly hoarse voice and the macabre words trickled through the serene old church, and this time Harry could hear a sly, gloating note in the voice, as if the speaker was relishing the lines. Earlier, he had been unable to decide if the rhyme was a warning or a threat, but standing here, he knew it for a threat.

The hooded head turned slowly from side to side again, and

Harry remained absolutely still, hardly even daring to breathe. For a brief moment, he considered stepping out of hiding and calling out, but he knew he would not. It was not so much that the figure was menacing – although it was – it was that unmistakable taint of madness that hung about it. Harry thought he was probably as courageous as most men, but he was certainly not going to confront an unknown madman in a dark old church, with no one likely to hear if he yelled for help. And surely, in a minute, the eerie chanting would stop, and he would be able to return to the barge.

But the chanting did not stop. The figure leaned its head forward again, as if peering into the shadows to see what might lurk there, then the rhyme started up again.

'*Wrapped in a cloak and hidden from sight,*
'*He's ordered by Catherine to steal through the night.*
'*Commanded to smother the secrets concealed –*
'*And stifle the murder she dare not reveal.*
'*For that royal Romanova – that murderess damned –*
'*Controls the Face Stealer and gives the command*
'*That those who might know or suspect or mistrust*
'*Are turned by the Face Stealer to stone and to dust.*
'*So never agree to the Face Stealer's game,*
'*Run for your life if he comes.*
'*For when the game's ending, you'll draw your last breath*
'*And the game will result in you meeting your death.*
'*As Peter met his death in Ropsha that night*
'*By Catherine's command and imperious might.*'

Dawn was not yet streaking the skies when Harry finally reached the barge, and it was too early for the servants to be around.

Reaching the privacy of the cabin allotted to him, he sat on the bed, staring through the tiny porthole at the dark river. I suppose I didn't dream any of that? he thought. I suppose I haven't been inside this cabin all the time, and had a nightmare? And even if it was real, how can I be sure I understood what that macabre creature was chanting?

It seemed an endless time before daylight began to streak the sky, and Harry finally made his way to Catherine's bedchamber. She donned one of her sumptuous robes, and

reclined on the bed, and Harry entertained the brief thought
that even at this hour, with her hair unbound, she was lovely
and graceful and compelling.

She listened in silence to his story of the robed and hooded
creature and the half-chanted, half-whispered lines.

'The royal Romanova – that murderess damned –

'Controls the Face Stealer and gives the command.'

And then, the final lines:

'. . . Peter met his death in Ropsha that night

'By Catherine's command and imperious might.'

At first, Harry thought she was stunned, and then he thought
she was furious, and there was a bad moment when he
thought the fury was for him – that she might be about to
have him thrown off the barge – even order him to be flung
into prison.

But he waited, and at last she said, 'Did you believe what
the rhyme said?'

'No.'

'You would say that, of course.'

'I believe you are capable of many things, but not outright
murder. And certainly not the murder of your own husband.'

'His death gave me the Imperial Throne,' said the Tsarina,
and gave him a very direct look.

Harry made a dismissive gesture with one hand, indicating
that he considered the acquisition of a throne unimportant.
'You have never heard of the legend?' he said. 'Or of the Face
Stealer?'

'I have never heard that name, but I know who it was you
encountered tonight. He has a darkness within him.' She looked
up sharply. 'You recognize that description?'

'Oh yes,' said Harry, softly, and was aware yet again of an
understanding between them.

'His name is Brother Quintus,' said Catherine, slowly. 'He
murdered my husband. He gave Peter poison to drink under
the guise of it being the wine of the last Sacrament.' A pause,
then, as if the words were being forced from her, she said, 'I
did not know about it until afterwards. It is almost ten years
now, but for most of those years, I have feared Quintus.' She
leaned forward, her arms linked around her bent knees, her

unbound hair tumbling around her shoulders. 'He was part of the Verkhoturye monastery all those years ago, and I think he will still be in there,' she said. 'I had hoped the story would remain shut away with him, but it seems it has not. It seems he has kept it alive.'

'For ten years?' said Harry, incredulously.

'Ten years will not mean so very much to him. He will have been schooled in patience in the monastery. Also, he may have made other attempts to bring the story out during those years,' she said. 'Attempts I have not heard of. And he would have been restricted in what he could do,' she said, thoughtfully. 'He would have to obey the rules of the Order. Once before, he tried to bring out what he saw as the truth. There were carved heads bearing an accusation – it is too long a tale for now, but I will tell you presently. That attempt was thwarted, but I have always known he would try again. He will have been focused on revenge ever since that day, you see.'

'Revenge? But why— Oh, wait, though – was this Quintus promised a reward for what he did? And was that promise later reneged on, and the reward never materialized?'

'You always understand things instinctively,' she said, gratefully. 'You are right, of course.

'Who was the real murderer? Who ordered Quintus to kill the Tsar?'

'It is better you do not know.'

He ignored this. 'It can only have been someone very close to you,' he said, frowning. 'Someone who thought he – for of course it was a "he" – would gain enormous advantage from the Tsar's death. Wealth and power and influence. Someone who had shared your bed? And who believed he could then share the throne?' He waited, then, as she did not answer, he said, 'There is only one person it can be, isn't there? Grigory Orlov.'

The assent was in her eyes, and Harry said, 'But if Quintus has already tried to bring out the truth, why did you not let him? Why did you not simply let Orlov face justice? Was it because you remained in love with him?' As he said this, he was aware of a wholly unfamiliar stab of jealousy. To push it away, he said, 'Or was it because the truth would have incriminated you?'

'It would not need to have incriminated me,' she said. 'Not unless Grigory had been minded to be very vindictive. But, Harry, whatever my feelings for him by then, I could not denounce him, because— Oh, because we had shared so much.' Her eyes slid away from him, and then, with sudden resolve, she said, 'There is a child. His son and mine. It is not known to many – emperors may have mistresses by the cartload and bastards by the dozen, but empresses must not. There has always had to be such secrecy.'

The spike of jealousy dug itself in more deeply. A son, thought Harry. And not a son from the royal marriage which would have been a business arrangement – but a son conceived within a love affair. I ought not to mind, he thought, angrily, and pulled his attention back to what she was saying.

'To have denounced Grigory,' she said, 'would have meant his death, and probably a bad death. Even I would not have been able to save him. We were no longer so close by then, but we had shared so much—'

'The boy.'

She made an impatient gesture. 'I seldom see him, but I am sent news of him, and I know he is being well cared for. Perhaps one day, I can acknowledge him openly. But I could not allow his father to be executed. You understand that?'

Harry stared at her, but when finally he spoke, he was relieved that his voice sounded completely normal.

'I cannot understand completely,' he said, carefully, 'but I can understand enough, Sophie.'

She raised grateful eyes to him and reached for his hand. In a different, brisker voice, Harry said, 'There will be a way to deal with this – to deal with Quintus – and we will find it.' He stood up, and said, 'And now, with your permission, Highness, I will ask for coffee to be brought to us.' He smiled at her. 'I am accustomed to going without sleep, but the night has been an unusual one. And while we drink, I should like you to tell me about the carved heads that bear an accusation.'

Finally making his way back to the room allotted to him on the barge, his mind was tumbling with everything Catherine had said, and with a great many strange and disturbing images.

This eerie creature, Quintus, must, of course, be dealt with, but without any suspicion falling on Catherine. Harry had no idea yet how it could be done, but he would not believe it was impossible, because he would not believe anything was impossible.

And tangled up in all of this were the carved heads – Stone Heads, Catherine had called them, and apparently Verkhoturye's Father Abbot had referred to them in the same way. There had been a letter, which Catherine had copied into her diary – 'You are the only person to whom I have ever shown these pages,' she had said, and Harry had read it with absorption, and had listened to the account of Catherine's secret visit to the monastery.

And so that, thought Harry, is the secret and the mystery that Verkhoturye holds.

Four carved heads – three of children, one of an older man. Four death masks, echoing, in reverse, each of the heads. And etched into the base of the heads were the words that, put together, levelled that damning accusation.

Catherine Romanova murdered her husband, Tsar Peter III, Ropsha 1762.

There was a bad moment when he wondered whether she had told him the truth – whether she had been more seriously implicated in the Tsar's death than she was admitting, but he was able to dismiss it fairly easily. I would know if she was lying, he thought, determinedly, and turned instead to consider the lure sent out by the Stone Heads of Verkhoturye. Was it a lure strong enough to tempt him to steal them? But, at once, his mind shied away from the idea. It's because they're being kept in a religious house, he thought, and I never steal from religious houses of any kind.

But he knew it was more than that. At some level of his mind, he knew there was something wrong, something dark and forbidding about the Stone Heads. Far better, thought Harry, and probably far safer and perhaps even kinder, to let them remain in their dark solitude.

Even so, he went on thinking about them.

TWENTY-FIVE

Quintus would never forget the day he had known that the legend he had spent so long in creating – the legend intended to deal out hurt and damage to the Tsarina and the Orlov brothers – had finally embedded itself into the little community below the monastery.

It had taken a long time for Quintus to rewrite and embellish Gleb the Rhymer's original brief chant, but that had not mattered. One day, Catherine Romanova would come to Verkhoturye – Quintus knew it quite certainly, because he knew the Tsar's murder bound them together, and she would be pulled back to him. When she did come, he would be waiting. The legend would be waiting, as well.

In the beginning, he had not thought that the Heads of the children and of Gleb could be used against the Tsarina and the Orlovs; it was not until sometime after he had completed them that he had had the idea of carving the accusation into the bases. That had been more difficult than he had expected, but he had practised on several odd pieces of clay and stone in his father's workshop, and finally he had mastered the trick of it. When the work was finished, without anyone seeing, he had left the Heads and the accompanying masks in Cympak's church, placing them just below the altar where they could not be missed.

He was pleased with this unexpected refinement to his overall plan. The Cympak priest, who was a stupid, sheep-brained creature unable to think or make decisions for himself, had gone running to Father Ignatius to ask what to do, and Father Ignatius had sent word to the Tsarina. Quintus knew all this, because it was laughably easy to slip into Father Abbot's study when no one was around and read any papers and documents that might be of use. It was something he did quite often, and no one ever knew, because he was sly and stealthy and clever. He had been especially watchful after delivering the Heads to the church, and his vigilance had been rewarded, because he had seen the letter written to Catherine.

After this, he kept careful watch for all arrivals and, sure enough, a few days later, from a small window overlooking the monastery courtyard, he saw the Tsarina's arrival. A single plain carriage it was, and Catherine herself dressed plainly. Quintus knew very little about ladies' garments, but it pleased him to realize this murderous bitch, who always appeared splendidly dressed and bejewelled, had searched out a plain gown and cloak, and eschewed jewels and embellishments.

Grigory and Alexei Orlov were with her, which was clear proof to Quintus that the appearance of the Stone Heads had created concern and anxiety. Exactly what he had wanted. He did not think either Catherine or the Orlov brothers would ever forget that they had ordered the murder of the Tsar, but he intended to make sure they did not – and to remind them that there was someone in the world who knew what they had done, and who might one day make a very public denouncement of them.

None of the monks had the least suspicion that Quintus was not an obedient, pious member of their Order. He had never expected they would; he had long since perfected the art of hiding his real self, and patience had become part of his life.

What he had not expected, however, was the hard, insistent excitement that engulfed him the first time he stole out of the monastery. Prowling the night streets of Cympak, softly chanting the rhyme he had spent so long in composing, he understood for the first time how it must feel to desire a woman and to do so with an intensity that drove out almost every other emotion. He understood, as well, why the elders of his religion advocated so strongly for prayer and fasting and resolve, preaching that it quenched such needs.

He had no intention of seeking out a woman, but in the deepest recesses of his mind was the knowledge that a woman was at the heart of this. Catherine. Wasn't she the reason and the spur, and wasn't she the one driving him on?

*   *   *

He knew the legend had burrowed its way into the minds of the local people when he heard it being sung quite openly.

He had spent an hour stealing through the streets, pausing at any lit windows he found, softly chanting the rhyme. When first he began his nocturnal prowlings, little groups of men came out into the streets to find whoever was behaving so sinisterly. They never found him, of course; Quintus had been born and grown up in Cympak, and he knew all the little alleyways and narrow passages, and the empty houses where a man might hide. After a while, the searches ceased, and he understood that when people heard him coming, they simply locked their doors and shuttered their windows.

But there came the night when he set off later than usual – it had been long after his usual midnight journey – and when he turned to climb the mountain path back to the monastery, the sky was already becoming streaked with faint dawn light. He thought it was too early for anyone to be abroad, but as he crossed the little square, he heard the rumble of cartwheels on the cobblestones and the chink of metal. Milk churns, thought Quintus, at once. It's the milk being brought in early from one of the farms. He stepped into the half-concealment of a corner doorway, and as he stood there, his heart pounding, across the deserted square came the sound of a jovial voice calling to someone to make sure the churns were not spilling over – that they did not want all that milk to be spread over the streets.

There was a clatter of metal again, and two voices – young boys' voices – called back that the milk was not spilling and everything was safe. Then, as if to brighten the still-dark streets, they began to sing.

'Beware, beware, the Face Stealer's hands,
'Run for your life if he comes.
'For he'll snatch you all up in his murderer's hands
'And carry you off to his lair down below,
'Where the iron teeth clang and the river-light glows
'And the water lies waiting for prey.'

The farmer's voice called out to ask if they did not know anything merrier to lighten their morning round, instead of that gloomy, frightening song that a madman sang every now and then. There were giggles from the cart, and one of the boys said something about it not really being frightening; it was the song everyone sang when they played the Face Stealer game. They played it in the schoolyard, said the other one. It was a good game.

The cart was rattling across the square now, towards the church, but Quintus could just hear they were still chanting, and they had reached the later lines.

'For that royal Romanova – that murderess damned –
'Controls the Face Stealer and gives the command.'

The chant sounded as he had intended – a simple repetitive rhythm and words, exactly the kind of thing children often sang. He had deliberately made it so.

The farmer's voice came again, saying the boys should not sing such things about the Imperial family – dear goodness, did they want them all clapping in gaol?

The cart rattled away, and Quintus could no longer hear the voices, but it did not matter, because it was clear that the legend had taken root. All he had to do was ensure it was not forgotten – that the robed and hooded figure continued to be seen and heard in the night streets.

And when Catherine returned to Verkhoturye – as Quintus knew she would – she would hear the rhyme and the legend of the Face Stealer, and she would realize it was being whispered that she was a murderess – the killer of her own husband.

And she would know Quintus was at the legend's heart. She would know he was waiting for her.

She did return. Her Court embarked on a gaudy glittering river voyage, and news reached the monastery that there was to be a detour so that Her Highness might visit Verkhoturye and the villages around it.

Quintus listened to the monks talking about it, some of them wondering if the Tsarina might even visit their House, and if Father Abbot might relax the Rule for some of them to go into the villages and watch Her Imperial Highness's procession. It would all be very splendid, they said – the word was that the Tsarina would have many of her powerful courtiers and that the people closest to her would be accompanying her.

Powerful courtiers and the people closest to her. The words were like the flaring of a brilliant light in Quintus's mind. Grigory and Alexei Orlov, he thought. The two men who had forced him to kill Peter III for Catherine's sake – who had blackmailed him into doing it, and then had thrown him out of the Winter Palace as if he had been no more than a piece of rubbish. Was it too much to hope that one or both of them would be here?

Until now, he had left long interludes between his visits to Cympak, and he had always waited until after the monastery's bell had chimed midnight. He made sure he was back in his own room long before the six o'clock call to Prime. The Imperial visit came when only three weeks had elapsed since his last foray, but that did not matter. On the night it was reported the Imperial barges had moored, he did not wait for midnight; he slipped out as soon as the monastery had sunk into silence.

From the outskirts of the village, he could make out the glimmer of light that would be the barges. It was a strange feeling to know *she* was so near. Quintus thought he would not risk approaching the barges – in any case, the riverbank would have little concealment.

There were quite a lot of people in Cympak's streets. He had no idea if this was usual at this hour, but it seemed possible that some of them were from the Tsarina's party, perhaps surveying the terrain for a procession through the villages or maybe simply curious. As the church clock chimed for eleven, a noisy, boisterous group of richly clad men – six or eight of them – came swaggering along the street. At their head was Grigory Orlov.

Quintus's heart leapt with a mixture of fear and excitement – it was no part of his plan to actually confront Orlov, but if ever there was an opportunity to let him know the Tsarina was talked of as a murderess . . . He stepped into the shadow of a deep doorway, and as the men walked past, laughing and trading friendly insults with one another, he began the chant. The words drifted on to the night, and although most of the men seemed not hear, Grigory Orlov stopped and looked back. He tilted his head in a listening attitude, then called to the men that he would follow them in a moment. 'Too much wine taken,' he said, reaching for the fastening of his breeches and stepping into a side alley.

But as soon as the group was out of sight and beyond hearing, Orlov emerged from the doorway and came towards Quintus. At once, Quintus darted out of the doorway and ran lightly along the streets. Orlov saw him, of course, and followed, but Quintus could outwit this one easily. He sped along the narrow streets, several times doubling back to confuse his pursuer. Once, he even chanted part of the rhyme to lure Orlov on, doing so more loudly than usual to be sure Grigory heard it.

He thought he had outrun him, but when he reached the foot of the mountain path to the monastery, he paused to look back and saw Orlov emerge from the cluster of buildings. It was all right, though – once he had reached the monastery and got inside he would be safe. He went up the steep mountain path, clutching his robe tightly around him, scarcely noticing the wind gusting into his face. He was starting to tire now, and the path was steep, but he was almost there, almost safe . . . Here were the immense stone pillars guarding the entrance; he went through them and across the courtyard. Stay in the shadows around the building, said his mind, and he'll never see you . . . Around the side, under the windows, and straight along to the little kitchen door . . . Almost there . . .

His hand had closed on the ring handle of the kitchen door, and he was just taking a breath of relief when the shadows came at him. Orlov's hand closed painfully around his arm, pulling him half to the ground. Something hard and heavy came down on his head, and a sick blackness began to descend like a smothering curtain. For a moment, it was shot with jagged lights, and somewhere beyond them was Orlov's face, the eyes narrow and filled with hatred. Quintus attempted to push the stifling blackness aside, but it was all around him, and he was aware that he was tumbling into a deep tunnel where there was nothing – no sound, no light – and where there might not be anything ever again.

*   *   *

He had no idea how long it was before he became aware of his surroundings again, but he sensed the blackness retreating and, little by little, he realized he was lying on a hard, cold surface. A thick, heavy silence pressed in on all sides, and there was an atmosphere of extreme age and isolation. The darkness was almost impenetrable, but gradually his vision adjusted, and he began to make out faint patches of lightness. He struggled to sit up, and, gasping from the pain that shot through his head and his neck and shoulders, put up a cautious hand to explore the source of the pain. As his hand touched his neck, he cried out, because the whole of his neck was swollen, and it felt like a huge throbbing bruise. His cry echoed and seemed to bounce mockingly back from the walls. As it did so, something stirred in the shadows, and Quintus's heart leapt with terror. He narrowed his eyes, trying to penetrate the blackness, and gradually one of the faint patches of lightness took on the recognizable form of a face – pallid, staring, the eyes unblinking. Quintus shrank back, pressing against the wall immediately behind him, then saw with mounting horror that there were two watching faces – and that one was turning slowly from side to side . . .

He was aware that he was clenching his fists and that he had drawn up his legs against his chest, and through the scudding terror, he could hear someone screaming – terrible, trapped-hare screams that reverberated through the darkness. It was some moments before he realized he was the one who was screaming.

Somehow he got to his feet, backing away from the dreadful sight, thrusting his hands out before him in defence. The heads moved again, slowly, and Quintus, whose eyes were becoming more adjusted to the dimness, saw that other heads were ranged behind them. Four heads – pale and remote, but not moving as the two he had seen were moving.

It was then that understanding came. These were the Stone Heads and the death masks – the sculptures he had created – that he had worked on in such secrecy, fashioning and shaping and honing, and then engraving with the accusation against the Tsarina. The movement had come from the death masks – someone had looped thin rope around them, and they hung from nails driven into the wall. The ingress of air caused by Quintus's movements had caused them to stir. It was that which had made it seem as if the masks were turning to look at him.

There was a moment when he drew in a deep breath of relief, because no one was watching him from the darkness. He knew about these faces – he was their creator.

The relief lasted for scarcely half a dozen heartbeats, then terror came scalding back, because he knew where he was. He was in the bowels of the monastery, locked inside the room with the Stone Heads. He could see the outline of the small barred window now – three steps took him to it. With one hand, he clutched the bars, his other hand searching frantically for a handle or a lock that would open the door from this side.

There was no handle, no lock. This was the room that was kept padlocked from the other side, and that was kept in perpetual darkness, as Father Abbot had decreed all those years ago. It was the room to which no one ever came. No one would come now, because no one – save the man who had tried to murder him – knew he was here.

Catherine's private memoirs, early 1770s

I have had a great many remarkable days in my life, and doubtless I shall have a great many more, but I do not think I shall ever be faced with days remotely resembling the ones I have just lived through.

I do know it is only two days since Harry told me of his sinister encounter with Quintus, but as I write this, it seems far longer.

This morning, Grigory came to my bedchamber (I will *not* refer to it as a cabin, not if fifty sea lords or admirals insist it is the correct term). To my annoyance, the moment he entered, my heart began to thud, because I knew he would have come to talk about Quintus – Quintus and Verkhoturye are inextricably linked. What I did not know, though – not immediately – was whether Grigory was aware that Quintus was prowling the night streets, sending that sinister chant – so

deceptively simple, so chillingly damning – with that terrible
statement in the last lines.

'. . . *the secrets concealed –*
'*And stifle the murder she dare not reveal.*
'. . . *the game will result in you meeting your death.*
'*As Peter met his death in Ropsha that night*
'*By Catherine's command and imperious might.*'

But Grigory did know. It seemed that two nights ago, he and
a few of my attendants had taken themselves ashore – as he
told me this, I instantly visualized them swaggering and
strutting their way through the streets, probably looking for a
local tavern where they could drink and carouse, wanting to
impress the local people. It would not have impressed them,
of course; it would have been offensive and infuriating, and
it would have served Grigory's party right if the local people
had turned on them and given them the beating they deserved.

It was when they were returning to the barge that Grigory
had heard the chanting.

'Eerie and spiteful it was,' he said, his expression and his
tone unusually serious. 'You could not imagine, Highness—'

I said, 'I can imagine, for I already know of it. It was
Quintus you heard, of course.'

'It couldn't have been anyone else. But—'

'Did any of the men with you hear it?'

'No. But I heard it, and I followed it, Catherine,' he said,
and his use of my name stirred at old memories.

Not taking my eyes from his face, I said, 'What did you do?'

'I followed him. All the way to the monastery. And once
there . . . I had to silence him,' he said. 'Once inside the
monastery, I hit him so hard he fell, senseless. I knew I would
have to kill him, of course, but I didn't dare do it there –
anyone might have heard and come along to investigate, even
at that hour.'

'You took him down to the crypt,' I said, Father Abbot's
words still vivid in my mind. *A small room deep within the
crypt*, he had said. *A grisly little place – it is rare for anyone
to go there.* 'You took him to where the monks had hidden
the Stone Heads.'

'Yes. I carried him through the stone corridors and the halls – with every step, I was afraid he would revive, but he did not. Even so, I felt as if eyes peered at me from the corners and whispers hissed from the darkness. But nothing stirred – it's a massive old place, as you know, and those thick stone walls soak up sounds. I found the crypt easily enough – it was simply a matter of looking for stairs leading down. And a grim old place it was, Catherine. Stone tombs – sarcophagi – with the bodies of all the long-dead monks . . . But at the very end, beyond them all, was the room I was looking for. It had a small barred window – God only knows what its original purpose was – and there was a bolt and a padlock. The bolt drew back with a shriek like a soul in torment. As for the padlock, it snapped off easily enough, and I opened the door and pulled Quintus inside. And then . . .' For the first time, his voice faltered, then he said, 'I strangled him.'

Seeing or perhaps only sensing my recoil, he put out a hand tentatively. I ignored it, and after a moment, he said, 'I should have liked to slit his throat and cut out his heart, but that would have meant blood, and blood is incriminating.'

'The Heads – they were there?'

'Oh yes. All of them blind and cold and dead, but somehow—'

'Watching,' I said, almost to myself. 'Seeing and knowing.'

He made an impatient gesture as if to brush aside such fanciful nonsense. 'I came away as quickly as I could,' he said. 'I closed the door and shot the bolt. I was able to snap the padlock back in place, as well. Then I returned to the barge. I have no remorse for what I did, Catherine. Quintus was peddling the legend and the rhyme like some evil street ballad seller. He wanted you – Alexei and me, as well – to be punished, and he was gradually spreading the story of how your husband died. It was . . . it was as if he was slowly dripping acid on to us, Catherine. He had to be silenced, or he would have destroyed you – all of us.'

'He was cheated of what he had been promised,' I said, half to myself. 'He wanted to be revenged on us.' But then I remembered that Quintus had killed Peter solely to gain wealth and perhaps power. And I believe dying from poison is a cruel and agonizing death.

Grigory said, 'I wanted to destroy the Stone Heads while I was there, but I dared not remain any longer for fear of being discovered. I returned here as quickly as I could.'

He fell silent, and I said, 'There's more to tell, isn't there?'

'When I strangled Quintus,' he said, slowly, as if choosing his words with care, 'I had to take off my gloves to do it. I put them on again when I came out, of course, but once back here, I realized my signet ring was no longer on my hand.'

For a moment, I did not understand, then, with a rush of horror, I understood all too well. His signet ring – the ring that most gentleman of any standing, and certainly all noblemen, wear most of the time, generally with their family arms or crest on it so that letters can be sealed or signatures verified by dripping softened wax on to the paper and pressing the ring's engraved outline into it.

Grigory said, 'It could only have slipped off in that locked room. While I was strangling him,' he said, and I repressed a shudder. He got up and began pacing the room. 'I must go back in there to find it,' he said.

'And Quintus's body?'

His eyes slid away from me. 'It could be a very long time before it is found,' he said. 'I replaced the padlock and bolted the door from the outside. It looks exactly as it looked before I put him in there.'

'But surely he will be missed by the other monks? They will look for him?'

'Yes, but that would take them time to arrange, and we will be long since gone from here.'

'They would search the monastery, though,' I said. 'And eventually, they will find his body – and they will find it in the room with the Stone Heads. Father Abbot will see a link at once – a link between Quintus and the Heads and me. The engraved words on the Heads, the fact that Quintus spent several weeks at the Winter Palace . . . Father Ignatius was loyal to the Romanov line and the Imperial Throne ten years ago, but I would not guarantee his loyalty in light of this. Grigory, Quintus's body cannot be left in that crypt. You must retrieve your signet ring, of course, but you must dispose of the body at the same time.'

He looked at me. 'You are right,' he said, at last. 'But I can't carry a dead body through the monastery and bury it or consign it to the river or a fire by myself. Someone will have to come with me.'

TWENTY-SIX

Whatever Harry might have expected from his sojourn with the Russian Empress, he certainly had not expected a request that he help with the disposal of a murder victim's body.

'There is no one else I can ask,' Catherine said, clutching his hands.

'Grigory Orlov,' said Harry, only just managing not to speak through clenched teeth. 'I've hardly spoken to him since I've been here.'

'He has stayed on the edges of most things during this trip,' she said, almost defensively.

Harry did not say that, as far as he was concerned, the edges of anywhere were a suitable place for Orlov. He said, 'I hope he and I are able to understand one another. Does he have any English?'

'No, but his French is very good.' She looked at him with such hope and she was suddenly so dreadfully vulnerable that Harry would have stormed citadels and torn down fortresses if it would ensure her safety. Disposing of a murdered corpse seemed almost trivial in comparison.

And alongside all of this was the knowledge that he would reach the heart of Verkhoturye's mystery – that he would see for himself the sinister Stone Heads.

Even so, approaching the monastery in company with Grigory Orlov, he had to suppress bitter hatred for this man who had been Catherine's lover, who had fathered a son on to her – a child she dared not acknowledge – and who was almost entirely responsible for this appalling situation.

Setting out, Orlov had looked Harry up and down with distaste. 'You look like the worst kind of ruffian,' he said. 'Those garments— Nor do you appear to have shaved for at least two days.'

'If we are caught,' said Harry, composedly, 'I shall be able to pass as a vagrant. An itinerant, even. Vagrants and itinerants do not shave very often, and they wear whatever garments they can find. I shall be able to blend with the landscape. You, on the other hand, present the appearance of a high-born nobleman, and if we are indeed caught, you will be recognized for what you are.'

Orlov stared at him. 'I suspect you are being impertinent.'

'You do not need to suspect – I *am* being impertinent. Is this the mountain path we have to take? Then lead on, if you will.'

The church in Cympak below was chiming the hour as they reached the monastery. Harry glanced at his companion and said, softly, 'The iron tongue of midnight. And midnight is traditionally the time any self-respecting villain chooses to commit a nefarious deed.'

Orlov shot him a startled look, clearly not seeing any irony, which pleased Harry. This one could never have shared the small amusements of life with the Tsarina. He was never really the one for you, Sophie, my love, he thought. I don't care if he was a rampant stallion in the bedchamber, I won't believe the two of you had that 'secret harmony of hearts' that we've had. And then he thought: I'm approaching an ancient monastery with a man I don't like or trust in order to hide the body of a villain he's strangled, and I'm quoting Milton's *Paradise Lost*!

Orlov was walking around the side of the huge dark building, pointing to a small side door ahead of them. 'It was unlocked when I was here,' he said.

'Probably, it will be unlocked now,' said Harry, not saying that it would not matter if it was not, since he could unpick the locks of almost any door.

'Careless housekeeping,' said Orlov, and Harry nodded solemnly, and refrained from mentioning that such careless housekeeping had facilitated many a burglarious exploit for him. Not that this was a burglarious exploit.

The door was not locked, and as they stepped inside, the stillness of the monastery folded around them. How must it be to live inside this quiet serenity, thought Harry, staring into the dimness, to spend your days in prayer and devotion and work, knowing you would never enter the outer world again? The prospect brushed silkily across his mind – peace, shelter, contemplation . . . Study, quiet companionship . . . There was a remarkable allure about it. But almost immediately, he remembered the excitement of planning a filch – of getting into the houses of the wealthy without them knowing, and abstracting jewels and objets d'art which could be sold profit- ably. There were other excitements in life, too, of course: the delighted anticipation that swept through you when you entered a bedchamber in which a lady awaited . . . Face it, thought Harry; you're not designed for a quiet life of celibacy.

Orlov was walking purposefully through the dim halls, neither of them speaking. He indicated a small side passage leading off a large, pillared hall, and Harry nodded and followed.

Steep, narrow steps that twisted sharply led down, making it necessary to keep one hand on the wall for balance. At the foot of the steps, Orlov produced a tinder box, and after a moment, a wavering light sprang up. In front of them were the rows of tombs – plain stone, each one bearing the name of its occupant.

They wound their way between the tombs, until Grigory held the light higher and pointed. 'That is the room.'

With the words, the candlelight fell on to the low oak door, and in that moment, Harry felt as if something had closed a constricting hand around his chest. He thought he let out a gasp, and he heard Orlov give a soft, horrified curse.

Near the top of the old door was a small, barred window. The light showed it clearly. But it also showed what was on the other side of the bars. A human face was pressed against the bars – a face that had wide, staring eyes, the pupils turned up, so that only the whites showed. A face whose mouth was stretched wide in a dreadful, silent scream . . .

The two men moved closer, and when Orlov held the light closer, his hands were shaking, causing shadows to move all around them.

After a moment, Harry managed to say, 'I suppose it is Quintus, is it?'

In a harsh, strained voice, Orlov said, 'Yes, of course it's

Quintus. But he was dead when I left him – I swear by every-thing I know that he was dead.'

'Clearly, he was not, though,' said Harry, bending to examine the padlock. 'This is only wedged in place,' he said.

'Yes, I snapped it off; I told you. I put it back in place so that it wouldn't look as if anyone had broken it. We only need to draw back the bolt to get in.'

The squeak of the bolt being drawn echoed loudly in the quiet crypt, and both men looked instinctively behind them. But nothing stirred, and taking a deep breath, Harry pushed the door open. It swung inwards, and there was the sound of the dead man's feet scraping over the floor. His hands were still clamped to the bars – the nails were broken and crusted with blood, and Harry forced down the dreadful image of Quintus struggling to get free, frantically clawing at the bars, probably beating at the stone surround of the window. In as practical a tone as he could manage, he said, 'We'll have to prise his fingers free.'

'All right.'

The sounds of the finger bones snapping as they forced them free was something Harry thought he would hear in nightmares for a very long time. But at last, the dead man fell to the floor.

Orlov spared him a brief look, and then moved the candle flame around the tiny room, suddenly letting out a small, satisfied sound and bending to pick up something that glinted in the light.

'The signet ring,' he said, and pushed it on to his finger. 'And now let's get the wretched Quintus out and find somewhere to bury him.'

Harry took the candle from him and held it up so that it fell into the dark corners. Cobwebs trailed from the ceiling, and the stone walls were worn and clearly extremely old. This would be a terrible place in which to die alone.

But Quintus might not have felt alone. On a narrow section of jutting stone were the objects about which the entire Verkhoturye legend had been woven. The Stone Heads. Blind and pale, and three of them with a heart-breaking trusting innocence. Children, thought Harry, and the pity of it wrenched at him. But then he looked more closely at the fourth, and there was no innocence there, and precious little trust. Dear God, he was a sly, spiteful one, whoever he was, thought Harry. And then he saw that behind the Heads, like watchful shadows, were what looked almost like reverse images of the faces. As if they were looking out of a mirror.

'Death masks,' said Orlov from behind him. 'I'd think whoever made the Heads took those impressions from the four dead bodies.'

'Would it have been Quintus?'

'Oh yes, almost certainly.' Orlov glanced uneasily towards the door. 'For pity's sake, let's get him out while everywhere is still quiet.'

It took more resolve than Harry had expected to lift Quintus and carry him out of the grisly little room, and once he paused, half doubling over.

Orlov said, caustically, 'If you're going to be sick, go and do it quietly in a dark corner.'

Harry was so angry at this that he straightened up at once, and as soon as they had Quintus's body out of the room, he snatched the padlock from Orlov and reattached it with a furious snap.

Carrying Quintus's body between them, they began a wary journey between the stone sarcophagi towards the stairs. Once Orlov stopped and tilted his head to one side, clearly listening, but then frowned, and they began the awkward ascent of the steps. They had reached the second curve, and Harry was just starting to think they were going to get out without being caught when overhead the huge monastic bell began to chime.

Harry swore in English, and almost dropped Quintus's body. Then Orlov said, 'It's calling the monks to some kind of night service – a vigil, perhaps.'

'Prayers for divine help to find their missing Brother?' said Harry, half caustically, but half seriously.

'They must have realized by now he's missing.'

'If you're given to praying on your own account, you'd better pray we aren't found,' said Harry. 'Clearly, the monks haven't searched down here yet, but I can easily see them emerging from their prayers, and telling one another they've been directed to explore the crypt.'

'Whatever they're directed to do, if we carry him out now, we run the risk of being caught,' said Orlov. 'We'd be seen – or, at best, heard.'

'Just the two of us might slink through the shadows unnoticed, but not if we're carrying that burden,' nodded Harry. 'Put him down on the stair for a moment.' He went down the steps again, and beckoned impatiently for Orlov to relight the candles. Then he directed it all the way around the crypt. Low, vaulted ceilings, stone pillars and the rows of sarcophagi with their stone lids.

The rows of sarcophagi . . .

Harry said, 'How difficult would it be to lever off the lid of one of those tombs?'

'It was one of the grisliest, most macabre things I have ever had to do,' he said to Catherine, the following morning. 'Is that hot chocolate you have in that jug – praise the gods, so it is. And some of whatever is in that dish under the cover. Thank you.'

He drank the chocolate gratefully, although he was aware of a sudden wish for coffee or tea as it would have been made in England.

'What remains of Brother Quintus,' he said, setting down his cup, 'is now sharing his last resting place with a former Abbot of St Nicholas's Monastery. At least, I hope it will be his last resting place.'

'You put him in one of the tombs?' said Catherine.

'We did. The stone lid was extremely difficult to raise – at first, we thought we wouldn't manage it. And if we had dropped it— That would have sent an explosion of sound through the whole monastery, for it was as heavy as – well, as the stone rolled back from Christ's tomb in Golgotha.'

'Your visit to a religious house seems to have planted a few religious thoughts in your mind,' said Catherine, dryly. 'But finish the story.'

'That was the finish,' said Harry. 'We dragged the stone lid half off the tomb – there was a moment when it seemed as if a dry dead breath gusted into our faces, and even Orlov flinched. I shan't chill your soul by describing what lay inside the tomb – it was mostly just bones and a few shreds of hair and cloth, in any case. Between us, we tipped Quintus in and dragged the cover back in place. Then we stole back up the stairs – in the pitchest of pitch darks because we didn't dare have the candle burning – and slunk through the monastery to the little side door. I don't think we were far from the monks' chapel,' he said, 'and I will admit that after all that had gone before, hearing the chanting of their prayers was extremely eerie. Even though I couldn't follow what they were chanting, it still made my skin prickle with – oh, with a variety of different emotions.'

He leaned back against the pillows that were piled up on the bed and looked at her.

For what felt like a long moment, neither of them spoke, then she said, very softly, 'The time has come when you are going to leave, hasn't it?'

Harry took a moment to reply, then said, 'I think I must, don't you, Sophie? We both knew I should do so eventually.' He pulled her against him. 'You know, of course, that there will never be anyone like you in my life again.'

'Nor you in mine.' She sent him the smile that lit her face like a mischievous cat. 'I wonder, Harry, how many times we have both said that to a lover.'

'I have never said it,' said Harry, meaning it.

'Nor I. Wait, though—' She slid from the bed and, taking a key from the desk, opened a small door in the elaborate cupboard near to it. 'There is no real way for me to thank you for what you did at the monastery, but I should like you to have this.'

Harry said, 'What I did, I would have done anyway. But it would be ungracious if I refused any gift you make. It would be false and hypocritical.'

'You should be able to sell them very profitably,' she said, coming back to the bed and placing several leather jewel cases in his hands. 'Although not in this country, please. They might be recognized.'

There were three cases: one long one contained necklaces –

glittering ropes of colour and gold; one contained bracelets and rings; and the third held two large ornaments, which Harry thought were brooches or hair ornaments. As he opened each of the cases, the contents caught the light and gleamed softly like cats' eyes.

He said, softly, 'The emeralds. Dear God, the Romanov emeralds. I know I said I would not protest, but this is far more than—'

'It is not far more,' she said. 'It is a small piece of what I owe you – and of what I feel for you.'

'I am tempted,' he said, 'to quote the Bible statement about the price of a virtuous woman being far above rubies.'

'But you will accept?'

'Oh yes,' he said, softly, still staring at the emeralds. 'Yes, I will accept.' He closed the cases and took both her hands. 'Sophie, dear love, I think you have made it possible for me to realize a long-cherished dream.'

'A piece of land of your own,' she said, nodding. Harry knew she did not entirely understand his dream, because no one who had been born into the rich palaces of her family and her ancestors could really do so. But he knew she understood enough. She said, 'And once you have that land, you will build on it – a place that will be your own for always.'

Harry said, 'I will. And woven into it will be memories of the lady who made it possible. Memories that will be everlasting.'

'Immortal,' she said. 'Like that flower – amarant. Never fading.'

'Amarant,' said Harry, almost to himself, and for a moment the word seemed to linger on the air between then.

'Yes,' she said, and they looked at one another. Harry thought: There truly will never be another like her in my life.

'And now, Harry Fitzglen,' said the Tsarina of all the Russias, the cat-smile lifting her eyes again, 'will you please make love to me one last time.'

TWENTY-SEVEN

Mallory Abbot, 1909

'I do know,' said Viola Gilfillan, seated on the stone floor of the Brundage mausoleum, 'that I've said more than once that I wanted you to play Romeo to my Juliet, but—'

'But neither of us actually expected to be playing it in reality.' Jack was sitting next to her, both of them leaning against an outer wall. The light from the two candles he had lit were keeping some of the darkness at bay, but shadows still clustered thickly in the corners and lay across the coffins stacked on their shelves. Each time the candle flames flickered, the shadows seemed to stir and reach out questing hands.

He said, 'I imagine, though, that we were visualizing balconies and impassioned dawn declarations, rather than the final scene with—'

'With the star-crossed lovers dying in each other's arms in the tomb-house,' agreed Viola, hugging her arms around her knees for warmth or comfort, or both. 'But I do think Shakespeare might have approved this place as a setting for that scene.' Then, in a different tone, she said, 'Jack, I know Simeon locked the door from the other side, and I know you've tried to get it open at least five times, but someone will miss us quite soon, won't they? Or, at least, someone will miss you and come out here? Did Gus or Byron know you were going to get in here?'

'They all knew,' said Jack. 'And when they realize I'm missing, this will be the first place they'll search.'

'What if they see the padlock on the door and think it's all locked up and go away, though?'

'They wouldn't. They'd make assurance doubly sure,' said Jack, firmly. 'In any case, we'd hear them, and yell like fury to them that we're here.'

'But supposing Simeon gets here first? We wouldn't have

any way of knowing who was out there, and whether it would be safe to yell like fury, would we?' said Viola. 'Because Simeon is going to come back, isn't he?'

'I'm afraid so. I think he'll have gone in search of something that will allow him to get up to that shelf and the Heads. He probably won't be able to bring anything out here until the morning, though, by which time Gus will long since have come to the rescue.'

'But will Gus be able to get in? Simeon locked the padlock in place, remember. We heard him do it.'

'Gus will get Ambrose or even Rudraige to pick the lock,' said Jack. He glanced at her, and smiled slightly. 'It's what we do, Viola – remember?'

'Did Simeon get in by picking the lock, d'you think?'

'Either that or he cajoled the key out of the Brundage woman,' said Jack.

'Whichever it was, if he comes back before we've got out, could we pounce on him? Overpower him between us?'

'It would depend on whether he's still got the revolver. But if he's going to be climbing up a ladder, we might manage it. And don't forget, he doesn't know we're here, which means we'd have the advantage of surprise. He'll certainly come back, though. It's clear that he wants those sculptures.'

'Twice over?' said Viola. 'That's immensely greedy of him. He'll have been paid for them once already. When he sold them to the Ecclesiastical Society, I mean.'

'Yes, he would, but it seems that he's decided to try selling them a second time,' said Jack. 'Stay where you are, and I'll light a couple more candles. I think there're enough to keep them burning for the night.'

'I suppose,' said Viola, as he lit the candles and wedged them in crevices in the stonework, 'that we aren't trapped in here indefinitely? I mean – they aren't likely to open the door in a week or so and find our dead and frozen bodies.'

Jack said, with more assurance than he felt, 'Of course we aren't trapped indefinitely. One way or another, we'll get out – even if we have to wrestle Saintly Simeon to the ground when he comes back. Which he certainly will.' He looked at her. 'But I think we're here for the night,' he said. 'And I'm afraid it's likely to get quite cold.'

'I don't suppose there's much we can do about that, though, is there?'

'At least you can have my coat,' said Jack, removing it, and wrapping it around her, turning up the collar in the process. 'Sorry,' he said, 'I've dislodged some of the pins in your hair – it's tumbling down around your shoulders.'

'I daresay I look like a street urchin anyway,' she said. 'It's dreadfully dusty in here.'

'You look like a lady from a pre-Raphaelite painting after a night on the tiles,' said Jack, taking one of the loose strands of hair between his fingers. He paused, then said, 'You know, there might be something we could do to keep warm.'

She had been watching the candle flames burn up, but when he said this, she turned her head and smiled into his eyes. His arms went around her.

The flaring candles were gradually burning lower, emitting the scent of warm wax which diluted the dry, stale air. The small flames altered the shadows from being sinister, crouching shapes into friendly blurs.

There were no longer any words – there was no real need for them – but presently Viola, said, in a breathless whisper, 'Jack, if you make use of the Fitzglen Pause now, I swear that once we're out of here, I'll tell the entire police force everything about your family.'

'I couldn't pause now if my life depended on it,' said Jack, and pulled her against him.

The darkness inside the Brundage mausoleum did not exactly lift, but patches of faint light trickled in from somewhere. Jack looked down at Viola, who was sleeping against his shoulder, and tightened his hold on her.

She smiled, half opened her eyes and said, demurely, 'I hope you realize, Mr Fitzglen, that I allowed this purely to keep warm.'

Jack said, gravely, 'I did realize it. And I expect you understood that, on my part, I acted from pure chivalry, nothing more.'

'Whatever you call it, you are a very parfit gentil knight, Jack Fitzglen,' she said, her eyes alight with amusement. 'Although there were times when "gentle" wasn't exactly the word I would have used to describe— Shall we continue to spar and scrap when we're back in the real world?'

'I expect so.' He smiled at her, then said, softly, 'It's still quite cold, isn't it?'

'Now you mention it, it is.'

'It would be sensible to do whatever we think necessary to keep warm.'

'It would,' she said, demurely.

'And I should think we've got at least an hour before it starts to be sunrise, and Gus and the others realize we're missing.'

'At the moment, I don't care if it's sunset next week before they find us,' said Viola.

Gus did not know when he had ever been so frantically worried, and this was saying a good deal, because during his years with the Fitzglen family in general and Mr Jack in particular, there had been a great many deeply worrying occasions.

However, this was a whole new level of what Miss Cecily would term worriment. Gus had known all about Mr Jack going out to the mausoleum in the church grounds, of course, and he had entirely understood that Mr Jack felt one person alone would be less noticeable than two. He would be back before anyone realized it, Mr Jack had said, and there would be a good tale to tell the family over breakfast, because he would have retrieved the Stone Heads, which was the whole purpose of this visit.

But when Gus went along to Mr Jack's bedroom shortly before the breakfast gong was due to sound, there was no sign of him, and the bed did not look as if it had been slept in. Gus abandoned his plans for helping with last-minute packing and assisting Bill the Chip to stow away the last few items of scenery and props, and although his first instinct was to go full pelt out to the churchyard and the grisly Brundage mausoleum, he thought he had better take someone with him. He would normally have called on Mr Byron, but his sprained ankle prevented him from walking more than a few steps. Mr Rudraige would certainly come along if asked, but it would take half an hour for him to find his coat and the muffler without which Miss Cecily said he should never venture forth, and there was also the point that he had the way of talking loudly, especially when he was agitated, which would attract attention and was the last thing wanted.

Miss Cecily and Miss Daphnis and the twins, Gus dismissed almost at once. Miss Cecily would fly into one of her flutters and have to be revived with sal volatile, Miss Daphnis would tell everyone she had always known Simeon Fitzglen would end in bringing doom and disaster down on the family, and the twins would either be terrified or see it as a huge entertaining adventure.

That left Mr Ambrose. He would certainly join in a search for Jack at once; the trouble was that Gus had a suspicion that Miss Viola Gilfillan might be involved, and Mr Ambrose had no idea that Miss Viola had played a part in any of this – or even that she and Mr Jack were on speaking terms, never mind any other kind of terms. He would be shocked and dismayed to find any Gilfillan tangled up in the filch. On the other hand, if they had to break into the mausoleum, Mr Ambrose was as good as the rest of the Fitzglens at picking a lock. With this in mind, Gus went along to his bedroom to explain the situation.

'Good God, of course I'll come,' said Mr Ambrose, snatching up a coat. 'And how about taking young Volkov with us – this is as much his province as anyone's.'

Gus thought this was a good idea, and they scooped up Mikhail, who had been about to go in search of breakfast, and went out into the dull morning.

'Mr Jack was going to the mausoleum at midnight,' explained Gus, as they headed for the church. 'But that's eight hours ago now.'

'What could have gone wrong?'

'Things do go wrong on a filch sometimes,' said Ambrose, as they went through the lychgate. 'But we usually find a way out, and Jack *always* manages to do so.' He paused just inside the gate and looked around. 'It doesn't look as if anyone's here,' he said. 'Let's hope there's no early morning service going on in St Osmund's.'

'Matins, it would be,' said Mikhail.

'Whatever it's called, let's try to look as if we're taking a pre-breakfast stroll. If anyone appears and questions us, we'll say we're here to collect a few items we overlooked from last night's performance.'

But St Osmund's was silent, and everywhere appeared to be deserted. Mist clung to the trees and moisture dripped from the branches. The Brundage mausoleum, when they reached it, crouched broodingly in its corner.

Mikhail said, 'The padlock is on the door.'

'Yes, and it looks as if it's locked in place, which either means Jack got in and came out and replaced it,' said Ambrose, 'or he didn't get inside in the first place. Or—'

'Or he's trapped in there,' said Gus, anxiously. 'Can you undo the padlock?'

'If I can't, I'm not worthy of the name of Fitzglen,' said Mr Ambrose, pulling from his pocket a small leather wallet, almost identical to the one Gus had seen Mr Jack use many times. He knelt down and slid a narrow, pointed instrument into the lock.

Mikhail, watching closely, said, 'Should we call out to ask if Jack is in there?'

'No, because if someone is in there, it might not be Jack,' said Ambrose, frowning and reaching for another of the implements.

'Who—?'

'Saintly Simeon,' said Ambrose. 'And if he is, it's a good thing there are three of us. Only I'm not sure— Ah, that's got it. Ever a Fitzglen.' He removed the padlock, glanced at the other two, then pushed the door in. 'Jack?' he said, cautiously. 'Are you in there? Because if you are, for pity's sake stop being melodramatic and say something.'

Gus felt as if light years whirled past before the familiar voice said, 'Of course I'm in here. And night's candles are almost burned out, so we're extremely glad to see you. What kept you?'

*   *   *

Gus thought it would be as well not to enquire too deeply into how Miss Viola Gilfillan came to be inside the mausoleum with Mr Jack, and he did not do so. Mr Ambrose gave her a somewhat startled look, but Mr Ambrose was always perfectly polite, and clearly he would not ask any questions that might be awkward or embarrassing. Not that Gus had ever seen Mr Jack embarrassed, but you never knew.

There was a murmured introduction between Mikhail and Miss Gilfillan – she shook hands with him and said good morning, as if, thought Gus, a rescue from all-night captivity in a mausoleum was an everyday experience.

Mr Jack said, 'Prop the door open, one of you, and let's get a bit of daylight in here. We've spent enough hours in the dark to be grateful for some light. Although,' he said, with a sideways glance at Viola Gilfillan, 'the hours were not as dark as they might have been.'

Gus saw her smile at him, and he also saw that her hair was loose and cascading around her shoulders, and hoped they were not heading for a difficult situation, because this, after all, was a member of the hated Gilfillan clan.

And then Mikhail said, 'Are they here? Jack, did you find them?'

'I found them, and they are here,' said Jack. He stepped back and pointed to a high shelf in a corner of the mausoleum.

To Mikhail, it was as if Time had seized him with both its hands and sent him spinning back to the crypt in the monastery – to the night when he had stolen through the dark, draughty passages, and finally stood before the locked room. The night when he had seen for himself what was locked away in that grim prison cell. He could still remember the feel of the iron bars at the little window as he grasped them, trying to see more clearly into the dark room. With a jab of fear, he remembered all over again the sick terror that had clutched him when the faces had seemed to look round and then move towards him . . .

As if from a distance, he became aware of Jack saying, 'There weren't just the Heads, as you can see. Whoever created them seems to have made what I think are masks – death masks.'

'Mirror images,' said Viola.

Mikhail said, in a voice he only just recognized as his own, 'They were all in the monastery. The masks, also. I saw them, and – oh, but someone must have hung them from nails or even hooks. They—' He paused, then said, 'They swung to and fro, as if they were trying to see me. I thought – you will think me absurd, but I thought they were coming alive – that they were coming towards me. It was one of the most terrifying moments of my entire life.'

For a moment, none of the others spoke, then Jack said, softly, 'So you did try to get to them.'

'Yes.'

'I thought you might have done. No matter,' he said. 'What matters now is getting them down and out of here, before that villain Simeon comes back for them.'

'That's a *very* high shelf, though,' said Ambrose, dubiously.

'It is, isn't it? Gus, what are the chances of bringing a stepladder out here? Without being seen, I mean?'

'Mightily difficult, Mr Jack. You can't,' said Gus, firmly, 'carry a stepladder through a churchyard in broad daylight—'

'Which it is by now.'

'—and not be seen.'

'How else would you get up there, though?' demanded Ambrose. 'Short of— Dear God, Jack, tell me you haven't been considering stacking the coffins up and climbing on to them?'

'Can you think of a better way?' said Jack, already going over to the ledge just under the high shelf. 'If I could have managed it last night, I would have done. Dammit, old Hornbeam had told me they had been put on a high shelf, but I thought I'd be able to get up there. Still, we should be able to reach them between the four of us.'

'Five of us,' said Viola.

'I think your role in this scene is to stand guard at the door,' said Jack.

'Banished to a walk-on part,' she said, with a mock sigh, but she went to the door and stood leaning against the side of it, scanning the forest.

As Jack reached for the first coffin, and Gus stepped up to

take the other end, Ambrose said, 'Of all the bizarre filches I have taken part in—'

'Never mind how bizarre it is, take that corner, and pray to all the gods of the dead that the wood holds firm. Mikhail, can you— Oh, good man,' said Jack, as Mikhail, who agreed with Ambrose that this was bizarre, but saw how the coffins could be arranged to form a kind of stairway to the high shelf, grasped the opposite edge.

'It'll end in disaster,' said Ambrose, as they lifted the coffin. 'One of these things will split and disgorge its contents over the ground, and we'll be faced with a huge bill from the Brundage family, not to mention bringing the wrath of half the English Church down on us.'

'Not if we're careful, we won't. That's the first in place – now for a second,' said Jack. 'Viola – is all quiet out there?'

'Nothing stirring, not even a mouse.'

It took some time to stack up the coffins so that they would reach the shelf, but it did not take as long as Mikhail had expected. He had no idea if this was pure luck or if it was that Jack and Ambrose – Gus Pocket, too – had previously had to gain access to high windows or awkward entrances.

There were a couple of heart-stopping moments when Ambrose almost lost hold of the third coffin, and only regained it just in time to prevent it from smashing on to the stone floor, and another when Gus's shoe caused a corner of it to split slightly.

But at last Jack had climbed cautiously up to the shelf and was reaching for the Heads and the masks.

'I'll hand them down one by one,' he said. 'All right?'

Mikhail, who had hardly spoken during the careful preparations, said, 'Not the fourth one. Only the children,' and saw them turn sharply to look at him.

He said, 'I am sorry – I had not realized I was going to say that, but—'

'But that fourth one isn't, somehow, part of it,' said Jack, studying the sculptures from his precarious perch. 'You're right, Mikhail. Whoever he was, let's leave him here. If Simeon comes back, he's welcome to the head and the mask of that one. But let's get the others down – we can each carry two, can't we? And then let's get out of here and lock the place up. Can we reaffix the padlock?'

'We can. What about the coffins?' said Ambrose, looking at them doubtfully, as Jack leapt down and brushed the dust from his trousers.

'I think we can leave them like this,' said Jack. 'Whoever comes in here next will realize the Heads have been taken, and if it's Simeon himself, he'll know he's been outwitted.'

TWENTY-EIGHT

'How long is it likely to be before anyone discovers the Heads are missing?' demanded Rudraige Fitzglen, as the family, together with Viola, Mikhail and Gus, sat round a late breakfast in The Swan's coffee room. 'Because we can't risk falling under suspicion.'

'I think it could be quite some time before anyone goes in there,' said Jack, eating a large plateful of eggs and bacon with appreciation. 'Ambrose replaced the padlock, and from the outside, the mausoleum looks exactly as it did before. I think we'll be long gone from Mallory Abbot before anyone realizes what's happened.'

'Simeon will go back in there, though,' said Ambrose. 'To get the Heads.'

'Yes, but he's hardly likely to advertise the fact that three of them have been filched,' pointed out Jack.

'Especially since he'll have gone in there to filch them himself,' said Byron, who had breakfasted earlier, but was not going to miss any of this, and was artistically draped on a small sofa in a corner of the room with his sprained foot resting on a cushion.

'The thing I find difficult to understand,' said Cecily, 'is why Simeon went into the mausoleum at all.'

'To get the Heads, obviously,' said Rudraige impatiently.

'Yes, but he had them once – and sold them at what must have been a very good price,' said Cecily. 'Why did he want to get them a second time?'

'Outright greed,' said Daphnis, buttering toast and reaching for the dish of honey. 'He simply wanted to sell the things twice over.'

'I wonder if he intended to inveigle that Brundage woman into some kind of sneaky plan for that,' said Byron, thoughtfully.

'Very likely. It was often his style to . . . well, entangle a trusting female in one of his plots,' nodded Rudraige. 'Disgraceful man, and I'm very glad we threw him out into Sloat Alley that day. Miss Gilfillan, can I pass you the marmalade?'

'You can indeed, but I wish you wouldn't be so formal,' said Viola. 'Especially considering I've spent the last few hours scrambling around in a mausoleum and clambering over ancient coffins along with half your family. That kind of behaviour breaks down barriers, doesn't it? In fact, I feel I've forged all kinds of new links.'

Gus, who was helping spoon out scrambled eggs, managed not to look at Jack.

'I have a feeling,' said Jack, 'that the reason Simeon is trying to reclaim the Heads is because when he sold them to the Ecclesiastical Society, he didn't know their entire history. I think he's since realized they're more valuable than he originally knew.'

'He'd know there were local legends and secrecy around them, though,' put in Daphnis. 'He'd have been constantly alert to the existence of anything rare and valuable while he was in Russia.'

'Yes, but I think it was only afterwards that he realized what lay behind all the secrecy,' said Jack. He looked at Mikhail, who was sitting between the twins. 'In the base of each one,' he said, 'someone – and presumably the sculptor – had carved a series of words. They're a bit worn, and I think they're in Russian, so I couldn't read them.'

'I saw them, too,' said Viola, eagerly. 'But it was so gloomy in that place that it wouldn't have mattered what language they were. I did wonder if they might be the name of each child, though.'

'Mikhail, could they be that?' said Jack.

'They are not the children's names,' said Mikhail. He hesitated, as if unsure whether to continue, then said, 'If the Heads are placed in the right order – and if the Head of the older one we left in the mausoleum is included – the carved words, put together, form a sentence. The first Head is inscribed with the name *Catherine Romanova*.'

'Catherine the Great,' said Daphnis.

'Yes. The second has the words "murdered her husband". The third Head says, "Tsar Peter III". And the fourth has a date – "Ropsha, 1762".'

He paused, looking at them, and Jack said slowly, 'Put in order, that would read—'

'"Catherine Romanova murdered her husband, Tsar Peter III, Ropsha 1762." Yes,' said Mikhail.

There was a sudden silence, then Byron said, slowly, 'I've read up a bit about that era since all this started, and the facts seem somewhat contradictory. Some sources do suggest that Catherine killed the Tsar – not with her own hands, of course, but that she ordered his death.'

'But other sources,' said Mikhail, who did not want to disagree with Byron or any of the Fitzglens, but who would defend his country's history if he had to, 'say she was innocent, and it was one of her lovers who planned the Tsar's death and actually killed him. Count Grigory Orlov is the lover generally thought to be the murderer.'

He saw they were considering this, and at last, Jack said, slowly, 'And that's why the decision was made to keep the Heads locked away in the dark?'

'Of course it was,' said Byron. 'That accusation against Catherine couldn't possibly be made known to the general populace.'

'That is so,' said Mikhail, eagerly. 'There was much unrest in the land then – as there is now, of course – but in those times, there had been the Seven Years War – the War of Austrian Succession – and people were resentful, many of them struggling to survive. If they had been told the Empress had murdered the Tsar, they would have believed it. They would have seized on it as a weapon for protests – violent protests. There could have been attacks on the royal palaces – on the Tsarina's life, even. You have the expression about setting fire to a tinder?'

'We do. You're saying the monks covered up the truth?' said Jack. 'Concealed the Heads?'

'I think it is likely. Peter III had not treated the Russian Orthodox Church well,' said Mikhail. 'The religious houses disliked and distrusted him because of it. Monks are not supposed to have sides in any conflict or alliances with anyone, but I think, for this, the monks at Verkhoturye would have wanted to protect the Tsarina.'

'But does it mean Catherine really did kill the Tsar?' asked Ambrose.

Mikhail said, carefully, 'I have read much about those days. When I was very young, I was schooled in the Verkhoturye monastery; later, I taught my own pupils about Russian history. I know there have been evil, greedy people who have done terrible things, and there have been many deep secrets that have been concealed. Even so, I am still proud of my country.' He spread his hands. 'I do not know whether Catherine was guilty of the death of Peter III, though,' he said. 'I do not think anyone ever can know.'

'I wonder if Harry knew,' said Byron, thoughtfully. 'I wonder if that was the secret he covered up for her. She wrote about "jealous people who might plot against him and cause him harm" in that extract Mikhail found, you remember. But I don't suppose we'll ever know that, either. A pity.'

'But you have regained the Heads,' said Mikhail. 'Because of that, I shall be able to prove my innocence to the people of Cympak. And I will never be able to express my thanks sufficiently to you all.'

'You'll take the Heads back there, of course?'

'Yes, I must do so. I will have to remove the carved words first, of course.' He looked at them hopefully.

Gus said, 'They're very deeply carved, but we might be able to burn them off. Or even cut away that part of the base, then sand it smooth. Bill the Chip's sure to have something in his workshop we can use.'

'Tell Bill you're adapting some props for a production next year,' said Rudraige. 'Although it wouldn't really matter if Bill saw the things – he won't know any Russian. But the Heads certainly can't be taken back with an accusation of murder against a Russian empress, never mind how long ago it happened.'

'I am going to ask if they can be installed in Cympak's church as a memorial to the three children who vanished all those years ago,' explained Mikhail. 'And while I'm there, I will try to teach the children some traditional English rhymes for their games, so that they can sing them instead of the Face Stealer song,' said Mikhail. 'Petronella and Phoebe are going to look some of your rhymes and songs out for me.'

'We thought,' said Petronella, 'that it might sort of squash the Face Stealer rhyme out of people's memories.'

'Oh, how lovely,' said Cecily, clasping her hands together, and Rudraige murmured to Daphnis, in not-quite-a-whisper, that whatever you might say about Lydia Fitzglen, the twins were turning out extremely well.

'Dear old Freddie would have been proud of them,' he said.

'And,' said Byron, thoughtfully, 'the Stone Heads will have emerged from that long, lonely darkness at last.'

'Oh God, he's going to write one of his odious odes about them,' said Rudraige. 'Pay him no attention, Mikhail, my boy. But listen now, you make sure you come back to us, won't you?'

Mikhail looked across the table to Petronella and smiled. 'I shall be very sure to come back,' he said.

My dear Mr Fitzglen

Firstly, and most importantly, thank you for the very generous donation you sent for our church funds. It will go a considerable way to restoring the bell tower, and the Parish Council think it can also provide two new pews in the church itself – the idea of a plaque on them mentioning the Fitzglen name has also been suggested. Your company would therefore have a small memorial within St Osmund's. I hope you will find that acceptable.

Once again, I send my thanks to you all for providing us with such a very entertaining evening at St Osmund's. It was a considerable departure from our usual fundraising events, of course, and I have already had many letters and messages from my parishioners, saying how greatly they enjoyed the performance and how much they would welcome a second such evening.

There is, however, a tragic and, I am afraid, macabre

post-script to your visit. On the day after you left, Mrs Brundage, whom you met while you were here, asked if I would accompany her to the Brundage mausoleum. You will perhaps recall that she had recently acquired several sculptures which she had thought might be incorporated into St Osmund's. However, on learning a little more of their history, she decided they were not suitable, and, at her request, I had placed them in the mausoleum for safety.

However, it seems she had formed a plan for selling them – although I do not know to whom – and had decided they would be more secure in The Manor. As I believe I mentioned, she had never cared to enter the mausoleum, but felt she must now do so, and asked if I would accompany her – which I was happy to do. I collected an oil lamp, knowing how dark it would be inside, and left a note for the verger to meet us there with the stepladder so that we might reach the high shelf where I had stored the sculptures.

Sadly, though, the visit had an unforeseen outcome.

You would expect the incumbent of a thirteenth-century church to be accustomed to the slight eeriness of churchyards, but as we approached the mausoleum, I was aware of apprehension.

It has always been kept locked, and as far as I know, Mrs Brundage has the only key. But as we drew near, we saw that the door stood slightly ajar. As I pushed it wide, the dull daylight slanted in and showed up the coffins – coffins that, until then, had been stacked neatly and respectfully along the sides.

They were not neatly stacked any longer, though. Several had been dragged out and stacked against one wall, clearly to form makeshift steps to the high shelf near the roof. But two of the coffins had tumbled down, splintering slightly in the process, although, God be thanked, not badly enough to spill out what lay inside.

We went forward cautiously, and as the light from

the oil lamp fell across the stone floor, I saw with a horrified shock a figure lying on the ground, among the broken coffins, directly beneath the high shelf. I have seen some distressing things during my years in the Church, but what met my eyes rendered me speechless for some moments.

The figure was sprawled on the ground, the limbs at awkward angles, and the back of the head smashed almost to a pulp. It lay on its side – dreadfully, most of the face was visible to us. Blood and splinters of bone were everywhere. But, most bizarre and macabre of all, almost a complete stone face – presumably all that was left of the Russian sculptures – lay close to the body. You will think me fanciful, but it was almost pressing into the dead man's own face, and it was as if the blind stone eyes were staring straight at him with a kind of malevolent triumph.

Mrs Brundage dissolved into sobs – in itself unusual, for she is normally a strong-minded, decisive lady. I escorted her from the mausoleum without delay, of course, and thankfully, as we went back through the church grounds, we met the verger who was bringing the stepladder as I had asked, and we were able to send him for the police.

It has been difficult to establish exactly what happened, but the conclusion is that the dead man somehow got into the mausoleum to steal the Russian sculptures. There had been much interest, locally, in the initial proposal to incorporate them into St Osmund's, and it seems probable that this wretched man, hearing of them, considered them worth stealing. It looked as if he had dragged the coffins across to the shelf in order to climb on to them and reach up to the sculptures.

But he must have missed his footing, or possibly one of the coffins slipped, and in reaching up, he brought the sculptures crashing down on his head. I do not know if it will be possible to establish if the Stone Heads themselves delivered a fatal blow – I imagine they were very heavy – or if the fall on to the hard stone floor was responsible for his death.

The police cleared away most of the debris, and the verger and I helped where we could. Everything was badly fragmented – there was sawdust from the coffins everywhere, and splinters of stone and clay from the Heads – so that it would have been impossible to piece any of it together, and we did not try. I am afraid the Russian sculptures are therefore gone beyond recall.

This is a sad and daunting story, but I have a reason for relating it. The dead man appears to have been a complete stranger to these parts, but in his jacket was a pocket book proclaiming him to be Simeon Fitzglen. I wonder, therefore, if there is any possibility that he is a connection of your family. If so, I would be very grateful if you could put me in touch with any nearer relations, so that suitable arrangements can be made for interment.

Again, I am so sorry to be sending this news, but with it come my very best wishes and kind regards to you all.

Henry Hornbeam, DD.

'I suppose,' said Jack, folding up the letter, 'that we should offer to foot the bill for the funeral.'

'I'm afraid we should,' said Ambrose, glumly. 'We'll have to say we think he's a distant cousin. It's no more than the truth, after all. And I daresay the funeral won't be a very lavish or expensive affair.' He jotted down a few figures and frowned at them.

'Ought one of us to attend the service?' asked Cecily. 'It might look peculiar if we didn't. If we're accepting responsibility for the funeral costs and claiming cousinship, I mean.'

'I'm not going to that villain's funeral,' said Rudraige, firmly. 'I'm sorry he's dead, but I'm damned if I'll join in the weeping and wailing and all that guff about "Letteth Now Thy Servant Depart in Peace".'

'But you have to admit there's a certain poetic justice in the way he met his end,' said Byron. 'Crushed to a pulp by the very items he was trying to filch. Well, by the fourth one, because we've got the other three, haven't we?'

'Look here, though,' said Ambrose, 'about Simeon's funeral—'

'I could go,' offered Cecily. 'You aren't opening the Pinero piece until next month Jack, and I'm not in it anyway, so I'd be free.'

'I'll come with you if you like,' said Ambrose, putting away his ledger. 'I expect we can fit around rehearsals.'

'Would you, Ambrose? You'd be the very person – you're so good at donning a funeral mien,' said Cecily, pleased.

'It comes of playing vicars in so many plays.'

'But Cecily, if you're considering wearing that dreadful black bonnet, for pity's sake, remove the feathers,' said Daphnis.

Cecily replied with dignity that she hoped she knew better than to wear a feathered hat to a funeral, and went off with Ambrose to consult train timetables.

My dear Reverend Hornbeam

Your kind words after morning service were most gratefully received.

I am afraid I was sadly deceived by the man styling himself as the Reverend Simeon Fitzglen, whom, to some extent, I had befriended. Mr Fitzglen – I no longer believe he is entitled to be styled 'Reverend' – had presented himself to me as having devoted his life to charity works in several countries. I now realize this was false. Indeed, there had been a hint of past guile on the night the Fitzglen company presented their play at St Osmund's. As you know, the author of the story on which it was based was among the audience– a Professor James from Cambridge University, and a charming and courteous gentleman. I was introduced to him, and he was most interested to hear of my own endeavours in the literary world. In discussing the Fitzglen company, the professor mentioned encountering an Archdeacon Fitzglen, who had later been discovered to be entirely fraudulent, as well as outright venal. It is not difficult to conclude that this bogus archdeacon was the man I had known as Reverend Simeon Fitzglen.

Rodger says I am far too trusting, and that I must take this as a salutary lesson. He is also of the opinion that we should now have the mausoleum demolished, and a churchyard burial for those whose bodies have been resting there.

I do not feel I can attend the funeral on Friday, and hope you will understand.

With kind regards,
Marjorie Brundage.

'You really are going to come back, aren't you?' said Petronella, perching on the window ledge in the Amaranth's costume room, where Mikhail was packing the Stone Heads into a small wicker skip that nobody seemed to mind being appropriated. 'I know you said you would when Great Uncle Rudraige asked, but that might have been just politeness.'

'It was not politeness,' said Mikhail. 'I am certainly coming back. Not just to England and London, but here, to this theatre. Jack has said there can be a place for me in the company.'

'Has he really? I didn't know that. That would be marvellous,' said Petronella. Mikhail had already discovered that when she was pleased about something, her eyes lit up and a faint flush touched her cheeks. It did so now, and he thought it was the image of her he would take to Cympak with him.

But he only said, 'I will not be away for much more than three weeks – Ambrose has worked out the arrangements for travelling there and coming back, and helped with booking seats for trains and ferries. It will not be very difficult.' He did not say it would be a great deal easier than the long and fragmented journey he had made to England. He said, hopefully, 'While I am away, I could write to you, to tell you all that I'm doing.'

'Could you?' said Petronella, at once. 'Really write, do you mean? Sorry, I know that sounds a bit— It's just that Cecily says people who go off on long journeys always promise to write, and they do at the beginning, but then their letters get shorter and shorter, and degenerate into the I-hope-you-are-well-I-am-very-well category, and eventually stop arriving altogether. She said it quite wistfully,' added Petronella. 'I think she might once have had a lost love who stopped writing to her.'

Mikhail considered this, then came to sit next to her on the window ledge. He reached for her hand and said, 'I promise I will not become a lost love.'

Byron had discarded the strapping around his sprained ankle, but had commandeered Great Uncle Rudraige's silver-topped cane to walk along to Jack's rooms.

'I'm glad you aren't rehearsing this afternoon,' he said, 'because I come bearing information and documents.' He lowered himself into the most comfortable chair, and accepted Gus's offer of a padded footstool. 'In fact, Jack, dear old Arthur Challis has finally allowed me to borrow the Deeds relating to Harry Fitzglen's purchase of the Amaranth land. And they'll be better read with a cup of tea, I should think—'

'Gus, make some tea, would you,' said Jack, at once. 'And bring in a cup for yourself, because you'll want to hear this. You're as much part of it as any of us.'

'More, in fact, since you unearthed those documents about the Heads from the Ecclesiastical Society,' said Byron.

'I'd like to hear it, but if it's legal stuff, I daresay I shan't understand very much,' said Gus, clearly pleased at being included.

'I daresay I shan't, either,' said Jack, frowning at the sheaf of papers Byron had handed to him. 'It looks formal and long-winded.'

'That's because lawyers in those days were paid by the line,' said Byron. 'The more words they could cram into a document, the more money they could demand. But clerks often marked out the salient points by making the initial letter larger.'

'Yes, I'm seeing that,' said Jack, studying the faded pages. 'And it does make it easier to find the way through hereditaments and enfeoffments and demesne – oh, and pannage. What's pannage?'

'The right to feed swine on beech mast and acorns at certain seasons in any woodland on the land in question,' said Byron, and grinned. 'Don't look so impressed – I looked it up. It's only mentioned to confirm that pannage rights weren't passed to the purchaser. Keep reading.'

'"The tract and parcel of land and all its appurtenances delineated on Plan A attached herein, situate in the Borough of London Town, bordering on to Sloat Alley on the west and Drury Lane to the East and Long Acre to the north—"' said Jack. 'It's nice to see Sloat Alley mentioned, and— Oh, good, here's our tea. Thank you, Gus.' He turned to the next page, stared at it for several moments, then said, 'Oh!'

'I thought that would get your attention,' said Byron, in a pleased voice.

'That's extraordinary,' said Jack. '"The land herein described was offered per auctionem, and the unsuccessful bidder, named herein, is hereby made the subject of an Order of Prohibition, such Order banning him from entering on to the parcel of land described herein or into any buildings that might thereafter be erected on it . . ."' He paused, as if assimilating what he was reading, then went on. '"The said person is most strictly prohibited from approaching nearer to the owner than one half-mile (forty chains, twenty rods, one hundred and ten yards), on pain of a fine and possible criminal proceedings." And the name of the unsuccessful bidder—' said Jack, slowly.

'Was Hugo Gilfillan,' said Byron.

'Yes.' Jack was still staring at the page. 'Then the feud between the two families goes back further than we realized.'

'Turn to the next part, and you'll see it not only goes back further, but it goes deeper than merely being outbid for the Amaranth land.'

Jack began to read the next page aloud, and as he did so, he felt as if Harry was reaching out to him.

'"I hereby declare and attest that the villainous Hugo Gilfillan is banned from entering on to the land delineated in the plan within these Deeds, after it has passed into my ownership, which will take place seven days from the date on this document, which will be the tenth day of this month.

'"Furthermore, the same Hugo Gilfillan is required, under pain of imprisonment or the calling out to a duel to the death, never again to express the view he voiced so publicly and raucously in the Maiden Lane coffee house, to wit that I, Harry Fitzglen, had concealed the truth regarding the death of the Russian Tsar, Peter III, in July in the year 1762, such statement being slanderous and very likely libellous, as well as malicious, damaging and most certainly untrue."'

Jack put the Deeds down carefully, and reached for the tea Gus had poured.

'You can almost hear Harry declaring that the dastardly Gilfillan was never to set foot on his land, and, more to the point, never to voice again that astonishing accusation,' said Byron.

'The accusation that Harry concealed the truth about Peter III's death,' said Jack, slowly. 'If he really did conceal that, it could explain how he got the emeralds that enabled him to buy the land.'

'A reward,' nodded Byron. 'Mikhail said it's generally believed one of Catherine's lovers was responsible for the Tsar's death, didn't he?'

'Count Orlov.'

'Yes. And that the monks might have covered up that accusation on the Stone Heads to protect her. Harry could have been part of all that.'

'If so, it would explain why he was so vehement in silencing Hugo Gilfillan. Gilfillan had probably just heard vague gossip, but was resentful at being outbid for the Amaranth land.' Jack looked back at the Deeds.

The final page said, 'I set my hand and my name to this on the date of the Conveyance.' Below these words was the signature. Harry Fitzglen.

Jack stared at it for a long time, then became aware of Byron saying, elaborately casually, something about Viola.

'Because, I suppose, as she's been involved in so much of this, and as Hugo would have been her ancestor—'

'Yes. I'd better tell her about it,' said Jack.

He thought Byron and Gus exchanged a look, but Byron

only said, 'It would perhaps be courteous,' and Gus merely asked if he should make a fresh pot of tea.

'It's really only a brief business meeting I'm suggesting,' said Jack to Viola the following day. 'But I'd like to tell you what seems to be the final act. The Stone Heads and Saintly Simeon's fate. Also, what seems to be the start of the Fitzglen–Gilfillan feud. I think you're owed it.'

'Yes?' She looked at him with interest.

'My evenings are free at the moment, because we're rehearsing, but your *Lady Windermere* is still running, isn't it? I wondered if we could have a late supper after you finish. I could book a table at Rules or the Café Royale for around eleven or half past. If it wouldn't be too late for you.'

'It wouldn't be too late at all,' she said. 'And either place would be a good deal more comfortable than the last time we were alone together, wouldn't it?'

'But,' said Jack, his voice very casual, 'it did occur to me that if we're to discuss our disreputable ancestors, it might be more discreet if we had supper in my rooms.'

'People do tend to overhear conversations in restaurants,' agreed Viola. She studied him for a moment. 'Late supper in your rooms,' she said, thoughtfully.

'I can have food sent in, or Gus could leave something out. Not if you hate the idea, of course.'

'No,' she said, slowly. 'I don't hate the idea at all. And, as you say, your rooms would be much more discreet than a restaurant.'

'Would tonight be a good night for you?'

'Tonight would be very good indeed,' said Viola, politely courteous, but then she smiled, and the smile held the memory of a cold, shadowy mausoleum where the only light was an erratic candlelight, and the only way to keep warm had been for them to lie in one another's arms.

Harry Fitzglen stood on the patch of land that, incredibly and marvellously, was his own, with the bustle and thrum of London swirling all around him, and a sheaf of legal documents bearing his signature in the pocket of his cloak.

Hold on to this moment, he thought; hold on to it and try to store it away, because even if you live to be a hundred, there will never be another moment like it. Even the memory of how Hugo Gilfillan had tried to get this land for himself, seizing the fragments of rumour and speculation that had clung to Harry after his return to London, could not mar today. And he could deal with the likes of Hugo and any other Gilfillans who might try their fortunes against him, thought Harry, and smiled.

He had been poor and he had been rich, sometimes in quick succession, but as he visualized the building that would one day stand on this land, and as he felt the rustle of the thick parchment document in his pocket, he knew he would never again feel as rich and as blessed as he did today.

And it had been made possible by a lady with whom he had shared an extraordinary, unforgettable time. A lady whose memory would never fade. With the thought, from the motley collection of phrases and words and legends that lay in his mind, a single word – Greek? – came unbidden to the surface. Amarantos. Harry smiled. Amaranthus. Meaning everlasting.

Final extract from the private memoirs of Catherine, Tsarina of Russia, c.1774

Today I received a package swathed in layers of cotton waste and linen, the whole wrapped in thick brown paper, and bearing so many requests to treat it with care that I am surprised it has reached me at all.

I waited until I could be alone before unwrapping it, for although I did not know the writing on the parcel, never having seen it, I knew, quite surely, who the sender was.

The floor of my bedchamber was covered with wrapping paper and sealing wax, and strewn with shreds of cotton before I finally lifted out what lay within.

It was a framed and glazed sketch, not large, perhaps ten

inches high and about twenty inches wide, and it showed a most beautiful building with porticoed front and stone pillars, and with steps leading up to a wide door. Even in the charcoal lines, there is the impression that beyond that door would be sweeping stairways and gilt balustrades and marble floors and ornate ceilings and arches.

Above the door is depicted a large plaque, the lettering ornate and graceful and easily readable.

The Amaranth Theatre.

AUTHOR'S NOTE

To use a genuine person from history in a work that is primarily fiction can present an author with an obstacle-strewn path. Proven facts cannot be changed or even manipulated – even though it can be annoying to discover that some people have died too soon and others too late to fit into the storyline. There is also the matter of how far contemporary accounts of events can be trusted, because it's undeniable that a number of chroniclers have had an axe of their own to grind, a grudge to promote or a score to settle. But short of toppling dynasties or unseating monarchs, of rescuing rebels and traitors from the scaffold, the plot and the characters of a historical novel have to be tailored to fit the records that are available.

During the writing of *The Face Stealer*, I made several assumptions about the infamous Russian Empress, known to most people simply as Catherine the Great. Involving her with the Fitzglen clan posed an intriguing challenge, although it also meant negotiating a tangle of legends and rumours, gossip and speculation. There is a wealth of primary source material about Catherine's life, not least within her own memoirs, which have been translated into several languages and analysed exhaustively, and which are still available today. She was also a prodigious letter-writer, communicating with luminaries of the day such as the writer and philosopher Voltaire, the diplomat and art critic Baron von Grimm and the French philosophers and encyclopaedists Diderot and d'Alembert. She numbered monarchs and heads of state among her correspondents, although she was not always respectful towards them or about them, having once likened the King of Sweden to Falstaff.

But from the complicated web of intrigue and rumour and fact, what stood out for me was Catherine's humour and humanity, and her energy and imagination and determination.

She introduced sweeping changes to the country, many of them inspired by the 'Age of Enlightenment' philosophies and beliefs of the seventeenth and eighteenth centuries. She was keenly interested in the renaissance of culture and sciences and the founding of universities and theatres, and new cities were created under her rule – notably, Sevastopol, Kherson and Yekaterinburg, which was named for Catherine and was later the tragic backdrop for the slaughter of her descendants in 1917.

Portraits show her formally posed, but in several it is possible to detect a glint of amusement and perhaps even of mischief, as if she might sometimes have found the adulation and the pomp amusing.

She was certainly on the fringe of many a plot, but no firm evidence seems ever to have been found of complicity in the assassination of her husband in 1762, in the sinister 'torture mansion' of Ropsha. Public opinion of the day, though, held her culpable, and she probably had to tread a very cautious path for a while after Peter's death – as suggested in the later parts of *The Face Stealer*, when she is faced with the accusation carved into the Stone Heads by the vengeful – albeit fictional – Brother Quintus.

Her son, Paul, who coveted the Imperial Throne and harboured a deep resentment towards his mother, spread colourful and often vindictive and bizarre rumours about her bedchamber activities. He finally succeeded to the throne in 1796, after Catherine's unexpected death at the age of sixty-seven. However, his mother's legend always overshadowed him, and in fact he only reigned for five years, being assassinated in 1801.

Even allowing for the scandalmongering of Paul and others, it is accepted that Catherine had a number of lovers. She is credited with having said, 'The trouble is that my heart is loath to remain even one hour without love.'

Her favourites were Prince Potemkin-Tauricheski – the ambitious dreamer, statesman and nobleman, with whom she is rumoured to have entered into a morganatic marriage – and Count Grigory Orlov, who figures in the plot of *The Face Stealer* and appears there as the prime mover in the assassination of the strange, eccentric and cruel Peter III – a belief strongly held at the time and since.

Adding up these facts and impressions, it seemed not too far-fetched to allot to Catherine a lover of my own creating – a gentleman who would secretly, if briefly, capture her emotions and her senses, and with whom – as Harry Fitzglen was to say – she shared for a brief time Milton's 'secret harmony of hearts'.

It is probably safe to say that Catherine Romanova and Professor Montague Rhodes James would not have expected to find themselves sharing the pages of the same book, even though they appear in different time sections of the plot. But the ghost stories of M.R. James fitted so beautifully into the Fitzglen plans to infiltrate the mausoleum that they seemed almost tailor-made. Jack Fitzglen and the rest of the family thoroughly enjoyed making use of his work – and I enjoyed letting them do so. For me, James is one of the great masters of gentle macabre – a writer who knew that the unseen is often more frightening than the seen. James knew about the midnight creak on the stair – when no one was there to have made that creak – and about the whisk of something sinister disappearing around a corner. As he says to Jack and Byron over lunch at Rules, it can be far scarier to glimpse the shirt-tail of a ghost than the ghost itself. I don't think he actually ever said this, but I do think it's an outlook of which he would have approved.

The Treasure of Abbot Thomas was first published in 1904, as part of an anthology. There have been many adaptations and dramatizations of it since then, as, indeed, there have been of the other stories.

I would like to think the Fitzglens' performance of their version of *Abbot Thomas* might have added an extra version of the story to that list and that the professor might have approved of it.

Sarah Rayne